Books by Phyllis A. Whitney

RAINBOW IN THE MIST
FEATHER ON THE MOON
SILVERSWORD
FLAMING TREE
DREAM OF ORCHIDS
RAINSONG
EMERALD
VERMILION
POINCIANA
DOMINO
THE GLASS FLAME
THE STONE BULL
THE GOLDEN UNICORN
SPINDRIFT
THE TURQUOISE MASK
SNOWFIRE
LISTEN FOR THE WHISPERER
LOST ISLAND
THE WINTER PEOPLE
HUNTER'S GREEN
SILVERHILL
COLUMBELLA
SEA JADE
BLACK AMBER
SEVEN TEARS FOR APOLLO
WINDOW ON THE SQUARE
BLUE FIRE
THUNDER HEIGHTS
THE MOONFLOWER
SKYE CAMERON
THE TREMBLING HILLS
THE QUICKSILVER POOL
THE RED CARNELIAN

RAINBOW
IN THE MIST

PHYLLIS A. WHITNEY

RAINBOW IN THE MIST

DOUBLEDAY

NEW YORK   LONDON   TORONTO   SYDNEY   AUCKLAND

Published by DOUBLEDAY, a division of Bantam Doubleday Dell Publishing
Group, Inc., 666 Fifth Avenue, New York, New York 10103.

DOUBLEDAY and the portrayal of an anchor with a dolphin are the trade-
marks of Doubleday, a division of Bantam Doubleday Dell Publishing Group,
Inc.

Library of Congress Cataloging-in-Publication Data
Whitney, Phyllis A., 1903–
    Rainbow in the mist/by Phyllis A. Whitney.—1st ed.
        p.   cm.
    I. Title.
PS3545.H8363R25   1989   88-18099
813'.54—dc19   CIP

ISBN 0-385-24954-3
Copyright © 1989 by Phyllis A. Whitney
ALL RIGHTS RESERVED
PRINTED IN THE UNITED STATES OF AMERICA
MARCH 1989
FIRST EDITION

BG

For Audrey Bershen,
who said I would listen when I was ready,
with loving thanks for years of friendship
and guidance.

My thanks to many friends in Virginia, who helped with this book.

Robert and Nancy Monroe opened the first doors for me. Jean Wallis sang to the cows, and let me adapt that wonderful scene for my story. Trew Bennett introduced me to her magical Sun Wheel, while Linda Jackson, Morrie Coleman, and Nora Murphy shared llama lore with me at their llama farm, which I can see out my windows. The character of Victor grew out of conversations with Maureen Littlepath, to whom I am grateful.

My special thanks to Tina Anderson who typed all those words.

Others read the manuscript when completed and I owe them my gratitude for watchful attention to detail: Phyllis and Arnie Popkin, Scooter McMoneagle, and Nancy Navarra.

RAINBOW
IN THE MIST

CHRISTY gripped the wheel of her car with a tension she hadn't been able to release in this entire daylong drive. Anxiety was needless, since only one person was aware that she had left Long Island, or knew where she was going. Yet the feeling of tightness between her shoulder blades persisted—as though an invisible hand reached for her.

It was like her dream, where there was always a follower . . . She *must* leave this behind her now. In a few more miles she could stop running and pour everything out to Nona, as she'd never been able to do with her mother. Nona believed in the existence of evil, while Lili didn't. That was only one of the differences between her mother and her aunt.

When Christy phoned, Nona had simply said, "Come!" and Christy had responded in joyful relief. There was no need to let her mother know where she would be, since they'd hardly talked in months. The basic disagreement between mother and daughter was hurtful but couldn't be helped. Christy knew she must follow her own path and not listen to Liliana Dukas. Besides, if Lili wanted to know where she was, she would find her—instantly.

As the road climbed through Virginia's beautiful Nelson County, high ridges rose ahead tinged with the hazy blue that gave the mountains their name. In the light of late afternoon, lower hills, crowding in, were delineated by shadow lines in their deep folds. Already she had the feeling that these blue-green arms would surround and conceal her, keep her safe even from herself. The season was spring and she could start anew.

Her Aunt Nona was the true mother who had raised and nurtured her ever since Christy had been a small child and Liliana Dukas's destiny had taken off on a surge of publicity—notoriety!—that had made her world-famous. These days Lili was in demand for talk shows and conferences everywhere, attracting thousands of devotees. As a mother, she had provided her one child with an intense, almost devouring love (whenever she was around), but the wider demands that engulfed her life caused her to forget much of the time that she had a daughter. Or so it had often seemed to Christy. Lili's "voices" told her that her destiny was to help the world, and apparently they didn't worry about the needs of one sometimes resentful little girl.

At twenty-eight Christy still shrank from her mother's fame. Lili had always used her maiden name of Dukas, so Christy could hide behind Loren, her father's name, even though he had left them so long ago. One regret in Christy's life was that he had died before she could ever get to know him. Lili would never talk about Kenneth Loren, or about her other husbands, and Nona had been almost as reticent.

While Nona Dukas had never married, she had gained a quiet distinction of her own, and she'd dropped the family name early on. For herself she'd chosen the curious name of "Harmony" with which to sign her paintings. From her aunt, Christy had received a restrained, undemonstrative love that had nevertheless been a rock to depend upon in her growing years—as she must depend upon it again now.

Nona's no-nonsense approach would enable Christy to relax, rest, be free of the terrible demands that had been placed upon her in recent years. She had never told Nona exactly what had happened to her in these last two years—though Lili had known immediately and had wanted to take part—to "help." It had been necessary for Christy to stand up to her mother and demand to be let alone. Unexpectedly, Lili had listened and tried to respect her daughter's wishes. Christy was sure that when Nona knew all that had happened she would give her full support to whatever course her niece decided to follow. There'd be no need to struggle any more, because she knew what that course must be.

Of course Lili had always hoped that the miraculous gift her Hungarian mother had possessed would manifest itself in her daughter. When the first hint of it had appeared in the year when Christy was five, Lili had been tremendously pleased and excited. From the first, however, Christy had hated the gift and wanted only to reject it. She'd always disliked the name she had been given at birth—Chrystal. A name her mother still used. Crystals were a part of Lili's life, not Christy's.

She would never forget that first searing flash of premonition that had warned her about her darling Puddles. She had seen with horrible clarity the moment when the little poodle had been struck by a car, and she knew exactly where it had happened. Her mother listened to every tearful word and drove her to the blind curve that Christy's vision indicated. Even as Lili tried to comfort her daughter, she had exclaimed over this evidence that the family talent had reached into another generation. But why, Christy wailed, why couldn't she have seen *ahead* of time what was going to happen, so that Puddles could have been saved?

For years after, her doubtful gift had let her alone, and she had tried to block out any thought of it. She had found work that pleased and satisfied her. Although she had no brothers or sisters, since Lili was too busy to raise a family, and was usually between husbands anyway, Christy grew up loving children. She had a special sympathy for the small ones, and since she loved books as well—Nona had seen to that—it had seemed natural to combine the two and become someone who put books into the hands of children.

The library she worked for on Long Island discovered that she was especially good at telling stories to groups of the very young. Her own small person never overwhelmed them, and they loved the way her brown eyes could widen dramatically; loved the feathery tricks her eyebrows played to make them laugh. A wide mouth that she'd always thought too big helped because it was expressive, and her voice was soft but very clear, and filled with cadences that seemed to hold and entrance a young audience. Of course all the marvelous children's books at the library gave her ammunition. For Christy, words always came first and she loved to say them aloud, so her listeners could relish the author's language.

The library system quickly recognized her special magic, and she'd been sent around to tell stories wherever small children gathered to listen. The work had been satisfying, and she didn't mind in the least that her mother thought it was all a waste of the "real" talents she should have been developing.

Christy had been delighted when Nona, using the name of "Harmony," did the illustrations for a favorite recent picture book by Rose Vaughn, entitled *The Little Red Road.* The author, a close friend of Nona's, had died recently, and Christy felt sad because there would be no more wonderful, Nona-illustrated stories from her pen.

Charlottesville was behind her, and the four-lane highway that rose into the foothills of the Blue Ridge Mountains led closer to the turnoff. Now the hills were an irregular, wooded jumble all around, and she liked the surprise views that appeared at every turn. Nona had explained that after Christy left the main road she must look for a Baptist church sign and then a green dumpster that would mark the gravel road winding through the hills to the small community called Redlands, where Nona had built her home two years ago.

Christy had wanted to visit her aunt before this, but it had never worked out. Not until this last disaster had struck did she know that she must disappear, escape, sever all ties with terrible recent events. She was thankful that Nona didn't ask her to explain over the phone.

Her library director had seen Christy's need and let her go immediately and without question. She had understood what was happening—and simply cut the red tape. This woman was the one friend who knew where Christy had gone, and she would never give her away. Whether it would ever be possible to return to Long Island was a decision for the future—perhaps when she had healed a little and recovered her equilibrium. For now, she must be away from any settled area where violence was prevalent and her clairvoyance all too active. At Redlands there would be nothing to awaken it, and she could let her awful experiences flow away into the past. The Virginia foothills of the Blue Ridge would be peaceful, quiet. She knew from her aunt that only a handful of families had been drawn together here by the beauty of the Redlands area and a desire to be away from cities. Though they came from different places, they were bound by a common affection for the beauty of the land and the protection of bird and animal life, as well as that of the plants and trees that shared the countryside with humans.

After turning into the widespread acres occupied by Redlands, the road narrowed and changed from pavement to gravel as it climbed steep curves and opened into a high, rolling valley of sloping meadows where cows grazed. Forested hills and higher mountains enfolded the deep cut of the valley.

"When you come to the 'Y' in the road," Nona had directed, "you take the right fork. The second driveway on your right is mine. I'll be watching for you."

The second driveway had been recently topped with gravel that was a little loose near the road. Christy took the turn carefully, avoiding deep red ditches on either side. The afternoon was still bright and sunny and the dogwood trees in the valley retained some of their white plumage. As she got out of the car and stretched luxuriously, she wished she could have seen their full blooming.

Nona's house reached along the top of the ridge, and from the front appeared to be all on one floor, its gray roof shingles framed by two big oak trees on either hand. A low deck of red planks followed the angular turns of the house beneath an overhang that would shield the many windows from summer sun. The pitch of the roof was broken by a gentle rise toward the front edge that imitated the mountain cabin roofs she'd seen on the drive from Charlottesville—except that this wide roof carried two tiers of solar panels, shining like silver in the sun.

More notable than the roof at the moment, however, was the man who straddled the ridgepole, securing some sort of metal device in place. He stared down at her openly without smiling, intent upon her every move. His look seemed to hint at caution toward strangers. A big man, with wide shoulders, he sat with his long legs dangling down each side of the roof. His face, already tanned by the sun, was angular in its planes, his black hair ruffled by the wind. He was dressed entirely in gray— slacks and shirt and scuffed boots.

"Hello!" Christy called up to him. "I'm Christy Loren, Miss Harmony's niece."

He tipped his head toward her in a nod but didn't speak, and having satisfied himself in that single long stare, he went back to his work, whatever it was.

Christy took her suitcase and small zipper bag from the car trunk and stepped up on the deck. Three full-length glass doors, spaced well apart, offered access to the house. She could look through the nearest one to a service entrance floored in red tile. Undoubtedly a place to scrape off red mud when it rained. Farther along, set at a jutting right angle that faced her, the next door opened on the kitchen. She needed to go no further, as Nona came through at once onto the deck.

She looked as she always did—tall and spare, with bones that seemed to protrude in awkward places, though somehow they'd always offered a small child a comfortable place to cuddle. She wore jeans and a western shirt with red embroidery against blue denim. Short boots covered her long thin feet, and her stride as she came toward Christy had not shortened in the years that had carried her into her sixties. Lately, since her hair had turned gray and thin, she'd taken to covering it with a flowered scarf wound about her head, the ends flowing over one shoulder. What was good enough for Louise Nevelson and

Georgia O'Keeffe was good enough for Nona Harmony, as she often said. A final touch—long turquoise earrings—danced as she moved her head. In some strange way, as Christy had often noted, no matter what she wore, Nona always created her own fashion and lived it with panache.

A smile lighted her face warmly, and she held out her arms to her niece with an embrace that was hard and quick. Christy caught the lemon-grass scent of verbena that she wore, which had always been comfortingly familiar to sniff.

"Come inside," Nona said. "My coffee has just stopped perking."

A little of Christy's burden flowed away and she was able to laugh for the first time in weeks. Nona always claimed that the family "gift" had passed her by—"Thank God!"—but nevertheless, she knew to the instant when to put on the coffee, and few visitors ever took her by surprise. She could stop in mid-sentence, when no one else noticed anything, and remark, "Somebody's coming."

The angled doorway opened into a red-tiled kitchen and dining area. A bay of windows encompassed the view of mountains, meadow slopes, and distant clumps of forest. Now that the brown of winter had been cast off, new green softened the land, with red earth showing through wherever grass was thin or a dirt road wound through. An oval table had been set before the window bay, and a galley kitchen cut off at right angles to the dining space.

Nona took Christy's suitcase and bag and put them out of the way. "Leave your stuff there for now, and later I'll show you your room downstairs. We're on two levels at the back because of the steep hill. There's a bathroom down the hall if you'd like a wash. I'll pour our coffee and then you can tell me everything."

It was like Nona to sense at once what ought to come first. There would be no chitchat about her trip or her health before they got to the main topic of why she had come. Christy paused only to ask about the man on the roof.

Her aunt answered carelessly. "That's Victor Birdcall. He's putting up lightning rods for me. Did he give you his silent once-over?"

"I think he did."

"Pay no attention. He plays make-believe Indian sometimes, though I think the blood is diluted a bit by now. Hurry and come back."

Christy hurried, liking the spacious bathroom with its gray tile floor and blue fixtures. When she returned to sit in the window bay opposite her aunt, the view had already changed with the light as the sun dropped toward the mountains—a view so still and peaceful that Christy began to feel more relaxed than she had in months. There was so much sky out there above sloping pastures that even the mountains were dwarfed.

"It's popped up in you again, hasn't it?" Nona said, and smiled. "No, dear, *I'm* not psychic. But I don't know anything else that could upset you so badly. The one or two times it's hit me, I fell apart. Luckily I could always manage to close off the avenue, and I've been safe from it most of my life."

"I wish I knew how to do that," Christy said. Even though the whole thing churned inside her, ready to pour out, she hardly knew how to begin—or even where the beginning was.

Nona saw her hesitation and offered a side road. "Why haven't you ever married?" she asked bluntly. "I'll bet plenty of men have been after you."

A spark flashed in Christy's eyes. "Not plenty. A few. But I don't know about love—that's never happened for me, really. Men like to look after me—I'm such a little thing, they think I'm helpless! They want to put me in a pocket, keep me for a pet—and I won't have any of that. Of course when they find out what I can do they run like rabbits. Besides, I'd never marry after Lili's terrible example. Three marriages, and not one of her husbands could take it! She's never talked about the first one—she just clams up. And you've never been willing to tell me much either. Not even about my father. You get that remote look in your eyes and I don't dare push."

Nona sighed. "I never wanted to prejudice you against your mother. Because of the critical way I sometimes felt, I knew what would come through."

"It came through anyway. So tell me now. Maybe it will help me understand—other things."

Nona always drank her coffee black, but now she stirred as though the liquid were full of sugar and cream. When she put down her spoon, it was with an air of surrender.

"All right. I've put it off too long. That first marriage of your mother's—they were only kids. She hadn't been *called* then, and I guess she really fell in love. It took that first man a year to find out about her, and then he skipped for his own sanity. Left her for an older woman who was quite ordinary and gave him the mother he wanted."

"My father came next?"

"Yes. Ken was okay. I liked him, and I think he tried to stick it out. He loved you very much as a baby. I've told you that, at least. When Lili *found* herself, as she calls it, she said he couldn't take it either. Though he didn't leave her for another woman. He left because she scared him. Who wants to live with someone who knows what you're thinking before you do?"

"She's not that good!" Christy protested.

"They only needed to think she was."

"But the third man must have known all about her?"

"Sure. He was in the 'business,' as he called it. But you see, no matter what they say about her, Liliana Dukas is real. She's radiantly real. You can almost see the light around her. But he was a fake, and out to use her to make money. She can go silly in the head about men and doesn't foresee a thing. But when she found out what he was up to, she divorced him. I don't think she'll try marriage again. But that's enough of Lili. It's time to talk about you. Aren't you happy in your library work?"

"I love it. I want to go on doing what I like, and I'm really pretty good at it, Nona."

"But there's something you haven't shared with me. I've sensed it every time we've talked on the phone, and I've felt it in your letters—the holding back."

"I know. Thanks for not pushing me. I thought I could work through what was happening by myself, but it kept getting worse—more powerful and more frightening. This time I nearly cracked up."

"Then it's time to talk. I'm always good for listening."

Tears of relief came into Christy's eyes, but she blinked them away. She must talk this through as calmly as possible.

"The first time the flash happened it seemed useful—something that might even save lives, though it didn't make me popular. I was out in the country on a picnic with some friends. We wandered into a subdivision of newly built houses looking for a grocery store. The minute I set foot in that little development—" She broke off as the horror swept back.

Nona spoke calmly. "You aren't going to crack up or fall apart. Just look out at the mountains and let them calm you."

The light was still golden, and red earth threaded through the green. So quiet and peaceful—safe. Christy took a deep breath and went on.

"I *knew* right away. I could feel the poison bubbling up underground, getting ready to destroy everything above. I had to tell the people who lived there in their new little houses. I had to warn them, no matter how shocking it was."

"Did they believe you?"

"They didn't want to, but I found a place where the poisons were breaking through—so I could show them. I wanted to save the children from all that awful pollution that was going to seep into their water and gardens. Nobody thanked me, but some of the people moved. The rest stayed behind and hated me because they couldn't sell their houses. As though I were to blame for the poisons underground. In the end I was proved right, and everyone had to get out and leave a ghost town behind. The fault, the real crime, went back to a chemical plant that had dumped in the area years before."

"I suppose the newspapers got hold of it? Your part, I mean?"

Christy sipped coffee, grateful for its warmth. Even thinking about what had happened made her shiver. "That was the worst aspect. People read about me and began to ask me to test localities where pollution was suspected. Sometimes I could even tell them that a place was all right—and that was wonderful. But mostly I gave them bad news."

"Does Lili know about this?"

"She always knows. And of course she thinks it's wonderful."

"My sister may *know*, but she doesn't always understand," Nona said. "She wears blinders when it comes to anything she calls negative."

"My mother thinks I've come into my own, and now I'm to use my gifts for the good of humanity."

"Lili's always very high on humanity." Nona's tone was dry. "But there's more, isn't there? Maybe more than even Lili knows?"

The shivery feeling was growing, deep inside. Christy clasped her hands about the mug and sipped again.

"Yes. She hasn't paid much attention for a while, since she thinks I'm fine, and she's busier than ever. But she must be getting inklings by this time. I haven't told her I was coming here. The last time I found pollution was nearly a year ago. After that, the feeling I'd get, the places I'd be led to, turned so ugly that I can't live with it. I'll go crazy if it goes on! Yet I don't know how to turn it off. Once it started, there wasn't any more of what you might call *normal* pollution. The first time the new thing happened, I could feel the horror all through me, and I could point out where they should dig. I even made someone call the police."

Christy covered her face with her hands, but she couldn't block the pictures in her mind.

"Of course no one wanted to listen—I was just a crackpot.

The young officer who came was sure I was nuts. So I took a shovel myself and I struck right down into bone on the first try —because the grave was so shallow. So then they dug her up. A pretty young girl—not dead for long. She'd only just been reported missing. She had been raped and strangled. *And I knew where she was buried.* It was terrifying that I should know."

Nona's long fingers with their turquoise rings reached out to touch Christy, steadying her. "It's okay. Relax. It's best if you get it all out and let it go."

"At first the police were suspicious of *me.* They didn't think I could know so much unless I was involved. But then there were three more—and I couldn't have had anything to do with them."

Parents and police had begun to find her because of someone missing. It was always a young girl—always found murdered. There had been death threats too. Perhaps from the guilty who thought they might be recognized.

"How does this come to you?" Nona asked.

"I'd be given some possession of the girl who was missing, and when I held it I'd *know* where to look. I would begin to feel ill and a headache would start. I didn't always know the name of the location, but I could *see* the place and, when I gave them details, someone would recognize it. I don't know how it happens. I just blank out and the pictures come—in a sort of mist. When the police take me to the place—it has always been in my general area—I can find the exact spot."

Memory was vivid, painful. Two of the deaths hadn't been recent. Even though the detective who now believed in her most tried to spare her as much as he could, it was awful. She couldn't stand it any more. The horrors were beginning to color her storytelling. Tales of witches and goblins and monsters crept in—the books seemed to leap into her hands—scary things. Some children loved such stories, but some didn't and were frightened.

"Did you get any messages about who the murderer was?" Nona asked.

"No! The police always pushed me for more details, but I was thankful not to be led in that direction. The anonymous threats began to be frightening. So I had to run away—to save *me*. When you said to come I got ready the next day—and here I am."

Christy looked out the window at shadows lengthening across peaceful meadows that sloped down into the valley. Someone was taking the cows back to their barn for the night. Against a sky that was still blue, banners of rose were spreading. Along the ridge where Nona's house stood, a small boy flew a dragon kite, running with the wind.

"It's so peaceful here," Christy said. "Not even a house in view on this side because of the trees along your ridge. It's wonderful to be where no one knows me; no one knows what I can do. I never want to go back to where crime is happening. I'd just like to be—ordinary. I'd like to fall in love and get married and have babies! But how can I, ever?"

Nona patted her hand—a solid, bracing pat. "You did some good, you know. It was better for those parents to be sure, and not go on forever hoping and wondering."

"I don't know if that's true. It's so final to know. Maybe hope is better. Anyway, that's not the point. Why couldn't I know ahead of time? Why couldn't I stop it from happening?"

"That's what you said about Puddles when you were little. But even if you knew, you'd only frighten people and they wouldn't listen."

"Then it's better to be where it can never happen. Whatever it is I have, it doesn't reach out over too many miles. I can be safe here."

The pat was repeated, more firmly. "Finish your coffee and then you can unpack and get settled while I start supper."

Christy looked at her quickly, sensing something. "There haven't been any crimes around here, have there?"

"Not that I know of. At least, not recently. This is Virginia, remember, and old places have histories of spilled blood. At least this area has never been thickly settled—maybe only farmers and Indians have crossed the land or lived here. But I can't guarantee the past."

"It's not the past that sends me messages. At least, not the distant past."

"I wonder if you're doing the right thing?" Nona said, not looking at her.

"You mean in coming here?"

"No—I'm happy to have you. I mean your running away from these messages that come to you, instead of seeing them through."

Christy had begun to relax, but now she stiffened. "What do you mean?"

"Nothing specific. And of course you must rest now—find relief from all your strain. But even if you run away, I don't think your visions will stop—and there may be a use for them. We have to do what we're put here to do—isn't that true?"

"Has something happened here at Redlands? Something you haven't told me?"

"Nothing that won't keep until tomorrow."

For a moment Christy stared at her aunt, all her sense of safety evaporating. Then she put her head down on her arms and began to cry. She had held back her fears for so long, not daring to let go, and now sobs came raggedly, despairingly. Nona pushed a box of tissues near her hand and let her cry.

Christy didn't look up until she heard the door to the deck open, heard a step on the tiles. When she raised her tear-streaked face, she saw that Victor Birdcall had come down from the roof. He filled the doorway, all in gray, except for the western belt he wore, its buckle heavy with silver and turquoise. He glanced at Christy and turned quickly away, speaking to Nona.

"Sorry to interrupt. It'll be dark soon, so I'll stop for now. I'll come back tomorrow and finish the job on the lightning rods."

"Thanks, Victor. This is my niece, Christy Loren, who'll be

staying with me. Christy, this is my friend and neighbor, Victor Birdcall. He lives across the valley on the opposite mountain."

Christy was in no state to rise to the introduction, and she regarded Victor with a certain caution, aware that she returned his own distrust. He was even bigger than he'd seemed on the roof—a man probably in his fifties. Weathering sun lines creased his face, and none of them seemed like laugh lines. In contrast to his black hair, his eyes were a burning blue. She had the sudden strong sense that this was a man who had no space left for other people's troubles.

Aware of Christy's growing tension, Nona spoke curtly to Victor. "I'll see you tomorrow—okay? Plan on having lunch with us."

He caught the peremptory note in her voice and clicked his heels. "Yes, ma'am!"

"Oh, come off it!" Nona said. "I'm just trying to get rid of you quickly. Christy has had a long trip and some unsettling experiences."

His grin came reluctantly—so he could smile. "I'm gone," he said. He didn't look at Christy again but gave Nona a touch of forefinger to temple as he went out the door.

"I shouldn't have been so short with him," Nona said as Victor went off along the deck, his boots light on the planks. "He looks so tough that sometimes I forget how he can curl up like a sensitive plant and take offense."

"He makes me uncomfortable," Christy admitted. "There's something—something dark—" She broke off. "No! I don't want to think about that."

"Then don't. Victor's okay and he's a good friend. So just slam that door when it starts to open. You'll go down useless roads if you dip into every human psyche you meet. Save your gift for where it's needed."

She didn't want to save it at all, but it was still possible to do as Nona directed, and she put Victor out of her mind.

"Let me set my casserole in the oven," Nona said, "and then I'll show you your room."

Christy stood looking out the big windows. These were the forested mountains of the east coast, beautiful with their long shadows flung across slopes of meadow, and rosy light tinting the western sky. In this quiet hour the birds knew that night was coming and they twittered busily in the still air, before settling down. The boy with the soaring kite had gone elsewhere. The scene was peaceful, quiet, yet Christy no longer felt reassured.

Nona closed the oven door and walked into the long hall that ran parallel with the front of the house.

"I want to see your studio," Christy said, following. "You're painting now, aren't you?"

"I certainly am. I've never felt more creative, and I've started a new series that I'm excited about. Come downstairs first, and when you're ready I'll show you."

Stairs slanted to the lower floor that dropped down the hillside at the back. A guest bedroom opened on a wide deck that Christy could see through sliding glass doors. Beyond the edge of the deck, dropping still farther down the steep hill, grew stands of poplar, birch, maple, oak, and dogwood, the latter still ghostly with remaining petals. With the sensation of being among treetops, Christy could see through the branches to the blue ridges of the high mountains not far away. Yet the contrast was great between the front of Nona's house and the view from the back. Out in front there were far-flung spaces of sky, cloud patterns, and changing colors over fields cropped close by cattle. Here at the back, trees hid all but patches of sky, and night came quickly, so that dark woods seemed to crowd in.

Nona slid a door open on its track and a light breeze came through the screen, breaking the early evening calm. "There's a stream down at the bottom, but don't go hiking in the woods unless someone's with you. The snakes will be waking up pretty soon. We don't have rattlers around here, and the black snakes are harmless. But we watch out for the copperheads. They like rocky ledges and woodpiles and thick grass. I manage to live with them peacefully, but you're a foreigner."

Christy drew back from the doorway uneasily. She'd had no experience with snakes, and the outdoor beauty seemed suddenly less appealing.

"There were always snakes in paradise," Nona pointed out, "and they do keep down the insect and rodent population. We share the land with them, but we also stay aware and we don't go putting a hand down on a log or rock without looking first."

"Is that a house down there across the stream?"

"Floris Fox lives down at the bottom. She and her husband used to have a small llama farm. Now that she's a widow, she only keeps a few animals that she can care for with a little outside help. Floris is local and she and Abel were here before the rest of us at Redlands. Most of us come from somewhere else."

Nona was trying to be cheerful in order to promise interest for her stay, but Christy knew her own story and fears had disturbed her aunt.

She turned from the view of tall trees to examine the room. Quilts on twin beds repeated the leafy green pattern outdoors, with touches of yellow sunlight cutting through the print. When Nona turned on a fluted bedlamp, the room's pine walls took on a warm glow.

Christy released a breath that was a sigh of weary contentment. "This is just the sort of room I need right now. The quiet is heavenly."

"When all the tree creatures wake up there'll be a noisy orchestra, but they haven't started yet. I'll see you later." Nona kissed her lightly on the cheek, but before she could turn away, Christy put a hand on her aunt's arm.

"This place *is* safe for me, isn't it? There haven't been any crimes around here?"

"I've already answered that. There's no way to reassure you, considering your present state of mind. But this isn't New York, and you'll feel better tomorrow. Change out of those wrinkled clothes and come upstairs."

It seemed to Christy that her aunt hurried off a little too

quickly, as though the answer she could give wasn't completely reassuring. All Christy's antennae were out and they quivered uneasily. Not just because of snakes. Nona would have had no way of knowing ahead of time the problem that had sent Christy into flight. But now that she'd been told, there seemed something a little guarded about her manner.

Never mind! She must not start up all the doubts and tremors again. It was natural to be edgy wherever she was right now, but this was a place where she could rest and heal all that throbbing, fearful sensitivity.

A green-tiled bathroom adjoined the bedroom, and a shower would be restful and help her to relax. Her mind must be taught new ways—and it would learn! As she stood looking around at the plain wood furniture, some of it undoubtedly handmade, she began to feel quieter, more reassured. Nothing stirred now at the back of her mind to threaten her. There were no flashes of light, no mist, no throbbing head.

She had just opened her suitcase when a sound outside broke the country stillness. This rear side of the house was darker than the front, where the sky still showed traces of brightness. A wrought-iron table and several chairs had been placed outside on the wide planks of the deck, and she saw what had made the sound. A small boy, perhaps six or seven, sat perched on the table, and he was staring at her through the screen. He was the same boy she'd seen flying a kite a few moments ago.

Boys and girls of this age were usually her friends, so she stepped out on the deck to join him. "Hello. I'm Christy Loren. What's your name?"

He stared at her solemnly, and she stood very still, waiting. The boy's fair, curly hair sprang back from a good forehead— sunny hair. But his darker brows drew down in a scowl and his small mouth seemed tight with disapproval.

"Go away," he said.

She nodded, still smiling. "All right. Maybe we can get acquainted another time. That was a great dragon kite you were flying out there."

This didn't soften him in the least. He slid down from the table and ran to the far end of the deck, where he jumped off and disappeared along the hillside. Christy drew green draperies across the sliding doors, trying not to feel disturbed. Small boys often had to be approached warily, and this one would be a friend once he got used to her.

Nevertheless, the intensity of the words he'd flung at her echoed in her mind. *Go away!* She must ask Nona about him when she went upstairs. But first she would take that relaxing shower.

She has come.

I have known she would come ever since I saw the clipping. She is her mother's daughter, and with Nona here, she'd be drawn to Redlands.

I met her once long ago and only by chance. She won't remember. We were in the same hall, listening to Dukas. The daughter is young—an innocent. What does she know about good and evil?

I know. And I know which I prefer. I know which is more powerful and compelling. And far more interesting. For now I will watch. There isn't any danger—yet.

2

EFRESHED by her shower, and dressed in jeans and a blue chambray shirt, Christy went upstairs, where Nona met her in the hallway.

"Supper will be ready soon, and a friend is going to join us. I hope you don't mind. There's time now for you to see my favorite room."

She didn't feel like meeting anyone tonight, but of course there would be visitors in her aunt's home. She couldn't be a recluse and hide from people, though she hadn't expected to meet Nona's friends so quickly.

"Who's coming?" she asked hesitantly as she followed her aunt.

They'd reached a big room at the rear corner of the house, and Nona paused to put a reassuring hand on Christy's arm.

"Eve Corey is a good friend. She's closer to your age, and I think you'll like each other."

"Of course," Christy said, and tried to dismiss her nagging uneasiness.

Nona's studio was a long, wide room, divided into two sections by a pair of Chinese screens. The nearer area served as a sitting room; the farther was where Nona worked at her painting. A slanting roof offered two skylights over her easels.

Nona went ahead, turning on lights. Weather windows, two panes thick, looked out upon darkening treetops at the back of the house. Several paintings stood about on easels—evidently work in progress. Nona had always liked to keep several projects going at once. She would move from one to another, until a painting absorbed her so completely that she worked through to its finish.

Breathing the familiar smell of oil paints and turpentine, Christy felt immediately comfortable. The seeming muddle of Nona's worktable, where brushes and palettes and bottles stood about, was a familiar disorder never to be disturbed by others, since Nona knew exactly where everything was.

One easel had been hidden by a green cloth flung over it, and Nona went to stand with her back to it, almost protectively. "Something new," she said. "Something I'm not sure of yet, so I don't want anyone to see it."

Christy turned to other easels and glanced at several finished canvases set against a wall.

"They're all on the same subject." She voiced her surprise. "Don't you paint anything but roads these days?"

"*Red* roads! They fascinate me and have ever since I moved here—the red roads of Virginia. Of course, these are back roads and there are endless variations. I'm to have a showing of this series in Charlottesville next month, and I'll need to complete three more before then."

In one watercolor a road of red earth ran beside a railed fence, beyond which cows grazed on a hillside meadow. In another, the road wound its way through high grass, to be lost among mountain folds. Still another road circled a small pond where ducks paddled. All were rural mountain scenes, with always a red road winding through. There were no human figures—and there seemed a loneliness and quiet about each scene. Settings that should have been serene and peaceful somehow were not. These were paintings deceptive in their country simplicity, the mood of each somber and mysterious. Where that quality came from Christy wasn't sure.

"What do you see when you paint these?" she asked her aunt. "Are they from life or your imagination?"

"Both, of course." Nona gestured toward a separate row of canvases set face out against the wall. "Tell me what you think of these."

In an oil with a twilight aura, the road came to a sudden end in tall weeds, going nowhere. In another, a ribbon of road climbed to the top of a wooded cliff, where it vanished into space. A third road led into a covered bridge but never emerged on the other side. In the lower right-hand corner of those she had completed was Nona's special signature, bold and clear: HARMONY. Yet these were not harmonious paintings.

"Well?" Nona was waiting. Not that it ever made any difference to Nona what others thought of her work.

"They're compelling. After the first bucolic impression, I want to go deeper into what they mean. I want to know where those roads go, and why some of them end so abruptly. They're unsettling. I'm not sure what you're doing or what you mean."

"That's the mystery of any road." Nona sounded pleased, and her turquoise earrings danced with the turning of her head. "You never know what lovely surprise or unexpected disaster waits for you around the curve. I didn't want to paint pretty country scenes—these reach much more unsettling depths. Of course *I* don't know where my roads go, and I'm not sure I want to. I'd like them to tantalize and promise, and pull the observer into them. You may not see the fantasy right away, but it's always there. These are secret roads and they keep their secrets, even from me."

"I'm not sure I like them," Christy admitted. "They make me uncomfortable."

"That's what I intend. You'll remember them and go on wondering what's going to happen in those hidden distances. Come and sit down and we'll talk a bit until Eve arrives."

On the Chinese screens that separated the sitting area from Nona's work space, waterfalls tumbled steeply down gold panels, to end in white spray over stylized black rocks. All was inked in with sparing lines. Formalized mountains poked starkly into the sky, and small figures on little white horses rode endlessly down precipitous paths between twisted pine trees. Beyond the screens, a small sofa upholstered in wheat-grained cloth with a faint rose stripe, a drop-leaf oval coffee table of polished wood, and several chairs invited the visitor to rest and talk.

"There's good energy here," Christy said. "I can feel it around me. There's no dis-Harmony here."

Nona nodded, pleased. "Sometimes when everything gets too tense with my painting I come here and let it all go away."

Christy went to stand before a cork board hung on the birch-paneled wall. Here were clippings about Harmony and her work, as well as snapshots of friends. She recognized a group photo she had sent her aunt, taken when she was dramatizing a story for children at a library back on Long Island. The rapt faces of the small listeners were a study in themselves. But all that had been before witches and goblins began to creep in.

The next color photo—an enlargement—arrested Christy's attention. Here was the touch of fantasy again, though this was the picture of an actual woman. Her face showed delicate features, with wide, startled eyes, as though she hadn't expected to be photographed. Long fair hair, caught back with a violet ribbon, had released a strand, lifted by a breeze to trail across one cheek. Her dress was long and white, with eyelet embroidery and a violet-ribboned yoke. A nightdress, perhaps? Her feet scarcely touched rough grass, and she raised her arms as if dancing to music only she could hear. Behind her a stand of woods seemed darkly secret—the trees very still, watching her.

A familiar sense of something about to be revealed stirred in Christy. "Who is that?" she asked her aunt.

Nona went abruptly to the board and removed the pins that held the picture. "I must put this away. Her name was Deirdre, and she was just as ethereal as she seems here. Never mind— we have other things to talk about. Come and sit down."

Nona spoke in the past tense of the woman, but casually, as of someone who had moved away, and the stir of warning died in Christy.

She chose an upholstered rocker and settled herself comfortably. Nona dropped onto the sofa, propping a cushion behind her and stretching out long legs on the coffee table. When a book was shoved aside by her foot and fell to the floor, Christy rose to pick it up and saw that it was Rose Vaughn's *Little Red Road* that Harmony had illustrated. She sat down to leaf through the familiar pages.

"Such a beautiful book! It's deserved the acclaim it's won. Children love the story, and they love your pictures when I show them the book."

"Rose's death was a tragedy. I still miss her, though it's eight months now since it happened."

"You wrote about her accident—a terrible shame. She lived around here, didn't she? I hope you'll do more work like this with other writers."

Nona took the book from her and closed it with a firm snap. "I haven't the heart to work with anyone else. Rose was working on something—a story about llamas. I believe she'd completed it, though she never showed it to me."

"Can't you still illustrate it?"

"It's disappeared, and Oliver, Rose's husband, says he couldn't find it among her things. Donny loves this book."

"Donny? Is he the small boy I saw outside on the deck downstairs? I tried to make friends with him, but he wouldn't talk to me—except to tell me to go away. When I said we might get acquainted later, he gave me a black look and ran off."

"I'm sorry. Donny has problems right now. He lives close by with his father, Hayden Mitchell. Rose was his special friend, and her death hit him pretty hard."

"You said it was a fall—how did it happen?"

"That's the miserable part—it never should have happened at all. Like most accidents. Rose loved to hike and often went out alone, since Oliver doesn't care much about physical activity. She should have known better than to go off without telling anyone where she meant to climb. They didn't find her for three days. As a matter of fact—" Nona broke off and shook her head. "Never mind. I can't really talk about it. Not yet."

"Did she live in Redlands?"

"Yes. Over on the mountain above Victor's cabin. Poor Oliver. He still lives in their house, and it's been a dreadful time for him. He teaches English lit at the University of Virginia in Charlottesville, and he's a writer himself. Though I'm not much in sympathy with his articles on parapsychology. His debunking is passionate and wrongheaded—I don't think he knows what he's talking about. Rose understood better—you can sense it in her stories."

"She did other stories?"

"Several earlier ones. If I ever illustrate another book for children I'd like to do one of Rose's tales. But Oliver doesn't want them published."

"Why not?" Christy was beginning to dislike Oliver Vaughn.

"They fly too strongly against all that down-to-earth realism he prides himself on. He doesn't approve of fairy tales for children. He doesn't understand that fantasy is right brain. It stretches the imagination and helps it to grow. His nothing-but-realism credo stifles it and builds walls around it. I've had a few rounds of argument with him, but we get nowhere."

Nona sat up, suddenly alert. "There—that's Eve coming now. Let's go meet her."

Christy had heard nothing, but Nona's inner faculty was working, and a moment later the door chimes sounded. Nona led the way out to the front deck. "Come around this way, Eve," she called, and added to Christy, "Eve works for Hayden Mitchell, Donny's father."

Eve Corey waved and started toward the kitchen door where Nona stood. She was probably in her mid-thirties and she dressed as though she cared very little about what others thought. The afternoon had turned warm enough for shorts, and she hadn't bothered to change. Patched denim revealed plump legs and well-padded hips. Her face was round and devoid of makeup and she wore her brown hair in a straight cut below her ears, with slanted bangs across her forehead. At the moment she looked upset and irritated.

"Come in and tell us about it, Eve," Nona said. "Christy, this is Eve Corey. Eve, Christy Loren. What's happened to upset you?"

Eve was tall enough to carry her weight fairly well, and she moved quickly, assertively. As she strode into Nona's red-tiled kitchen, Christy could sense her vitality—an excess of energy that surrounded her—at the moment, angry energy.

"Want me to fix the salad?" Eve asked. Her Virginia accent was only a hint—musical and pleasing. "Maybe tearing up lettuce will make me feel better. I just had a run-in with Victor Birdcall. How you can stand to have that man working for you I don't know."

Nona raised an eyebrow at Christy, undisturbed. "We keep out of Eve's way when she gets mad. What did Victor say to upset you?" She handed Christy woven place mats to arrange on the table set in the bay of windows, and opened a drawer to indicate silverware.

The refrigerator door slammed as Eve took out salad greens and carried them to the sink.

"Victor thinks Hayden should drop the search for Deirdre and let her stay missing. Of course he's wrong, and I said so. He shouldn't go telling Hayden and Donny stuff like that. Even though we've combed the woods and hills around here and haven't found a trace, we can't give up."

Nona cast a wary look at Christy. "It's been two months, hasn't it?"

"Six weeks."

Christy repeated aloud the one word she'd focused on: "Missing?"

"Let's not talk about this now," Nona said quickly. "We don't want to spoil our meal."

Moving automatically, Christy finished setting the table, thrusting back a new wave of anxiety. She'd sensed something evasive in Nona ever since she'd told her aunt what had brought her here.

"It doesn't matter, Christy." Nona watched her uneasily. "This has nothing to do with you. Don't even think about it."

Eve went right on. "Doesn't it seem strange that we've had two disappearances in less than a year?"

"Rose was found," Nona reminded her. "That was a fall—an accident. While Deirdre could have run off anywhere in her whimsical way."

"Helpless little Deirdre, who needs her husband and even her young son to look after her?" Eve shook her head vehemently. "Not likely. Besides, nobody can stop Donny from looking. Not after what happened with Rose. That's what scares him. He'll go on and on until there's an answer. And now Hayden's letting his work go, which means that I'm taking on most of it at the plant nursery. Donny's staying out of school on various pretexts, and things are going to pot. It would be better to find her dead than to go on like this."

"I'm lost," Christy said. "I don't know what you're talking about."

"Sorry. I suppose I should have explained." Nona lifted an earthenware casserole from the oven and set it on a trivet. "As soon as your salad's ready, Eve, we can eat."

"Explain *now,*" Christy insisted. "Please."

"Oh, all right." Nona gave in. "Hayden Mitchell runs a tree and plant nursery not far from Redlands. He's put in all these flowering bushes for me, and he's really creative, imaginative —an artist with growing things. Eve works as his assistant, and she's pretty good herself at all this horticulture stuff."

"I just have a knack for getting things to grow," Eve agreed. "But you're marking time, Nona. Tell her about Deirdre."

"Not now." Nona was firm, and Christy understood her aunt's reluctance, though Eve didn't. She thought of the photo she'd seen of a slim, almost ethereal woman in a white gown and bare feet, her long fair hair lifting in a breeze.

"Why did what Victor said upset you?" Nona asked Eve.

"Victor always upsets me. But this time I started wondering if he knows something he's not talking about. I asked him right out, and he scowled as though he'd like to hit me. He has a vile temper, and I don't think you should trust him the way you do, Nona."

Eve mixed salad greens as she talked, and now she brought the big wooden bowl to the table.

Nona gestured them both to chairs. "I'm not worried about Victor." She pulled off the flowered scarf she'd tied around her head, and graying hair sprang up in little clumps, somehow making her look less indomitable—as though the scarf provided her with an armor, a defense.

Christy sat where she could look out the window toward the ever changing view. In growing darkness the mountains formed a black silhouette, like a scalloped cutout set against the backdrop of a lighter sky. Far across the dip of the valley, house lights shone among the trees. Houses that weren't visible by day.

Eve followed the direction of her gaze. "That's where Victor lives. He built his own log cabin over there in the woods. Oliver Vaughn's house is higher and a little farther along on the right. He's stayed there since Rose's death."

Through open windows a breeze stirred the good scents of Nona's cooking. She had baked chicken with broccoli and mushrooms in her own special stock, seasoned with lemon juice and dill. Hot corn bread added its own appetizing aroma, and Christy found that she was hungry in spite of her uneasiness about all she was learning.

"Now tell Christy about Deirdre Mitchell," Eve repeated, undeflected by Nona's hesitance to explain. "You really must, you know. Sooner or later she'll meet Hayden."

Nona set down her fork and gave in. "What happened was sudden. One night Deirdre got out of bed while Hayden and Donny were asleep—and simply disappeared. She put on sandals and slipped a coat over her nightclothes, but she didn't take anything else. Which makes her disappearance seem all the more ominous. She intended, obviously, to return to bed."

"It wasn't all that unusual for her to go outdoors in the

middle of the night," Eve said. "We all knew that. She'd stay out for a half hour or so playing her games—dancing with her spirits—barefoot on the grass in the moonlight! That's what she claimed. She was one of those full-moon people. Or sometimes she'd go out at dawn when the sun was rising on the dew. It's a wonder a copperhead didn't get her!"

"That was Deirdre's style," Nona said tolerantly. "Just as it's mine to paint red roads. As for snakes, Deirdre always claimed they were her friends and she was safe with them. She really did seem to have an affinity for wild things. I sometimes thought that cat of hers was half wild."

"That's another funny thing," Eve said. "That Siamese disappeared along with Deirdre."

Nona explained to Christy. "That's something that worries us. The cat always stayed close to her—so why hasn't it been found either? Anyway, Christy, I never meant to have all these unhappy events spill out on your first night here."

The stirring under the surface was alive now in Christy, as though something dark waited to spring out at her.

Nona knew what was happening. "Don't, Christy. Don't let it take over. You *can* stop it, you know. Give yourself a little breathing space."

"What does that mean?" Eve asked bluntly.

Christy raised her hands in a helpless gesture. "Tell Eve, if you like. It doesn't matter."

Reluctantly, as they ate, Nona related the story of what had happened in Christy's life during the last two years, and Eve listened intently. When Nona was through, Eve regarded Christy with growing excitement.

"Perhaps you were sent!" she cried. "Perhaps it was meant that you should come here and help Hayden and Donny."

Nona said nothing and her silence made Christy all the more uncomfortable.

"I haven't any talent for finding people who disappear because of accidents," she told Eve.

"But what if something worse has happened to Deirdre?" Eve persisted.

"That's enough for now." Nona pushed back from the table. "If you're through, let's clear the dishes and I'll fix the dessert."

Eve gave up for the moment. "Okay. How does it work, Christy? You can talk about that, can't you? How do clues come to you?"

Christy carried dishes to the sink, wishing she could sidestep all of this.

"It's not idle curiosity," Eve added. "I feel terribly sorry for Hayden and Donny—so if there was any chance of your helping—"

"I can't tell you how it happens," Christy broke in. "I don't know where the pictures come from or why they come. They're suddenly there, whether I want them or not, and I begin to sense something. I don't feel anything now about Deirdre, and I don't want to. When it happens it can be shattering. Worst of all, I never have any feeling that I've helped."

"You don't need to think about any of this until you're rested," Nona assured her. "Eve, why does Victor feel that the search should stop?"

Eve scowled. "Who knows? He gets hunches, but he makes me mad the way he acts—as though he has some deep, inner knowledge that nobody else can have. I don't know if he really knows something or if he's putting me on. I just wish he'd go back to New Mexico, or wherever he came from."

"I'll talk to him," Nona said. "For dessert we're having yogurt with honey and nuts and a sprinkle of carob. Agreeable?"

Nobody objected, and when she'd spooned the mixture into sherbet glasses, Eve carried them to the table.

"I'd better fix an extra dish," Nona said. "Someone's coming."

A moment later they heard a car on the gravel driveway, and Eve rolled her eyes at Christy as Nona switched on the outside lights.

"I don't know how you do that." Eve went to look out toward the driveway. "It's Oliver Vaughn."

"Oliver was Rose's husband," Nona reminded Christy as she went out on the deck.

A moment later she returned, followed by a tall, slender man, perhaps in his early forties. He carried a tote bag filled with books that he set down on the tiles as Nona introduced him to Christy.

His interest as he took her hand seemed especially intent. "You're Liliana Dukas's daughter, aren't you? Nona has told us about you, though I gather you haven't followed in your mother's footsteps."

"Sit down, Oliver," Nona directed. "I know you hate yogurt, but have some anyway. At least you drink coffee."

Oliver Vaughn was good-looking enough to have been a movie actor out of the past. Today's actors were stamped in no such beautiful pattern. His pale, silky hair contrasted with dark eyes as heavily lashed as a woman's. His straight, classic nose looked as though he might be disdainful of much that came under it.

"I brought over the extra copies of Rose's book you wanted," he told Nona. "I'm clearing out her things, and I know you can use more copies of *Little Red Road.*" He sounded matter-of-fact, but Christy sensed that Oliver Vaughn might be suppressing a great deal of emotion under his cool demeanor.

Seated, he didn't seem as tall—it was his legs that were long. Under a blue pullover his shoulders rounded a little, as though from bending above a desk.

"Thanks," Nona said. "I'm very glad to have these."

"Can you use any help, Oliver, sorting through Rose's things?" Eve offered. "I can manage the time."

He shook his head. "I want to do this myself. I'm going to put my house up for sale and move into Charlottesville as soon as I can."

"Must you move?" Nona asked. "I should think Redlands would be ideal for a writer."

"You mean because it's so quiet that nothing ever happens here?" He raised an eyebrow derisively and turned to Christy. "You may have heard that this hasn't been a happy place lately. I lived here because of Rose—because she loved the isolation. Now I'd rather get away. I don't want to be here when they find Deirdre."

"What makes you think she'll be found?" Nona asked.

"It's inevitable, isn't it? Where could she go in sandals and a nightgown?" There was something about the way he spoke that made Christy look at him quickly, but his bland expression told her nothing.

He ate a mouthful of yogurt, made a face, and went on. "I saw your mother in an interview on television last week. What do you think of her work?"

"Before you commit yourself, Christy," Nona put in, "you'd better be aware that Oliver's second vocation is the exposing of fake psychics. Lili would really baffle him."

Christy smiled, sidestepping his question. "My mother lives her life as she pleases, and that's fine with me."

"I'd like to meet her," Oliver said. "I've just finished writing an article about this so-called channeling—where spirits who come from God knows where and have special identities are supposed to speak through human channels."

"Perhaps God does know," Nona said mildly. "Even though you don't think it's for real."

"Oh, I'm sure some of these people get carried away by their own fantasies," Oliver said. "I've checked some of the prophecies psychics make at the beginning of every year, and mostly they're wrong."

"Of course there are phonies in every field," Eve put in. "But *you* see what you want to see, Oliver. Rose heard her own voices—"

"Rose was different." Oliver dismissed her words. "Every artist, every writer, experiences inspiration—something that comes from the unconscious. How, we don't know. But these aren't voices from outer space, or put into us mysteriously."

"How do you know that?" Christy asked. "Who really knows where inspiration comes from?"

He regarded her with his cool, rather distant air, and again she sensed some tension in him, barely suppressed. Oliver Vaughn was far from being an open, easily read person.

"People like Dukas speak with changed voices and claim that entities are speaking through them—coming from elsewhere. The scientific mind knows that this is nonsense." He was emphatic.

"Then you think my mother is a fake?" Christy asked.

"I don't know enough about her. That's why I'd like to meet her, perhaps put her through a few tests, if she were willing."

"She wouldn't be," Nona said. "I know my sister and she wouldn't waste her time. She uses whatever she has for purposes that count. It doesn't matter to her if there are those who don't believe."

Oliver smiled without warmth. "All of which brings her a great deal of publicity and wealth. That's one of the things that makes me skeptical. Forgive me, Christy, but this sort of enterprise can become pretty big business these days, taking money from the gullible."

"You only see one side!" Eve protested. Her attitude toward Oliver seemed an odd mixture of affection and impatience. "We all have to earn a living, and sometimes money comes more easily in one profession than another."

"Except," Oliver pointed out, "that this pretends to be an altruistic gift—all for the benefit of mankind."

Even though this man put her off a little with his skepticism, Christy had always shrunk from these very aspects of her mother's work. Lili, of course, dismissed the money earning airily. All that was incidental, she said, and she couldn't help or control those who handled her scheduling and programs. There was a large staff who had to be paid, and she trusted all of them. Yet it had seemed to Christy that the entourage that surrounded her mother might be all too willing to sop up whatever came their way. Perhaps they even used Lili, but this was not something Christy could do anything about. She was sure that her mother was not the greedy one in the picture.

Nona glanced at her watch. "I didn't know whether to mention this or not, but since we're talking about her, Lili's to be on a program that's coming on TV in about five minutes. Shall I turn on the set? Would you like to watch, Christy?"

Watching Liliana Dukas "perform" was not Christy's favorite way of spending time, but Oliver Vaughn's attitude and remarks had rankled. It might be interesting to see her mother answer him herself.

"It's fine," she told her aunt.

Eve jumped up eagerly. "Do let's! Dukas always fascinates me. So here's another chance to check her out, Oliver."

He didn't seem particularly eager as he trailed after them to the living room. His aloof manner gave him an air of being removed from whatever was happening around him. Yet Christy, walking beside him, could sense the vibration of some inner turmoil. She felt a curious urge to put a quieting hand on his arm to reassure him. A disturbed and unhappy man was masquerading under the guard he wore.

Nona's living room was large, with cream walls and a high ceiling. An electric fan hung beneath the central light fixture, its blades quiet on this cool evening. Soft green wall-to-wall carpeting gave the room a sense of quiet and peace, even though small tables and bookcases were busy with dozens of ornamental objects that Nona had collected in her travels around the world. Christy remembered the African pictures brought from the French Congo before it became an African nation, the lacquer boxes from Japan, and the great carved fish of gray Vietnam marble.

"This is my museum room," Nona told Christy. "It's the first time I've had a place to set out all my treasures. Do sit down, everyone."

Christy moved away from Oliver, whose tension continued to make her uncomfortable. She chose a hassock near Nona's armchair, while Eve and Oliver sat on the couch. Nona touched a button that raised a screen over the television set in one wall. A satellite dish outside brought in the world, and Nona began to change galaxies. Perhaps Lili's "channels" were just as real as these, Christy thought, if one possessed the ability to understand such mysteries.

Nona found the proper channel, and Bill Mathison's middle-aged, affable face came on the screen. His show had the special quality of being live in these days when most programs were recorded. So one never knew what might happen next, and he often invited controversial guests who dealt in the esoteric.

Once the commercials were out of the way, Mathison introduced his panel. The only man was Thomas Ardle, "debunker" of psychic matters, and a man Christy detested for his prejudice and ability to twist everything to his own views. She wondered if Oliver Vaughn was like that, and found herself watching him across the room. There seemed a deep suffering in this man who had so recently lost his wife, and she wondered if his mind could be opened to the help and comfort he might receive from someone like Lili. Probably not, since Rose, with all the sensitivity and awareness that showed in her writing for children, hadn't been able to convince him.

"Get on with it!" Eve told the screen, squirming with her usual impatience. "Let's have Dukas!"

Christy had never heard of the woman who was next introduced—rather wispy and other-worldly—perhaps given force by the entities who spoke through her. Liliana Dukas, secure in her fame, came last on the screen in the introductions, confident, smiling warmly, exuding a quality that Christy thought of whimsically as "electric serenity."

How strange, she thought, that the old childish longing could arise whenever she saw her mother after a lapse of time. Memories swept back—memories of a vibrant, beautiful whirlwind of a woman who swept lovingly into her daughter's life— and then flew off on her own affairs, leaving Christy lonely and empty. Now the unwelcome longing was almost as sharp as when she had been a little girl.

From her chair, Nona watched her knowingly, and Christy smiled at her aunt. If it hadn't been for Nona, she'd have felt even more bereft through all her childhood.

Once the introductions were over, Dukas was to be interviewed first, and she smiled kindly at the critic, who scowled back, determined to remain unimpressed. There was a radiance about Lili, an outgoing generosity that always brought a sense of helpless admiration to Christy, no matter how much she might want to resist and resent all that charm.

Dukas was still beautiful in an old-fashioned way, not minding a few extra curves to her full figure. She could wear timeless clothes that enhanced her voluptuous appeal, and tonight her long dress was of a royal blue that the camera loved. A shimmering blue that contrasted with heavy coils of dark hair that she had never allowed to turn gray. Lili's face seemed as smooth as that of a young woman, and even her hands appeared flawless, devoid of wrinkles or conspicuous veins.

"Dukas sure takes care of herself," Eve murmured, hiding her own bitten nails under the hem of the man's shirt she wore over her shorts.

With her usual grace, Lili answered the host's questions and then settled herself in her chair and closed her eyes. She could do this very quickly, as Christy knew. In only a moment or two she began to sway a little—an almost infinitesimal movement that stopped as she began to speak.

The voice was of a different caliber from Lili's, and the entity who came to Lili was called Josef. He could be outspoken and was not one to suffer nonsense gladly. Lili herself had none of his acerbity. The host's questions were of no great depth, meant to entertain, and Josef disposed of them almost carelessly. Nothing of particular importance was said, until Thomas Ardle was invited to ask a question.

"What does Dukas do with all the money she takes in because of you, Josef?" he asked.

"That is not our concern," Josef said loftily, removing himself from the plane of such earthly matters. His interest, he went on curtly, lay in how he could help, through Dukas, those who needed him.

Christy smiled, almost sorry for Thomas Ardle, who would be no match for either Lili or Josef. Ardle's debunking talents might work on haunted houses, or the bending of spoons, or other feats that might or might not be trickery. But how did you "expose" someone who was channeling? Lili didn't often make prophecies that could later be proved or disproved. Her gift lay in healing, in offering advice and comfort to those who had suffered a loss or needed guidance.

Josef went on in his slightly stilted way, ignoring the next question Ardle asked him. "There is someone listening now who is suffering greatly. A man who has lost his wife in recent months. He needs to take care and be warned. We wish to warn him that her death may not have been an accident."

Josef stopped speaking and Lili opened her eyes, immediately with them again. She would know what had been said—never an unconscious channeler.

Ardle burst into angry words. "What kind of thing is that? Means nothing! There must be hundreds of men—thousands! —listening out there who have lost their wives. It's harmful to warn of something that may not be true at all. How do you know who will take this to heart?"

Christy looked intently at Oliver Vaughn and saw that his hands were tightly clasped and white at the knuckles. He looked as angry as Ardle did. The other woman had come on the screen, but in Nona's living room no one watched her.

A note of malice crept into Eve's voice when she spoke. "Maybe Dukas meant you, Oliver. I've always felt that Rose would never have fallen when she was out hiking. She was never the careless type."

Oliver looked positively ill, and Christy knew that Eve's words and her mother's had struck home.

The doorbell chimed suddenly, startling them all.

"I'll see who it is," Nona said. For once, she hadn't been aware of someone coming.

Oliver was staring at Eve as though still listening to her words, but now he chose to deny them. "That's crazy," he told her roughly. "Everyone loved Rose. There isn't anyone who wanted to harm her."

"I suppose not." Eve sounded unexpectedly contrite. "Forget I said it."

But none of them could forget what Liliana Dukas had said, and little attention was paid to the second woman being interviewed. Nona rejoined them, bringing with her a man whom Christy hadn't met, though the others knew and greeted him.

"This is Donny's father, Hayden Mitchell," Nona told Christy.

Hayden was not as tall as Oliver, and he was more sturdily built, with wide shoulders and strong cheekbones in his tanned face. His eyes were dark brown, intent in their regard, and his brown hair showed a bit of unruly curl. At least, he smiled more readily than his son, though the relaxing of his wide mouth was fleeting.

"I'm sorry," he told Nona. "I didn't realize you had company until I saw the cars on the driveway. Then I thought I might as well come in anyway and show you what has turned up."

Ardle had appeared on the television screen again, his voice cutting through the room, compelling attention, so they all turned to watch.

"I'll switch it off," Nona said. "Then we can listen to Hayden."

Prompted by some inner urging, Christy spoke abruptly. "No—please. Lili will be on again and I'd like to hear her, if Mr. Mitchell doesn't mind."

At Nona's bidding, Hayden sat down reluctantly, and the television stayed on. Christy, however, found herself watching the man instead of the set, and when no one explained what was happening, Hayden took something white and soft and filmy from his pocket.

"Donny found this today," Hayden said. "It's a scarf that belonged to his mother. He came across it near the stream below this house. I went down there with him to look around, though we didn't find anything else. Donny says this was caught under a bush, so searchers missed it, but Deirdre must have been down there. The water's low in the stream, so it's not deep enough for her to have fallen into. I don't know what to make of this."

Hayden spoke without expression in his face or voice—a screen, perhaps, for whatever lay beneath, though his dark eyes seemed intensely alive and, Christy thought, strangely wary.

"Christy"—Nona spoke hesitantly, a note of pleading in her voice—"if you would just touch the scarf . . ."

Christy jumped up from the hassock and started toward the door. "No! You can't do this to me, Nona! Take it away—I won't touch it!" She understood now what her aunt's talk about not running away had meant.

"What are you talking about?" Hayden demanded, his voice ragged. "What are you up to, Nona?"

Christy backed toward the door, her hands behind her. On the screen Lili appeared again and she closed her eyes as Josef's voice emerged, answering Mathison's last question.

In her mind Christy breathed a quick prayer for help— perhaps to her mother. There had been telepathy between them a few times in the past. At once Lili's eyes opened and she looked straight at the camera. In Nona's living room there was sudden silence.

Josef was gone, and Lili spoke in a soft, penetrating voice. "Christy is in danger. I want her to leave that place as soon as she can—tomorrow at the latest. There are clouds around her —a dangerous mist!"

Mathison jumped in at once. "Who is Christy?"

Lili only shook her head and returned to the program as though there had been no interruption.

Christy cast a frightened look at the screen, aware of Hayden's fixed attention, questioning and curious. But she had nothing to give him and she couldn't face any of them a moment longer. She rushed out of the room, unable to respond except by flight, and hurried down to her bedroom.

There was no key or she would have locked the door. She threw herself across the flowered quilt and closed her eyes, covered her ears with shaking hands. She *had* to shut herself away. Lili's power had reached out to her in response to her own plea, and Lili was usually right. Not for anything would she touch the scarf that had belonged to Deirdre Mitchell. Nor could she face that stark look in Hayden's eyes. Her instinct was to distrust him entirely, and for some reason to be afraid. A reason that had nothing to do with the scarf.

Upstairs in the living room the four who remained stared at one another, and Nona went to turn off the television set. Quietly she explained to Hayden why Christy had come and why it was probably wise if she never touched Deirdre's scarf. It had been a mistake, she admitted, to ask that of her niece. Then she looked toward the windows. "Someone's out there."

A moment later they heard a tapping on a window to the deck.

"May I come in?" Victor Birdcall asked, and Eve, at a nod from Nona, went quickly to the door to let him in.

There's no need to fear her. Even if she holds the scarf it will tell her nothing. It's been washed three times, so she can't sense anything of Deirdre. It's only a red herring I put there for Donny to find. They'll never look in the right direction now.

If she listens to the warning from Dukas she'll leave tomorrow. Then everything will be safe. For all of us.

3

CHRISTY had left a lamp burning beside her bed, and she'd closed the curtains against the black night outside. She had just fallen into a light, uneasy doze when Nona tapped on her door. Some insistent dream took wing and Christy was glad to see it go. She sat up with a sudden awareness of the wooded hill that dropped steeply down behind this house—to the stream near which Deirdre's scarf had been found.

"Are you asleep?" Nona called softly.

"I'm awake. You'd better come in."

She wanted no more stirring of those dark mists tonight, but Nona couldn't be sent away. Lili's force, that dynamic energy she could summon, had been frightening. Lili *knew*—something. So it was best if Christy told her aunt at once that she must leave tomorrow. Redlands was no longer safe for her.

Nona had put on a quilted yellow robe and her short, spiky hair gave her an air of alarm—though she seemed calm enough outwardly. She had brought a tray with glasses of hot milk and wheat wafers on a flowered plate. Her sharp features seemed softened by lamplight, and she looked safe and familiar to Christy, who could remember all the times when Nona had brought hot milk at bedtime to heal the upsets of the day.

"I'm sorry about everything that happened tonight," Nona said, helping Christy to sit up and take a glass, as though she were still a little girl. "It was all too sudden, and I shouldn't have pulled you in. Tomorrow night we'll keep for ourselves."

"I won't be here tomorrow night," Christy told her. "You heard Lili. For once I must listen to her. I must leave as soon as I can."

Nona sat down and sipped from her own glass. "If that's the way you feel, of course you must go. Though I'd hoped for a longer visit. I'd even hoped that you could help *me*. My work's been taking a strange turn lately, and your perception—"

"How could I help anyone when I can't help myself?"

Nona puzzled aloud, "Sometimes I seem to put more into my paintings than I expect. I even have the feeling sometimes that I'm trying to tell myself something."

She sounded so uneasy that Christy began to pay attention. "What could I do that might help?"

"I'm not sure. Perhaps I thought you might find an answer if you studied one or two of the paintings that trouble me. There's one I did of Deirdre in the woods—one you haven't seen—that seems especially insistent whenever I look at it. As though it were trying to tell me something—though it came out of my own consciousness and from my own brush."

"Perhaps I can look at it in the morning before I leave." Hot milk had soothed Christy and made her a little sleepy. But before she could settle down on her pillow, Nona went on.

"If there's anything there, I suppose it will surface eventually, one way or another. After you left, Christy, Victor Birdcall showed up. I suspect he'd been watching us from outside, and he seemed concerned about Deirdre's scarf, and the way you ran off. He told us in that prophet's voice he sometimes adopts to let Deirdre go. He said she was never of this earth—only loaned to us for a little while. So it would be best not to look for whatever remains of her. If there's a great stir and much suffering, it might draw her back to this earthly plane—and that wouldn't be good for anyone."

"How did Hayden Mitchell react to that?"

"He didn't, outwardly. There's a lot of deep, angry emotion there, and he just sits on the lid. I'm not sure of its cause. He holds back so much that sometimes I'm afraid there'll be an explosion."

Christy was glad she wouldn't be here long enough to see the outcome of any of this. All her hopes for peace and safety had vanished, and she knew she must escape before that darker shadow that pursued her made itself known. She'd sensed at once that the threat was connected with Hayden.

"What happened after that?"

"Oliver laughed. Hayden said nothing at all—and even his silence can be upsetting. Sometimes I wish he would let go."

"And Eve?"

"She stayed out of it for once, though I think she was annoyed with Oliver for laughing. She thinks Victor is up to no good, and that we all ought to take him more seriously. There's some interesting background that I haven't told you about Eve and Rose. Perhaps it doesn't matter, since you're leaving."

The sleepiness was passing as they talked. "You might as well tell me now. You're dying to gossip."

Nona grinned. "You know me too well. All right—it's a bit of a story. Eve and Rose were friends as children. Their families had neighboring farms here in Nelson County. Rose's father raised horses, so she rode a lot as a young girl. Eve would come to ride with her. They went to the university together in Charlottesville, where they separated for a while because they were taking different courses. Oliver Vaughn was a young professor in one of Eve's classes, and I think they became what is called involved. Oliver is only a little older. They were going to be married when Eve finished school. Only she made the mistake of introducing him to Rose—and that was that. Rose was beautiful and warm and utterly trusting. Eve could hold her own with Oliver, and still does, but Rose looked up to him in a way he couldn't resist. There's a vanity in the man I've never liked. Anyway, he fell in love with Rose and whatever he had with Eve was over."

"How did she take it?"

"I guess she tried to talk Rose out of marrying him. She knew Oliver pretty well, and she knew Rose could never handle him. But Rose was always ready to forgive Oliver anything. She would bear with his sullen moods and be comforting and admiring. So of course she was the one he had to have. I saw her in tears a few times when we were working on *Red Road* together, so I don't think she was entirely happy. Strangely enough, Eve and Rose remained friends after Rose married Oliver, and it wasn't Rose whom Eve blamed or resented."

"That seems to Eve's credit."

"I'm still wondering how Oliver took what happened tonight with Lili. He has always been opposed to everything that hinted at the psychic. Though I don't think he has the single-track mind that Thomas Ardle has."

"How did Oliver take Rose's death?"

"He shut himself off up there in his house in the woods and wouldn't see anyone for weeks. Now he's planning to move away, and I suppose he'll try to forget everything that's happened here. Except that Deirdre's disappearance has opened it all up again. He's sure she'll be found dead, just as Rose was, but he doesn't think either of them was murdered—as your mother seemed to be hinting about Rose on the air tonight. Victor had another surprise for us. Are you sure you want to hear all this tonight?"

"Go ahead. You always used to tell me bedtime stories." Christy ate another wheat wafer and finished the milk.

"All right. It's on your head. Victor took something out of his jacket pocket and showed it to us. It was a slipper that he'd found covered by leaves on the bank of the stream near where Donny picked up the scarf. At first Victor had only wanted to show it to me—not the others."

"Why not?"

"I suppose his feeling connects with letting Deirdre go and not stirring up her earthly remains. The only problem is that, according to Hayden, the slipper isn't Deirdre's. It isn't even her size."

"What did the others say?"

"Nobody claimed it, and they don't trust Victor, so they didn't say much of anything. I took the slipper and said I'd keep it for a while. It's black velvet, flat-heeled, worn in the sole—ready to be thrown away. Not something Deirdre would wear, even if it had been her tiny size. And certainly not out in the woods."

"So who is running around shedding one slipper?"

Nona raised her hands helplessly and stood up. "Who knows? Let me tuck you in again. You'll go right to sleep now."

"What are you really up to?" Christy asked as her aunt moved to the door. "You didn't tell me all this for nothing."

"I thought I'd give you some new ideas to stir around in your dreams. So you can see what comes out. I'd like you to stay long enough to get to know Hayden Mitchell a little. Not that you'll like him. He's too sure of himself, too macho for your taste. But there's a vulnerability there too, and a deep love for his son. He needs your help, whether he'd ever admit it or not. Good night, Christy."

She went off quickly, and Christy lay awake for a time, listening to the beginning of the loud cricket orchestra outside. When drowsiness came, the dream began—the old dream of a red-floored corridor with high walls and the only escape far ahead. As always, she heard the sound of footsteps following, and something menacing seemed to lie around the next turn. Something that meant her own death. Of course she never rounded the turn—she always woke up in time.

The night seemed long before the insect chorus turned into the trills and twitterings of birds waking up. A pale light appeared at the glass doors to the deck, edging the draperies.

Christy lay still, trying to fling off the tormenting effect of the dream. It had begun to repeat itself soon after she'd found the first murdered girl, and it was nearly always the same. After she woke up from this faceless pursuit, her heart would pound for a time. She waited now for it to quiet before she got out of bed.

As she showered and dressed, she held to the thought of her car waiting for her out on the driveway—a friend and ally that would enable her to get away promptly. She would have breakfast with Nona, and then she would go.

When she'd dressed in corduroy slacks and a jonquil-yellow

blouse, Christy went upstairs to find Nona whistling cheerfully in the kitchen. The front windows drew Christy to the tremendous spread of mountains that rimmed the deep cut of this little valley. Its sloping folds of meadow showed red wherever the earth was bare of grass, and cattle were already browsing where green came through. Here the trees had been banished to the high, blue-green mountains, and to isolated clumps that separated the houses along this ridge. Downstairs she'd sensed only the darkness of trees that closed in the house, crowding the lower deck, where the hill fell steeply away in a carpet of dead brown leaves. In contrast, this upper side of the house was open to the sky—open and free.

Christy went out on the front deck and raised her arms, breathing deeply of fresh crystal air, banishing night dreams. Here, surely, she could find peace and goodness and a quiet that could shut out the clamor of a world going all too quickly insane. If only this too were not an illusion, so she might stay and bring her own life forces back to recovery.

She went inside, smiling at her aunt.

"Good morning, Christy." Nona returned her smile warmly. "We're having blueberry pancakes—your favorite. I can see you slept well. Everyone sleeps in this cool mountain air."

"Some of the time I slept," Christy said, and didn't mention her dream as she sat down at the table.

Nona's red-tiled kitchen seemed utterly peaceful this morning, with no waves of uneasiness stirring. The view continued to draw her, and Christy looked out through glass at a light that was still misty with early morning. Shreddings of fog drifted between mountain folds. Part way up the opposite slope, lights shone through the trees around Victor Birdcall's cabin, though no lights could be seen higher up in Oliver's tree-hidden house.

When she'd heaped their plates with steaming pancakes, Nona sat down beside Christy. She wore a blue-flowered smock over jeans, and a length of matching material had been tied jauntily around her head. No earrings this morning, but the scent of verbena was familiar and reassuring.

"Where does Eve Corcy live?" Christy asked.

"She left the family farm, and is staying in the little house Hayden and Deirdre built out at the plant nursery when they first came here. Eve's found a place for herself working for Hayden, and her green thumb is a help to him. After she lost Oliver to Rose, Eve married some years ago, but her husband died in Vietnam, so she's a widow."

"Is she still interested in Oliver?" The question was an idle one, but Nona hesitated a moment too long before she answered. Once more, Christy sensed the stir of something disquieting.

"I think she may be. But she wanted to show both Oliver and Rose that she didn't care when she made her short marriage. Don't be upset by Eve, Christy. She can speak her mind pretty openly, but she's okay. And she really did care about Rose."

Christy had no intention of being upset by anyone here. In spite of the deceptive lure of this place, she meant to be gone for good in a little while.

Nona pushed the butter plate toward Christy. "I love to sit here in the early hours and watch lights come on across the valley," she mused. "I enjoy being alone in my own little world —yet with human companionship not too far away, if I need it."

Christy began to eat without comment. The pancakes were delicious and took her back to childhood when she'd lived with Nona on Long Island.

As the light strengthened and the mists lifted, the strong red earth color showed through on meadow and mountain. The red boards of Nona's decks echoed the very shade of burning red—the red of the path in her dream.

Nona, who always claimed to have no interest in cooking, made the best pancakes ever. Christy spread on butter and ate with gusto. The dream was only a dream. She had never told Nona about it, or Lili—for fear of portents and warnings, and she wouldn't tell Nona now. In a few minutes she'd be in her car and on her way.

"I hope you've changed your mind about leaving," Nona said. "We need you now."

"I don't want to be needed that way!" Christy drank the last of her coffee and pushed back her chair. "Please understand that I'd love to stay with *you,* Nona darling, but because of all that's happened here, and is still happening, I don't dare."

"Where will you go? Where can you be safe?"

She really hadn't thought about that. Her one thought had been to get away from those footsteps that might come close in this place; to escape from the horror she might bring to Hayden and Donny Mitchell if she stayed and found Deirdre. There was even that darkness in Hayden that she didn't want to fathom.

"I'll just drive off along some country road and find a cabin I can rent. Then I'll stay for a while and be anonymous—until I'm healed."

"Listen to me." Nona reached across the table to touch her hand. "I don't care much for the direction Lili has taken with her life, but I believe in some power out there that guides us. Whether we call it God, or whether we call these beings our guides or our guardian angels—I do believe that roads are opened to us every day of our lives. We can make choices that send us ahead on our course—whatever it is. Or send us backward toward regression. Sometimes it requires courage to take a chance and move ahead on the risky, unknown course. Those who are too cautious seldom go anywhere, and they miss a lot. They only avoid. That's what you're doing now, Christy—avoiding. It isn't like you. We all have a destiny to follow, and your way has been pointed pretty clearly. Not to stay where you were, working with the police, but to follow your road here. Though neither of us could know why until you came."

"You don't know now! Lili spoke to *me* last night. She knew my danger and warned me. I have to listen."

"Lili's given to dramatics and sometimes she gets a mote in

her eye. Ardle was right when he said that it's not wise to make predictions of danger. Where there are lessons to learn in our lives, we'd better learn them without interference and not run away."

Christy had heard all this before, since Nona could grow evangelical at times. She wanted only one thing—blindly!—to escape whatever it was that hovered just out of sight in this expanse of valley and mountain.

She stood up and hugged Nona lovingly. "Please want what's best for me."

"All right," Nona said. "You'll have to choose your own course. You'll have to learn in your own way. But before you leave, I want to show you something." She opened a cupboard and took out a tissue-wrapped parcel. "Don't worry—it's not that scarf of Deirdre's."

Christy took it doubtfully and unfolded the paper. Inside was a single slipper—flat-heeled and worn. A black velvet slipper embroidered with tiny, frayed flowers in pink and green silk. There was no way to avoid the sensation that flooded through her from the object she held in her hands. This was not the energy of a living thing but a freezing wave, a tremor that swept up her arms and enveloped her body.

"Whoever wore this is dead!" Christy could hear her own voice as if it came from far away—as though something else spoke through her. She let the worn slipper fall from her hands and sat down weakly.

"This isn't Deirdre's slipper, is it?" Nona asked softly.

"I don't think so."

"Do you know anything about the woman who wore it?"

"The slipper might tell me, but I don't want it to!"

"Was her death violent?"

"Murder is always violent." The chill had warned her, not only of death, but of a vicious fury striking without mercy.

"Then you *must* stay," Nona said. "You know you must. You're committed to stopping whatever has begun. First Rose, and then perhaps Deirdre—neither of whom ever hurt anyone. This could be Rose's slipper, though if it is, why didn't Oliver say so? I've never seen her wear a slipper like this, but she could have worn them just around her house."

"Why would it be found near Deirdre's scarf, and why just one?"

"Maybe these are questions you can find the answers to—and if you do, perhaps you'll find the murderer you sense."

Christy shook away the deadly cold. "I've never tried to find a murderer, and I don't want to. This is what Lili is afraid of—that I'll put myself in the way of something dangerous. I don't have that kind of courage, Nona."

"I suppose I'll have to let you go"—Nona spread her hands—"but you'll remember this, Christy. You won't be able to shake it off. Do you want to live with that sort of guilt—the guilt of running away?"

"I'm guilty of nothing except trying to save my own peace of mind—maybe my life."

Something fell to the floor with a crash in another part of the house and for a moment Nona and Christy stared at each other. Then Nona ran into the hall, with Christy on her heels. They were in time to block the small figure that ran out of Nona's studio into her arms. For a moment Donny struggled and fought, but Nona held him until he went limp and started to cry.

"It's okay, Donny," she told him. "If you broke something, it doesn't matter. Let's go and see what the damage is and then you can start feeling better."

He came with her, no longer struggling. "I didn't b-b-break anything. But you lied to me! You were my friend, and you lied to me!"

Christy followed them through the sitting room and into the studio beyond. A large easel had fallen backward on the floor and Christy saw that the painting it held was the one that had been covered by a green cloth which had now slipped from it to the floor. This was the painting Nona had claimed was unfinished.

Her aunt let go of Donny and set the easel on its legs. The boy stood watching dejectedly as she put the painting in place, this time without its covering. Nona had again painted one of her red roads. This road ran through a hemlock forest, winding between tall trees. The focus of interest was a dancing figure in gauzy white. The woman seemed to flit ahead on the path, with mists floating down from the treetops to soften her outline, so that she became part of the mist herself, with only her bright face clear and visible as she looked back over one shoulder, laughing.

There was no doubt in Christy's mind. Nona had painted Deirdre, and the picture was certainly finished. Yet she had hidden it from view. Perhaps because it was too prophetic?

"When did you paint this?" Christy asked her aunt.

Nona sighed. "At least four months ago. This is the one I wanted you to see. I didn't know what I was painting—it just came. I covered it up because it made me uncomfortable. Especially after Deirdre disappeared." She turned to the boy, who had been listening intently. "I've never lied to you, Donny. I don't even know what you mean about lying."

He stared at her, tear marks streaking his cheeks. "You said you didn't know what happened to my mother. But you do— you painted her before she—she went away into all that mist."

"I painted this out of my imagination, Donny," Nona said. "Just the way I do most of my paintings. It's true that I painted this before your mother went away. But I didn't know that was going to happen. Deirdre saw this herself and she liked it. She liked the idea of drifting away as though she were part of the mist. You believe me, don't you, Donny?"

His dark head seemed too heavy for his thin neck as he stared at the floor. "I guess I believe you." Then he raised his head to look at Christy with a suddenness that startled her.

"Why did *she* come here?" he asked Nona.

"Perhaps she was sent to help us find your mother," Nona told him. "So I think you should make friends with her."

"I don't like her," Donny said. "She's—creepy."

"That's silly. You don't know her."

"What do you mean by creepy, Donny?" Christy asked.

He twisted his body away from her, not meeting her eyes. "You can see things—bad things."

Christy looked at her aunt in astonishment.

"Sometimes children know," Nona said. "Anyway, Donny, I think you should give Christy another chance—you might like her."

He looked at Christy then—a strangely searching look for a boy so young. "Don't make my mother be dead," he said softly.

There was no answer to so terrible a thought. In a moment, Christy knew, he would pull away from the hand Nona had placed on his arm and run from them both—leaving his frightening plea to hang on the air behind him. Prompted by one of her sudden urges, Christy moved quickly, picking up the copy of *Little Red Road* that Nona had left on a table. She held it out to the boy.

"This is one of my favorite books, Donny. Did you know that I work in libraries back home, reading stories to children? I've read this book by Rose Vaughn any number of times, and children always love it. I understand that Rose was your friend."

Donny gave her a black look and ran out of the room.

"Bad timing," Nona said. "It's my fault. I should have told you that it was Donny who found Rose. He went to a favorite place they used to visit together—and Rose was lying there dead, at the foot of a rock cliff. He climbed down, thinking he could help her—so it was all pretty awful. He's been a different child ever since, pulling into himself. And now it's much worse, since Deirdre is missing too. That's why his father is letting him stay out of school for a while. Though I think it might be better for him to be occupied and distracted."

Donny's horror and grief seemed to pour along Christy's own sensitive nerves. She had to do something.

"I want to try an experiment with him, Nona." Christy ran outside after the boy and found him sitting at the edge of the front deck, his legs dangling. She dropped down beside him, still holding Rose's book. Nona followed, but she stayed back, watching.

"There's something I've always wanted to try," Christy told the boy. "I wonder if you would help me? I don't think I can do this alone."

Donny looked up at her and Nona nodded. "I think you ought to help Christy if you can."

Without much interest, Donny let Christy pull him up and they started down the driveway together. Fresh, clean morning air and the sight of new green, slashed here and there with red, brought a lift to Christy's spirits, and a slow excitement started in her. More than anything else right now she wanted to reach this small boy who walked so gloomily beside her.

"We're going right down the road," she told him, pointing. "Once, when I was a little girl, Nona took me to spend a month on a farm and I learned something interesting about cows. The poor things get terribly bored and they enjoy unusual happenings. Just a car going by can be something to watch. You've noticed that, haven't you?"

"Yeah, sometimes they try to stick their stupid necks through the fence to see better."

"Do you know any of the cows in that field across the road?"

There seemed nothing strange to Donny about being personally acquainted with cows. "Sure. Some of them have names."

"That will help. Cows are curious animals. So when something new comes along, they're interested. And I have something *very interesting to try.*"

Donny had begun to be curious too and he went with her more willingly. They hurried along the road and crossed to where wooden rails fenced in the cows. One animal was grazing placidly nearby and Donny spoke to her.

"Good morning, Ophelia."

Ophelia turned her head to look at him, her chewing uninterrupted.

"That's Juliet over there." Donny indicated a plump cow who examined him thoughtfully and then lumbered over to the fence. A third, whose name, Donny said, was Rosalind, joined her sisters. Rosalind tried at once to put her head— unsuccessfully—between the fence rails.

"Has somebody been reading Shakespeare?" Christy asked Donny.

"My mother named them," he said. "She could always pick wonderful names."

"Let's begin," Christy said quickly, avoiding dangerous ground. "The other cows will probably come over because they won't want to miss anything."

She opened the book to the first page of Rose's story and Harmony's pictures and began to read aloud. She knew every word by heart, but she always used the book, since her business was to interest her listeners in books—though that wasn't exactly her goal now.

" 'Once, not very long ago' "—she spoke clearly and loudly —" 'there was a little red road. It ran through a countryside where mountains and forests opened their arms to let the little road through.' "

The cows stared at her, riveted. Christy gestured widely with one hand to indicate the curling road, and other cows came over to push against the fence. Donny giggled, and she knew what she was doing would succeed.

She went on, even more dramatically now, as people in the story came along the road. Since it loved company the little red road was very happy. One of the cows forgot to chew. Christy had never had a more rapt audience for her reading, and she was caught up in the narrative, not forgetting to turn the open pages toward the cows to show them the pictures. Donny thought that was funny, and whenever she paused for breath, he filled in the words, reciting to the cows himself, equally successful as their absorbed attention shifted to him.

As it climbed into the mountains, the little road ran into a terrible storm. A river rolled along beside it, overflowing and washing out the only way by which people could get to town. A donkey that was carrying a boy and a girl was swept right into the swirling water. The little road tried to hold them, but its surface had turned slippery with mud, and the donkey's hooves slid right into the stream that poured across the road.

Several more cows had forgotten to chew. Ophelia's large, liquid eyes were wide with interest, and Donny climbed to the top of the fence. "It's all right," he assured the cows. "The road knows what to do!"

This was the part of the story Christy always liked best, because what *could* the little road do? It had no voice to call for help, as Rose pointed out in the story. It couldn't reach up and save the children. It could only go on its way, climbing, climbing. And that was enough. The water was very deep where it had washed across the road, but the hill beyond was steep and rose above the water level. Someone had dumped gravel there, and when the donkey swam desperately to the place where the road rose out of muddy water, it found its own footing and climbed up to where the road went on, dry and safe. The children were carried happily to their destination, and one had the feeling that the determination of the little road to help had drawn the donkey's hooves to safety.

Christy had no patience with stodgy critics who deplored anthropomorphism in writing for children. Stretching the imagination in every possible direction was what mattered, and Rose Vaughn had done this with sensitivity.

At this point Christy's listeners usually clapped. Applause, surprisingly, came from behind her, and Christy turned to find that a Jeep had driven along the real road and stopped near the fence. Hayden Mitchell, Donny's father, sat at the wheel and he was clapping his hands together gravely, with no more of a smile than he'd shown last night.

"Finish the story," he directed. "You don't want to disappoint your audience."

In spite of the applause, he showed no other approval, his tone flat. She hesitated, the mood spoiled, not wanting to perform for this cold, probably critical man. Donny, however, was waiting, so she went on. Now the boy recited the words in unison with Christy as the little red road wound its way up the mountain and into the town, where people rushed out of their houses to help the girl and boy, who were, of course, soaking wet. Now the little road could continue through the town on its own, gaining new travelers and wandering over the mountain to reach new sights, new places, and new people to help.

Christy closed the book. At once Ophelia blinked and moved away, sensing that the show was over.

Donny looked at his father from his perch on the fence. "Christy reads real good. Though not as good as Rose."

"This is Rose Vaughn's story," Christy agreed, "so she would read it best."

"But she never read it to the cows," Donny said, giving credit where it was due.

"I'm going down to the mailbox," Hayden told them. "Do you want to come along—both of you?"

Since Donny seemed eager, Christy agreed, and when the boy climbed into the front seat, she got in beside him. She must, she thought, make allowances for Hayden Mitchell's state of depression that made him so curt and unsmiling.

"How long will you be staying with Nona?" he asked as they drove down the road.

"I'd planned to leave early this morning, but Donny changed my mind. I expect I'll be going soon."

He said nothing more until he'd pulled the Jeep into a parking space above the row of mailboxes. "The flags are down, so the mail has come," he told Donny. "Do you want to pick it up?"

Donny clambered over Christy and ran down the incline toward the boxes.

His father stared ahead through the windshield as he spoke. "After you took off last night, Eve told Oliver and me about you. I can understand why you'd want to run away from Long Island."

He couldn't possibly understand. Christy gripped Rose's book tightly, knowing what was coming, and bracing herself to resist.

"You know, don't you," he went on, "that Donny found Rose? And now he's sure he'll find his mother dead too. I don't feel the way Oliver does about psychic matters, but I'm not filled with confidence either."

"Yet you'd break down and take a chance with me?" Christy asked dryly.

His smile was sudden, totally unexpected. One side of his mouth lifted, and his eyes mocked her with their curious intensity. The effect was disturbing, irritating. It was anything but a friendly smile.

"If you have the talent Nona claims, aren't you obliged to use it?" he challenged.

"I'm not obliged to do anything! I never asked for any of this, and—"

"And it's safer not to get involved?" The twist of smile had vanished as though he had removed himself to some distant plane. "Here comes Donny, so don't say anything. I'll drive you back to your aunt's."

The boy came running over to the Jeep and tossed his armful of mail into the back seat. "Move over," he ordered Christy, sounding as curt as his father. "Please" was a word he apparently hadn't learned. Perhaps Hayden seldom used it.

She had to sit closer, though she tried to lean toward the boy so as not to touch his father. She was sharply aware of the jarring vibrations that seemed to surround this man. There were hidden depths that made her uneasy. Hayden Mitchell needed help, but not of the sort she could give him. Lili might have been able to calm and restore him just by reaching out her hands. Christy had no such healing gifts. What he might get from her was far more destructive. She wanted only to have this grim clairvoyance leave her forever, so that she could be like other people.

As the Jeep passed below Nona's house before turning up the

drive, she looked up to see that Victor Birdcall was again perched on the ridgepole, working on his lightning rods.

Donny saw him too. "There's the Thunderbolt Man!" he cried. "Dad, I want to go talk to him."

Hayden stopped the car. "Go ahead. Though I don't think Victor will like that choice of a name."

"He doesn't care. He knows I call him that." Donny hopped down again and went running along the drive toward the house.

"Shall I drive you up?" Hayden asked Christy. "Or will you come over to my place and tell me whatever you can?"

He spoke without emotion—as though he didn't care one way or another. The flash of challenge she'd seen in his eyes was gone, yet the very suppression of emotion reached through her defenses. There was very little she liked about Donny's father, but she knew he was suffering deeply, and this she couldn't refuse.

"I'll try," she said. "Though I'm not sure there's anything I can do."

Silently, Hayden put the Jeep into gear and drove on.

Will she go away, or will she stay?

If she stays, sooner or later someone will give her the scarf. I wonder what she'll make of it? Soap and water will surely defeat her. Besides, even if she senses something, it won't lead anywhere. All the secrets are safely hidden.

I don't want to harm her. She's only an incidental interference. But if she persists, it may be necessary to stop anything she tries to do— even to stop her. There is too much at stake.

4

HAYDEN Mitchell's house had been built next along the ridge that ran high above the road, and it was hidden from Nona's by a thick stand of pine and oak. The steep gravel driveway wound up to a cleared parking space in front of the garage. Christy, looking ahead, saw Eve Corey sitting on the low front steps studying a sketch pad propped against her knees. As usual she wore faded denim shorts, a bit tight on her plump legs, and a man's shirt hanging outside. Thonged leather sandals left her bare toes free.

Eve looked up as they approached from the car, thick eyebrows beneath windblown bangs, raised and faintly derisive.

"Hi," she greeted them, and then to Hayden, "So you've persuaded Christy to do her thing after all?"

Hayden ignored her words coolly. "You have something to show me?"

"Right," Eve said, unchastened. "You aren't exactly on top of things lately, and Mrs. Hampton is annoyed. She's a good client, and we want to keep her happy, so you'd better look at what I've suggested for plantings in the front area."

As Hayden sat down beside Eve on the steps, Christy studied the house he and Deirdre had built a few years before. Like Nona's, it was gray, with a red deck running its width, but this house was two stories at the front, and built foursquare, with big windows offering a sweep of mountain and valley from a slightly different angle than Nona's.

Eve looked up from her sketches at Christy. "I hope you got some sleep last night, after all the excitement."

"I did fine." Christy resisted the probe.

"Rhododendrons should look well in this corner where the deck jogs." Eve held out her pad for Hayden to see. "Farther along we can plant gumpo—those Japanese dwarf azaleas. The deck's low, and Mrs. Hampton doesn't want anything growing too high in front. Around the oak tree over here on the right we might use spiraea. Gold flame, maybe? But she wants to see *you* about all this. You really haven't been on the job as you should be." Eve sounded both critical and impatient.

"I'll talk to her," Hayden said and handed back the pad.

Eve's curiosity hadn't lessened and she was still interested in Christy. "That was some get-together last night! Especially with Victor showing up like the spirit of doom after you left. Did Nona tell you? Oliver was pretty upset. When we went out to our cars afterward, I tried to talk to him and calm him down —but he hardly listened. I'm not sure why he was so upset, but the sooner he gets away from all these bad vibes and moves to Charlottesville, the better."

Hayden said nothing, and neither did Christy. Eve finally took the hint and stood up. "I'd better run along. Good luck, Christy, with that scarf of Deirdre's." Clearly she'd guessed why Christy was here and would have liked to stay. But with no encouragement from Hayden, she gave them both a mocking salute and walked toward her car.

As they went through the front door into a long stretch of living room that ran the width of the house, a woman came through from the rear.

"Hello, Leonie," Hayden said. "This is Miss Loren. Christy, this is Mrs. James, who takes excellent care of us."

Leonie was a tall, handsome woman with warmly golden skin and black hair that she wore in a coil at the nape of her neck. Her skirt, bright with tropical flowers, was topped by a scoop-necked white blouse. Gold hoops in her ears danced as she moved, and she acknowledged Hayden's introduction with dignity, though her concern was elsewhere.

"Have you seen Donny, Mr. Mitchell? He went off right after breakfast and didn't tell me where he was going."

"It's okay," Hayden said. "We have to let him run free for now. But I'll speak to him about letting you know when he goes out."

Leonie nodded and returned to whatever task she'd dropped when they came in.

Hayden explained as she went off. "It was Deirdre who found Leonie for us, and we need her more than ever now. Her father was local, but her mother came from Haiti. She's older than she looks, and has retired as a schoolteacher. Deirdre liked her to dress in island colors and Leonie enjoys a bit of drama after all her staid years. She's very good with Donny and he talks to her more than he does to me these days."

Hayden was marking time, Christy knew—perhaps postponing whatever might happen, now that the moment was upon them. He probably dreaded the outcome as much as she did.

"This is a beautiful room." She gestured, looking around. The floor was red-tiled in a herringbone pattern. Woven swivel chairs upholstered in royal blue could face the conversation area of sofa and bookcases or swing around to command the stunning sweep of mountains. Once more, Christy's eyes were held by the view. Shreds of mist topped trees across the valley, while the rest of the green land, with its patches of red, dreamed in morning sunlight. Nothing appeared to move anywhere.

On the opposite side of the room, more windows looked out upon the same stretch of woods that plunged down the hill behind Nona's house.

Hayden came to stand beside her. "There's a stream running through at the bottom of the hill. That's where the Llama Lady, as Donny calls her, lives. Nona has told you about Floris Fox?"

"She's mentioned her."

"Sometimes I think Floris likes animals better than she does people. Deirdre didn't get along with her too well in the last months." He turned from the window abruptly. "Let's go upstairs and I'll show you the scarf."

"Not yet," Christy said quickly. "I mustn't go too fast. I need to feel my way a little. Did Deirdre have a room of her own—a private space she enjoyed?"

"Yes. Her room's upstairs. Do you want to see it?"

"Please. It might tell me something about her—something that might help before I touch her scarf."

As he led the way upstairs she could sense his uneasiness, his distrust. He was clearly doing this against his better judgment —perhaps at Nona's urging.

"Deirdre chose the room with the balcony at the front of the house for her own," he said as they reached the upper hallway.

When he opened a door Christy stepped across the threshold and stood very still, waiting for whatever might happen. A single narrow bed had been placed where Deirdre might lie against pillows and look out at the mountains by day, and the stars and moon at night. It was not a bed to share with a husband, and the room itself surprised Christy. Somehow, from what she'd heard about Deirdre, she'd expected frills and fancies. But this might have been the room of a nun. The wood furniture was plain oak, straight and severe. There was no upholstery—one sat on hard boards, and there was little in the way of decoration. A patchwork quilt on the bed offered the only splash of color, except for a single large painting over Deirdre's small, plain desk.

Recognizing Harmony's work, Christy went to stand before it. The painting had been done in recent years, since it featured a red road. Trees grew on each side in the foreground, and the road climbed between them, curving out of sight at the top of the picture. Nona had caught the particular blue of a Virginia sky when the haze lifted, with only a trail of mist smoking between the mountain folds. The central theme of the picture was not the road, however, but the tremendous rainbow that arched above it, one end lost in mist, while the other seemed to touch the road itself where it curved to one side of the picture. All the rainbow colors were there in the wide band that held them, yet they blended one into another in the nebulous way of a real rainbow—soft-focused, yet distinct at the same time.

"It's—magical," Christy said softly. "One of Nona's best."

Hayden glanced at her. "That's the word Deirdre used. Though for some reason Nona didn't want me to buy it for her. She said at first that it wasn't for sale, because the rainbow meant something special and she wanted to keep it herself. But Deirdre coaxed and coaxed, and Nona wound up making it a gift. Deirdre would sit for hours staring at the painting—so that her behavior made me uncomfortable. She said voices spoke to her out of the rainbow. Deirdre had a strong mystical cast to her nature. I knew that was part of her, and I tried to understand her whimsical side. In the end, I failed."

His voice had dulled, and Christy shrank a little, knowing what she must do. She moved close to the painting, shutting Hayden out of her mind, willing herself into the scene Nona's brush had caught—as if she might step beneath the arch of the rainbow. Nona had said that she didn't always understand what she herself had painted.

"Yes," she said softly. "I think this is where Deirdre wanted to go—out to the rainbow's end. I wonder why she wanted to—to escape?"

"She always wanted something that was beyond reality. She could never accept the fact that rainbows have no end."

"I'm not sure that's true." Christy tried to speak lightly. "I think Nona has seen the end of a rainbow in her imagination—so she could paint it."

"Imagination is one thing. Believing is another." Hayden turned his back on the painting. "I don't like it. Sometimes Donny comes here and sits on that stool staring the way his mother used to do. As if *he* wants to go to the end of the rainbow—the way he thinks she has done. Sometimes I wonder if I'd better take it down."

Again Christy could sense darkness in him—something even more troubling than sorrow.

"Show me the scarf," she said. "I'm ready now."

He crossed the room. "It's right here in Deirdre's desk."

"Then let me go outside first. Take it to a neutral place and leave it. I don't want anyone nearby when I touch it."

Every clairvoyant had his or her own way of working, and this was Christy's. But now she sensed increasing resistance in Hayden. It would take very little to turn him away from what she must do, and perhaps that might be safer for all of them. But it was already too late. She could feel the inner stirrings begin—following a course that could never be stopped.

Hayden gave in. "All right. Go and wait on the deck downstairs, and I'll come and tell you where I've put it."

She ran down the stairs with an odd sense of flight. Leonie James stood near the bottom step, watching her. Her dark eyes were wide with awareness, and Christy knew she sensed something.

"Be careful, Miss Loren," she whispered.

Christy nodded understanding and went out onto the red deck. The morning had warmed and a small breeze shivered in the oak tree, sending a crisp brown leaf from last winter skittering across the boards. She breathed deeply of the high, clear air, bracing herself against what might come; feeling, as always, unprepared and defenseless. Down on the road a car, traveling too fast, raised a cloud of dust that drifted upward.

A moment later Hayden joined her. "I've put the scarf on the bookcase in the living room. I'll stay here until you want me."

She had to offer him—and herself—one last chance. "You're sure you want me to go ahead?"

"I'm sure."

"Oliver Vaughn doesn't believe in any of this," she added, still delaying. "Even though he was married to Rose, who must have been sensitive to mystical vibes—as she revealed in her writing."

"I'm not Oliver." He sounded sharp and disapproving. "And I always thought Eve would have made him a better wife than Rose was able to."

From Hayden, who had seemed reticent and not given to revealing what he thought, this was unexpected. Christy couldn't help retorting.

"That's a man's viewpoint—which woman would make the best wife."

His mouth twisted in what seemed to pass for a smile. "I expect Oliver made no more of a husband for Rose than I have for Deirdre."

This was a new and distracting thought, but she thrust it aside to be dealt with later. The moment had come. She went again into the long red-tiled room and walked directly to the bookcase, where for a moment she stood with her eyes closed. When she had time, it was best to go down inside herself and achieve a mild trance before she touched anything from a missing person. The quivering had stopped, as it always did when she emptied herself and allowed whatever pressed in to come through.

Now a deep inner stillness possessed her. Behind her eyelids colors flashed yellow and green—against deep black. She reached out with both hands and picked up the scarf. The silk seemed to twine about her fingers as though it were alive. Shockingly alive, so that the very touch of it seemed to burn her skin. She wanted to drop it and run from the room, but she made herself stand where she was and let the scarf flow through her hands in a stream of white fire.

The impressions in her mind came thick and fast. A sense of horror that she had never before felt to this degree seemed to surge through her very veins. The intensity was far stronger— and it was different. She received no picture of Deirdre in her consciousness, or of where she had gone, where she might be found. Something else was there—an appalling sense of evil, of wickedness. Anyone who continued this search would be faced with an ultimate terror. Never before had this shattering awareness of a murderer swept her as it did now. In the past she'd seen only the sad, mutilated girl, and there was no wickedness, no evil residue left—but only the vision of a place where men could go to find the body. Never before had her vision reached out to the person behind the crime.

This was different and far more terrifying.

Perhaps she had made some sound without knowing it—perhaps she'd even cried out—for Hayden was suddenly in the doorway, watching her.

"Are you all right?"

The silk was no longer fire and ice, and it slipped from her fingers, floating lightly to the floor.

"I need to go outside," she told Hayden. She heard the trembling in her own voice, felt the throbbing begin at her temples.

Alarmed, he put an arm about her and she leaned into his strength, seeking support and human reassurance—anything that would wipe away that awful knowledge of human vicious-ness that existed at the other end of the scale from goodness and love.

Outside, Hayden led her to a porch chair and she dropped into it. "I'm sorry—I need to rest for a moment." The throb-bing would stop—it always did, but right now she felt ill.

He drew over another chair and sat beside her, waiting. She knew he held back the questions that must be brimming in him, and she tried to speak, though her words came haltingly.

"I—can't help you, Hayden. I'm sorry—but I can't tell you what you want to know."

"But you felt something—you're frightened. At least you can tell me why."

"I don't know how to tell you, because this has never hap-pened to me before. I only know that someone truly evil has held Deirdre's scarf. Perhaps so evil that all that remains of Deirdre in the silk has been burned away."

"I don't believe in an abstraction called evil."

She could sense his disapproval, his withdrawal, and there was nothing she could offer. "Lili—my mother—doesn't be-lieve in it either, but I'm afraid I do."

"You mean angels and devils and hell?" He sounded scornful, and the antagonism she felt in him from the first, had grown stronger.

"No, I don't mean evil in the old biblical sense," she told him. "I can't explain. But I'd like to talk to Nona about this—talk to her right away. I'm really sorry I can't help you, Hayden."

"I never really thought you could," he said. "I'll drive you back to your aunt's now, if you like."

Christy shook her head. Her need to be alone was too urgent, the danger she'd felt too great.

Hayden paid no attention, but came with her when she left her chair. He kept a wary eye on her progress as they followed the path to Nona's, though he didn't touch her, even when she stumbled.

An empty field of red earth and rough grass separated the two houses, and it took only moments to reach Nona's. Victor Birdcall had come down from the roof to work at the near corner of the house, running a cable from one lightning rod into the ground. He looked at neither Christy nor Hayden as they went by, returning Hayden's greeting with only a nod.

In the single moment when she came near Victor, Christy tried to sense any current that might emanate from him, but she knew instinctively that the evil that had woven itself into the scarf in some moment of fury couldn't be discerned now in its human beginnings. The intensity would have long since been dissipated—perhaps even wiped out at its source by the act of murder?

Nona was in the kitchen fixing lunch when they came in. She looked at Christy and Hayden with sharp understanding.

"You've touched Deirdre's scarf, haven't you?" she said to Christy.

"I wasn't able to help," Christy told her. "I need to talk to you—please. And I need to see that painting again—the one of Deirdre going off into the mist."

"I'll come too," Hayden said. "What painting is this?"

"I haven't shown it to anyone, Hayden," Nona explained. "This morning Donny knocked it over and discovered it. I'd hidden it from view because I didn't want to show it to anyone after Deirdre disappeared."

"Is Donny here?" Hayden asked as Nona started ahead down the long hallway to her studio.

"Not now. He came back and stayed with the painting for a while. I had the feeling that he recognized something in it— something physical." She paused in the doorway of her studio. "He even asked me about the pile of rocks I'd painted beside the road. I could only tell him it was out of my imagination and didn't represent any real place. After a time he decided to go down to visit the llamas, so I made up a bag of sandwiches and fruit for him and let him go. He enjoys those animals and he and Floris Fox hit it off very well."

Nona moved to where the painting stood on its easel, uncovered now. This was a very different painting from that of the rainbow that hung in Deirdre's room. Even the pigment in the earlier painting had seemed filled with light and hope and promise. This one of Deirdre was a darker scene—dark in its implications, somehow, even though the haze that wreathed her was light in tone. The great pile of granite that formed an outcropping at one side of the path rose somberly, and beyond it Deirdre's figure flitted into misty air. Her very dress seemed like vapor, and only her face was clear—laughing as she looked back over one shoulder. Viewing the painting for the second time, Christy could fancy the eerie laughter that might be coming from her open lips. At least the throbbing torment of Christy's headache had lessened.

Hayden studied the painting for a moment. "You knew, didn't you, Nona? I mean that she'd disappear into the mist. Something in you knew, so that you were seeing the future."

Nona flung out her hands in denial. "If that's what I was doing, I certainly didn't know it at the time."

"What if you painted her now?" Hayden persisted. "Would anything more come to you?"

Nona shook her head impatiently. "I can't work coldly and deliberately. I need to be prompted by some vision in my mind. Or by the insistence of something that *wants* to be painted. As that picture did. There's nothing right now to make me try."

When Hayden turned away, Christy had the feeling that he avoided looking at her again—as though the very sight of her added to his unhappiness. "Anyway, thanks," he told them both, and walked out of the room.

"Hayden has lost a daughter as well as a wife," Nona said.

"What do you mean?"

"Here—let's sit down," Nona pulled a stool for Christy before the easel and drew up a chair for herself. "You need to understand what Deirdre was like, if you're to help him."

"I can't help him at all—I know that now."

Nona went right on. "Deirdre was woman enough for him, I suspect—passionate and high-spirited. Men were always drawn to her—perhaps because she eluded them, slipped out of reach. She was also a child who never quite grew up—and so was at the mercy of those who didn't respect her innocence."

Once more Christy studied the gracefully turned head in the painting—the bright look of that face peering from the mist, the parted, laughing mouth. Somehow there seemed little of innocence in that face. Perhaps the portrait—though only a glimpse—was more true than Nona realized. More and more, Deirdre seemed to be composed of a confusion of qualities that made her enticingly mysterious. Christy thought of what Hayden had said about not being a good husband for Deirdre, and wondered if any man ever could have been.

"I wonder if she was all that innocent?" Christy spoke aloud. "You didn't catch innocence in what you painted here. I'd say you revealed a woman with secrets."

"Sometimes my brush makes judgments I'm not aware of," Nona admitted.

"Did you like Deirdre Mitchell?"

"I try to give everyone the benefit of the doubt." Nona sounded wry. "I don't think I succeed as well as Lili does. Perhaps some deeper feeling that I don't even recognize got into that painting. Perhaps what I felt about her wasn't altogether fair. I don't think she was always good for Donny, because he wanted so much more from her than she could ever give as a mother. That wasn't her fault, any more than it was his. It's a wonder she could ever bear a child, when she was so much like one herself."

"Do you know of anyone who hated her enough to kill her?"

"Of course not! This is a peaceful place."

"The place is peaceful, yes, but I wonder if the people who live here really are!"

Nona let that pass. "You held her scarf, Christy—what did you feel? Tell me."

Christy swung about on the stool, her back to the painting. "I felt something more terrible than I've ever experienced before. Even when I was working with the police, I never felt anything exactly like this. But I don't believe it was Deirdre I felt. There was no quick vision of where she might be found. Only a sensation, as though whoever had held the scarf was driven by some vicious intent. Something almost inhumanly evil that made the silk feel as though it scorched my hands. I don't think Donny found it where Deirdre dropped it originally. But I have no clue as to who might have put it there."

"What about the velvet slipper that Victor picked up near the same place? Is there a connection?"

"I can't tell. I received the strong impression that whoever had worn the slipper was dead. There was a superimposed male impression that could have meant Victor Birdcall, since he found it. What do you really know about Victor, Nona? Your friend Eve seems to disapprove of him."

"She's that way toward a lot of people, and he's never made any effort to make friends with her. I'm afraid he has a way, sometimes, of dismissing with indifference those who don't interest him. I know where he comes from and what he's running from. All that's in the past and doesn't matter any more. It has nothing to do with what's happening now, so you needn't look in Victor's direction. He claims that he found the slipper by chance, and I believe him. Will you try again with it, Christy, and see if it might tell you anything more?"

There was no point in refusing. The escape she'd intended when she got up this morning seemed further away than ever. It was as though the dreadful experience with Deirdre's scarf tied her here with its silken strands.

Turning the slipper about, touching the frayed embroidery, slipping her fingers into the toe, Christy tried to let the male impression go. She wanted something else to come through. She sat very still, letting everything but the slipper fade away. And suddenly the sense of evil was there again. With it came the conviction that the same person who had left Deirdre's scarf in the woods had put this slipper there as well. To confuse? To set down false trails? This time the feeling was far less intense than when she'd picked up the scarf, and no burning sensation came with it. As she continued to hold the slipper, the second layer of personality faded and left a sad truth behind.

"I'm sure this slipper belonged to Rose Vaughn," she told Nona. "I knew Rose through her writing—and there's some essence of hers that I can recognize. But last night no one claimed the slipper. What do you know about Rose's husband?"

"Oliver's a bit too opinionated for my taste, and he's totally scornful of anything that touches on the mystical or psychic."

"Yes, I got that impression."

"But I can't think he's the one you're looking for. I can't imagine Oliver committing a violent crime. Physically, he might, but not emotionally."

"How could anyone else get the slipper?"

"It wouldn't be hard. Around here we don't lock our doors. I suppose anyone could have slipped into Oliver's house and taken it. Since he teaches at the university in Charlottesville, he's away a good part of the day. Sometimes he seemed to dislike Deirdre—they were really at opposite poles—and I think sometimes she liked to tease him, just to see him squirm.

She could be almost cruel—in the way a child is cruel, with no real recognition of what she was doing."

"Nona, do you believe that evil actually exists? Lili doesn't."

"Of course I believe. There are evil men and women—evil nations, since they can be led by evil human beings. You don't question that, do you?"

"I don't know how we can ever judge. Maybe there are only those who are weak and mistaken and programmed in the wrong direction in childhood. So that evil is only a *result.*"

"Perhaps. But then do we go on forgiving terrible acts? I suspect that the most dangerous aspect of evil is that it never recognizes itself. The blame must always be put on someone else, or on outside circumstances, so the guilty can believe themselves innocent."

"That's pretty frightening."

"We all have a dark side, Christy. Only rainbows are made of light. Wait until you see a rainbow out there against the mountains—it will lift you and wash away all that's wrong in the space around you."

"But only for as long as it lasts—seconds? Minutes?"

"That can be enough if we carry the effect with us afterward."

"I saw your rainbow painting that Deirdre hung in her room. Hayden seemed to think it had special significance for you."

"He's right. The rainbow is becoming a symbol all over the world. Something that brings together people of good will from different religions and races—perhaps a vast coming together in time to save the planet. Though I'm not sure Deirdre was ready for such harmony. Perhaps I should never have given her the painting. She set too much importance upon it—as though it were real and she could find the rainbow right there within its frame."

Christy turned to the painting to study Deirdre's laughing face, its expression somehow all-knowing—the very opposite of innocence. Who had Deirdre so tormented that some punishment had been dealt *her?*

Nona left her chair abruptly. "We'll talk about all this again. Right now we'd better get lunch. Victor's joining us—remember?"

Christy hadn't remembered. For one thing, she hadn't expected to be here, and she still wanted to get away. She had done what she could for Hayden Mitchell—which was very little—and she had glimpsed something threatening and terrible.

Nona was watching her. "Honey, stay a few days longer. We need you more than you know."

But *she* didn't need any of this, Christy thought as she followed her aunt to the kitchen that was Nona's family room. When salads were set out, cold chicken forked onto a platter, and rolls put in the oven, Nona went outside to call Victor. He washed in the laundry room and joined them in a few moments.

"Seeing how you have company, I could have brought my lunch and eaten outside the way I always do," he said.

"Don't be grumpy, Victor," Nona told him. "Sit down and turn on your charm."

This was apparently a joke between them and Victor smiled grudgingly. Because she felt uncomfortable with this man, Christy made an extra effort to be pleasant.

"Birdcall's an interesting name. What tribe were your ancestors?"

"One of them danced the Highland fling under the name of MacLeod," Victor told her, and then relented. "It's not a real Indian name. The family name was Man-Who-Calls-Birds, but my grandfather thought that was a mouthful in the translation. So he shortened it to Birdcall."

"It's good that you can carry the name on." Christy was still trying.

"I haven't. It's my grandmother's name. I just took it for myself."

Because his own birth name had become known in some

unpleasant way? Christy thought with that intuition that could come in a flash, and was often to be trusted.

"Some of Victor's ancestors were Plains Indians—Sioux," Nona said.

Victor corrected her. "Sioux is the language. They called themselves Dakota, or Lakota." After that bit of information he addressed himself to eating his lunch, the subject obviously closed.

Nona passed him the basket of rolls. "We think that the slipper you found in the woods, Victor, might belong to Rose Vaughn. Christy had the feeling that whoever had worn it was dead."

Victor gave Christy the same blank stare with which he'd regarded her when she arrived yesterday. Perhaps it was a look more searching than antagonistic. As though he tested people in some way.

"If that's true," he said, "why didn't Oliver claim it when I brought it over here last night?"

Nona shook her head doubtfully. "It seems strange, but perhaps it was too painful for him to talk about. I know he's trying to put all reminders of Rose away from him. I feel that it's a good idea—his moving to Charlottesville."

"What about Donny?" Victor shifted his searching look to Nona.

"What do you mean?" she asked.

"I saw him running through the woods a little while ago, and he didn't answer when I called him."

"He was off to see the llamas," Nona said. "They're Donny's road to Oz. Victor, have you any idea what's going on in Donny's head? Sometimes he talks to you."

Victor went on eating silently for a moment. Then he seemed to make up his mind. "The kid thinks he's seen his mother. He thinks she's come back to tell him something."

Nona put down her fork, dismayed. "That will be hard for Hayden to handle. Of course Donny's head is full of what he imagines. He wants so much to believe that Deirdre's alive that he's brought her out of my painting."

"Except," Victor said quietly, "that I've seen her too. I've seen her drifting in the woods in her white dress—just like Donny says. I had to tell him so, just to let him know he wasn't making it all up."

"Go on, Victor," Nona urged, but now he wouldn't meet her eyes.

"That's all about that," he said flatly. And then, to Nona, "Did you know Sinh has come back?"

"Deirdre's cat? It's been gone ever since she disappeared."

"Right. But she turned up at Floris's early this morning—half starved and scrawny. Sometimes I go down there to help with the llamas. I was there when the cat crawled to the bottom of those steps up to Floris's house and began to yowl. I went down and brought her up to the kitchen. Usually she won't let anyone but Deirdre and Donny touch her, but she was too weak to claw me. Of course Floris talked to her in the way she talks to her llamas, so maybe Sinh will tell her something."

He looked a bit sly and mocking, but Nona paid no attention. "That's Sinh with an *h*," she told Christy. "Do you know the story, Victor?"

"Something about a sacred cat?"

"Yes. Deirdre loved all sorts of exotic lore. The Burmese and Siamese kept temple cats—they still do to this day. They believed that when some holy human being—usually a priest—died his soul was temporarily housed in the body of his favorite cat. It might live there for years, until the cat itself died. I remember Deirdre's excitement when she talked about this. She said such cats were often put in gilded cages and given special offerings of food. In the beginning, legend has it, they had golden eyes. But then one was portrayed in a statue with eyes of sapphire, and all the eyes of the temple cats were miraculously turned to blue. Sinh was the name of one of the first cats of legend, and Deirdre thought it perfect when Hayden brought her a Siamese kitten."

It was a strange and entrancing story, and added a bit more to the growing "legend" of Deirdre herself.

Nona wondered aloud. "Where can Sinh have been all this time? Christy, I think we'd better go down and see Floris and the cat. Then we can talk to Donny too. I'll get my jacket."

Victor, at home in Nona's kitchen, rose to clear the table, and Christy helped.

"Did you really see Deirdre?" she asked.

He piled dishes onto one long arm expertly and gave her his strangely searching look. She was aware of the contrast of blue eyes (like Sinh's?) in his dark face.

"Maybe I only thought it was Deirdre," he said. "Sometimes the mists out there can fool you."

Rose is gone and Deirdre's gone, so I should be safe enough. I can have what I want, and there is no one to oppose me. Except Dukas's daughter. She hasn't gone away yet, and she's held the scarf. But I can't be everywhere and hear everything, so I still don't know exactly what happened.

At least there's a way to find out. An open channel. Not the kind of channel Dukas talks about! I must push a little harder now—make a real move.

It was fun meeting Donny in the woods. I'm not sure if Victor saw me, but at least the white dress gave the right illusion. And misdirection. I've been laughing ever since.

5

THE PATH winding through the trees at the back of the
house was steep, but Nona was surefooted in jogging
shoes. Christy stayed close behind as they went down. Nona
had brought along a walking stick she used for balance, to help
herself down rocky places and fend off springy vines.

"What about snakes?" Christy called after her. "You said—"

Nona paused to speak over her shoulder. "I expect they're
waking up by this time, and they're out there. But mostly you
won't see them. They don't want to mix with us any more than
we do with them. When they're not threatened they don't
attack."

"But copperheads—?" Christy was still nervous.

"They're not aggressive like rattlers, though they're plenty
dangerous if annoyed. Just watch where you put your feet and
your hands and you'll be all right. The black snakes are scary-
looking but harmless."

Once Christy stopped to look back at the house on its high
perch near the treetops. Victor was up on the roof again, his
head turned as though he followed their progress down the
hill. Christy went on, watching the ground, since even a
twisted root could look threatening. Where a large boulder
barred their way, the path turned and ran along the hill, almost
level for a distance before it turned down again. Nona had
already rounded the far turn, and Christy found herself alone
on the red, uneven path, looking ahead through a corridor of
oak and poplar. The reminder was sudden, arresting all movement.

This could be the narrow way of her dream, with high walls

on either side and a blood-red floor! Were these the woods where her dream would come true? Where that fatal, relentless pursuit would take place? She *must* leave—she mustn't stay.

She hurried now to keep Nona in sight, her own heartbeat loud in her ears. Foolish, of course. She had only to stay out of the woods when she was alone, and nothing could reach her. The dream had no reality. One simply vented fears in a dream. Still—she must get away as soon as possible. She wasn't sure why she hadn't escaped right after lunch.

At the foot of the hill the stream came into sight, flowing placidly, and Nona stood on its bank waiting for her. A wooden bridge led across to the enclosure where llamas grazed.

"Raising llamas is a big craze these days, all over the country," Nona said. "Here in the east the first herd was brought over from Peru to some place in the Catskills. On the west coast William Randolph Hearst introduced them on his acres at Hearst Castle. Floris says all those in this country are descended from these two original herds."

Christy had never seen such animals close up, and she stood on the bridge watching them. They were large in size, though smaller than camels, their heads held high on long necks, and their ears pricked forward.

"They need water for their feet," Nona explained as Christy joined her. "That's how they keep cool—through that cleft in their toes. There's Floris out there now at her grooming chores. She doesn't keep as many llamas as she used to when her husband Abel was alive, but they require a lot of work and attention. Loving attention."

Farther along the enclosure Donny Mitchell sat on the top rail of the fence, where he could meet a long-necked llama on his own level. At the moment Donny's attention was focused on the barrel-bodied creature that stood beside him. He saw Christy and waved.

"Come over here and let Snow White kiss you. She'd like that."

Christy laughed as she joined him at the fence. "Snow White?" The llama was a bright orange-red and Donny grinned.

"The people who raise llamas always give them names before they sell them. She really used to be white, but around here, whatever the original color, they all turn into the same shade—what Floris calls Virginia peach—from the red earth that gets into their coats."

Christy offered her cheek at Donny's insistence, and Snow White breathed against it affectionately.

The woman who had been grooming another llama with a hairbrush, stroking down its legs, turned to greet them. "Hi, Nona. This is Christy Loren, isn't it?"

Floris Fox was younger than Nona, perhaps in her fifties, but weathered, brown, and long of neck—a little like the beast she cared for. Her eyes were brown too, but not as large and liquid. She reached one tanned hand over the fence to grasp Christy's in welcome. But though she smiled readily, showing slightly crooked teeth, her eyes seemed to weigh and appraise, as though something in her stood back, with none of the quick, friendly acceptance of the llama called Snow White.

There were only five animals in the enclosure, and two younger ones stood off by themselves, chewing and watching. Snow White, however, loved the spotlight, and she snuffled at Donny as he fed her a reward pellet.

Nona had not come down here to admire the llamas, however. "Can we talk a minute?" she asked Floris.

"Sure." She patted the flank of the animal she'd been grooming, and it moved away.

"That's Orion," Donny said. "Sometimes he spits—but only at other llamas. Spitting is a terrible llama insult."

"Come on up to the house," Floris invited, "and I'll make us a pot of tea."

Donny scrambled down from his perch. "Sinh's come back," he told Nona. "So my mother must have let her go. Can I come inside too, Floris?"

"I suppose." Floris rolled her eyes at Nona. "If Sinh's been with Deirdre, she sure wasn't taking care of her. The way she looks, I don't think Deirdre can be—" She glanced at Donny and broke off, shrugging.

Floris's house, brown and weathered, had been built on a granite outcropping, well above flood level if the stream rose.

The two women walked ahead toward the high steps, and Christy followed, noting the contrast between them. Both were tall and a bit rangy, but there was something about Nona that gave her a special individuality. Even the scarf about her head was tied with a distinctive twist, and the earrings she'd put on never seemed incongruous with jeans. She would always make her own style.

Floris, on the other hand, wore shapeless brown pants with bits of llama fluff clinging to them, and a faded shirt that was outsize and might have belonged to her husband. She carried herself with as straight a back as Nona's, however, and they matched strides as they walked toward the house.

Donny came with Christy. Since the episode of reading to the cows, he had accepted her. "Sinh looks sick," he told her. "Floris says she hasn't had much to eat. There are plenty of field mice, but she's been a persnickety house cat. My mother says temple cats need special food."

The railed steps reached a landing and then turned upward to the front deck of the house, set high above the stream. Floris led the way to a large kitchen that was clearly the heart of her house, as kitchens seemed to be around here. Its windows looked out upon woods and stream and llamas. Down here in the ravine the mountains were invisible, though Nona's roof could be glimpsed among the trees far above.

In front of a wood-burning stove—cold at the moment—lay what looked like a skein of dirty wool. When Donny dropped to his knees beside it, the skein produced a head from under one paw, looking more like a cat, its sapphire eyes strangely knowing.

"I wish that cat could talk," Floris said. "I wish she could tell us where she's been and what happened to Deirdre."

"My mother's all right," Donny said with confidence. "I don't have to search for her any more."

Nona exchanged a look with Christy. "I'd like to telephone Hayden," she told Floris.

Floris nodded and Nona went to a phone set on a far corner of the kitchen counter. She spoke softly when she'd dialed so that Donny couldn't hear what she said, and he went on stroking Sinh and crooning to her.

Christy bent to touch the cat's roughened coat, but Sinh raised her head again and gave her a look that was anything but friendly.

"She doesn't let many people touch her," Donny said with pride. "Just my mother and me. And sometimes my father and Leonie."

"She was glad enough to see me," Floris said, putting a kettle on the electric stove. "She used to come down here a lot, and she even made friends with Ambrosia."

"Ambrosia?" Christy asked.

Floris looked toward the door to the living room. "Meet Ambrosia," she said and grinned.

To Christy's astonishment, a full-grown llama of the same Virginia peach color as the others, stepped delicately through the open door from the deck, her ears high, and with what was surely an angelic smile on her wide mouth.

She advanced carefully into the room, knocking nothing over, and came to where Sinh lay outstretched. Bending her head, she nosed the cat gently, affectionately, and Sinh didn't object.

Nona turned from the phone, laughing at Christy's expression. "They make wonderful house pets. Though I think I'd find one a bit big to live with. They're very clean and completely housebroken, since they have their own toilets outdoors and always go to the same place."

"Unfortunately, Ambrosia likes to eat my house plants,"

Floris said. "I think you'd better go outside for now, pal. Donny, take her down to the pen, will you?" When Donny had gone, she explained further. "Llamas are very gentle when they're field raised and used to human touch. Ambrosia never breaks anything or even knocks things over, big as she is."

"I reached Hayden and he's coming down," Nona broke in.

Sinh went to sleep again, curling into a dirty-looking ball. When Donny returned he drew a book from a case in the dining area of Floris's kitchen, and held it out. It was another copy of *The Little Red Road,* and he began to tell Floris about reading it to the cows.

"Maybe I could take this out and read it to the llamas too?" he suggested.

"You could try," Floris said, "though llamas are a lot more nervous than cows, and they don't pay attention too long. They're plenty curious, so you can go ahead and try if you want."

Donny clattered down the outside steps, carrying the book.

"Sit down, both of you," Floris invited, spooning loose tea into an earthen pot. "Tell me what you wanted to talk to me about, Nona."

They sat at a rustic table of long boards, watching Floris place mugs and spoons before them.

"Let's wait until Hayden gets here," Nona said. "I want him to hear this too."

Through an open window Christy caught Donny's voice rising clearly as he began reciting the little road's adventures to the llamas.

"You did a good job, Christy, making friends with Donny," Nona commented. "The book made a perfect bridge. Floris, there was another manuscript Rose was working on—do you know anything about it?"

"She was using my llamas, and I think she had the whole thing nearly done."

"I'm sure there was a manuscript," Nona agreed, "but it seems to have disappeared. Oliver told me it wasn't among

Rose's things. If it could be found, I'd still like to illustrate it and see it published. I know Rose came down here to see the llamas several times, and once when she visited me afterward, she seemed upset. Do you know what happened?"

Floris brought the sleeping tea to the table and set the pot on an iron trivet. "What happened wasn't important as far as I was concerned. It was only Deirdre I was peeved with—not Rose. But Rose got upset and went off in a huff, and she never came to see me again. Though if she'd lived, I'm sure she'd have gotten over whatever upset her. It was foolish of her to defend Deirdre."

"What had Deirdre done?" Nona asked.

"It's all water under the bridge—let it go. You like your tea with lemon, don't you, Nona?"

Donny gave up with the llamas and came back inside. "They just want to eat, and Snow White kept kissing me," he said in disgust.

At the sound of his voice Sinh lifted her head, and Donny poured her another saucer of milk. The cat lapped without much interest and went back to sleep.

Nona wasn't ready to let the matter of Rose and Deirdre drop, however, and she returned to what Floris had said. "How could anyone fight with Rose or manage to offend her? I've never known a woman more gentle or more generous about her judgments."

Floris ran a hand through her short, untidy hair. "That's what you think. She was also loyal to her friends and those she admired. Rose had a notion that Deirdre was made of—of—"

"Rainbows and magic?" Nona said softly.

"Or cobwebs and cotton wool!" Floris sounded tart.

Christy found herself watching Donny for any reaction to the words spoken around him, but all his attention seemed focused on stroking Sinh.

"What did *you* say to upset Rose?" Nona persisted.

Floris too gave Donny a wary look. "I said I thought Deirdre was being mean to my llamas."

"That's hard to believe." Nona stirred the tea Floris had poured into her mug. "Deirdre loved animals. Did you ever see Deirdre do anything unkind?"

"Not actually. The funny thing was, they reacted to her in different ways. Sometimes they loved her, and sometimes they didn't."

"Do they make any sounds if they're frightened?" Christy asked.

"They'll hum if a strange animal is around," Floris said. "If they're really alarmed they can sound like geese. Ordinarily the presence of a human wouldn't bother them, but there were occasions when Deirdre made them restless and they wouldn't come near the fence if she was there. Of course, nobody goes inside the pen unless I say so."

Donny was very quiet. Little pitchers, Christy thought. His focus might not be quite so intent upon the cat.

"So what did you tell Rose that upset her?" Nona persisted.

"I told her that Deirdre was teasing the animals, and I wished Rose would talk to her."

"Why couldn't you tell Deirdre yourself?"

"I did! But she got that misty-eyed, wounded-doe look and I felt like a bully. Just the same, I know she was doing something to upset them and I wanted Rose to find out what it was. It's even possible that Deirdre didn't realize what she was doing."

Donny looked up from stroking the cat. "She pinched their ears," he said calmly.

"That's impossible!" Floris cried. "Llamas are terribly sensitive about their heads. They wouldn't let her."

"How do you know that, Donny?" Nona asked quietly.

"Sometimes she could do things nobody else could." Donny remained undisturbed. "She didn't mean to hurt them. She was just testing them for earrings."

This was too much for Floris. "Earrings on my llamas! That's crazy! What on earth are you talking about?"

"I told her it wouldn't work and they wouldn't like it," Donny said. "But she thought they'd look nice with those big pointed ears and little button earrings in them. Not the dangly kind."

"My God!" Floris said.

Nona leaned toward the little boy. "Donny, are you making this up? Are you making up a story the way you and Rose used to do?"

"Of course not." He looked offended. "Here—see this!"

He picked Sinh up and she went limp and unresisting, resting her head along his arm. Attached to the cat's ear, Christy could see the sparkle of a tiny rhinestone.

Floris said, "That's terrible!"

"Why?" Donny asked. "My mother said if I was a girl she'd have had my ears pierced for earrings. She had a whole box of them herself and she always wore them. I don't think it hurts much."

"But you can't explain that to a cat," Nona said. "*Or* a llama. I don't understand why Sinh hasn't clawed that thing out of her ear."

"Deirdre *did* explain to the cat," said a voice from the deck, and Christy looked around to see Hayden Mitchell in the doorway. His gravity seemed to have an angry underside at times, as though something no one understood might be driving him.

"Donny's telling the truth," he went on. "Deirdre had a way of getting Sinh to do whatever she wanted. She'd whisper to it in her own cat language and Sinh listened as though she understood. She seemed to accept that thing in her ear because Deirdre wanted her to."

"The witch's familiar," Floris said, not quite under her breath.

The dark fire seemed to light in Hayden's eyes and he stared at her. She met the challenge and stared back. "You allowed that?" she said.

Nona spoke for Hayden. "Allowing Deirdre was like allowing a cloud to float. We all know that."

"Who found Sinh?" Hayden asked abruptly, his attention now on the bedraggled cat. Sinh raised her head again, and this time her tail twitched as though she might spring into motion. Donny spoke to her soothingly and she was quiet again.

"Don't stand there in the doorway looking like a thundercloud," Floris said to Hayden. "Come in. We're having tea, but you can have coffee if you like. Sinh showed up this morning when Victor was here, and he brought her into the house. She was pretty nervous at first and didn't trust us. But milk and bits of chicken quieted her down. She was half starved, but she would hardly let me touch her until Donny came. Who knows where she's been?"

Donny crooned to the cat as it lay in the curve of his arm.

"My mother's not really gone. She'll come back when she feels like it."

For a moment no one said anything. Then Hayden sat down near Donny and Sinh. "What do you mean by that?" he asked gently.

"I saw her, Dad. I saw her yesterday near those woods across the meadow. It was getting kind of dark and clouds were floating in, but I saw her white dress and I called to her. She only waved to me and went off into the trees. I ran after her, but she wasn't there any more." His eyes were bright with tears of disappointment, but his gloom and dejection had lifted.

Floris took the cat from Donny's arms and returned it to its padded box on the floor. Hayden drew his son between his knees, looking deeply into his eyes.

"I'm sorry, Donny, but I think this was a dream you had. It's easy, you know, to see things that we want terribly to have happen—but we need to keep what's real and what is just a dream separate."

Donny twisted from his father's grasp. "I *did* see my mother! I *saw* her!"

"There's something you ought to know," Nona said quickly to Hayden. "Victor Birdcall told us a little while ago that he's seen Deirdre too—the same white figure in the woods."

"There—you see!" Donny cried. "Victor wouldn't make that up."

"I don't know that you can trust Victor," Floris said, filling a coffee mug for Hayden. "Oliver's been checking up on him. Some pretty bad things happened out in New Mexico."

"Oliver's been down here?" Nona sounded surprised.

"Why not? He used to come with Rose sometimes when she was watching the llamas and getting stuff for her book. He was here just a few days ago. He's writing some sort of article he thought I might help him on, and he hinted around about Victor. Though he wouldn't explain. I guess he has a friend in Santa Fe, where Victor comes from."

"I don't like this," Nona said. "Victor's had enough to deal with. All he wants now is peace. He's not harming anyone, and Oliver has no business stirring things up."

"But there hasn't been much peace around here, has there?" Floris asked, her eyes bright with something like malice. There was a scrappy side to her nature, Christy thought, and remembered Hayden saying that she liked animals better than people.

Donny was still indignant. "Victor's not lying! He's not making anything up, and neither am I! If you don't believe me, I don't care!"

Before Hayden could stop him, the boy rushed out of the room and down the steps of the deck.

"Let him go," Hayden said wearily. "I'll talk to him later."

Nona said, "Do you mind going back to the house alone, Christy? I'll see you in a little while."

Clearly she wanted to talk to Floris. Christy thought of the narrow path up through the woods—the red corridor of her dreams—and her hesitation must have shown.

Hayden stood up. "I'm going your way," he offered, though his tone was cool, as though he performed a duty reluctantly.

"Thank you," Christy said stiffly—better Hayden than snakes—and they went outside together.

He had left a forked stick near the foot of the steps and he picked it up as they started toward the bridge.

Three llamas stood near the fence, watching—Snow White, of course. She was the Mama Llama, as Donny sometimes called her. She always seemed affectionate toward humans, and very inquisitive. A smaller animal stood beside her—one whose fur was pale brown, which indicated a newcomer, since the original color still showed in the fur. Three curious faces looked over the fence at Christy and Hayden, and there was no uneasy humming now. The one male in the group stood back from the others, observing with a paternal air. The three at the fence had small, pursed mouths that looked as though they were about to smile.

"These days," Hayden said, "Floris keeps just one male, and lets them breed according to nature. With more, they'd be in separate fields. When Abel was alive they had a large farm and sold the wool. They even trained some of the llamas as pack animals. Now, when Floris takes care of them herself, she just keeps a few as friends."

Christy paused beside the fence and permitted Snow White to salute her. But she had no food pellet to reward her with and the animal lost interest.

"Deirdre was wonderful with all animals," Hayden said. "Just as Donny is. She used to say she must have been a llama in a past lifetime. At first they took to her and seemed to understand what she was saying."

"In spite of the earrings?" Christy asked.

The life went out of Hayden's voice. "She could be whimsical at times and get carried away."

Christy groped futilely for anything that would make the scattered fragments of Deirdre come together. "Floris said they hummed in the last weeks as though Deirdre were some strange animal."

He let that go. They had reached the bridge and were crossing it. When he stopped midstream and stood looking down into the rippling water, she paused beside him.

He spoke without looking at her. "Are you going to look for Deirdre?"

His words sounded more like a challenge than a request, but she could understand his pain—his reaching for anything that came to hand.

"I wouldn't know where to start," she told him. "I don't even know much about what Deirdre was like. I don't think there's anything I can do."

He left the rail and walked on and she went with him.

"I thought psychics received answers from their own sources," he said.

She sensed mockery and ignored it. "I don't think of myself as psychic. What comes to me is limited. It's only an occasional clairvoyance."

"The scarf wasn't enough? You reacted pretty strongly to that."

"Whatever was there of Deirdre had been erased and some other personality superimposed."

She didn't want to think about the scarf, and they walked on in silence, her resistance growing. They had started up the steep path through the woods, and he went ahead now. She found herself looking for snakes, not sure she could even tell one from a broken branch unless it moved. When she hesitated because of a twisted tree limb, Hayden looked back.

"We'll probably never see a snake, but I carry this stick with me, just in case. I can hold one down with the forked end."

"Then what?" Christy asked.

"The copperheads we kill—though I don't like to. Unfortunately, there's not always a peaceful way to let a copperhead go."

It was not snakes alone, however, that troubled Christy about the woods. A pressing sense was growing in her—of something unseen following. Something that caused a prickling at the back of her neck. Halfway up the hill, she turned to look down through tall columns of oak and poplar and maple that crowded each side of the path and stretched away thickly on either hand. Nothing moved and the woods seemed still and empty. Around her, gray trunks thrust into the sky, their high canopies blocking the sunlight except where it fell through to the ground in golden-brown patches. Far above, their green heads swayed gently in a wind that never reached the ground. Down here the stillness seemed eerie and there was only the red path and the gray columns to give her a frightening sense of her dream. But this was real. This was where it might happen—if she stayed.

Without warning, panic seized her, and she tried to run past Hayden up the hill, only to stumble over a rock. He caught her by the arm and saved her from falling.

"What's really bothering you?" he demanded. And then more gently, "Do you want to talk about it?"

Not to him. Not even to Nona. Not to anyone! The haunting lay deep inside herself and only she could deal with it.

When she didn't answer he walked ahead, speaking over his shoulder. "We'll stop for a break in a minute. It's a long climb back—worse than coming down. There's a rock outcropping around the next turn where we can sit for a while. You sound winded."

His tone was impersonal, but at least he was being considerate.

Only once after that did she look back, and there was still nothing to be seen. The follower of her dream existed only in her mind, and she must deal with it—not allow it to become a prophecy she believed in.

The great pile of granite made an opening in the trees, with only seedlings clinging here and there to its crevices. One side rose in a gentler slope, and where they would first set foot to climb up, a large coiled snake lay in a spot of sunlight.

"It's only a black snake," Hayden assured her. "They're harmless and they do a lot of good, eating mosquitoes and insects. Look—he's not unfriendly."

Hayden set the end of his stick down beside the snake, not pinning it, just nudging a little. After a moment the creature uncoiled itself and investigated, recoiling gracefully up this new attraction. Hayden tossed the stick away into brush, and pulled Christy up the sloping surface of the rock.

"I'm not sure I'd try that with a copperhead," he said, and Christy shivered.

The high slope of rock was free of invaders, and Christy sat down beside Hayden, pulling up her knees to rest her cheek against them, closing her eyes. The man beside her was quiet, no longer an antagonistic presence—but merely a listening one. What if she could tell him, after all? One reason she'd never told anyone about her dream was the sense that if she put it into words she would make it real. Now, however, the place itself was real—perhaps the very scene of her dream. Something had been put into motion that she might not be able to stop, and it might be better to tell someone about it.

She began to speak without preamble. "I have a dream that recurs. In it I'm always running down a corridor with a floor that's the color of blood. Like that path down there. On either side of me are high gray walls closing me in—like the walls those tree columns make. There's no way for me to go except ahead, and I'm always running because something is forever coming after me. I know if I stop I'll be caught and something awful will happen. But my lungs are bursting and I can't breathe. Of course that's when I wake up. But it's a terrified awakening because I can't throw off my fears right away. Sometimes I'm almost afraid to go to sleep at night—though the dream only comes once in a while."

When she raised her head, Hayden's look was grave but not unsympathetic.

As though she were still running, Christy went on breathlessly. "Of course I can just stay out of the woods, but I'll dream anyway. I'll dream until it's over. I'm sure now that I've come to the place where it must end, one way or another. Perhaps I can't run away any more, even though I want to. Perhaps I have to let it happen, before I can ever be free."

Hayden spoke calmly, accepting. "If this happens in real life, you'd certainly better run."

But in the dream her feet turned to lead at the same moment that all the breath went out of her.

For a while they sat in silence, though Christy's thoughts were busy. Perhaps it was the very fact that Hayden seemed distant and impersonal that had enabled her to tell him. Strangers on a train! But when the silence grew too long, Hayden began unexpectedly to talk about himself.

"I've had a repeating dream too, though it's recent, and it's not about a place. There's only darkness—like a starless night. And out of that void a voice calls for help—always the same voice." He paused for a moment and then went on. "It's Deirdre calling. Sometimes I think her spirit is very near, trying to reach me so it can be released. But I don't know how to let her go until I know what has happened to her. Can you at least try to help me, Christy?"

For the first time he had spoken simply, no longer on guard against her in some way she didn't understand. And now she knew there was no other way except to try. His need was too great, and even though she had no confidence in her own ability to help him, she could no longer choose to go away. Always before, she had wished that her talent could be used to help—instead of offering only the knowledge of death. But she had not felt that Deirdre was dead—though she might very well be. There was Donny's need as well, and there her sympathy and longing to help came easily.

"This is untested ground for me," she said. "My mother has always told me that I ought to develop whatever talent I have —instead of turning my back on it. So all I can say is that I'll see what develops. Perhaps there's something I can try. Will you take me back to Deirdre's room? I won't touch her scarf again, but there may be something else there that will speak to me."

"We can go any time you like," he said. Strangely, now that she'd given in, he sounded stiff again. It was as though he must

resist kindness, gentleness. But his reaction no longer mattered. She had chosen her way, and there might even be times
ahead when she would need to oppose him. She must find out
how to go down into some dark place ahead, not only to find
Deirdre but to unmask the one who might have harmed her.
Whether she had the power to follow through on this she had
no idea. Or any idea what might happen to her if she did.
There could be a psychic risk when one became open to evil.
Yet this was a risk she would now have to take—might be
compelled to take.

For a little while longer they sat quietly, Hayden waiting for
her to move. Finally, to break her own reverie, she asked a
question.

"Tell me what you think about Donny's and Victor's belief
that they've seen Deirdre in her white dress."

"I don't know what to think. She wasn't wearing that dress
when she left, but neither is it in her closet. I don't remember
having seen it for a while, but I'm not sure what Deirdre might
have taken with her—in case her leaving was deliberate."

"Have you any reason to think it might have been deliberate?"

The darkness in him that she had sensed before came down
like a blind to shut her out.

"I can't believe it's Deirdre they've seen," he said curtly.
Now he stood up on the rock and held out his hand. "Shall we
go?"

She let him pull her up from the rock. One of the difficulties
that might lie ahead could be the barrier that Hayden himself
was so determined to raise against her. When he started down
toward the path, she spoke to him quietly, daring a great deal.

"Do you really want to find your wife?"

His face was tight with anger as he looked up at her. "That's
not a question you need to ask."

Neither was this an answer, she thought, but when he went
ahead down the rock, she followed, with no help from him. At

the bottom Hayden picked up the stick the snake had abandoned, and they went on in single file, climbing the hill—separate and on guard against each other. This would not be an easy alliance.

She's stirring everyone up and I must use this confusion. It can lead them in all directions and conceal the truth. I have the real power on my side. Her so-called gift is nothing. Dukas would be a stronger threat.

Though it was a close call with Victor. Apparently he did see me. Less so with Donny. He thinks his mother was made of mist—so it was easy to get away. Victor is suspicious, but he keeps his thoughts mostly to himself. He has too much at risk to be open. But after this I must be more careful.

I think she heard me in the woods today and was frightened. And that's fine! She'll be wary now. The illusion of the white dress was perfect. Perhaps too perfect—a mistake? But of course not—I don't make mistakes.

Perhaps I indulged my anger too quickly with Rose. But Deirdre had to be subdued—I always knew that. She was afraid of me, but never strong enough to stand against me. I can only laugh when they search for her. The place where she is hidden couldn't be more secure.

6

WHEN CHRISTY and Hayden reached his house, they found Oliver Vaughn in a rattan chair on the front deck, smoking a professorial pipe. He greeted them with a wry smile, and Christy was struck once more by his almost perfect good looks. She wondered why they put her off. Perhaps they gave him an arrogance that she reacted to and resented.

"I've been hoping you'd show up, Hay," Oliver said, rising to greet them. "I hiked over here to have a talk with you about Victor Birdcall. I've recently learned some pretty interesting things about him. Perhaps information that may have some bearing on what's been happening around here."

Hayden had chosen his own direction, and for the moment wasn't interested. "Later, Oliver, please. Have you seen Donny?"

"He's upstairs. Eve was here, also waiting for you about some problem at the nursery. I'd hardly come up the steps when Donny dashed out of the woods and tore into the house. Eve thought she'd better find out what was going on, so she went inside after him. This must have been a half hour ago, and I haven't heard a peep out of either of them since."

"Will you wait for me, Oliver?" Hayden asked. "We shouldn't be too long."

Oliver settled in his chair again rather sullenly. This was Saturday, so he had no classes, and would probably rather be doing something else with his day.

Hayden gestured Christy into the house. She could still sense his anger because of what she'd asked about Deirdre. Yet she couldn't regret her question. *Did* he want to find her? She wasn't sure what had prompted her to ask him that, except that she needed to smoke *him* out of hiding. His bristling was useful to him as a screen, but she needed to know what lay behind it. Whether Hayden resented her for probing wasn't important.

The red-tiled central room was empty when they went into the house. Hayden called out for his son, but there was no answer, and he motioned toward the stairs. On the second floor Christy heard Eve's voice from the direction of Deirdre's open door.

Hurrying after Hayden as he entered Deirdre's room, Christy felt at once a rush of negativity that she hadn't felt before among Deirdre's things. Perhaps its source was Eve Corey, who sat jauntily cross-legged on Deirdre's bed, watching Donny. The boy had perched on a stool before the rainbow painting and he didn't look around.

Eve glanced at them and shrugged helplessly. "I'm glad you've come. I've been trying to persuade Donny that he won't find his mother in that picture."

Donny kept his eyes on Nona's painting. "My mother loved rainbows. She always wanted to go into this picture herself. So if I look hard enough, maybe I'll find her there. I think there's somebody hiding in those woods—you can see if you look!"

Christy crossed the room to study the painting. Had Nona painted more than mist beneath the rainbow?

"If you do find her there, Donny," Eve said, "she won't be real. She would only be a bit of paint that Nona used when she created that scene."

"What do *you* know!" This time the boy swung about on the stool and faced them all, his eyes alive with a fury that was nearly out of control. An echo, perhaps, of what Christy had seen in Hayden. "I *did* see her!" he cried. "I saw her *really* in the woods—not in a picture. She's not dead—like Rose!"

"I hope that's true." Hayden came to put an arm about his

son. "But we can't count on it, Donny. We mustn't fool ourselves."

Christy, still searching the painting, saw what Donny had
seen—not merely mist but a tiny face—or something very like
a face—peering out from thin shrubbery, the faintest indica-
tion of the body beneath, lost in shadow. There was no telling
whether Nona had known what she was painting.

Eve got off the bed and stretched plump arms over her head.
"If I'm off duty here, I'd better go downstairs and tell Oliver
what's happening. See you later."

It was a relief to have her leave, Christy thought. Eve wasn't
insensitive, but she viewed the world in a totally opposite way
from Deirdre's mystical approach. Like Oliver, she was tied to
what she believed was real, and she left others little room for
choice, too quickly condemning.

With Hayden's eyes upon her, Christy began to move about,
allowing her senses to turn inward to where the *knowing*
might begin. With Eve gone, the negative quality Christy had
sensed might evaporate. She needed to be quiet, needed to
resist the turbulent feeling that had charged the room. Behind
her, both Hayden and Donny watched, and she could sense
their tension. She paused before Deirdre's dressing table,
where everything personal had been put away. If she opened a
drawer she would probably find Deirdre's lipsticks, makeup,
the perfume she'd used. Her perfume had a heathery scent,
light and woodsy, and it still lingered in the room. She avoided
touching the drawer.

Other items in the room had been left as they were—a lacy
blue shawl that had been thrown over a chair and allowed to
stay, as if awaiting Deirdre's return; a square of needlepoint
she'd been working on. Without touching this, Christy studied
the pattern of stitches. Deirdre herself had been creating a
rainbow, though it looked as though one end flamed into
earthly fire, while the other grew out of a black thundercloud.
A curious, rather violent conception—symbolic of what?

"Donny, did your mother ever talk to you about this needle-point she was working on?"

The boy thought for a minute. "I don't know if she was talking about this, but she told me once that you could never tell where a rainbow began. She said nothing was *all* beautiful, because there was always another side." He left his stool and came over to Christy. "Her closet's here. If you want, I'll open the door for you." It was as if he understood that Christy wasn't ready yet to touch anything Deirdre had used when she was last in this room.

"Please, Donny," she said.

Hayden watched them both, but Christy avoided looking at him—wanting only to be open to whatever impression of Deirdre might come to her in this room.

The closet offered an array of the long gowns Deirdre had liked. There were a few dresses, as well as skirts, blouses, and jeans. On a rack were high-heeled slippers, hardly worn, an array of sandals, and three pairs of walking shoes that bore the stains of red dust on the leather.

Nothing spoke to her. Nothing demanded to be examined, and she didn't want to dispel whatever might come to her by needless handling.

Donny said, "There's one thing my mother liked especially. A sort of—magic thing. Would you like to see it?"

"Very much," Christy said.

He went to a teakwood chest that stood at the foot of Deirdre's bed and raised the lid.

"Of course!" Hayden still watched intently. "Deirdre's jewel case is in there and it might tell you something."

But what Donny took out was a small, dark blue velvet pouch, tied with silver cord. He offered it to Christy, and this time she didn't hesitate. At once she sensed a faint pulsing in her hand as though she held something with a life of its own. When she opened the drawstrings she found that the bag contained a crystal. Somehow she had known it would be a crystal —but what a crystal!

It lay heavily in her palm, more than two inches long from point to base, its planes filled with rainbow lights. It was a polished crystal, such as healers sometimes used in their work.

"My mother said there was a spirit in the crystal," Donny said.

"Even rocks have their own life," Christy agreed, "and I'm sure this is special."

"Can it lead you to Deirdre?" Hayden asked skeptically.

"I don't know." Christy returned the stone to its pouch. "May I borrow this—take it with me for a day or so?"

"I suppose." He seemed indifferent. "Is there anything else in this room that might help her, Donny?"

The boy shook his head, but as they went downstairs he followed close on Christy's heels—as though she carried a bit of his mother with her in the crystal.

Out on the front deck Oliver and Eve sat talking, and they broke off when the others appeared. Christy had a faint sense of conspiracy between them.

"Can you spare me a minute now, Hay?" Oliver asked.

"Of course." Hayden sat down beside him. "I'm sorry you had to wait. I was concerned about Donny, but my son is fine." When he ruffled Donny's hair, the boy drew away and followed Christy as she moved toward the far steps.

"Can I go with you when you look for my mother?" he asked.

"I'm not going to look for her. At least, not now, Donny. I just want to see whether this"—she held up the pouch—"will tell me anything. I promise I'll let you know when there is something I can talk about."

"Okay." He caught her hand suddenly, pulling her along the deck so the others couldn't hear. "I—I guess I ought to tell you . . ." He broke off doubtfully.

"Whatever it is, I'll listen," Christy assured him.

He reached out to touch the blue velvet pouch as though it would help in what he meant to say. "It was my fault that my mother went away."

"How do you mean, Donny?"

"Something happened." He glanced toward his father and lowered his voice to a whisper. "Something awful. I know it was my fault, but I can't tell you. I don't want to talk about it. Just so you know."

"I don't believe," Christy said, "no matter what it was, that you were really to blame. Perhaps if you talked with your father about this . . . ."

"You don't know!" he cried darkly, and pulled away from her to run to the far end of the deck, where he jumped off to the ground. In a moment he had disappeared into the trees.

Troubled, Christy returned to Eve and the two men. When she could see Hayden alone, she must tell him about his son's feeling of guilt.

"Can you tackle this alone—make a start, Eve?" Hayden was asking. "I'll get over to the office as soon as I can and straighten it out."

"It's about time," she said grumpily. "I'll get back now. Thanks, Oliver, for telling me about Victor. Let me know what happens."

Her manner was brusque with both men, but there seemed a special edge to her tone with Oliver, and Christy wondered if any of her old affection for him remained. The edge could be a defense she put up to hide what she might really feel. Certainly there was some sort of friction between those two.

Oliver nodded, not looking at her. "Sure. I'll see you later." Then, as Christy started to move away, he stopped her. "Christy, wait. I think you ought to hear what I have to tell Hayden."

She sat down on the steps to listen, though Oliver's antagonism toward Victor made her uneasy.

"I have a friend in Santa Fe," Oliver went on, "and I sent him what little I knew about Victor Birdcall. The name didn't mean anything, because of course he adopted it when he got out of prison and came here two years ago. It was my description of him, and the fact that his work is putting up lightning rods, that gave my friend a clue."

Oliver paused to puff at his pipe, and once more Christy sensed the tension in him and wondered why he was so down on Victor.

"Prison for what?" Hayden asked.

"Murder." Oliver seemed to relish the word. "Doesn't that make you uneasy? It does me."

"I've always liked Victor," Hayden said. "I'd need to know more about the circumstances, and why he was freed."

"How do we know he was freed? He killed his wife—shot her! And when it's a crime of passion, what does a murderer look like, anyway? We could hardly tell."

"Let's have the rest," Hayden said. "Do you know any more details about what happened?"

"I don't know any more. Maybe he's escaped—who knows? He's been pretty secretive—changing his name and all. And he must have felt safe enough here. Though perhaps others haven't been. Rose was much too kind to him."

"Don't stretch it, Oliver," Hayden said. "I don't think you ought to spread this around without talking to Nona first. I have a lot of confidence in her judgment, and I'm sure she knows all about Victor. Obviously, she trusts him."

"The police might be interested."

"They've talked to him, just as they have the rest of us," Hayden pointed out.

"But this information about him never came out. He certainly didn't tell them."

"You'll do as you like, of course," Hayden said. "But why not get a few more facts first? You might even talk to Victor."

"As though he'd tell us anything!"

"If that's all," Hayden said, standing up, "I'll get along to the office. Can I give you a lift, Oliver? It's begun to look like rain."

"No, thanks. I'll chance it," Oliver said. "But you'd better think about Victor. Don't dismiss this too easily." He gave Christy a sudden smile that surprised her. "I know *you* will think about him," he added, and went off with a wave of his hand.

She watched him go down the driveway with his long stride, surprised by both his smile and his words.

"What did he mean by that?" she asked Hayden.

"Maybe you're supposed to come up with something psychic about Victor. Oliver gets under my skin sometimes, though I suppose we must make allowances because of Rose. He's hurting a lot, and he can take it out on other people."

Just as Hayden himself was hurting, she thought.

Now she took the opportunity to speak to him about Donny. "I've just learned something. Donny believes that he's guilty of sending his mother away. Do you know about that?"

Hayden looked startled. "It's nonsense, of course."

"I'm sure it is, but that doesn't mean it won't be hard to shake. Sometimes children take on blame that isn't theirs. Can you think of anything that might have happened to cause this?"

"Not offhand, but I'll talk to him. Thanks for telling me. Did you get any sort of lead from Deirdre's room, Christy?"

"I don't know yet." She held up the blue pouch. "I'm going to spend some time with Deirdre's crystal now, so I'll walk back to Nona's."

"Then you'd better get started. The sky doesn't look good, and storms can blow up fast around here."

Always, on this ridge she had a sense of woods on one side and open space and sky on the other. But now, across the valley, everything had changed. One of the near meadows still shone green in sunlight that slanted through darkening clouds, but the wooded slopes above stood like black cutouts against an ominous lemon sky.

"Thunder weather," Hayden said. "I'd better drive you."

But she wanted to be alone. Wanted to escape from the troubling emotions that filled both Donny and his father and clouded her inner vision. He walked with her somewhat absently as far as the path to her aunt's house, then returned to his car.

As she hurried toward Nona's, she tried to empty herself of

everything except the sense of Deirdre that must come to her through the crystal.

A sudden gust of wind blew through woods that covered the ridge on her left, and she walked faster against its thrust. The yellow sky had grayed by the time she reached Nona's house, and she saw that lights had been turned on inside. But she didn't want to talk with her aunt now about anything that had happened. She must give the spirit of Deirdre's crystal time to speak to her. It no longer seemed to pulse with its own inner life through the pouch in her hand, and she would need to be quiet and alone to awaken it again. It wouldn't matter if rain caught her—she was close enough to shelter so she could turn back quickly to Nona's and run if she had to.

Past Nona's house the hill that flowed downward on the right was bare of trees and offered a clear view of mountains and sky across the deep cut of the valley. Now all that open space made her feel exposed—vulnerable. Somewhere a calf bawled for its mother, and the sound traveled and echoed in air that was suddenly still. High above a far mountaintop, lightning slanted, followed after a long count by rumbling thunder. The storm wasn't close as yet, but hilltops and sky that had seemed serene were suddenly darkened with roiling, moving clouds.

The path led toward a wooded area that shielded another house beyond. Nona had told her that the people who lived there were away. So she wouldn't bother anyone if she followed the path. She wanted to find a place where she could take shelter if the storm broke—a place where she could be alone with her own inner senses. A porch would do.

An awareness that someone was coming behind her cut through her preoccupation, and she turned quickly. But if anyone followed, he had stepped into near woods out of sight. She felt no particular fear. This wasn't the place of her dream, and nothing would happen to her out here in the open.

The next flash of lightning was bright, and thunder followed immediately with a tremendous clap and a great rolling of kettledrums. Before she knew what was happening, someone rushed out of the woods and hurled himself upon her. She was thrown bruisingly to the ground and lay with her cheek in a patch of red earth where grass was sparse. Struggling to free herself, she looked up at her captor and found that it was Victor Birdcall who had hurled her to the ground. He lay beside her, whispering angrily—as though the storm could hear!

"Don't you have any sense? Out in the open in a thunderstorm! Lie still—don't move."

Once Donny had called him the Thunderbolt Man, she remembered. Thunder and lightning were his business, and she lay obediently still, oddly reassured by his presence.

Rain—big crystal drops—slanted out of thunderclouds above, sounding through the woods like a rushing train. The sky had turned blue-black, with lightning flashes crackling through.

After a moment Christy protested. "I'm getting soaked, and the earth is turning to mud! Do we have to lie here?"

Victor raised his head cautiously, almost as though he sniffed the sulphurous air. "There's a house a few yards away. When I tell you, we'll make a dash for it."

The next thunderclap indicated that the storm had moved farther away. Victor waited for the next lightning flash and said, "Now we go!" He dragged her up roughly and they ran toward the log cabin in its clump of woods. Once on the porch, Victor took out a key.

"I look after the place when the owners are away," he said, and unlocked the front door. "They won't mind."

Christy moved inside gratefully, too cold and miserably wet to worry about Victor and the things Oliver had said about him. She viewed the big fireplace with joy.

"Oh, good! We can build a fire. There's plenty of wood."

"You crazy?" Victor shouted through a roll of thunder as the storm moved back upon them. "You better stay away from chimneys in a thunderstorm. Come over here to the middle of the room—it's safest here."

Reluctantly she let him pull her away from the fireplace, to stand dripping on a rag rug. "Why? Why here?"

"There's a cellar under us, and an attic overhead. Soot in a chimney can be a conductor, and so are all those iron shovels and pokers by the hearth. This is the best place unless a lightning ball comes down the chimney—then we take our chances."

He actually sounded frightened and his fear was contagious because it grew out of knowledge of this particular danger. Christy did exactly as she was told and stood shivering and dripping in the middle of the room.

"They haven't bothered with lightning rods here, though I've warned them they'll be sorry one of these days. I just hope it's not today."

Rain clattered on the roof, making an uproar of its own, and Christy held the wet blue pouch that contained Deirdre's crystal against her body, as if for protection.

"What's that?" Victor asked suspiciously.

"It's a crystal that belonged to Deirdre Mitchell. I've borrowed it for a little while."

"My grandmother knew about crystals," Victor said.

He too was dripping as he stood beside her, and he raised his head when thunder crashed at the same time that a lightning bolt struck nearby. This was a new view of Victor Birdcall. Storms were his element, even though he feared them, and she could feel his excitement and glimpse a blue fire in his eyes— his own sort of lightning. He was a strange, rather terrifying man, and yet she didn't feel in the least afraid of him. He had followed her and saved her from those wild elements out there. If he had really murdered his wife . . . but she wouldn't think about such things.

"That last one struck real close," he said, sounding almost pleased. "An oak tree, probably. Oak attracts all that anger from the sky."

Somewhere in the house a telephone tingled—a brief burst of sound.

"It's not ringing," Victor told her. "That happens to our phones in these mountains. It's the storm. Never touch a telephone in a thunderstorm."

She was beginning to realize that thunderstorms in the Blue Ridge were very different from milder Long Island storms, and certainly to be respected.

Victor went on admonishing. "Always stand away from walls. They're good conductors. Even better than a man. When you're outside stay away from tall men and cattle and trees. A man is even better as a conductor than a tree. So just put your face in the mud and stay safe."

Christy chattered her teeth in response. He crossed the room to pick up a patchwork quilt that lay on the sofa and threw it around her.

"Not much help till you get out of those wet clothes. But it will do for now. I think this will be over soon."

"How long have you been putting up lightning rods, Victor?" she asked, pulling the quilt up to her ears.

"Most of my life. When it's done properly, it's an art. I've made the connections on Nona's house practically invisible. When I do a good job it doesn't show, so of course nobody looks up and tells me how beautiful it is. But when the house stays safe in storms, I know I've done what I do best."

The storm appeared to have brought him to life, so that he seemed a different man—expansive on the subject he knew so well, and less suspicious and guarded. From what Oliver had said, he had reason to be guarded. However, she had stood enough of shivering wetness.

"It's stopping now, isn't it?"

"Hard to tell. The wind can change in a minute and then everything comes crashing back." He listened intently. "Maybe we can chance a fire now. It's still raining too hard to go out."

To Christy's relief, he busied himself at the hearth, lighting wood already stacked, now and then pausing to listen to make sure the storm hadn't returned. In a few moments the kindling caught and flames speared upward, crackling yellow and red. Christy pulled over a stool and sat as close as she could to the warmth and cheery brightness of the fire.

"In a little while I'll make a dash for Nona's," she said, shedding the quilt. She'd given up any thought of communing with the crystal for a while. That would have to wait until she was dry and comfortable.

"First we talk," he told her abruptly, and dragged a bench over, to join her at the fire.

"This isn't the time for talking," she said, suddenly uneasy.

"It's the time. Maybe it's the only time we'll have alone. You need to listen because you're the one with the gift."

"What do you know about that?"

His smile was slyly amused, more like a grimace. "I listened out on Nona's deck last night."

"All right." Christy gave in. "What do you want to talk about?"

"It's about seeing Deirdre in the woods in her white dress. I said what I did because I wanted to reassure Donny. Somebody needed to support him. And he believed he saw her."

"You mean you didn't see anything after all?"

"Oh, I saw someone in a white dress like Deirdre's all right. But it wasn't Deirdre."

She stared at him, reaching cold hands toward the fire. "Go on."

"I always watch the way people move—and that wasn't Deirdre."

"But Donny said she just drifted away in the mist."

"When I saw her she was walking toward me and she didn't move the way Deirdre did. Deirdre was like a dancer. On tiptoe! This person was more awkward. When whoever it was turned and ran, I knew it wasn't any spirit. She—he—it—didn't want me to come too close."

"Who do you think it could have been?"

Victor reached forward with the poker and prodded a chunk

of wood, so that sparks flew upward. "I couldn't begin to guess. That dress is a loose, cover-up sort of thing. Like a tent."

"A caftan?" Christy asked.

"I suppose. Anybody could have been under it—man or woman. Donny saw what he wanted to see—what he made up inside his own imagination, because he wants his mother to be alive."

"You didn't see a face?"

"No. There was a hood pulled over the head—white like all the rest."

"Why have you told me all this?" she asked.

"Because you're the one who will find out what happened— what *is* happening. You're already on the road and you won't stop now." He stood up with his back to the fire, looking down at her. "You won't stop because it's your *way*—your road—to help Hayden and Donny."

His eyes seemed darker with the fire-shine behind him—a deep, dark blue, and very wide and open, as though they searched her mind, her spirit.

"I'm not sure what I can do," she told him, letting the dark fire of his eyes hold her own gaze. She felt a little spacy, as though he might be hypnotizing her—perhaps influencing her mind for some purpose of his own.

She pulled herself out of the spell she'd begun to feel and stared into the fire, where a log fell, sending more sparks up the chimney. Away from the fire, the rest of the cabin seemed dark and chill, with shadows that flickered unsteadily up the walls.

"Did *you* like Deirdre?" Her sudden question came as a surprise to Christy herself—prompted by some inner voice?

"I don't know," he said. "She couldn't be counted on. She was like smoke, and you could never be sure from one minute to the next where she'd be or what she'd do."

"Do you think she's dead?"

"I only know that someone was masquerading in her dress."

"Will you tell Hayden?"

"Somebody will," he said cryptically, and glanced out a window. "You can leave now," he told her abruptly. "It's stopped raining."

Victor Birdcall ceased talking as suddenly as he'd begun. It was as though he'd closed a door and shut himself away from her. Reluctantly, she left the fire. In spite of Victor's strangeness, heat and light made the hearth seem a safer place than the cold, shadowy room.

She could see through the windows, however, that the sky had lightened, with clouds shredding away and nearby mountains turning green again. Mist rolled into the folds, soft and fluffy as cotton, making the crests float like the etched hilltops in a Japanese print. When she reached the door, Christy turned back.

"You ought to know," she said, "that Oliver Vaughn has been investigating you. He has learned where you've been for the last few years and why you were there. He's telling everyone."

When he faced the light, Victor's eyes were no longer dark but that intense blue again, and the lids came down to narrow them. He said nothing at all.

"I think you ought to know that Oliver wants to take some action against you," she went on, a little fearful because he'd turned silent and distant. "I don't know whether Hayden believed him or not, but he told him to stop talking."

Christy had taken her hand from the doorknob, and Victor reached past and pulled open the door. He made no response to anything she'd told him, but merely waited for her to leave. She went quickly out onto the wet path with its patches of red mud. Now she ran without looking back, and once she slipped, smearing herself with red.

Nona was waiting for her on the front deck, and she shook her head in reproach. "You shouldn't be out in a storm like that!"

"I know." Christy was out of breath. "Victor rescued me."

"Good for him! Take off your shoes, Christy—don't tramp that stuff into the house. Then go and take a hot bath and change into something dry. I'll bring you tea and honey, and we'll talk about a few things."

More talk! She wanted only to be alone where she could let whatever was clamoring to be released by the crystal come through. It was ready to speak to her now and she wanted to listen.

Deirdre was right to be afraid of me. Now she's gone—in the mist and rocks and rainbow, where she always belonged.

The dress must be got rid of, and I think I know how. There is a game I can play—perhaps a deadly game. But that's the kind that always fascinates me.

7

N ONA'S ADVICE was sound. After a hot bath Christy
felt warm and human again. The water ran faintly red
before she was through—a distressing color, and too symbolic,
as though her veins had bled. She washed every trace from the
tub and dressed in dove-gray slacks and a blouse of pink
checks. Now she was ready for the crystal.

She carried the little pouch outside to the rear deck. Chairs
and table were wet from the storm and she wiped them with a
towel and sat down. This was where she had first seen Donny,
but the long deck was empty now and shadowed by the dripping canopy of green treetops close to the house. A patch of
blue shone between branches where the sky had been washed
clean. All around, drops pattered from leaves, as though it
were still raining. In the woods below, where the sun slanted
through, tree trunks shone with their own golden-brown light
—well-spaced trees, with leafy, red-gold earth between—the
leaves left over from many autumns. High above, wind still
rushed through the treetops, scattering wetness, and Christy
sat quietly, entranced by the overhead ballet. The pattern of
the dance seemed almost choreographed, with the nearest
treetops bending green heads in one direction, while those
behind, as if stirred by a different current, bent the opposite
way.

The thought of Victor Birdcall was sharp in her mind. A
strange man. For a time she'd felt comfortable with him, even
safe. She'd listened to his talk about storms and lightning, and
she was glad he had told her that the figure seen on the path
had not been Deirdre. Then, when she talked to him about

Oliver, he had changed into someone more ominous and frightening. She'd sensed that he was a man of deep passion, but even when he was angry she couldn't believe he was a murderer.

She mustn't think of Victor, however, or Hayden, or anyone else now. She must be quiet and empty her mind. The crystal was waiting. Once more she opened the silver drawstrings and took out the stone. Deirdre had treasured this, Donny said, and it ought to be able to tell her something. The faint pulsing was there again, and she could sense the power of the crystal's spirit in her hand. It *wanted* to tell her something. Not everyone was sensitive to crystals, and she was glad she could respond.

Its faceted sides rose to a point, and she held it up to sunlight, so that rainbows sparkled in the stone. Then, as she turned the obelisk shape in her hands, something strange caught her eye. Some elusive shape seemed to move within the crystal as a shadowy image appeared in its very heart. It seemed to be a phantom that vanished as she turned the facets, only to reappear inside as a shimmering ghost that eluded her quickly at the slightest movement. No wonder Deirdre had treasured this, since it held a magic of its own at its very heart. She had heard of phantom crystals before, and she knew this to be rare and beautiful.

Ever since she'd touched Deirdre's scarf and sensed its evil, her own power had seemed diminished—as if it had gone into frightened hiding. Now the spirit of the stone reached out strongly to restore her.

Leaving her chair, she moved slowly toward the far end of the deck in the direction of Hayden's house—Deirdre's house. Strangely, the stone in her hand seemed to grow colder, as though it didn't want to go back to Deirdre's room and the chest that had been its home.

Caught up in the strength of this feeling, Christy walked toward the other end, where the deck ran below the windows of Nona's studio. At once the crystal responded and grew warmer in her hand—as though this was the direction she must take.

Just then Nona came through a lower doorway and stood regarding her for a moment. "What on earth are you doing?"

Christy held out the stone, shining on her palm. "This belonged to Deirdre. Donny would understand. I'm sure he's played the old game of hot and cold. *Now you're getting close —now you're far away!*"

"Crystals certainly have natural vibrations and forms. Where did you get that one?"

"Donny gave it to me—from a chest in Deirdre's room. He said it was a special treasure of hers. I have the feeling that it might guide me to her. Can you sense anything when you hold it?"

Nona took the crystal from her and turned it about in her fingers. "Sometimes the power speaks only to certain people. It seems inert to me. What happens when you hold it?"

Christy took it back. "When I move toward Hayden's house, the stone cools in my hand. But when I walk the other way, it gets warmer. There's something in that direction—something connected with Deirdre. I need to follow wherever it leads."

"This isn't the time. Let it go for now, Christy. You mustn't go traipsing off in the wet woods by yourself. There are matters we need to talk about right away."

She'd had too much of talk, Christy thought. The crystal was urging her to follow where it led, and she knew with growing conviction that the stone would bring her—if not to Deirdre, or to where Deirdre's body lay—then to something that had to do with Deirdre. The trail should be followed before it grew any fainter. But before she could step off the end of the low deck, Nona put a hand on her arm. "Lili is coming and we need to get ready."

Her aunt turned and went ahead into the house, and Christy could only follow, speechless. She didn't recover until they were in the sitting-room area of Nona's studio and she'd dropped onto the small couch, staring at her aunt.

"Have you actually talked to Lili?"

Turquoise earrings atremble, Nona stood with her arms folded. "Of course I didn't talk to Lili herself! You know how she operates. Someone else always does dreary things for her, like making phone calls and travel arrangements. Her secretary phoned to let me know that reservations have been made, and that Lili will arrive tomorrow. We aren't being consulted—this is an edict from on high. Fortunately, she'll come without her usual entourage. She had that much sense, at least. She's flying up from Palm Beach and her plane will be met in Charlottesville by a limousine that will bring her here. All she wanted of me was directions—which I had to give."

"But why is she coming?"

"Who knows? I wasn't told. We'll receive her as gracefully as we can, and find out what's up. Mrs. Brewster, her secretary, had no instructions to tell me anything except that Liliana Dukas is to materialize here tomorrow. Of course this means that her Voices have spoken, and Lili does what they tell her. The feelings of more ordinary mortals seldom concern her. I wouldn't mind if she used this advice she gets to guide *her,* but when she reaches out to govern everyone else, we part company."

Even as she listened, Christy sensed the old ambivalence in her aunt. Nona often sounded impatient with Lili, and easily critical, yet under her bluster about her sister there could also exist a reluctant respect.

Unexpectedly, Christy found herself defending her mother. "I don't think she means to be high-handed. She just sees her goal and goes for it in the most direct way possible. Maybe she'll even be able to help us when she comes."

Nona's, "Humph!" sounded halfhearted.

Christy had carried the crystal inside the house, and now she slipped it into its pouch and closed her fingers over it. *Be still for a little while,* she whispered in her mind, and the pulsing impatience of the stone—that only she could feel—seemed to subside.

A sound from the studio end of the room—a cat's mewing—startled them, and they looked around to see that Sinh had recovered sufficiently to climb the hill to Nona's house. She sat erect as a temple statue before the painting in which Deirdre slipped away into the mist.

Nona moved toward the cat cautiously. "How on earth did you get in? There's not a door open, or a window without a screen!"

Sinh turned her head with its dark, Siamese markings that she wore like a mask, and twitched her tail—that tail with the distinctive kink that some Siamese cats had carried throughout the centuries. Legend had it that a deity, wishing to punish, had once tied a kink in a temple cat's tail, and the Siamese had carried it ever since. Sinh's creamy coat looked much less rough and ragged by this time, so she must be giving it her own tongue treatment. As they watched, she began to wash her face showing indifference to their presence, even though she'd asked for attention by mewing.

"Come, kitty-kitty," Nona invited uncertainly.

The kitty-kitty gave her a scornful look from large blue eyes.

"She knows I don't like her," Nona said helplessly. "I don't mind ordinary cats, but this one puts on airs and gives me the creeps. Deirdre used to bring her to my studio sometimes, but she's never come on her own, and with everything closed, I can't think how she got in. We can't leave her here. I don't trust her not to be destructive when Deirdre's not here to control her. But she'll never let me pick her up."

"Let me try," Christy said. She knelt near the cat and began to speak soothingly. "Did you come to look for Deirdre, Sinh? She isn't here, but we're all looking for her, and we wish you could help us. Come now. Trust me, Sinh."

Sinh stayed haughtily where she was, looking as if she occupied some special royal place—a temple cat indeed! Christy remembered the legend and felt uneasy. The cat Sinh had been named for had been the receptacle for its master's soul, when his earthly body was abandoned in death. Was this why

Christy could get no inkling of where Deirdre might be—because her spirit now resided in this small animal?

"Don't do that, Christy!" Nona was watching her. "Whatever you're thinking—don't!"

Christy shook herself. "You're only a cat-cat," she told the Siamese. "Come here—I won't hurt you, and you're not going to hurt me."

She held out her hands and the cat looked her over, making up its mind. It moved its thin body, slinking toward Christy and mewing plaintively.

"I know," Christy said. "You're looking for her. But Deirdre isn't here with us. Come now—please."

Apparently her tone was quieting, so that the cat allowed herself to be picked up and stroked. She clung to Christy's shoulder, digging in with claws. Still whispering soothingly, Christy carried Sinh out to the front deck. When she detached her and set her on the ground, Sinh gave her a dismissing look and stalked off with dignity, lifting each paw carefully as though she disliked soiling it with red mud.

Now she would find her way back to the Mitchells' or down to Floris and her llamas, and Christy returned to the studio. Her aunt waited before the Deirdre painting.

"Thanks," Nona said. "How do you suppose Sinh picked this picture to stare at? Cat's can't recognize paintings."

"How do you know?" Christy asked. "I wouldn't put it past Sinh to have special talents. I just wish she could talk."

"The witch's familiar? But Deirdre was no witch. She was a sweet, charming, rather elusive young woman. Perhaps she never really grew up, but she adored that cat. Floris said it had been mistreated and starved. Deirdre would never have done that. Perhaps only Sinh will ever know what happened to her."

Christy was no longer sure of anything. The cat's presence in the studio signified something. Perhaps, even, that Deirdre herself had brought her here? There were so many contrary reports about Deirdre that bewildered and confused. Donny believed fervently that he had seen his mother. Victor said someone else was masquerading in her dress. But where had the cat been all this time?

"Come on back!" Nona said. "We're really talking about Lili, remember?"

"I'm sorry. What sort of plans do you want to make?"

"At least we won't have to entertain her. Lili always has her own ideas and manages everything. She'll tell *us* what to do. We're not being asked to put her up. A suite has been reserved for her—Brewster didn't say where. I suppose in Charlottesville. Probably at the Boar's Head Inn. I'm not to concern myself—all is being arranged. Though she will have to be fed, of course, if she comes here. Even Lili doesn't exist on rainbows and air—the way Deirdre thought *she* did. Is this meeting going to upset you, Christy?"

Meetings with Lili were always upsetting, though they could be rewarding as well. It was difficult not to slip back into a little-girl pattern of trying to please her mother, even when this attitude disturbed the grown-up Christy.

"I won't let it bother me," she said. "It's just that she sometimes pushes me in directions I don't want to go."

"I know. She never leaves much room for the beliefs of others, because of course whoever's in authority speaks directly to her. We'll just have to let her do her thing, and then gently encourage her to leave as soon as possible."

"Perhaps she *will* help us," Christy mused. "It's possible that she can pick up the trail I seem to have lost. Maybe that's why she's coming."

"Maybe." Nona began to walk about impatiently. "I suppose we'd better invite everyone in to meet her—so she can pick up whatever vibrations there are. I mean all those connected with Deirdre and Redlands."

"And with Rose?" Christy asked.

"I suppose so. Though I'd like to think the verdict there was correct—an accident. We'll invite Hayden, of course, and Eve, Oliver, and Victor—if he'll come."

"What about the Llama Lady?"

"Floris hates gatherings, but I'll get her here somehow."

"You'd better include Sinh," Christy said, only half joking.

Nona threw her a look that was hard to interpret. "Don't go overboard. Sinh is only a cat. Maybe, as you say, Lili will come up with something. I've never discounted what she can manage when that entity she talks to—Josef—comes through. Of course she's doing this because of you, Christy, so you should feel flattered."

"Not flattered," Christy said. "A little alarmed, perhaps. She must have canceled all sorts of engagements, which means that she's really disturbed about something."

"Well, we'll find out tomorrow. In the meantime, let's go shopping and get ready to kill the fatted calf. There's a grocery store in Nellysford, so come with me and we'll see what our nearest metropolis, population three thousand plus, has to offer."

Christy went downstairs for her purse and put the crystal into it. When she returned, Nona was backing her station wagon out of the garage—a long blue car with a remarkable decal of a rainbow on each of the front doors.

"We'll take the back way over the mountain," Nona said as they followed the dirt road out of Redlands. "There's a faster highway, but I like this better."

Adial Road followed S-turns over the mountain, climbed and dipped and climbed again, with woods and small houses along the way. The Blue Ridge Mountains were close now, rising thirty-five hundred feet and more in this part of Virginia.

"Nelson County hasn't a single stoplight," Nona said contentedly. "There used to be one in Lovingston, the county seat, but when it blew down, they never put it up again. Do you see that long, very high mountain rising out there? That's Wintergreen—a posh ski resort. Though now it's open the year round for other sports as well."

The road made its last long descent down a steep hill that dropped to a bridge across the Rockfish River and into Nellysford.

"Legend has it," Nona went on, "that Nelly drowned fording the river, and the place has been called by her name ever since. This goes back a century or so, of course. Another tale says Nelly was a horse—but it's apocryphal."

A few old farmhouses were left, but most of the scattered dwellings had been more recently built. The shopping center stretched along the Rockfish Valley floor, consisting of a strip of shops, open on one side, that served the area and whose architecture suggested an older, rural Virginia. Nona pulled into the parking lot and they got out.

For a time Christy had allowed her mind to drift peacefully. Grocery shopping was harmless, and for the moment she wouldn't think about Lili's coming, or all that was disturbing that might lie ahead. This peaceful state didn't last long, however, because they met Hayden and Donny Mitchell coming out of the store, a bag of groceries in Hayden's arms.

"Good!" Nona said when she saw him. "We want to talk with you, Hayden. Are you in a hurry?"

His expression was guarded. "I'll put this stuff away and wait for you by the car."

"While I shop, you can tell him," Nona said to Christy. "Will you come along and help me, Donny?"

As his son went off with Nona, Hayden put his bag in the back of his Jeep, and Christy got into the front seat. When he'd climbed in beside her, he seemed to study her again, and under his scrutiny she felt uncertain and uncomfortable. She was always aware of him as a strong, all too compelling presence, and the feeling was unsettling.

"Nona wanted you to tell me something?" he asked.

Christy looked off toward the mountains to break the intensity that had seemed to rise between them—as though he always challenged her in some way.

"It's so beautiful here," she said, not answering his question.

"It will be hot soon," Hayden said. "We'd better enjoy this cool weather."

He had sensed her disquiet and was giving her time, but she had to open up about what was troubling her.

"My mother will be here tomorrow," she told him. "We don't know why she's coming or how long she'll stay. Her secretary phoned Nona."

"And you're upset about her coming?"

"I keep telling myself I'm not, but it's true—I am," Christy admitted. "If Lili is willing to drop everything and come here because of me, she must feel that I'm threatened in some way."

"Perhaps you should pay attention," Hayden said.

"I don't know. My mother has a way of taking over. *Her* way is the only right course, and it's not always the one I want to follow. She behaves as though she's guided by a higher force than the rest of us can tap into."

"You don't believe in her—whatever they are—powers?"

"I used to believe more than I do now. If I'd taken all her advice, I'd never be able to be me. I need to learn in my own way at my own time."

"What do you think about your own gift?"

She was suddenly vehement. "I never asked for it—I don't want it! I don't even believe in it. Something happens and I'm forced to follow a road whether I want to or not. Now—with Lili's coming—"

Christy leaned back in the seat and closed her eyes. She wasn't sure why she was afraid of her mother's coming. She hadn't told Nona how strongly she felt, even though Nona would sympathize.

Hayden was watching her again thoughtfully. "Perhaps Liliana Dukas will find something we've all missed."

There was no answer to that—he might very well be right. But her uneasiness didn't abate. It was also possible that Lili, with her high-handed approach, might make everything worse. That could happen too.

"She has a way of hypnotizing everyone," Christy said. "And that includes me. I'm not sure I even think clearly when Lili's around and I hate sinking under her spell. But never mind that

—before Donny comes back with Nona, I want to tell you something that happened today. Victor Birdcall found me when I went for a walk and the storm came on. He took me into that cabin near Nona's house. At first he was full of warnings about thunderstorms, and then he spoke of seeing that figure in the woods, just as Donny did. Only Victor claims now that it wasn't Deirdre but someone who was masquerading in the sort of white caftan she used to wear. Have you any idea what this could mean?"

He shook his head soberly. "If I could guess at a motive for her leaving—and staying away—I might have an answer. I wondered about that dress when Donny described it. If it's Deirdre's I think she gave it away months ago. She often gave her clothes away when she tired of them."

"Who did she give it to?"

"I don't remember—if I ever knew. Perhaps Donny might recall. But if I ask him he'll be all the more upset, since he's so sure he saw his mother in the woods. I don't know how to let him down easily." Hayden sat stiffly beside her, his hands on the wheel, looking ahead through the windshield.

"Have you thought any more about Donny's feeling of guilt—that it's his fault his mother went away?"

"I've tried to figure it out. The night before she left, Deirdre and I had a quarrel. Maybe Donny heard something. Some of it concerned him. Just find her, Christy. Whether she's dead or alive, we need to know. So use whatever it is you have and find her!"

She had to answer him as honestly as she could. "Look—I don't read minds or crystal balls. I don't see the future, or consult tarot cards or tea leaves. I can't foresee anything. I can only wait for whatever comes. Nothing is coming through right now. My mother says I've never used whatever I have—never trained it. Perhaps something in me is resisting because when it happens it's shattering for me too."

He had seen her when she held Deirdre's scarf—he'd had a glimpse. "I'm sorry," he said. "I suppose I'm reaching for any help I can find, and I haven't thought about how this might affect you."

She tried to soften her words. "I do understand how you feel, and if I can help I will. I know how much you must love and miss your wife."

His hands tightened on the wheel. "You *don't* know—how could you? But if you're to help me, perhaps you'd better understand. This last year wasn't a happy one for Deirdre and me. It may be that I drove her away. So if something has happened to her, I'm to blame. There hasn't been much love between us for a long time, though I've tried to protect and advise her—when she would listen."

Christy had never wanted to help anyone more than she did Hayden. His suffering went deep, and she didn't need to understand to want to help. Perhaps she wanted this more than was wise—yet there was so little comfort she could offer, and no promise she could make.

After a moment he went on, speaking now of Lili as though there had been no sudden revelation, no opening of himself in those few moments.

"Perhaps your mother really will help. Has Nona made any plans for her coming?"

"Nona wants to invite those who are most concerned to come to her house tomorrow night. That will give Lili a chance to do her thing."

"You sound as though you don't like the idea."

"When my mother touches us as Liliana Dukas, everything will become too dramatic. She can't help being theatrical. But sometimes I think she puts too much trust in whatever voice speaks to her."

"You don't believe in her voices?"

"It's not that I don't believe." Christy smiled wryly. "I'm just not sure that every one of those entities out there is equally wise and all-knowing. Perhaps there are mischief-makers among them too, and Lili must make a wonderful playground."

He thought about this. "I wonder if that's what Deirdre was —a playground for mischievous spirits? She was always vulnerable—open. Often too trusting. Once she said something strange that I've never forgotten."

"Anything you can tell me about her might help."

"You remember the story of Undine—who was a being from the sea?"

"And not to be loved by mortal man? I remember."

"Deirdre said she was like that—that she had a home somewhere else, but she didn't know where it was. Sometimes she could laugh and make funny little jokes—she laughed a lot with Donny. But her jokes were never about herself—so when she said that she was serious."

Christy felt a twinge of sympathy for Deirdre. "It's not comfortable to be born different from everyone else."

"I suppose you've felt that too?"

"Yes—it makes me a stranger, wherever I go."

"But you're not haunted—not the way Deirdre seemed to be. You manage to live with—whatever it is you do. I've never felt that you were a stranger here, Christy. It's as though this is the place where you were intended to be."

That startled her even more—it was so unexpected from Hayden Mitchell.

"All I really want is to run away," she admitted. "What happens to me is more like a curse than a gift. No one wants to be close to a person who sees what others don't. When they believe, it alarms them. And if they don't believe, they think I'm offbeat and weird."

He was looking at her, studying her, as though there were some question he needed to have answered. "I'm sorry all this is adding to your own difficulty."

She hadn't intended to be so revealing about herself, and she stiffened against his sympathy. For her this was quagmire. She'd already been drawn toward something in this man— something she felt wary of.

He sensed the change in her and returned to a calmly impersonal manner. "What about the satisfaction of having your gift used to help others?"

"What satisfaction—when it brings misery to those I try to assist? If I could stop something dreadful before it happens—that would be satisfaction."

"Would anyone believe even if you were able to warn them?"

She could only shrug helplessly.

"Perhaps the very fact that nothing has come to you means that Deirdre is still alive. She could have run away from me—from the things I said to her that last night. I'd begun to be afraid that she was harming Donny."

"Would she run away in her nightclothes, taking nothing?"

He shook his head. "I'm not sure what she might have taken. But I go round and round over that."

Divided though his feelings were about Deirdre, she could sense his pain. She remembered Nona telling her that Deirdre was rather like a daughter to him—and one could suffer over a wayward daughter.

The crystal, tucked away in her purse, seemed to call to her silently. When she took it out and held it up to sunlight, white fire danced around the phantom at its heart. No rainbow colors now—just pure golden light. Was the crystal a charm against dark forces? A charm that Deirdre had forgotten to take with her?

"Today," she told Hayden, "I had the strong feeling that the energy in this stone wanted to lead me somewhere. Nona stopped me from going off into the woods to follow where it urged me to go. She said I must wait until someone could go with me. If it happens again, will you come?"

"If I'm around," he said. "Of course."

Nona came out of the grocery store, with Donny pushing her cart.

"Let's go help," Hayden said, and then touched her hand. "I'm glad we talked a bit, Christy. Thanks for being concerned. That's all I have any right to ask."

His touch was only meant to reassure, but it made her all the more aware of him, stirring sensations that had been asleep, giving her a feeling of vulnerability.

They left the Jeep and Hayden went with Nona to unload her bags into the trunk of her car. Donny stayed back with Christy and tugged at her sleeve.

"I need to tell you something."

She stopped beside him. "Of course, Donny. What is it?"

He looked uncertainly toward his father and Nona. "If I tell you, will you tell *them?*"

"Not if you don't want me to. Anyway, not without asking you first."

He seemed satisfied with that. "I know where Rose hid the llama story she was doing."

For a moment she didn't remember. "You mean the manuscript, Donny?"

"Yes. She had it all finished and she let me see it. But I didn't like it much, and she said I was right and she would have to do it over. She didn't want anyone to know about it until she'd fixed it. So she said she would hide it, so no one could see it until she'd done it better. She only told *me* where it was." He watched Christy anxiously. "We were real good friends," he added, "Rose and me."

"Of course. She did the right thing to trust you."

"But now she's been—gone—such a long time. And everybody talks about how they can't find the book. So I wondered— should I get it and give it to somebody? Even though she'd changed her mind about it?"

It seemed strange that he hadn't told someone about this before. His mother earlier, or his father. Or even Nona, who had meant to illustrate the book, and might still want to do so.

Donny sensed the question in her mind. "It wasn't like the *Red Road* book. The llamas in the story all had people's names. They weren't named like the real llamas."

"So?"

"The names were of the people who live around here. One was even named Rose, and a young one was named for me."

"That could be fun," Christy said, feeling her way cautiously, because there was something here she didn't understand.

"No, it wasn't any fun at all." Donny looked away from her. "Rose made the llama people mean and—and scary. It was like she changed into somebody different when she worked on that story."

Here was a possible lead. If the warm and loving Rose Vaughn had kept secrets that she'd released into this book, something useful might be revealed in her writing.

"It wasn't really a story," he went on. "Not yet. She could draw sort of cartoon pictures, and she put labels on them. But I guess she didn't really want to write the story yet."

"It might be a good idea, Donny, if you let us all see this manuscript," Christy said.

"No! It's not for the others. Because they're in it, and they won't like the way she's drawn them. But maybe you could look at it and tell me what to do?"

"You coming, Christy?" Nona called. "We need to get back."

Christy waved her hand. "Right away." Then she spoke to Donny again. "Bring the book to me when you have a chance. When I've looked through it, we can talk together about what to do."

She wasn't sure he was satisfied with this plan, and before he could rejoin his father, she asked a question that had been puzzling her.

"Donny, did you bring your mother's cat to Nona's studio this afternoon?"

He looked surprised. "Isn't Sinh down at the llama farm with Floris? I thought she was too sick to go anyplace."

"Then she must be well again, because she managed to get herself up through the woods and into Nona's studio where we found her." She didn't mention the puzzle of closed doors and screened windows.

"Where is she now?"

"We couldn't leave her there, so I carried her out to Nona's front deck. I think she went off in the direction of your house."

"Then that's probably where she is," Donny said, and ran toward his father's Jeep.

Christy joined Nona in the station wagon with its joyful rainbow decorations. On the way home Nona talked steadily about plans for Lili's coming. Christy watched mountains and ravines and forest flow past, lost in her own thoughts. She would certainly look with interest at this manuscript of Rose's.

No one's found the dress yet. I'll try a new place. Of course I want her *to find it and be all the more disturbed. If she's frightened enough, her own fears should hold her. I really thought she'd give up before this.*

Today she almost caught me when I was watching her out on the lower deck. She came right toward where I was hiding, and it's a good thing Nona came out and took her away.

The cat was a nice touch. Of course the animal hates me, and it spit and clawed when I carried it up through the woods. But I know how to handle the little beast, and it doesn't want to go back to where I've been keeping it. For a while I needed it because of Deirdre, but I don't need it any more.

When I put the cat in front of Nona's painting, it settled right down. Of course I closed everything up carefully when I left, so they're probably still wondering how Sinh got in. A locked room mystery!

They're all in a turmoil now about something. I'll have to find out what's happening—and find out soon. I'm not safe yet. Rose can't come back, but Deirdre might. I'm still not sure about Deirdre. I don't think she would go near any of the others—not after what she's done—but she might come just to spite me. Whatever space it is she occupies, if the pull was strong enough, she might come back.

8

THERE WAS no opportunity to be alone with Deirdre's crystal for the rest of the afternoon. Nona's preparations to receive Lili showed a certain respect for her sister. Not until after dinner was Christy able to escape to her room for a period of time that would be uninterrupted.

Now she could be still and hold the bright, faceted stone in her hands, trying once more to sense its energies. This time, however, there was no pulsing in the crystal, no sensation of warmth to guide her. The stone felt heavy in her hands and there was no response of any kind. She should have followed where it led earlier, before the impulse died.

After a time she opened the sliding glass doors to the deck and went outside, still holding the crystal. It had warmed a little, but only from the heat of her own hands, and no matter which way she turned, it remained quiet, sleeping, indifferent to her urging.

Her gift had never been as strong and certain as Lili's, and in a way she'd been grateful for its very uncertainty. What Lili possessed governed her whole life so that she had to live for it, and this was never what Christy had wanted. Now, however, there was a need for any power she could summon, and this was no longer impersonal. By this time she knew that she couldn't leave Redlands until she had found the answer to Deirdre's flight. Once that was done, she would be free to go.

This needed to happen quickly. Hayden's presence had become increasingly vital to her. His quiet strength and deep sadness sparked a response, a longing that could be neither denied nor satisfied. It was better to get away as soon as she could.

So let it be, she told herself. *Think of something else.* She left the deck and returned to her room.

Nona, who was a mystery buff, had stocked a small bookcase in her guest room with both hardcover books and paperbacks in the crime field, and Christy picked out a Barbara Michaels novel and sat down to read until she grew sleepy.

Here, close to the woods that dropped down the hill at the back of the house, she could hear little from upstairs. Once the sound of a car door slamming reached her, and she wondered who had come to visit her aunt in the evening. But nothing up there need concern her now. Tomorrow, when her mother arrived, no one would have much to say, because Lili Dukas would consult her own sources to solve the grim problems of Redlands, and Christy could only hope she would succeed.

Though, in Lili's sunny philosophy, the perpetrator of wrongdoing was never to blame. Circumstances formed each individual, and the wrongdoer was only working out his or her particular karma. Cause and effect—on and on until all the lessons had been learned, perhaps through thousands of life-times. But pretty uncomfortable for those who must suffer those effects now. Christy remembered the moment when she'd held Deirdre's scarf and that chilling sense of evil had flowed through her. There was more here than Lili accepted.

Weren't there human beings who were genuinely evil? Or was evil only a matter of perception? One person's stated evil could be perceived as another's good. The deeply religious sect that considered all other beliefs evil made a good example.

She had no answers. She tried again to concentrate on her book, but her thoughts would not be quiet. All mystery novels dealt with good and evil, and their conclusions were simple enough. The murderer was evil, while the victim might or might not have been evil. Those who tracked and exposed the murderer were obviously good. Or were they?

In a life without testing, who could grow? Dark surely balanced light, and everything in nature had its opposite pole. In a life that was all lightness and calm, there would be nothing to wake one up in order to reach out and learn. So perhaps growth required a whip from the dark side. Without pain, nothing happened, and evil might be the whip to spur humans on to oppose it for their own strengthening and—that term psychics often used—"higher enlightenment." Lili was great on higher enlightenment, but right now Christy didn't feel in the least enlightened.

She would get undressed and go to bed, though it was only nine-thirty. She stood up, stretching widely, yawning—and was suddenly aware of how black the nighttime woods were beyond the deck. There were curtains, but no draperies to pull, and that made her uncomfortable. She wasn't used to a house where no one locked doors or bothered to draw shades. Nona had said no one came up through the woods back here—there wasn't even a path on this part of the hill.

So why did she feel as though she were on a lighted stage—with someone out there watching?

The crystal winked at her in the lamplight from the dressing table where she'd placed it, but she paid no attention. It could keep its impulses to itself right now. All she wanted was to escape into sleep.

She went to the closet to take out her night things, and at that moment a scattering of sound reached her—as though someone had thrown a handful of light gravel across the deck. At once she was alert. A switch near the sliding doors would turn on outside lights, and she went quickly to touch it. But when she looked out between the curtains, nothing stirred on the lighted deck. Nearby tree trunks shone satiny brown beyond red decking planks, with only thick darkness beyond. Up through the trees the stars were pale. Unlocking the sliding door, she stepped cautiously outside and looked around.

Something white shone against the darkness below the embankment that shored up the earth of the hill. For a moment she thought someone crouched there—but the whiteness didn't move, and she realized it must be a garment of some sort flung across bushes. As far as she remembered, it hadn't been there before.

Outside, nothing stirred for the length of the deck, and there was no one on the stairs to the upper level. As she moved, cool night air touched her face, and gravel crunched beneath her feet. That gravel was the answer. Someone had wanted to get her attention—someone, perhaps, who had left that white thing near the edge of the deck for her to find.

Except for crickets and tree frogs, the night was quiet, and no wind stirred the silent trees that reached into a misty sky. Only the lighted deck and the inky hillside below formed her world of contrasts. The dark and the light—good and evil?

"Is anyone there?" she called, knowing the futility of such a challenge. Anyone who didn't want her to know of his or her presence wasn't going to answer.

Uneasily, she crossed the empty deck. There were other guest rooms down here, with their own sliding doors, but they stood dark and quiet—as far as she knew. Distant voices came from the front of the house above, so Nona had company. She had only to call out if she needed help. But first she wanted to see what that white garment might be. If it had anything to tell her, it would be better to touch it while she was alone.

The embankment below the deck consisted of flat, zigzag spaces filled level with fine gravel and shored up with wooden beams. Christy climbed down to the gravel and leaned over a beam to reach whatever lay below. The stretch was a long one, and just as her hand touched the cloth the push came in the middle of her back, sudden and strong. She pitched over the parapet, briefly aware of flying past tree trunks until she struck something hard and lay still in floating darkness.

How long she lay there, stunned and unmoving, she didn't know. Cold seeped through her, reaching her consciousness, and the insect chorus was an uproar in her throbbing head. Making an effort, she sat up and looked toward the house above. The deck was still empty in the outside lights, and nothing moved anywhere. A faint radiance showed at a hall window on the second level, and she could still hear the sound of voices.

She called out weakly, but there was no response. She would have to get out of this place on her own as quickly as possible, fearful now that her assailant might return. This meant collecting herself both physically and mentally.

As her senses cleared, she could remember the thrust of hands on her back, pushing her over the edge. The white thing she'd seen was still there. Low growth had broken her fall, and her head had struck a tree trunk. A lump was rising on her forehead and she touched it gingerly. Somehow she must climb back to the deck and go upstairs to find her aunt.

Her legs held her shakily when she stood up, and she clung to a sapling for a moment until she could endure an upright position. The white garment lay nearby and she picked it up and threw it over one arm. In touching it, no chill of evil came to her. But of course she hadn't psyched herself into a receptive state—not in this condition. With difficulty, she managed to climb over the parapet and onto the deck. Whoever had been there, hiding in shadows, was probably long gone.

Not until she reached her room did she examine the white dress that had probably been used as bait.

She knew at once what it was—the white caftan that had probably belonged to Deirdre, and which both Donny and Victor reported having seen on someone walking in the woods. Now, as she held the woven cotton garment, she opened herself, became very still, and at once the surge of horror came through, as it had with the scarf. This wasn't the misty, rainbow essence of Deirdre. *This* was evil. Not something abstract that one philosophized about—but someone with a wicked intent to harm. To kill?

For an instant she wanted to drop the gown, toss it away from her, but she resisted the impulse. Now that her senses were awake, she must try to follow through, let the gown tell her whatever it wished. Beneath the sense of horror that filled her, a picture began to form in her mind. A quick vision of rocks, a high place—a cliff? All this was sharp for an instant, and then gone. Even the chill was gone, and what she held in her hands was only a white caftan, stained with red earth and the juices of green leaves and grass. The vision hadn't been like the sure, clear scenes that had come to her when she was working with the police. There would be no body to find in this place that she'd glimpsed, and yet she knew she must go there, if it was possible. But only by daylight, and when someone was with her.

At least the throbbing in her head had abated, once she was on her feet and moving. She hurried toward the stairs with the dress in her arms and went up toward lights and voices from Nona's kitchen.

In the doorway she paused, wanting to view the scene quietly, and if possible sense whether her assailant was in the room. They were all there, sitting around Nona's oval table, drinking coffee and talking. Eve, Oliver, Victor, and Hayden. Even Floris was there, and only Donny was missing. Apparently, Nona had decided to call them together before Lili arrived.

Which one? Which one could have had time to attack her downstairs before joining this gathering? One thing she knew with certainty—and never mind Lili's views!—the powers of evil must be taken seriously. Destructiveness toward life *was* evil. To wave this aside and forgive was to fall prey to its intent. Not accepting, not opposing evil had always led into pits of darkness and death. She knew now that she was dedicated to the exposure and defeat of whatever wickedness was loose in this place.

They were all staring at her. The thoughts that flashed through her mind took only seconds, and before anyone could move or speak, she held out the white caftan.

"This is Deirdre's gown, isn't it? Someone else has worn it. I've just glimpsed a place that's important to what has happened here. It wasn't clear enough in my vision so I could identify it—though I'd know it if I saw it. Just rocks, a path, a high cliff. And these could be anywhere." She spoke quietly, in control of her emotions now—firmly in control.

Hayden came to take the caftan from her hands. He examined it carefully and then laid it over a chair back. There seemed a finality about the gesture. As though he had finally accepted that Deirdre was gone. His concern was now for Christy.

"You've been hurt—what's happened?"

She was suddenly aware of how wild she must look—with a bruise swelling on her forehead, a torn blouse, and streaks of red earth on her slacks.

"Someone pushed me off the lower deck." She could still speak quietly. "First, whoever it was threw gravel across the deck outside my room to attract my attention. When I went outside, I saw Deirdre's gown shining in the darkness below the deck. I climbed down to where I could reach for the dress, and someone pushed me over so that I fell and lay unconscious."

She waited, watching for a reaction from anyone. They all looked variously concerned, shocked, alarmed, except for Victor, who never showed what he was feeling.

Nona was the most indignant, and worried under her anger. "Come over to the sink, Christy, and I'll wash that abrasion. You've scratched your arms too. I'll put some antiseptic on them."

Christy held back. "Not yet, please." She closed her eyes and stood very still. *Tell me,* she whispered in her mind. *Tell me which one.* But the vision that had come to her so briefly was gone, and nothing spoke to her about anyone in this room. Even when she thought of each one in turn, not one of them shone brightly with an aura of either guilt or innocence. Each had a dark central core that was secret from the others. She must have that same dark core herself.

But real evil had a gift for disguise. It could wear virtue as its best defense, believing in its own false gods. Somehow she must find a way to penetrate this masquerade, as Victor had called it, to expose whatever lay beneath. Only then would her gift have served a real purpose for once in her life.

"I have to know," she told them softly. "I can't hide or run away any longer."

She went to Nona, whose hands shook as she ministered to bruises and scratches. This in itself was not like Nona, and rather alarming.

"Lili will be here tomorrow," her aunt reminded Christy. "That's why I asked everyone to come here this evening. So we could make some sort of plan to use her help. Then we'll all meet again, and Lili will know what to do."

It seemed all the more disturbing to find Nona, who had never approved of Lili, suddenly surrendering responsibility to her sister.

Hayden pulled a chair over to the table for Christy and she sat down beside him, grateful for his concern. Once more she looked from face to face, and her own tension returned. Floris appeared angry, while Oliver seemed guarded, not meeting her eyes. Eve's edginess showed as one hand tapped the table nervously. Hayden seemed quietly watchful, as though he too were on guard. It was he who spoke first.

"Have you any idea, Christy, how long you were unconscious?"

"I don't really know," she told him. "I did have a sense that time had passed when I came to, down there under the trees."

"We haven't been in the house very long," Hayden pointed out, "and we didn't all come by car."

His inference was clear. Any one of them might have slipped around to the back of the house to push Christy from the deck. Someone who had planted the dress there earlier? In which case, intent was evident. A plan. The dress really had been used as bait.

"The llamas have been humming on and off all day," Floris said. "That means they're uneasy about something. They're sensitive animals and they know when anything is wrong. I only wish one of them could tell me who came into my house and took Sinh away. I don't think that cat was strong enough to go far from milk and food. But you said she turned up in your studio, Nona, which means that someone must have carried her up to your house and left her there."

"Cats! Llamas!" Oliver dismissed both impatiently. "The question is, who pushed Christy off the deck and why?"

He could be dissembling, Christy thought. Any of them could be dissembling.

"The caftan is really the key to all this," Nona pointed out. "Someone used it to coax Christy to investigate. Do we know anything about this gown? Anything that would help us?"

Eve stopped drumming on the table. "Deirdre gave me that dress months ago. She knew I admired it. But after she disappeared I didn't want to wear it, even though all those folds would cover me up nicely. Anyway, I put it in the back of my closet, and I'd thought it was still there."

"It's the same dress whoever I saw in the woods was wearing," Victor said. "Since it's like a tent, anybody could have put it on."

"Including you," Oliver pointed out grimly.

"This isn't getting us anywhere." Nona quietly took charge again. "Lili will help, and we need to consider how to assist her. I'm not sure when she'll arrive tomorrow, but we'd better arrange to meet with her here tomorrow evening, if you can manage it."

"I've got other things to do beside attending a séance," Floris said. "Count me out."

Oliver agreed emphatically. "Waste of time. No séance for me either. I've investigated a few and found them all fakes."

" 'Séance' is an old-fashioned term," Christy said quietly. "My mother may be able to help us, as Nona says, so I think we should meet here and see what happens. Unless, of course, someone feels that it's too much of a risk to face her."

That seemed to startle them, though no one spoke until Hayden took the lead again. "The sheriff should be notified of this attack on Christy. But we might as well take whatever Lili Dukas offers as well."

"Let's skip the police for now," Nona said. "There's not much to tell them and Lili won't want them around. What about you, Victor? You'll be here?"

"I might like to watch," he said grudgingly.

"Good!" Nona approved. "So will you change your mind, Floris? And you, Oliver?"

Floris agreed reluctantly. "Okay—I'll come if I must."

"You might as well change your mind too, Oliver," Nona urged.

He shrugged elaborately. "All right. Though I still think it's a waste of time."

Victor moved toward the door to the front deck. "Let me know when you want me," he told Nona.

Oliver said, "Wait a minute, Victor! You came later than the rest of us—so how do we know—"

Victor returned to the table where Oliver sat, and stood looking down at him. "Anything more you want to say?"

Oliver flushed angrily, but he didn't pick up the challenge, and after a moment Victor went out of the room.

"That fellow's going to explode one of these days," Eve said, clearly on Oliver's side. "Maybe he has already." She went to where the white dress lay across a chair, but when she reached to pick it up, Christy stopped her.

"Wait—please! It might be better if no one else touches that caftan until my mother gets here. Perhaps it will tell her more than it's told me. In the meantime we'd better not impose any more impressions on it."

"We'll leave it right there," Nona agreed. "Now then—" The phone rang and she took it at the kitchen counter. When she'd answered, she nodded to Christy. "It's Lili's secretary, Mrs. Brewster. Your mother wants to speak to you. You can take the call in my studio, Christy."

This time she must resist, Christy thought as she went out of the room. She must hold on to her own identity and resist her mother's hypnotic spell. She switched on lights and went to the phone at her aunt's desk.

"Hello? Mother?"

"Darling!" The voice that was like rich velvet seemed to envelop her, pour love and warmth around her. There was no escaping its effect. "Something dreadful has happened, hasn't it, Chrystal? I could feel it this evening when it stabbed through me. Are you all right?"

"I'm all right," Christy said, wincing at the name she'd always disliked. "Are you coming tomorrow?"

"I'm flying into Charlottesville in the morning, and I'll drive out by limo. Be sure to say your words of protection tonight, Christy. Nothing can happen to you if you put a shield around you. There is no evil—only good for *you*. You know that, don't you, darling?"

"I know someone pushed me off Nona's deck tonight," Christy told her grimly. "I hit my head on a tree and was knocked out. But I've recovered, except for some bruises."

Lili poured the warm elixir of her voice around her daughter again. "You *are* protected. Nothing can harm you. Tomorrow we will work through this darkness—whatever it is—together. Good night, darling."

She was gone, and Christy sat for a moment allowing the echo of those melodic tones to comfort her. In some strange way she really did feel protected. For the moment. If only she could believe, as Lili did, that protection from harm was so easily achieved. Lili herself moved in an enchanted space. No matter what the outer circumstances, no matter what danger others might feel—Lili was spared. The knowledge Christy had had as a child, that her mother possessed the power to keep her safe, touched her again. The Dukas healing could flow out toward whoever needed it. It could also be a soporific and something she must guard against, lest it weaken her own resolve.

At least, when she returned to the kitchen, Christy felt calmer and more at peace, yet more determined than ever to follow through on exposing what lay behind all that had been happening here at Redlands. Her mother hadn't succeeded in blanketing her resolution.

Only Nona and Hayden sat at the table—the others had gone, Floris down through the woods with her flashlight, knowing her way well, while Oliver had driven Eve home in his car.

Nona looked up from her coffee cup and caught the change in Christy at once. "She's done it again, hasn't she? I wish I had Lili's talent for pouring anesthetic over whatever she chooses to touch."

Christy sat down beside her. "I do feel better for having talked to her. But she isn't going to change my course." She met Hayden's eyes resolutely.

He pushed his own cup aside. "I've been talking to Nona and we both think you must get away from Redlands as soon as you can."

"I can't leave now," Christy said quietly.

"Look!" Hayden tried to control his impatience. "Someone is afraid of you. That's evident. Afraid of your particular sensitivity. If you stay, you'll ask for a lot worse than a push in the dark. Your aunt and I agree now that I shouldn't have asked for your help in the first place."

Nona reached out to touch Christy's hand. "Please listen, dear. Stay until your mother comes, if you like. She won't be here long, if I know her. We'll see what she has to offer—and then you must leave as you meant to when you knew what had occurred here."

"Once you asked where I'd go," Christy reminded her aunt. "I didn't have a good answer then, and I don't now. Besides, I know I must stay and see this through. I don't know if I can help, but I have to try."

She didn't look at Hayden. She'd never asked for this feeling of involvement in all that concerned him, but she had no way to stop it from happening.

Nona gave up trying to persuade her. "At least, you'd better sleep upstairs tonight, Christy."

She managed a smile. "No, I'll lock the doors to the deck and I'll be fine. Nothing more is going to happen for a while. I think someone only wanted me to find that dress."

"That's what worries me," Nona said. "There's a—a madness in all this, and we haven't a clue where to look. Madness is like evil. It can wear disguises."

But she did have one clue, Christy thought, and not something psychic either. There was still the llama manuscript that had so disturbed Donny. He'd said that real names had been used, and perhaps real characteristics. So Rose's make-believe llamas might echo the behavior of the humans who lived here. As soon as she could, she would get Donny to show her the book.

"I'll be going along," Hayden said. He stood for a moment looking down at the white caftan where it lay across the chair, and Christy wondered what painful thoughts might be stirring in his mind. Then he turned to her with a look so unexpected that it caught her breath. A look that was warm and approving —grateful. He held her eyes for a moment, and then he was gone—off into the darkness to the house where he had lived with Deirdre.

Nona sat looking into her cup, elaborately unaware. But Christy knew she had seen that look.

"Good night," she said, and kissed Nona's cheek before she hurried downstairs to her room.

Deirdre's crystal gleamed in its place on the dressing table where she'd left it. She picked it up and sat down to warm it in her hands, so that she could feel its power flowing through her. The stone could tell her something, if only she knew how to listen. It seemed willing now, pulsing faintly with the rhythm of her own blood. But if it wanted her to go outside, that wasn't something she would try again tonight.

She fingered the swelling on her temple and tried not to remember those wicked hands pushing her. What hidden madness among them wore a disguise?

Dukas is coming. I'm not sure what this means, or what she can do.

At least I've frightened Christy. There couldn't have been a better way for her to find the caftan. I wonder what she makes of it?

So let them gather around Dukas! There's nothing she can do. Not even Dukas can find Deirdre. But Christy must be watched. There's a perception there that I can sense. I wonder what she's decided to do? Probably nothing, since Dukas is coming and will take over.

That will be interesting for me. Perhaps I can expose her for the performer and charlatan she really is. I would like to be the one to do that.

9

T HEY STOOD on the front deck, watching as the limousine came up the driveway. Again, Christy was aware of the wonderful sense of sky and open space, before mountains blocked the horizon. No darkness of crowding trees threatened here.

"I wonder which incarnation she's adopted this time," Nona said, and Christy smiled.

Lili claimed to have been a priestess in Egypt, a gypsy chieftain in a male life, a lady of the court during the French Revolution, where she'd lost her head, and many other people whose lives she couldn't always recall.

When the sleek gray car stopped near the garage the driver got out and opened the rear door for Liliana Dukas.

"It's her *female* gypsy phase," Nona commented as her sister stood looking out at the mountains. The day was beautifully blue and sunny, with floating piles of cloud, and Lili stretched out her arms in greeting to the universe.

She wore a long peasant skirt of garnet red, embroidered deeply around the hem in green and yellow swirls. Her white blouse was rounded at the neck, with eyelet trimming, and strands of beads clattered softly as she moved—amber, lapis, carnelian and jasper. Her brown-blond hair hung free to her shoulders, and gold hoops swung from pierced ears. Her eyelids were carefully tinted in green, and her lipstick was a dark red that matched her skirt. Lili had never held with a fashion that decreed pale lips. Both mouth and eyes reflected character, she said, and the lips should never be neglected.

Nona and Christy went toward her down the deck, and she

held out her arms again widely in greeting. Christy ran to her mother as she always had, drawn by this vibrant woman whose child she still found herself to be—when her mother was present. Hugging Lili, she breathed her elusive scent. Nothing prosaic like verbena—but a delicate water lily essence that was made up especially for her.

Lili and Nona never hugged, but a look was held between them for a moment of recognition. Then Lili turned to speak to the driver of the car. "I won't need you until tomorrow afternoon, Albert—say around three. Please leave my bags on the deck there. Then you can go back to Charlottesville and do whatever Mrs. Brewster would like."

So apparently she wasn't staying in Charlottesville, after all.

Albert said, "Yes, Miss Dukas," respectfully, and returned to his car.

Lili linked her arm with Christy's and went up the steps in a swirl of red skirts. Though she was in her sixties she moved like a young woman, her red-sandaled feet stepping lightly and with assurance. The chauffeur carried two handsome pieces of luggage into the entryway, left them, and drove off.

When Nona led the way along the deck to the kitchen— always the most accessible and informal room—Lili looked about, admiring everything.

"It's time I visited you," she told Nona, and sat down at the kitchen table. "Now then—how are you, Chrystal?"

"Except for a bump on my head and a few scratches, I'm fine," Christy told her, and didn't mention the flashes of fearful clairvoyance that still came at unwanted moments.

"Good! I'll treat that bruise for you later on." She turned to Nona. "Tell me what you've planned."

"Not very much," Nona said dryly. "We've left that up to you."

"That's fine. We'll go up to Wintergreen tonight," Lili said airily. "Brewster has made arrangements, and we can leave right after lunch. This will give you both a change from what seems an unhappy atmosphere around here."

This was typically Dukas, Christy thought. Wintergreen, she remembered, was the resort Nona had pointed out earlier on top of the mountain.

"You really might have told us *your* plans, Lili," Nona said.

"What difference would that make? It will all work out as intended." As always, Lili was confident of guidance. "Now, if you'll give me a cup of your cinnamon-apple tea, I'd like that. And of course I want to hear your version of everything that's happened here. You gave me a fright the other night, Chrystal, when I was on television. Right in the middle of the program, I knew you were asking for help. I tried to send you a message. You were watching, weren't you? So tell me everything!"

The name she'd been given at birth always made Christy a little restive. But while Nona made tea and served it with honey, she sat beside her mother and began with Rose's death. She told her of Deirdre's disappearance, and the events that had occurred since her arrival.

Lili listened intently. "I want to meet all these people."

"I knew you would," Nona said. "So I have invited everyone to come over here this evening."

"Then you must call and tell them we will all be dining at Wintergreen tonight. I suggest six-thirty at the Coppermine. There are other good restaurants up there, but this is at the Mountain Inn, and convenient. Brewster can set everything up. She'll be phoning me at any moment. I've arranged for a condominium for tonight—one of those cliff places that I've stayed in before you ever moved to this locality, Nona. So you and Christy will spend the night with me there. After dinner we can all have a quiet time to consult with Josef about these problems that face you at Redlands. Those who are involved in any way must be there, and solutions will emerge."

Nona and Christy looked at each other with wry understanding. Lili was behaving exactly as expected, and it was easier for everyone to go along with whatever she wanted. There would be a "séance" after all—and perhaps that was a good idea in the atmosphere Lili would create.

When the phone rang, it was the invaluable Mrs. Brewster. Lili took the call in the kitchen, checked the arrangements her secretary-assistant had made, and added instructions for dinner at the Coppermine Restaurant.

When she hung up, she paused for a moment of what she would call "focusing"—her eyes closed, her palms cupped. Nona and Christy were silent, waiting.

Returning to them, Lili went directly to the white caftan where it still lay across a chair. "This is the gown that belonged to Deirdre?" She didn't wait for an answer but picked it up and held the white folds against her body.

Christy had seen her mother do this before, and it wasn't quite the same ritual she used when she'd worked with the police. Lili bent her face to the dress, breathing deeply. She held it to her forehead, as though she searched past the surface with the vestigial third eye that could still be used by those who had learned to draw on its power.

When she looked at Christy again her expression had sobered. "What did you feel, Chrystal, when you held this?"

Christy remembered all too well. "A cold, horrible sensation came over me. As though I held something really evil in my hands. Something wicked and destructive."

"You misinterpreted," Lili said with assurance. She stood with the white caftan bright against her gypsy skirt, smiling sadly at her daughter. "Too many people confuse death with evil. Death frightens those who haven't accepted that it is only a doorway to the next adventure. Whoever wore this garment is dead."

"How did she die?" Nona asked flatly.

"I can't see that. There's the sadness of death as a loss of those left behind, but after that everything is misty. I can't tell what has happened. This is your province now, Chrystal."

Before Christy could refuse, Lili thrust the caftan into her hands. At once the chill came again, and she wanted only to drop the dress and run out of the room. This was not death but something far worse. Lili could never deal with evil, and it was she who had misinterpreted.

Her mother's hand on her arm stopped her. "Don't give up this time because the feeling frightens you. Stay with it. Let yourself go down deeply into the place and the time and the happening."

The Dukas voice, for all its honeyed quality, could compel, and Christy sat down in the nearest chair with the folds of cloth in her lap. She closed her eyes and let her hands play over the garment. It was as though she could sense without sight all that had marked the cloth. Here was red earth, here the green of grass stains. But none of this was pertinent. These stains hadn't occurred while Deirdre was wearing the dress. Christy pushed the knowledge of them away and held off the chill of horror that wanted to move in, refusing it as well, so that a deeper thought might surface. Now it was beginning to come—the sense of a particular place. It came vividly—a cliff, a red path, even a mound of rocks that towered on one side—all this came through distinctly in greater detail than her previous sensing. But even if what Lili said was true, Christy still couldn't tell how Deirdre had died. Always before, this had appeared in her mind sharply and clearly, when she was helping the police to find a body. But it was missing now. So—as Hayden had suggested—did that mean Deirdre was still alive?

Nona put the thought into words. "Can you tell, Christy—is Deirdre alive or dead?"

With a quick gesture of repugnance Christy pushed the dress from her lap. "I can't tell. The place was clear this time— so clear that I would recognize it. But there was nothing else. It all faded into mist and disappeared."

"Never mind," Lili said cheerfully. "It will come if you give it time. Rest yourself now. Nona, please show me what you've been painting. I read a fascinating piece about you not long ago —all those red roads you've been doing! I'd love to see them."

No one picked up the caftan, and it continued to lie in a heap of soiled cotton on the floor.

In Nona's studio a familiar visitor waited for them. Donny Mitchell sat on a stool before the painting of Deirdre, his heels hooked over a high rung, with Sinh draped languidly over his knees.

Lili seemed more interested in the cat than in the boy. "A Siamese temple cat! Where did this come from?"

"Sinh—with an *h*—belonged to Deirdre," Nona said. "She's looking better, isn't she, Donny?"

The boy glanced around, his attention focusing on the exotic figure of Lili Dukas. He held on to Sinh tightly, as though he expected her to leap away. Instead, when Lili reached out gently to stroke the cat's cream and brown fur, Sinh began to purr. She even reached out a tentative paw to touch Lili's hand.

"She never makes friends like that," Nona murmured. "But of course she'd take to you! You're probably part feline yourself."

"We recognize each other," Lili said lightly. "Her name is suitable, since there really was a temple cat by that name, but she shouldn't be called Sinh here. This is a magical cat—not a sinful one."

Lili's attention lifted from boy and cat to the painting of Deirdre disappearing down a misty road, her laughing face turned so she could look over one shoulder. "I would like to have known your mother, Donny."

The boy spoke quickly. "You can still meet her if she'll let you."

Lili had heard the story of Deirdre's appearance, and she answered carefully. "That would be very nice. If you see her again, will you tell her I would like very much to talk with her?"

"Sure," Donny said. "But I don't think she wants to talk to anyone right now."

As Christy studied the painting again, sudden realization struck her. In some strange way Nona's fingers had been guided as she painted. Nona herself had denied that this was a real scene, but now Christy recognized it fully.

"That's the place I saw just now when I held Deirdre's caftan! Do you know where it is, Donny? Is it a real place?"

Donny looked suddenly alarmed. He jumped down from the stool and the cat flew out of his arms and dashed for the door, as though more than his sudden movement had frightened her.

For a moment the boy stood looking at Christy, shaking his head. "No! I don't know anything about that place. I never saw a place like that!"

He ran after the cat in the same pattern of wild flight.

"Let him go," Lili said quietly. "He recognized it, but he doesn't want to tell us. It is a real place you painted, isn't it, Nona?"

"Not that I know of. I was making up that pile of rocks as I imagined it—though I remember that everything came easily at the time."

"You were probably channeling. Artists and writers often channel when inspiration is flowing. *You* don't know where it comes from when you create. You didn't think about this with your conscious mind—but suddenly it was all there."

"I suppose that's true," Nona said reluctantly. "Though *I* call it my unconscious. I've never known myself to paint a real place that I've never seen. That picture was done some time before Deirdre disappeared, so how could I—" Nona broke off, and Christy knew that her aunt had had enough experience with the mystical to stop her denial of foreknowledge in midair.

"Do you think you could find this place, Chrystal?" Lili asked.

"I'd recognize it if I saw it, but I don't know how to look for it. I wouldn't know where to begin."

"Then let's put the caftan in your hands again," Lili said decisively. "This time you'll find the way."

Reluctantly, Christy followed her mother and aunt back to

the kitchen. Donny stood there, holding Sinh in his arms, staring at the folds of his mother's gown, white against red tiles.

"That's my mother's dress," he said to Nona. "How did it get here?"

Christy answered him quietly. "I found it last night lying across a bush behind the house."

"Then she was there! I know she was there!"

"No, Donny. I don't think so." Christy didn't believe for a moment that Deirdre had pushed her off the deck. And she was sure that nothing of Deirdre's essence was left in that garment.

Lili spoke to the boy gently. "I'd like you to try something, Donny. Sinh was Deirdre's cat, wasn't she? So will you put her down for a moment—put her down on your mother's dress."

Donny hesitated. Then he set the cat carefully upon the caftan and stepped back, watching. Sinh seemed to stand on tiptoe, as though something burned her feet. Her fur stood on end, her tail twitched, and her eyes looked wild. In an instant she leapt away, and Donny ran to open the door to the deck, lest she hurl herself against the glass. Then he threw an agonized look at the three women and tore after the cat.

"Interesting," Lili said. "That was a strong reaction."

"Sinh felt what I did," Christy said. "Someone really wicked has worn that dress recently. Not Deirdre."

Picking up the caftan, Lili held it in her own hands, closing her eyes. "Whoever has worn it is confused and frightened and very much to be pitied," she said, and handed it to Christy. "Discover the place for us if you can. We must find the compassion to help someone in terrible need."

There was no way to refuse, and now, as she held the gown, no chill touched her, no sense of horror. In fact, a strange sense of happiness came as she closed her eyes and let herself drift. She had gone down deeply to something earlier that had woven itself into the very threads of the garment. Was this what Lili meant by compassion? She was Deirdre now, running along a path that followed the side of the hill where she had gone yesterday with Victor during the storm. There was the log cabin that belonged to neighbors, and into which he'd taken her for shelter. The path led on for some distance and then turned downward into the woods. Only a lovely freedom possessed her. If Deirdre had been running to her doom, she hadn't known it.

She opened her eyes and looked at Lili and Nona. "I think I can find the way. I believe Deirdre was happy when she followed the path that led to that place. I don't think she expected anything bad to happen to her."

"We must go wherever the trail leads," Lili said. "Now you are using your gift as you were meant to use it, Chrystal. We must be on our way."

Nona spoke firmly. "Not without Hayden. He's at the plant nursery today, and we will go there and pick him up. I'll telephone first and make sure he's free."

Christy was not sure this was right. Whatever happened might leave Hayden more miserable and uncertain than ever. She lacked her mother's confidence in the outcome of events in that place, if she found it.

Between them, however, Lili and Nona had settled the matter, and when Nona had made her phone call, they drove out of Redlands in Nona's car and Christy sat in the back seat with Deirdre's caftan beside her. She avoided touching it again.

"Hayden's Rockhill Nursery is only a little way," Nona explained as she drove. "He built the small house for Deirdre and himself when they were first married, and he was just starting his business. Now Eve Corey lives upstairs and uses the office downstairs as his assistant."

A narrow dirt road ran through thick woods, with no houses in view. After a couple of miles they emerged above the wide acreage of the nursery. Low, wooded hills enclosed a level stretch of earth dotted with rows of young trees.

Nona explained to Lili. "Hayden has planted shade trees—maple, oak, sweet gum, and others. Flowering trees too—pear and crabapple and dogwood. Virginia's climate loves flowering trees and they're glorious all around here in spring. Though the blooming is about finished now."

Over toward the house, smaller plantings had been started in flowerpots, being readied for new lives elsewhere. The house, brown-timbered, seemed to grow from its hillside, with oak and birch and poplar closing in at the back. A lovely, quiet, totally secluded place, Christy thought. A place where nature was respected and nurtured. This was Hayden's true side— clearly where he loved best to work, and where his spirit must find some sanctuary.

On the driveway Hayden stood talking to a man about to pull out with a truckload of dirt intended for the landscaping of a new house. He waved at them and motioned them toward the house.

Nona parked near stone steps and they went inside. The lower floor opened into an L-shaped room with a high, beamed ceiling and wide planking on the floor. At the back, stairs ran up to a section that formed the second floor. The downstairs area was arranged as part office and part rustic living room, with a desk at the front. A small galley kitchen made a divider behind, with a round dining table at one end. On walls above the desk hung framed photographs of homes that Rockhill had landscaped.

Eve Corey sat at the desk and she rose in surprise to greet them. "Hello, Nona, Christy. And of course this is Liliana Dukas?" She held out her hand and Lili took it with a look Christy knew very well. A sensing look, indicating that her mother was learning a great deal about Eve from this first contact.

"We've come to see Hayden," Nona said, and didn't explain.

Her slanted bangs gave Eve's face a pixie look that didn't quite suit her, and from beneath the bangs she studied Lili with cautious interest. Again, she wore her usual informal dress—jeans and a red plaid shirt, with thonged sandals on her bare feet.

"How do you like our corner of Virginia?" she asked Lili.

"It's beautiful!" Lili's arms reached out to embrace all she saw. "But under the circumstances I find Redlands a sad place."

"I hope you'll be able to help." Eve sounded as if she expected nothing much from Lili's "spirits"—since she'd undoubtedly been influenced by Oliver Vaughn.

"We're all invited to dinner at Wintergreen tonight." Nona interrupted the exchange. "Lili has rented a condominium up there, so that's where we'll meet with her after dinner. We can count on you, of course, Eve? And will you let Oliver know? We're all to meet at the Coppermine."

"I'll take care of it," Eve said. She pulled open a drawer of her desk. "Perhaps we can begin by having somebody explain this—if anyone can." She drew out a tissue-wrapped object, opening the folds so that the contents shone in sunlight from a window.

Startled, Christy said, "That looks like the crystal that belonged to Deirdre—the one Donny loaned me yesterday. But it can't be—I left that piece on my dressing table at Nona's today."

"Have a look," Eve said. "How it got into my desk I haven't a notion."

The stone felt cold and inert as Christy picked it up, as though it had withdrawn into itself. She held it to the light, turning it slowly. The floating phantom at its heart came into view, disappearing elusively when she moved the faceted stone.

"This is certainly Deirdre's crystal," she said.

"Interesting." Eve was laconic. "I don't think Deirdre's spirit is running around moving her possessions. So who is trying to spook us?"

"May I see?" Lili extended her hand, and Christy put the stone into it. Lili too held the crystal up to the light. "It's a beautiful stone—a rare one. But I think the last person besides ourselves to handle it must have used a cloth, or worn gloves. Crystals are sensitive—they know who holds them, and they know when the owner is right. Some stones respond to me, and some don't speak to me at all. This one seems to be sleeping."

"Waiting for Deirdre to return?" Nona asked.

Christy moved about the room to hide her deepening distress. Someone as mischievous and playful as Deirdre might have done this. Or it might be someone who wanted them to think it was Deirdre.

A framed color photo on the wall near Eve's desk caught Christy's eye, and she went to look at it more closely. She could identify the three people in the picture, even though it had been taken when they were younger. The two girls were laughing, while the man to whose arms they clung wore a sober expression—as though reluctant to pose. The man was Oliver Vaughn, and one of the girls was Eve Corey. The second one had married him—Rose Vaughn. Christy had seen her picture on book jackets, and she knew that warm, laughing expression. This must have been taken when the two young women were attending the University of Virginia and the man had been a professor there. In fact, the columns of one of the buildings Thomas Jefferson had designed showed at a corner of the enlargement.

Eve noted her interest. "That's an old picture, but I do like it of Rose, so I've kept it out. We were all young and happy then."

"Oliver doesn't look happy," Christy said.

Eve laughed with a hint of malice. "How could he be, when both those women were trying to marry him?"

Christy set the picture down, feeling uncomfortable, as though she'd trodden on dangerous ground. She was glad when Hayden came up the steps into the room.

Nona asked at once if he would come with them on a short drive. Obviously, she didn't want to reveal what they intended while Eve was listening. However, it wasn't necessary. Hayden acknowledged an introduction to Lili with interest, and agreed to leave with them at once.

Christy picked up the crystal from Eve's desk. "If you don't mind, I'll take this with me—since I'm the one Donny loaned it to."

"Of course," Eve said. "It has nothing to do with me. I never did go for all the fuss about crystals."

"We'll see you at the Coppermine at six-thirty," Nona reminded her as they went out, and Eve nodded, promising again that she would get in touch with Oliver.

When they walked to Nona's car, Lili studied Hayden for a moment with her usual sensing, her smile warm and compassionate.

"We want very much to help," she said simply.

Hayden's guard was up, however. He said, "I hope you can," indifferently, and got into the back seat beside Christy.

"How do you feel?" he asked her. "Are you all right?"

"I'm fine. Just a bump on my head, and Lili will fix that. We've been busy ever since she came."

He saw the caftan she had taken into her lap, but he said nothing.

As they started off, Nona driving, Christy began to tell him what they intended, but Lili broke in with quiet authority.

"Christy feels that she can now lead us to the place where your wife disappeared. I'm afraid she is dead, Mr. Mitchell. That was the message that came to me through the dress that belonged to her. Christy has seen the location clearly, and she believes that Nona caught the very spot in her last painting of your wife."

Afraid to look at Hayden, Christy put her hands on the dress in her lap but, like the crystal, it seemed to be sleeping now—only a stained cotton garment. She waited for Hayden's reaction to Lili's words, but he seemed lost in his own dark thoughts and offered no response.

"Donny recognized the setting too," Christy told him gently. "When we went into Nona's studio this morning, he was there with Deirdre's cat. But when we tried to ask him about the location of the scene in the picture, he became upset. I think he doesn't want to admit what he may really know."

Hayden stared out the car window, and Christy was aware that he had stiffened against them all.

Since those few open moments yesterday when they'd gone shopping in Nellysford, he had retreated a long way into himself.

Not until they reached Redlands, and Nona parked her car did he offer an objection. "There's something wrong about all this. How can Deirdre's dress tell you anything about what happened to her—when she gave it away months before she disappeared?"

"That really doesn't interfere with the impression I received," Lili said with assurance. "No matter what has happened to the dress since, something of Deirdre remains because she wore it most often. Something of her lingers in the very cloth. I can feel that, and I'm sure Chrystal can too."

Hayden got out of the car. "Then let's find out if this means anything." He spoke as though he had removed himself emotionally from whatever might happen.

As they started off on foot, Christy held the caftan against her body and kept the crystal in one hand. The others let her lead the way past the log cabin and trees that crowded in beyond. Now she had no more doubt than Lili did that she would find her way.

After a short distance, the path turned away from sky and space, dipping downward through a stand of oak trees she hadn't entered before. The crystal had grown warmer in her hand—not from her own body warmth but from something more. It was no longer asleep.

Treetops swayed in a breeze far overhead, shutting out any sight of mountains and valley. Sunlight slanted through the branches and lay in spangled patches on either hand, and the red color of the path was strong. She felt no fear of snakes now. It was as though something protected her, led her on to the fateful place that nothing must stop her from reaching.

The path curved as it descended, and the others followed close behind—first Hayden, then Lili, who sometimes grasped for his arm when her footing was uncertain. Nona came last, always sure on her feet, and Christy was glad of her strong presence close by on this uneasy expedition. Lili moved in her own spaces, and how much they had to do with the real world her daughter wasn't sure.

The crystal had grown very warm and, rounding a turn, they saw the great outcropping of rock ahead. It rose straight up from the ground in a series of granite ledges. Its high top stood boldly against the sky, and Christy knew at once that this was the rock pile in Nona's painting—this was the place. The crystal almost burned her palm, throbbing. Behind her, Nona exclaimed as she too recognized where they were.

Hayden's voice cut through and Christy heard his strange anger. *"This* is what you've brought us to?" he asked.

Lili ignored him. "You're right, Chrystal. This is the scene of Nona's painting." She came to stand beside Christy and put her hands on the white folds of cloth Christy still held in her arms. "I'm sorry to tell you, Hayden, but I must. This is not only a place to which Deirdre came, but I'm sure she died very near here. I can feel death all around me. The release from suffering, the escape into a new dimension, the wonderful blaze of light—it's all here, engraved forever on these rocks and trees and ground. The tragedy is only for those who are left behind —not for the one who dies. So you mustn't grieve, Hayden. Deirdre is safe, happy."

Hayden's anger spilled over. "Your voices are way off base! It's not Deirdre's death that's engraved on this spot—it's Rose Vaughn's. Christy has brought us to the exact spot where Donny found Rose—after everyone else had given up looking. Probably that's why he ran away from the painting when you asked him about it today. He knew that Nona had painted the place where he'd found Rose."

For once, Lili sounded upset. "No—this can't be! Chrystal— what do you see?"

Christy had begun to tremble. She dropped the caftan to the ground, and Lili, recovering herself, put a quieting hand on her arm. "Tell us whatever you can," she said gently.

Deirdre's crystal still burned with its own throbbing heat. Christy sat down on a rock and closed her eyes, waiting for the crystal to speak to her. Hayden was silent now, though she knew his anger still ran deep—as though her bringing him here was somehow a betrayal.

After a moment she raised her head and looked upward—far up to the top of the tall mound of granite—and began to speak quietly without conscious volition.

"It's true," she said. "Rose died here. I have held her slipper, and perhaps that's what led me here. But Deirdre's death is here too. Not down here where Rose fell, but up at the very top of the rock pile."

Her own words seemed to well up from some store of knowledge that her conscious mind seldom tapped. Hearing herself, she knew they were true. Yet there was confusion as well. A confusion of time. Had this happened already—or was it still to happen in the future? If it was the latter, could Deirdre be saved?

She could answer none of this and opened her hands to allow the crystal to cool. It had ceased to pulse—it had nothing more to tell her.

Hayden's impatience increased, his anger smoldering. "This is foolish! What could have harmed Deirdre up there? Besides, this area is one of the first places we searched for her, after what happened to Rose."

"I'm sorry," Christy said. "I can't tell you anything more."

Again the sense of evil filled her. If Deirdre had died up there, and Rose down here—there *had* been violence, wickedness in both cases. But she couldn't speak to Hayden about this until she knew more. She'd received a sense of lines being crossed—as though something wrong interfered with the pictures in her mind. They were true, yet out of focus at the same time. Even as she sought for clarity, mists wiped everything away and the vision was gone, leaving only weariness behind. She sighed in unhappy defeat.

"This isn't something I can command," she told Hayden sadly. "Sometimes I know *who,* but not *where.* Or I know *what* but not *when."*

"You're tired now," Nona said. "We'll go back. Another time you can take the path to the top, Christy. This is enough for today."

Lili understood better than anyone else. She bent over Christy where she sat and touched her forehead, pressing gently, her fingers cool on the darkening bruise. She spoke as though they were alone.

"You must learn to use your gift," she said. "It may be frightening, and sometimes disappointing. But now you'll stop fighting what is there. Just allow it to surface. You want to help—and you can."

When she took her hands away, a sense of calming, of healing, remained, and Christy relaxed a little.

"Let's go back," Nona repeated.

But before they could start up the hill, a voice called to them from high above. "Wait!"

They all looked up in surprise, and Christy saw that Victor Birdcall sat on a ledge where the rock face curved around to the left. His gray work clothes blended with the granite, so he was nearly invisible, and she had no idea how long he might have been there.

"I have something for you, Nona," he said, and started to climb backward down the wall of granite, its irregularities forming steps and handholds, so that he came down easily. When he reached the ground he took something from his jacket pocket and held it out to Nona. "I found this in a crack up there on top."

Nona took the velvet slipper from him in bewilderment. "This is Rose's matching slipper. But why would it be up there?"

"Perhaps she lost it when she fell," Victor said. "It looks as though it's been rained on a few times."

"And she lost the other one a mile away in the woods!" Nona cried. "This makes no sense at all. In the first place, she would never have worn those slippers out walking."

"You're right," Hayden said. "When Rose was found, she was wearing boots."

"What do you know about this, Victor?" Nona said. "You're the one who finds the slippers. Is there something you haven't told us?"

He returned her look calmly and said nothing.

Nona introduced Victor and told Lili how he had found the first slipper in the woods, where Rose would surely never have left it. Lili traced the frayed embroidery thoughtfully with one finger and then handed the slipper to her daughter.

Christy took it and waited for any pictures that might form in her mind. There were mists again—no particular scene. And then three figures gradually emerged—two women and a man. But only Rose was clear, wearing her velvet slippers. Both women seemed angry, though Christy couldn't distinguish their words. The man remained silent in the background, taking no part. Rose and Eve and Oliver? But this was her conscious mind building its own fantasy—intruding. Haze swept over the three, erasing the vision, and Christy found herself staring at her mother.

"I'm sorry—there was nothing I could identify that had any meaning," she said, and gave the slipper back to Nona. "Something is trying to come through, but I don't know what it is."

"Perhaps you're not being receptive," Lili said. "I still feel that you fight this every step of the way."

"I've been trying to help!" Christy cried. "I hate all this. It makes me feel ill and helpless. I don't even want to try any more—it's all so awful."

For once, Lili's calming hands had no effect when she touched her daughter, and Christy drew away.

Hayden put a stop to what was happening. "Christy's had

enough. Nona, you'd better get her back to the house. I'll see you all tonight—whatever good that will do."

He went off up the hill alone, and Lili shook her head, looking after him. "That is an angry, troubled man," she said. "Perhaps we can help him tonight."

Nona told Victor about the planned gathering at Wintergreen, but now he seemed undecided as to whether or not he would come. He'd been watching Lili Dukas, and suddenly she reached out and took his right hand in both of hers and looked at him intently.

"The flames are behind you," she said. "But you must still be careful. Your own nature leads you into dangerous ways."

Christy had often seen her mother do this with someone she'd just met—dipping back into the past, suggesting the future—and she knew how alarming it could be. Lili never seemed to recognize that the whole world wasn't tuned in to her way of being. Though perhaps that very fact gave her a quiet assurance that was seldom shaken. Victor, however, didn't seem to mind. He looked deeply into her eyes for a moment, and Christy sensed that these two were more of a kind than she'd expected.

Victor withdrew his hand, nodded to them all, and walked off without haste, choosing the downhill way.

Lili looked after him. "Victor must come tonight. Nona, make sure that he is there. I feel he is close to the heart of all that is happening, and his presence is vital. Perhaps he is closer than he knows."

"I'll do my best," Nona said, "but Victor chooses his own way."

"What did you mean about flames?" Christy asked her mother.

"I saw flames all around him—but they died away, and I knew they belonged to the past."

They'd started back up the hill and Christy asked another question of her aunt as they walked. "Does what Lili saw have something to do with Victor's being in prison?"

"How do you know about that?" Nona asked in surprise.

"Oliver found out, and he's been spreading rumors about Victor. But why flames?"

"Because his house burned after his wife was murdered. Probably in an attempt to cover the crime. He was accused and sentenced, though he always claimed there was an intruder. Such intruders have been used so many times to explain a murder that he wasn't believed. After he'd served two years, the real murderer was caught and confessed. So Victor was set free. He told me all of this when he came, but there was no need to explain to others, and there wasn't any further publicity. I'll talk to Oliver and set him straight. I knew Victor long ago and always admired him. So when he had a need to go to a new place, I suggested that he come here. I don't want the peace he's found to be disturbed."

Lili had listened closely, and now she stopped on the path, facing her sister. "There's still some cloud around that man. I want to see what happens tonight when we are all quiet together. Perhaps his Indian ancestors will help me."

"Do you mean to invite in devils or saints?" Nona asked tartly.

Her mother's laughter was something Christy remembered —high, light laughter, musical and confident. Something to dispel darkness.

"I don't *invite* either. I ask for knowledge, wisdom. Help from higher sources who know how to advise me. Of course I always guard against anything that might harm us."

Christy followed her mother and aunt along the upward curving path, thinking again of Hayden, and wondering how she might reach through to him. Of them all, he needed help the most, but she didn't know whether it could come from Lili. Nor did she feel that she had any power to help him. He had been angry over her bringing him to that particular spot. But she'd had no way of knowing that the place she would lead them to would be the scene of Rose's death.

Above all else, there still remained the strong feeling she

had received about Deirdre—that she had died up there on top of that granite pile. Present, past, or future? She lacked faith in her own power to produce anything useful.

"Look who's waiting for us," Nona said over her shoulder.

At the place where the path took its next turn before reaching the top, Eve Corey sat on a rock, watching them approach.

"I saw Hayden," she said as they reached her. "He told me where you were, so I came along to wait for you. No use climbing all the way down. He seemed pretty unhappy."

"Why did you come? Has something happened?" Nona asked.

"It's Oliver. He's upset about your Wintergreen plans. He wants to talk to you, Nona, and he's waiting up at your house. He wants to call everything off for tonight." Eve glanced at Lili apologetically. "He thinks Liliana Dukas is dangerous and should be stopped."

"Then by all means let's go talk to Oliver Vaughn," Lili said cheerfully. "I always like to help skeptics in their search for truth."

Oliver was less eager to meet Lili Dukas. When they reached the house, he sat waiting for them in a chair on the deck, and while Lili and Nona joined him, Christy and Eve sat on the steps just below.

"You can count me out," Oliver announced curtly as soon as introductions were over. "I don't want any part of this."

"Do I frighten you that much, Mr. Vaughn?" Lili asked gently.

He looked indignant. "I don't like to be manipulated. I don't believe in your so-called powers, Miss Dukas, and there would only be unpleasantness for you if I were present. I wouldn't hesitate to expose any trickery."

"Then let me reassure you." Lili smiled at him kindly. "I have come here to see my daughter and make sure she is well. Now that I know she's fine, I'll be leaving tomorrow. So all I intend is to invite Nona and her friends for dinner and then to an evening of talk and friendship in the place up at Wintergreen where I'm staying tonight. I *am* concerned about the terrible things that have happened here, and if I could help in any way, I'd like to. But only if you all want me to try."

Christy watched her mother with the same amazement she'd felt in the past. When Lili exerted herself to calm and reassure and win over, no one could resist her. Perhaps this worked because she herself never realized the performance she was putting on. It all seemed natural and convincing to her, first of all. Oliver Vaughn was no exception. He relaxed, melted a little in spite of himself, and let his antagonism subside. Lili was first of all a beautiful and charming woman, and even Oliver was not immune to her spell. Especially when her seeming interest in him was so flattering. What Lili intended to do tonight, and how Oliver might react, was something else. But for now he gave in.

"All right, I'll come," he agreed. "Though if I don't like what is happening, I'll leave at once."

Eve had been watching, entranced. She left the steps, smiling ruefully at Oliver. "This should be interesting. I wouldn't miss it for anything."

When they went off together to their separate cars, Nona regarded her sister thoughtfully. "I don't know how you do it, Lili. Oliver is practically a fanatic when it comes to anything psychic."

"He is also a disturbed and suffering man," Lili said. "I'm not sure that his suffering is entirely due to his wife's death. Is he interested in Eve Corey, by any chance?"

Nona smiled. "You don't miss a thing. But you've got it turned around. It's Eve who has always been interested in Oliver Vaughn. They were engaged once long ago, before Rose came into the picture and captivated him."

"He is too susceptible," Lili said. "But don't tell me any more. I must stay open and wait for whatever comes from higher sources."

"What will you do tonight exactly?" Nona was persistent.

But Lili only waved a hand in airy dismissal. "That isn't up to me. What will happen will happen. Right now I think we must deal with something troubling that is coming to us from Hayden Mitchell's house."

Christy and Nona turned to look in the direction Lili indicated. Leonie James, Hayden's housekeeper, was coming toward them with her free stride, managing to look exotic in spite of the slacks and plain blue shirt she wore today. Gold hoops in her ears danced, catching the sunlight with a certain gaiety. But her expression was anxious, and she spoke at once to Nona.

"It's Donny, Miss Harmony. He's done something very upsetting. I don't know how to handle this, and I can't reach Mr. Mitchell by phone. So will you please come?"

"Of course," Nona said. She glanced at Christy and her sister. "You may be needed too. We'd better get over to Hayden's right away."

Where had Hayden gone? Christy wondered. He had been on foot, without a car.

Dukas is here and spreading her useless spells! It was clever of her to decide that Deirdre is dead—but it doesn't really matter. Not unless she could find her.

The Wintergreen affair should be interesting, and it may upset a few people. But, at the same time, this is pointless too. There's nowhere Dukas's spirits can take her that will touch me. Even if they try to tell her, they'll talk in such riddles that no one will understand. If it wasn't all so dangerous, it would be funny.

Donny troubles me. I wish he would be less persistent in his search for his mother. He must not become a troublesome little boy. I'll need to find a way to head him off and turn him in some new direction that will distract him and remove him from the trail.

Perhaps Deirdre's needlepoint will help to accomplish that. I believe I have an idea.

W HEN THEY reached the house, Leonie hurried upstairs to Deirdre's room. The door stood open and she beckoned them in.

An upheaval had struck the room. Drawers had been opened and their contents strewn on the floor. Deirdre's desk was piled with its own contents. The bedspread had been pulled off and wadded at the foot of the bed.

In the midst of all this confusion Donny sat cross-legged on the floor. Tear streaks had dried on his face, and he stared at them bleakly. From the top of a bookcase behind him, Sinh watched with cold unblinking blue eyes—thinking her own strange thoughts?

Nona sat down opposite Donny. "Would you like to tell us what has happened?"

He shook his head, scowling.

"He won't tell me anything," Leonie said from the doorway.

Lili spoke softly in her musical voice. "I am Chrystal's mother, and I know you're Donny Mitchell. We'd like to help you, if you'll tell us what's the matter."

Lili's charm had no effect at all on Donny and he turned his head away.

Christy tried, keeping her tone matter-of-fact and calm. "You know, Donny, when something gets really bad, everybody needs help. Can we help you find what you're looking for? Maybe we can all look together."

Perhaps because she had read Rosa's book to the cows, Donny trusted her a little. "It's gone!" he told her. "I've looked everywhere and I can't find it. So maybe my mother came and took it away. She always told me there was something magic about it. But if she came, she didn't stop to see me—and when I met her in the woods she just ran off in the mist."

There was so much pain and longing in his voice that Christy ached for him. "Tell us what is missing. If we know what to look for—"

He got up from the floor and went to his mother's armchair. "It's that embroidery she was making. My mother left it in this chair the last time she was here. And Dad said to let everything stay as it was, so when she came back she'd know where her things were. That's what he thought at first."

Sinh raised her head and mewed plaintively. Perhaps she missed her mistress's presence in this room.

"Do you mean that rainbow needlepoint she was working on?" Christy asked.

He nodded gloomily and she dropped to her knees beside him.

"I remember that very well," she told him. "It was nearly finished, wasn't it? A rainbow with all the colors worked in. One end of the rainbow seemed to be on fire, and the other end was lost in a storm. Did she ever talk to you about what it meant, Donny?"

He seemed pleased that she remembered. "She told me one time that a rainbow could rise out of trouble and still be bright and beautiful. That's why I wanted to find it—so I could see if that was true."

"I can understand how you feel." Christy pushed a little harder. "Did she talk to you about what trouble the rainbow was rising from?"

"I asked her, but she wouldn't tell me. She just began to cry."

"Do you think she was afraid of something, Donny?" Nona asked.

This touched some chord, for Donny raised his head and looked past them at Leonie, watching in the doorway.

"Sometimes she seemed real scared about something. Leonie knows. Tell them, Leonie!"

Sinh leaped suddenly from the bookcase, startling them all. She landed on Donny's shoulder and rubbed her head against his, as if to comfort him. Christy thought of her whimsy about the spirit of the master (or mistress) entering the temple cat.

"Leonie?" Nona said. "Is there anything you can tell us?"

The woman stayed in the doorway, earrings trembling against the golden skin of her cheeks. "There was one time when I brought tea to Mrs. Mitchell in the afternoon. She always waited for Donny to come home from school so he could join her. He came with me to her room, and we found her lying on her bed crying. Donny went to hug her and he asked what was the matter. I set the tray down and waited to see if there was anything I could do."

Now Donny took up the story. "She cried and cried! But she wouldn't tell us why."

"She really seemed to be afraid of someone or something," Leonie said. "She—she said something very strange—that she might have to go away, and she didn't want to."

Donny's tears came again. "She said I should never forget her if that happened—and that she would never forget me. Not ever! That was when she showed me the needlepoint again. She said both ends of the rainbow were in danger, and she must find her way through the arch in time."

"That really worried me," Leonie said. "I asked her what she meant by 'in time,' and she just told me to leave the tray and go away. She wanted to be alone."

"She wouldn't let me stay either." Donny turned his head to Sinh, who looked into his face as though she understood, and mewed in sympathy. "Never mind," Donny told her. "I know she'll come back. It must have been my mother who took the needlepoint. All the spools of thread are gone too."

"Did you tell Mr. Mitchell about this, Leonie?" Nona asked.

"I told him, but he said that sometimes his wife made up little stories. She loved make-believe, and he didn't think anyone would want to harm her. Everyone loved Mrs. Mitchell, even though she—she—" Leonie broke off, hunting for words.

Lili had been moving quietly about Deirdre's room, touching nothing but looking at everything. Now she supplied her own words. "I believe that Deirdre Mitchell had her own mysterious spiritual life. It's possible that she even attracted entities that meant her harm. That could happen if she didn't protect herself. There are always prayers, words of affirmation that ask for help and protection."

"That doesn't help us now," Nona said impatiently. "Is there anything practical that speaks to you in this room, Lili?"

"Not what you would call practical, dear," her sister admitted.

"Or to you, Christy?" Nona asked.

"Not right now." Christy's feelings about Deirdre's room matched its state of confusion. Her real concern was for Donny and his grief. Grief that might be justified.

"Would you like me to help you put back your mother's things?" she asked the boy.

He turned to her, Sinh in his arms. "I don't care. It doesn't make any difference. Not if she's really gone."

With a touching dignity he walked past them out of the room, and no one tried to stop him.

"I'll pick everything up," Leonie said. "Thank you for coming over, Miss Harmony. Donny's not as upset as he was, and now that I know what he was looking for, I'll watch out for it."

"Have you any idea what might have become of it?" Nona asked.

Leonie shook her head. "Perhaps Mr. Mitchell has put it somewhere else. I'll ask him."

Lili seemed more solemn than usual. "I don't think so. To-night I'll ask about the needlepoint, among other things."

"Ask whom?" Nona demanded, still impatient.

"Josef, of course. I'm sure he will help us tonight. We should be on our way to Wintergreen soon. Let's have a sandwich lunch, Nona. I want to get up there early, so everything will be ready before we bring the others to Laurel House. That's where you and Chrystal and I will stay tonight. And I'd like time to rest before dinner."

"What about Oliver?" Christy asked. "He'll be upset when he finds out what you plan to do."

Lili seemed not at all worried about Oliver. "There are secrets in that man, as there are in Victor. He's not as sure of himself as he pretends, and I don't think he'll fight me. We may learn something useful."

If she hadn't been so concerned about Hayden and Donny, Christy might have been an amused spectator, watching her mother. As it was, she couldn't be sure what was going to surface, not only in the others but in herself as well. From past experience she knew what unexpected turns Lili's channeling could take, once Josef came in. Sometimes he seemed to have a prankish sense of humor, and Christy didn't trust him. She wished there had been time to ask Donny more about Rose's llama story, but that would have to wait until Lili was gone.

Right after lunch they started on their way in Nona's car. Lili exclaimed delightedly over the rainbows on the car doors.

The road to Wintergreen crossed Rockfish Valley and began to climb in a gradual rise. The long, high mountain loomed ahead, greening in spring rains and warmth, so that the curving road above was invisible among the trees. As the way steepened and began to loop back and forth in sloping turns, Christy could feel the changing pressure in her ears.

At the last minute, before leaving Redlands, they had acquired an unexpected passenger. Floris Fox had phoned to say she was having car trouble and would like to come with them. Someone else could bring her home tonight. . . . So she and Christy sat in the back seat, with Liliana Dukas and Nona in front. Lili had never learned to drive, since there was always someone eager to take her about, or else there were limos to be summoned.

Earlier, Christy had watched her mother's preparations uneasily. Lili's cheerful confidence usually overcame all obstacles, but her efforts were usually directed toward healing and life-counseling—not with the deviations of a possible murderer.

Lili had packed her costume for the evening in a suitcase—black crepe trousers and a gorgeously embroidered Chinese jacket in emerald green. She would add jade earrings, black satin sandals, and her own water lily perfume. Josef could be strangely sensitive to odors when he occupied Lili's body, and Christy had wondered about his past lives when there would have been fewer deodorants.

Once she had dared to tell Lili that she didn't trust Josef—he could be too worldly at times, and probably fallible for that very reason. Lili had said, "Of course he is worldly. He has lived through several past lives, and he knows all about humans because he's been human himself more than once. That's why he is so wise and I can trust him."

Now that they were on their way up the mountain, Christy was glad to leave Redlands behind for a few hours. Though this might be false security if whatever danger existed came with them. At least Lili's presence was some protection, and she was grateful for that.

In the car Floris seemed as twitchy as one of her llamas. Like Oliver, she didn't hold with Lili's performances, but at the same time she didn't want to stay home and be accused of concealing something—as she announced to them all a bit fiercely. A voluminous tote bag accompanied her, and now and then she fiddled with its contents as though she were undecided about something.

The car had left the Wintergreen gatehouse to follow the upward windings of Wintergreen Drive. Signs for side roads began to appear—all with woodsy names like Chestnut, Dogwood, and Milkwood. They passed villages of condominiums—or "villas," as Wintergreen preferred to call them. These had names of their own, which appeared on the map they'd been given, along with the keys to Laurel House.

The car turned onto Blue Ridge Drive, and now the great ski

slopes were visible, slanting steeply below the road. They drove past outlooks, where miles of the entire countryside were visible. One side of the mountain looked toward Stoney Creek and the Rockfish River, the other out over the Shenandoah Valley.

Nona knew the mountain well and she found her way with ease through the maze of lanes that cut through forests of chestnut oak. Laurel House was a duplex, with the other half unoccupied at the moment. Knowing the privacy Lili required, Mrs. Brewster had arranged well. They left the car in a parking area and crossed a little wooden bridge over a gully to reach the front door. The house dropped down the mountainside for two stories, with the main living quarters on the top floor. Nona unlocked the door for Lili, who walked in like the vibrant gypsy she was impersonating at the moment. Everything about her breathed happy assurance that all would be well, all questions would be answered, and no evil would touch any of them. Nona cocked a somewhat derisive eyebrow at Christy, who looked quickly away. Right now she wanted only to believe in what her mother could do.

The living room was furnished in semirustic luxury, with overhead beams and birch-paneled walls. Curving sofa and plump chairs were comfortably modern. Over the mantelpiece hung a painting of autumn woods, aglow with color, and opening upon a vista of valley and distant mountains; wide glass windows framed the tremendous view. At the far end, a glass door offered access to a balcony.

Christy went outside at once. The day was beautifully sunny, though up here the air seemed cool. Beneath the balcony rail, the cliff went straight down for thousands of feet. Spread out below lay the vast miles of the Shenandoah Valley— a checker board of cultivated fields and wooded country, its spring greens darkening into summer. Far away, the river, a dark, curving thread, wound through this old, old land of Virginia.

Up here the air was thinner, and far clearer than any glass. Christy breathed deeply, savoring the scents of high mountain growth. Without warning, the thought of Hayden was sharp in her mind. For too many years her heart had seemed a dry well, but now, when she didn't want it to happen, it was filling too fast with a warmth of new longing. Futile longing.

Beautiful places made her feel lonely. Tonight there would be a glorious sunset out there—and sunsets should be shared. But there was no one for Christy Loren to share anything with, and she'd better not start feeling sorry for herself. Hayden was involved with his own terrible problems, and it was certainly best if he never suspected the way she had begun to feel about him.

Nona came outside to stand beside her. "I still like our smaller mountains and closer views at Redlands best, but I enjoy coming up here where I can see far horizons. Lili loves horizons, so of course she had to bring us up to Wintergreen for her show. Everything is more spectacular up here, and that's what she thrives on. What's up with Floris, Christy? Have you any idea?"

So Nona too had sensed Floris's nervous state. "Let's go in and see if we can find out," Christy suggested.

In the big central room Lili was busy rearranging furniture to accommodate her plans for the evening. A larger half circle of chairs and sofa now extended around the fireplace, with a place for Lili at the center of the curve. Floris sat in a corner in a small, straight chair away from the others, her tote bag grasped on her knees as though she feared to let it go.

"Will you help me move this coffee table, Chrystal?" Lili asked.

When they'd set the table out of the way, leaving a thick rug before the hearth empty, Lili looked suddenly into her daughter's eyes. Christy had often wondered how well her mother read her thoughts. There had been moments between them over the years when Lili seemed to probe past any guard Christy might put up, quite aware of what her daughter might prefer to keep hidden.

But Lili only said, "Let's talk to Floris." Perhaps that was all she'd picked up—what Nona and Christy had been thinking about. Christy had no wish for either Lili or Nona to suspect the painful waking up that seemed to be taking place inside her.

Nona made the first direct move. "Floris, why don't you tell us what's troubling you? You've been edgy ever since we left Redlands."

Floris, more accustomed to jeans, smoothed her dark brown pants and crossed her knees, swinging one foot in its heavy boot. "I don't know what you're talking about."

"What have you brought in your bag?" Lili asked, dropping gracefully down on the carpet near Floris's chair, her wide skirts bright against the wheat color. Growing older hadn't changed Lili's ability to curl up on the floor.

The flush that moved up Floris's rather swarthy skin was painful to watch. It revealed too much. She *had* brought something unusual in her tote bag, and she was upset, perhaps even a little afraid, and not sure what to tell them.

In her own gentle, loving way, Lili placed both her hands over Floris's clenched fists and sat quietly, saying nothing. After a moment, Floris began to relax, to let go. Even the tight lines in her face smoothed out. Lili could calm the inner spirit as well as heal the body, and Floris gave in with a helpless shrug.

"I'm upset because I don't know what this means, and I hate to get involved," she said. She opened the wide mouth of the bag and pulled out a rolled wad of material. As she spread it out across her knees, Christy recognized Deirdre's rainbow needlepoint. Now, however, stains of red earth streaked the material. Stitches had been snagged, and the fabric was torn in one place.

"When did you find this?" Nona asked. "And where?"

"This morning. It was in the llama pen and it had been trampled and probably nibbled on out of curiosity."

The flames at one end of the rainbow had disappeared into smears of the same red as the earth of Redlands's fields and roads. The other side was torn so that the far end of the rainbow had vanished—leaving it a bridge to nowhere.

"This belonged to Deirdre," Floris said. "She brought it down to my house with her several times and worked on it while she visited me. Though after I scolded her about her earring idea and told her to stay away from my animals, she stopped coming. She's been missing for weeks, so why should this suddenly appear among my llamas? It wasn't there yesterday and I don't like this at all."

Lili might weigh her neck down with amber and turquoise and crystal, but she never wore rings, and her slender fingers were free of any metallic vibrations. She rubbed her palms together vigorously, gathering electricity, then held them over Floris's hands. Finally, she touched the woman's forehead, calming, soothing.

"It will be all right," she assured Floris. "Tonight we'll find some of the answers we need. Perhaps even from Deirdre herself, if she is allowed to come through."

This time, however, Lili had gone too far for Floris. She dropped the needlepoint on the floor and jumped up from her chair. "I don't aim to stay. I don't go for all this mystical stuff, and I never took part in anything that happened. Not anything! I shouldn't have come here today."

Her eyes following Floris's nervous movements, Lili drew her knees under her chin and clasped her hands around them. "You believe more than you know," she told her softly. "You talk to your llamas, don't you?"

Floris paused on her way to the door. "Most everybody talks to animals."

"But the way you talk to them is different, isn't it? *You* have a gift. When you talk to them it's sometimes in your head, as well as in spoken words. And you can hear them responding. Isn't that true?"

Again Floris flushed with emotion. "How'd you know that?"

"Perhaps I have my own gifts. I'd like to use them tonight, if

I'm allowed. But the circle mustn't be broken, and you are part of it. So please don't run away."

"Spooks!" Floris said scornfully.

Lili smiled. "I really don't think it was spooks who planted Deirdre's needlepoint in the llama pen. I don't believe it was Deirdre, either. Though perhaps someone who placed it there was trying to make you think that."

Floris gave in grudgingly. "Okay, I'll stick around. But right now I'm going for a walk. Fresh air is what I need."

"Of course." Lili rose with fluid grace. "Nona, I'd like to rest awhile before it's time to dress for dinner. The bedrooms are downstairs, I believe."

"Right," Nona said. "Go ahead." She turned to Floris. "I'll come with you for that walk. Want to join us, Christy?"

Before she could answer, Lili put a hand on her daughter's arm. "Stay here, Chrystal. It's necessary for you to be here—though I don't know why. Just be careful, dear. Be very careful."

Lili waited until Nona and Floris had gone and then picked up Deirdre's stained embroidery. Christy sensed what she intended and backed away.

"No—I don't want to touch that!"

When her mother had gone downstairs without insisting, Christy went out on the balcony and stood at the rail, pushing away all that was disturbing and saddening, letting her mind empty. Why she must wait here she had no idea, but Lili was too often right to be disputed.

Unfortunately, her mind would not focus on the view or stay empty for long. The thought of Hayden filled her too easily, so that he seemed close and real. Yet she didn't hear him when he knocked on the outer door, or sense his presence when he walked through the house.

"Hello, Christy," he said from the balcony door. "You've gone pretty far away—out across the valley?"

She whirled about, startled, and flushed as darkly and foolishly as Floris had done. His sudden appearance—out of her very thoughts!—brought a rush of emotion she didn't know how to handle.

He seemed not to notice her confusion. "Where is everybody?"

She explained, and he gestured toward a metal and canvas sofa, upholstered in green stripes, that stood at the far end of the balcony. "Come and sit down, Christy. I'm glad everyone's gone—we need to talk."

Christy sat down uncertainly and he sat beside her. "Leonie told me what happened with Donny, and that he's been searching for Deirdre's needlepoint. Can you make any sense of this?"

She was glad he was matter-of-fact and not really paying much attention to her.

"It's pretty complicated," she told him. "That piece of needlepoint has just turned up in Floris's llama pen. It's a bit worse for wear, but Floris doesn't think it was there until this morning. She brought it up here with her to see if anyone could explain it. No one could."

"Did this tell you anything?"

"I didn't touch it," Christy said. "I didn't want to."

"Will you do it now? Please."

There was no way to refuse him, however much she wanted to. "All right—I'll try. But nothing's likely to come through, the way I feel right now."

They returned to the living room, where Floris had put the needlepoint back in her bag before going out. For a moment Christy hesitated, and then reached in and pulled it out. To her relief, the only impressions that came to her were of the animals who had trampled Deirdre's beautiful work so heedlessly.

"There's nothing human left," she said. "This has been with the llamas long enough to erase everything else."

Nevertheless, as she held the square of cloth and turned it about in her hands, a strange picture began to form in her mind—not of a place but of something faceted and shiny that gleamed where sunlight fell upon it.

"I don't know what I'm seeing," she told him. "I don't think it's connected with the needlepoint. It's something like a crystal, but different. I'm not able to see it clearly. I just have a sense of something I'm not able to identify."

Hayden stared at her for a moment in surprise and then drew something from his jacket pocket and held it out. "Is this what you're sensing?"

What he held on the palm of his hand was a roundish, chunky crystal, an inch or more in diameter, with clustered points and facets. White sand had caught in its crevices, and there was a trace of red earth on the flat base. She knew what it was at once.

"That's a Herkimer diamond. It could be what was coming through. They're powerful stones."

As she stood beside him, she was intensely aware of more than the crystal. She was aware of *him*. They stood so close that, if she moved the hand she'd reached toward the stone, she would touch his fingers—and there was a longing in her to do just that. But if Hayden was in the least aware of her as a physical presence, he didn't show it, and her hand fell to her side.

"Victor Birdcall let me borrow this," Hayden said. "What *is* a Herkimer diamond?"

She spoke almost by rote, thinking more of the way his hair grew over one ear than she did of the stone. Hair that would feel springy to her fingers, with one lock that would cling if she touched it. "Herkimers are one of the oldest formations of crystal—hundreds of million of years—and they're found in Herkimer County in New York State. They're based in anthracite—coal. The same type of formation. What was Victor doing with this?" As though she really cared!

Hayden moved restlessly. He never liked the confinement of walls. "Let's go for a walk too, Christy. I don't care for all this synthetic atmosphere. There's a place not far away that you might enjoy. And we can talk more easily outdoors. I'm not comfortable here."

She was eager to go with him—just to *be* with him. A walk at least would be a sort of shared experience. They went outside together and followed along the winding lane for a short distance, and then turned up a path that climbed roughly over rocks and tree roots and ran between stunted oaks that had taken the full effect of high winds on top of Wintergreen. Their twisted trunks and gnarled branches all leaned in the same direction the gales had blown. Wooden steps opened to the view ahead, and they climbed to a platform built over a huge outcropping of rock. Planks formed the floor, and wooden rails zigzagged in geometric patterns and angles. On one side Christy could look down a cliff of tumbling rocks to the ravine far below. On the other side, the Shenandoah Valley spread away to the horizon, while overhead white cloud shapes piled in high floats against a blue sky.

Just a little while ago she had been thinking that beauty like this should be shared. But such a sharing was for lovers, and she and Hayden were as far apart as though they stood on opposite banks of the river that flowed through the land down there.

"I like to come up here," Hayden said. "There's a restful quality, and walls are a long way off. It was strange, but Deirdre, who often seemed about to take flight on her own, was afraid of heights. Sometimes she had dreams of falling—nightmares that made her wake up screaming. So she seldom came to Wintergreen. She even avoided high places around Redlands. That's one reason I couldn't accept what your mother said about Deirdre dying up there on top of that pile of rocks. She would never have gone there in the first place."

Christy didn't want to talk about Deirdre now. "Tell me about the Herkimer and Victor Birdcall," she said. Leaning on the wall beside him, she was all too sharply aware. She didn't want to think of the way his dark hair blew over his forehead in the wind, or the look of his chin and nose in profile. She'd never noticed before, but his nose had a little dent on one side of the bridge—somehow endearing, softening the stern outline.

"Yes—I want to tell you," he said. "Though it's pretty strange and it concerns Deirdre too."

When he'd left them this morning, he explained to Christy, he'd been without a car, but he'd caught a lift to the nursery and had gone to work loading plantings into a truck, enjoying physical effort that kept him from too much thinking that led nowhere. Nevertheless, he kept remembering their curious encounter with Victor Birdcall, and the memory wouldn't let him be. Finally, he got into the Jeep, drove back to Redlands and up along the dirt road that led to Victor's log cabin.

"When I got out of the Jeep, Victor wasn't out in front, so I walked around to the back and saw something that had been constructed behind his cabin. I knew at once that it was Deirdre's work, though I hadn't known it existed. She'd wished she could make a Sun Wheel at our place, but she wanted a large one, and there wasn't enough level ground. So Victor had let her build this one behind his cabin. Neither of them had told me about it—though I'm not sure why. Perhaps only because Deirdre loved her little secrets, and Victor is closemouthed about everything."

Hayden looked out over the pattern of sunlight and cloud shadow that filled the wide valley. Against a patch of clear sky, contrails streaked white ribbons across miles of space.

Christy waited in silence until he went on.

"It must have taken her a long while to build that wheel. I know now that sometimes when she would disappear she must have been working on it at Victor's. He never gave her away. Donny must have known too, since he is everywhere, but she must have asked him to keep her secret too. Now I've been wondering if there was something else up there that she didn't want me to know about."

Christy had learned about Sun Wheels through Nona, though she had never seen one. "Some of the stones that made it up had to be special, didn't they?"

"Yes. It must have taken her weeks, months sometimes, to find exactly the stones she wanted. She'd rimmed the whole thing in white sand, with special rocks set into it around the circumference. The whole thing was perhaps fifteen feet in diameter, and she'd divided the enclosed area into four segments with a cross of white stones. The big central stone was white too, with other rocks inside the rim representing the colors of the rainbow.

"While I stood there looking at the Wheel, Victor came outside and told me how Deirdre had hunted for those rainbow stones. Sometimes a lump of quartz would show a streaking of purple. Or a rock with iron in it provided the red. Victor helped her find some of them himself. There were other rocks inside the circle that represented all human life and all religions on earth. Each quadrant marked off by the stone cross apparently has different qualities attached to it."

"The Herkimer diamond was part of the Wheel?" Christy asked.

"It was a stone someone had given her, Victor said, and she'd placed it in the circle. From time to time she borrowed it from the Wheel for some purpose of her own. Herkimers have their own special qualities, Victor told me, and he said that Deirdre would sometimes sit in one of the quadrants and hold that stone in her hands—as though it had some special protective virtue that helped her. But she never told Victor what she needed to be protected from."

Again, Hayden was silent at the rail beside her and Christy waited until he was ready to go on. When he spoke again, he held the stone up to the light as though it would tell him something.

"There's more. Victor's an early riser and he went out one morning before daylight—about a week before Deirdre disappeared. He found her sitting inside the Wheel on a straw mat, with a blanket around her shoulders. She was holding this same stone, and she was looking at the sky, watching the dawn spread across the hills. It was especially beautiful and filled with color that morning, and Victor watched it with Deirdre. When full daylight came, she replaced the stone in the Wheel and told him some of its virtues. She said it was often given to the dying to hold because it calmed and helped them to an easy passage."

Hayden drew in his breath sharply before he went on.

"Victor said she wasn't unhappy that morning, but quite serene. She thanked him for letting her build the Sun Wheel and allowing her to use it. Victor realized that she wasn't sitting in an east, west, or south segment, all of which are supposed to have benign qualities. Instead, she'd chosen the north quadrant, and he told me that north stands for black light, for the unconscious, for dreams and death—for all those mysteries that men can never know or understand until they cross over. Yet before she left, she told him happily that she was a child of the rainbow and that she would be safe. At the very last moment, before she stepped out of the circle, she picked up a small black stone from the north and took it with her. He didn't ask why. He said she'd moved away into her own mystical place and probably wouldn't have heard him."

Christy was aware that the hand that didn't hold the stone was grasping the rail tightly, revealing the emotion that tore Hayden apart and wouldn't let him rest. She wanted to reach out to touch one strong, tanned hand—just to offer human comfort. But she didn't dare. If she touched him she might reveal too much of her own feelings at that moment.

When he continued, his voice was tight, controlled. "This morning when Victor went outside, he noticed that the Herkimer was missing from its place in the Wheel. Later, when he started breakfast, he found the stone on his counter top. He had no idea how it got there."

Hayden held out the chunky stone to Christy. "Victor said I should give it to you and see what it told you."

Once more, Christy moved away from the test. "I'll take it if you want me to, but give me a little time. Why do you suppose Deirdre trusted Victor with any of this, when she was so secretive otherwise?"

"Perhaps because of his Indian heritage. Perhaps the Sun

Wheel is related to the medicine wheel of Western tribes. Victor said Deirdre never really talked to him much, but sometimes she would come into his cabin for a cup of his herbal tea. He knows how to be quiet, and that was all she seemed to need. Just to be still. But he sensed how troubled she was—sometimes even afraid."

Hayden's voice changed.

"I could have done more if I'd paid attention. She could be like a child—a child who lived in her own imaginary world. And I let her alone and didn't concern myself. I only noticed when she came out of that mood to throw some unreasonable tantrum, and then I was impatient with her. We didn't have much of a marriage any more, and I just let her go her own way."

So now, Christy thought, Hayden would carry his own guilt because he'd never reached Deirdre or truly tried to understand. Guilt like that could be carried forever, unless Deirdre was found and all the questions answered. Christy turned her back on the view, looking into the green of mountain laurel, still showing a few blooms. It was time now and she held out her hand.

"Will you give me the stone, please?"

He placed it on her palm, and at once all her uneasiness evaporated. The Herkimer had given its allegiance to someone who was good. Perhaps a loving dreamer, not wholly of this world, but who meant harm to no one.

Christy turned the stone in her fingers, touched its planes and tiny protruding points that stood up like little mountain peaks—miniature ice cliffs of crystal. The stone was rather heavy, and it possessed none of the grace of the phantom crystal Deirdre had treasured. Yet it too was filled with mysterious light. Pinpoints of light sparkled at its heart, and she could look through flat planes as if through windows and see the inner life of the stone. Here and there, as she turned it in the sunlight, she caught a tiny glint of green, a hint of rose—

the rainbow that hid its colors deep within. At another point the light was golden with no trace of any other color. She could imagine Deirdre sitting in her safe, beautiful Sun Wheel, protected and happy, holding this stone and allowing it to comfort her.

That last morning, when she'd watched the dawn with Victor, perhaps she had known that it was the last dawn of her earthly life. Perhaps she'd felt that death was coming, though she hadn't seemed afraid.

But now something else had happened to this stone. Someone driven by malice or mischief had played this trick. Or had this, perhaps, been a cry for help?

There was no easy answer, and Christy's power was too weak to seek deeply into the stone. Yet before Hayden could be free of his own haunting, all these questions must be answered. She gave the stone back to him regretfully.

"I wish I could help, but while this tells me some of the good qualities Deirdre possessed, it doesn't give me any other lead. Perhaps Lili will understand better than I do. You must show this to her tonight, Hayden. Has Victor any notion as to whether it was a man or a woman who put this in his kitchen?"

"He didn't say. It seems a bit too playful for most men—but rather like Deirdre herself."

There had been other indications that were seemingly like Deirdre—or, as she'd thought before, someone who was imitating her.

"Let's go back," Hayden said abruptly.

He looked so sad and remote that she longed again to offer some touch of comfort. But she couldn't know how such a gesture might be received, and she didn't dare risk it.

They returned together to the road, and there was no touching between them, Christy suffering her own silent despair. So much seemed to hang on what Lili might accomplish tonight, but Christy's belief was not as strong as she wished it could have been. Lili refused to recognize the power of evil, and if one didn't recognize something wicked, how could it be vanquished and dispelled?

They walked back to Laurel House in a silence that set them far apart, and Christy knew she had failed him.

Laurel House was a good choice—out there on top of nowhere. It will be interesting to see what nonsense develops there to-night. Dukas and her idiot Josef! As if they could be a match for me.

That was a good touch on my part—leaving the Herkimer stone for Victor to find. I need to mislead him at every turn. Otherwise, he might be sensitive enough to find answers— before I am ready. I should have been ready before this, but Dukas's coming has stirred the pot too much. There is a lot of fear around now—and fear can lead to foolish actions. Of them all, Victor could see the truth, if he really looked. Fortu- nately, his own torments keep him blind.

Deirdre cried when I took away her needlepoint. I'd brought it to keep her happy—give her something to do. To pretend to do. Of course she couldn't work at needlepoint, any more than she can cry real tears. How can a spirit woman cry or work at embroidery? She must stay that way, and materialize only when I say. Of course, I allowed her to take the Herkimer diamond to Victor's cabin herself. She hoped he would find it and understand—perhaps come looking for her. She still isn't sure which world she's in. I went with her and brought her back again.

Is Hayden becoming interested in Christy? I wonder. That would not be a good idea. So far, she's been harmless enough. Of course she has probably fallen for him —women often seem to. I wonder what he has to draw them to him? If I were in

Christy's shoes, I would never look at him twice. But then, I never understood why Deirdre married him in the first place. At least, she's still afraid of me, and under my control. I'm the only one who can reach into that other world for her.

It was a clever idea to leave the rainbow needlepoint in the llama pen. No one will ever know I put it there. It's too unlikely.

There are those, of course, who would say that I am mad. I can laugh in their faces because I know better. I'm wiser than any of them, except perhaps Victor. I must watch Victor. How I would like to destroy the Sun Wheel—but it's not time yet. I wonder what Victor did with the Herkimer when he found it? My trick with the crystal that I left in a drawer at the nursery office must have puzzled them.

11

DINNER at the Coppermine was a strange affair. Christy found herself more observer than participant, and Hayden Mitchell, seated on Lili's right hand, seemed lost in himself and hardly present. This could be no lighthearted social occasion, as Lili had suggested. Not considering what might lie ahead for them tonight.

They had all met at the Mountain Inn and walked through the lobby concourse to the open flagstone area beyond. Here rustic architecture made a half circle two stories high, with miles of valley view opening on one side. Once, of course, there had really been copper mines up here, and the entrance to the restaurant suggested the entrance to a mine.

Inside the big dining room, with its beamed ceiling and mountain lodge aspect, a large round table had been reserved for the Dukas party. While there could be no head to the circle, wherever Lili sat was obviously the center. Tonight she looked stunning in her black crepe trousers and embroidered green Chinese jacket. Dangling jade earrings beneath her dark, up-swept hairdo reminded Christy of the times when she'd been allowed to touch those earrings.

Beautiful as Lili looked, however, she couldn't match Nona for dramatic elegance. Nona's pearl-gray chiffon gown showed touches of autumn flame in its folds when she moved, and her garnet choker and earrings added a darker fire. Tonight her hair was hidden by a flame-colored turban knotted with an imaginative twist. Under the flowing gown her spare boniness had disappeared, and she always held herself with a special dignity. Lili could be commanding and exuberant, and she could carry everyone along on her own tide of energy—but she was never as grand as Nona when her sister really made the effort. As she had tonight.

As always a subtle rivalry existed between the two, and Christy knew very well that she was the center of their conflict. Though Lili had given her daughter over to Nona years before, she expected to return on any one of her flying visits and claim her child completely. Christy had learned to remove herself from this tug-of-war. She loved Nona, and she was on her side—but then there was Lili in all her enchantment, behaving like a loving mother, and hard to resist.

As she grew older Christy had learned to recognize that Lili had her own special reality. She possessed a talent for healing that reached out widely and that she could never deny. This had been hard for a child to understand, and even now the grown-up Christy sometimes felt old resentment creeping in.

At the table a large menu folder was brought to each diner, and when Christy, feeling indifferent to food, had made a choice of something light, she studied the rest of the group Nona had gathered here.

Floris still looked edgy and had clearly been unwilling to dress for an affair she didn't want to attend. Her plain brown pants suit and windblown hair flung a certain defiance at her hostess. Eve, who was also more comfortable in jeans, wore a pink-flowered print that didn't flatter her, and she looked uncomfortable. Oliver's presence seemed to absorb her, and she watched him covertly much of the time.

Oliver looked handsome in a gray jacket over a blue turtleneck, with well-cut gray trousers. His manner was remote, as though he too wished he were somewhere else.

In this country atmosphere, Hayden had come as he pleased in dark slacks and a Norwegian sweater with reindeer running diagonally across the front, but he seemed anything but relaxed. Later on, Lili was going to have her hands full with these crosscurrents ready to surface.

Christy had put on a slim black frock with a single strand of pearls that had belonged to Lili's mother—the Hungarian grandmother Christy had never known. She'd learned long ago never to dress in competition with her mother. Lili must always play center stage—a position she took gracefully as her natural right, ignoring Nona's dramatic presence.

Perhaps of them all, Victor Birdcall seemed most in character. His fringed western shirt with a turquoise bola tie, black strings tipped in silver, and hand-tooled leather belt with a beautifully crafted turquoise buckle, all suited him. Victor seemed the calmest, and most in control of his feelings. Perhaps only because he knew how to hide his emotions successfully?

When they'd ordered and the appetizers were served, it was Victor who threw a rock to stir the already ominous waters. Literally a rock! Hayden had apparently returned the Herkimer diamond to him, and he took the chunky stone from his shirt pocket and rolled it into the center of the table. It landed on a flat plane, its heart fires winking at them beneath its surface.

Lili was delighted—or pretended to be. "A Herkimer diamond! And such a large one! Where did it come from?"

"That's what I'd like to know," Victor said. "It belonged to Deirdre, and she'd put it among the rocks in the Sun Wheel she built out behind my cabin. But this morning that stone turned up on my kitchen counter."

"May I see?" Lili held out her hand.

Nona reached for the stone and passed it to her. Lili turned it about in her long-fingered, ringless hands, as though she drew some physical impression from it. Watching her mother, Christy sensed Lili's sudden rejection of the Herkimer. She set it down quickly, as though it had told her something she didn't want to know. It was a gesture Christy recognized—a movement away from anything distasteful. As far as possible, Lili wanted only sweetness and light around her, and Christy wondered sometimes if her mother held some deep-seated fear of the evil she always rejected as non-existent.

"What did you feel?" Christy challenged.

Jade earrings caught the light as Lili shook her head. "There's confusion. Too many people have handled this stone, and I can't tell anything about it."

Christy persisted. "This afternoon when Hayden showed me that stone and I held it, I felt that someone good had owned it. So what do you feel that's different?"

Lili went down another road, speaking to Hayden. "If this belonged to your wife, do you know where she got it?"

Oliver, who clearly wished himself somewhere else, seemed startled by the question—and he answered before Hayden could speak. "*I* know where she got it. Rose—my wife—gave it to Deirdre a long time ago."

This seemed to mean nothing to Lili. "The stone has been contaminated. It should be bathed in spring water, with a pinch of sea salt, and then allowed to dry in the sun and air. But not where small animals can find it, or it will be stolen."

Oliver snorted impolitely, and Eve, following his lead, laughed.

"I think you should wait," Victor said quietly. "Let the contamination, if that's what it is, remain until it can tell you something. Perhaps there's meaning here that shouldn't be erased. Different people seem to have different reactions to the stone."

"I've always been interested in Herkimers," Nona said. "Do they have the same healing power as crystals?"

"I've never used them for healing," Lili told her sister. "But I have found that they bring peace to those who are ill. When death is near, a Herkimer can help make the passing easy and welcome."

Christy glanced at Victor, remembering what he had said about Deirdre sitting in the dark north quadrant of the Wheel.

He took the stone back, and spoke as quietly as before. "Perhaps you can ask about this crystal tonight, Miss Dukas."

Lili nodded agreement, but Floris, who had been attacking

her salad with apparent indifference to what was going on around her, suddenly broke in.

"I had a dream a couple of nights ago. I saw Deirdre standing beside my bed—just as real as could be! She was wearing one of those white things she liked to drift around in, and she had a sparkling diamond in her hair. It just came to me that it looked like that Herkimer stone. I don't usually remember dreams, but this hung on afterward. I haven't got a notion what it can mean."

Lili drew them all away from discussion of the stone. "Let's forget this now and enjoy our dinner. Tonight I will certainly ask Josef if there is anything we should know about this particular stone."

Oliver pushed his plate aside as though he'd lost his appetite. "So this isn't to be the friendly get-together you promised, Miss Dukas? Now it seems we're to have a séance after all."

"Please, Oliver—not that word!" Lili remained unruffled. "Few psychics hold séances any more. If Josef chooses to come in there are questions we can ask him. If he doesn't, they will go unanswered. There's no table-tipping, no ectoplasm floating around. All that belongs to a time in the past when our friends from other planes were having difficulty reaching us. Now the channels are open, and they come in easily."

Oliver looked as though he wanted to get up and leave, yet he was also torn by a desire not to miss whatever might happen. Eve watched him anxiously, and followed suit when he seemed to give in and relax.

By the time the entrees were served, the dinner conversation had turned guardedly polite, with everyone slightly on edge. Laurel House and whatever would happen there hung over them like a threat as the time drew near.

Just before dessert and coffee could be served, however, Lili suddenly pushed back her chair. "I'm sorry. A message has just come through. An urgent message. We must leave at once."

Since no one had approached the table, there was no doubt about her meaning. One of her "guides" had spoken. Oliver looked more skeptical than ever, and Eve, who had come with him, stayed close as they all went out to their cars. Sometimes she behaved almost protectively toward him, Christy thought. But what did Oliver need to be protected from?

In any case, there seemed to be enough dry kindling here to set off a fine blaze, and she wondered how Lili could possibly keep everything cheerful and bright—and *good.* Yet Christy still couldn't tell the source of the hostility that seemed to lie just below the surface. It wasn't necessarily emanating from Oliver, but possibly from unseen energies that hovered around them all.

Nona led the way to Laurel House in her car—a drive of only a few minutes. Lights burned in the upper living-room windows—as Lili had left them—and it was she who was first across the short wooden bridge from "the mainland to our island," as she put it. The door she'd left locked stood open, though this didn't seem to surprise her.

"We've had visitors," she said. "That's why I was called. Let's see if they are still here."

The living room was empty, and nothing seemed to have been disturbed.

"I'll look downstairs," Hayden offered, but Lili shook her head.

"There's no need. It's only this room that has been visited. Please be quiet, everyone. Let me see what I can sense."

Floris sniffed her distaste for such nonsense and sprawled into an armchair. Eve had grown uncertain and uneasy, and she put a hand on Oliver's arm. Nona glanced at Christy and touched a finger to her lips. Clearly she wanted to give Lili every chance to do her thing. Of them all, only Victor seemed comfortable and not ill at ease. He had remained near the door that opened from the entryway into the living room, so that he would have blocked anyone who might have wanted to leave. Now he spoke directly to Lili.

"*She* has been here," he said.

"Yes," Lili agreed. "It was Deirdre. But we didn't arrive in time. She's gone now."

Hayden looked angry. "What are you talking about? You've already claimed she was dead."

"There are different kinds of death," Lili said. "Tell them, Victor."

Victor fingered the strings of his tie. He never liked the spotlight, but Lili must be answered.

"Deirdre's perfume," he said. "That heather scent she always wore. I caught it the minute I came into the room."

"I did too," Lili agreed. "Haven't the rest of you noticed?"

Hayden was still angry. "I know her perfume very well, and there's not a trace of it in this room. You're imagining it! Or else you're leaning on suggestion."

"I agree," Oliver said. "The house is so full of incense you must have burned earlier, Miss Dukas, that something as faint as Deirdre's perfume couldn't possibly be caught."

Lili smiled, dismissing his words, and waited for the rest of them. Christy had closed her eyes to let all her senses turn inward. Yes—the heather scent was there, even if only because Lili had suggested it. Under the sandalwood something else lingered—but perhaps only to the sensitive nose, like her own. Odors of plastic and foam rubber, the smell of new rugs, all could be filtered out when she concentrated, leaving only that slight trace of Deirdre's outdoor scent.

Christy met her mother's eyes in agreement, aware of the tenuous bond that existed between them. Of the others, only Victor had shared the experience of catching Deirdre's perfume. He took out the Herkimer diamond and gave it to Lili.

"Perhaps you can call her back with this. Perhaps she will speak to you now."

Hayden stirred restlessly, but he didn't object. Christy watched her mother turn into Liliana Dukas as she chose the central armchair in the half circle about the fireplace. Without being asked, and perhaps to conceal his own indignation, Oliver knelt to light the fire, not looking at the others. Nona knew what her sister wanted, and she went about relighting the sticks of incense that had been placed in brass holders around the room. She also turned off all but one of the lamps, so that the room was illuminated mainly by the new fire, whose flames were reflected in the black glass of the windows.

"Thank you, Oliver," Lili said. "Thank you, Nona." Then she gestured to the chair beside her, speaking to her daughter. "Please sit here, Chrystal." And to Hayden, "You on my left, if you don't mind. The rest of you may sit where you like. There's no special formality about this. I really don't know what will happen. We merely invite, and a quiet, peaceful setting helps."

"And as dark as possible!" Oliver complained.

"If we can all relax, everything will happen more easily." Lili told him calmly. "Bright lights are a distraction."

Each one found a place, except Victor, who seated himself cross-legged on the floor, with his back to the fire. Christy remembered what Nona had told her about Victor liking to "play Indian." Only she didn't think he was play-acting now. Perhaps something old stirred in his blood to make this strange Blue Ridge Mountain scene familiar, and the position he'd chosen on the floor was the one most natural to him.

Hayden remained irritated, as though his own hurting stirred an exasperation that he was barely able to contain. "Perfume!" he repeated. "There wasn't a trace!"

Oliver laughed. "They're talking about a psychic scent, Hay. Ordinary mortals like us wouldn't catch it."

"You're quite right, Oliver," Lili told him. "Though *you* are far from ordinary. I have a strong feeling that something is troubling you that you may want to bring into the open to-night."

"That sort of remark"—Oliver turned on her sharply—"is cheap and easy. Those words would apply to anyone here."

He would have liked to stalk out of the room and turn his back on whatever might happen here, Christy thought. But nevertheless, he stayed—perhaps because he was afraid to leave and miss what was about to take place?

Lili let his comment pass. "Please talk, all of you. Conversation is natural and there's no pressure of anything to happen. You'll know when it's time to be quiet." In one hand she held the Herkimer Victor had given her.

After her invitation, some of them tried to talk, though a bit self-consciously. Not Victor however, and not Oliver. Hayden managed to speak casually to Nona about some problem he was having with a dying rhododendron. Eve asked a question about llamas and that freed Floris's tongue, so that she told them about a llama baby that had been born that spring and was thriving.

All Christy's senses were like antennae now—she had no control over them, so that what came to her was a disturbing rush of scattered thoughts, fears, anger, a jumble that seemed to gather in the room around her. Only a few times before had this happened to her, and it was difficult to endure. Lili had often said that her own psychic powers were stronger at night, so perhaps that was happening to Christy now. Her sensitivity was waking up, aware of the warring emotions that lay just below the surface in this room. If Lili wanted a serene, peaceful atmosphere, she wouldn't find it here.

Lili's eyes were closed. This would be the moment when she said a short, protective prayer—for herself, and for all those gathered here. One could become too open and vulnerable to restless spirits seeking a doorway into human life—so Lili would always ask for help and protection from a Higher Power, whatever name mortals chose to give it.

Except for Lili, perhaps the one truly serene person in the room was Nona. She would let all negativity flow away from her, so that she could open herself to whatever might happen. She might have moments of scoffing at her sister, but she was one of them, and psychic in her own way, whether she admitted it or not.

The sort of psychic who could dip into people's minds might have read the secrets in this room, but psychic skills come in all shapes and sizes, and Christy's own visions were not of others' thoughts and motives, except as they came jumbled into this senseless bombardment that she longed to escape.

After a little while the talk died away of itself. Lili's eyes were still closed, and she had drawn her trousered legs up into the lotus position. A hand rested on each knee, with the palms upward, receptive. The Herkimer held winking flames at its heart, where it lay upon one palm.

When Josef began to speak, they were all aware of his presence. The voice was different from Lili's—a little deeper, and not as resonant. Like the flat tones of one unused to human vocal chords. His speech forms were stilted and a little antique, since he had lived in another time on earth.

"Good evening, friends," he said.

Christy and Nona responded, knowing the ritual. No one else spoke. Victor seemed immobile, his back to the fire as he stared into shadows stirred by the flames behind him. Thrown into silhouette, he seemed a large and formidable figure. The room was quiet now, and even the turbulence of emotion that had swirled around Christy had grown still, as if in breathless waiting.

"You have pertinent questions to ask?" Josef inquired.

An awkward silence followed, until Nona spoke. "We are seeking someone who is no longer with us. A woman named Deirdre Mitchell. She has disappeared and we wish to find out what has become of her."

"She is with you," Josef said.

"You mean in reality? You mean she is alive?" The exchange was entirely between Nona and Josef now.

"Her reality is not your reality." He elaborated a bit on this, as though he enjoyed the opportunity to be wordy.

"Is she happy, Josef?" Lili pulled him back.

"She is not happy. She seeks release."

"Can we help her? Can we find a way to release her?"

Josef was silent for a moment. "I do not know. It is not clear at the moment. There is confusion."

Hayden broke in, his voice harsh, and Nona, on his other

side, put a quieting hand on his arm. With an effort he lowered his tone and went on. "I need an answer. A *real* answer. Is my wife alive or dead?"

"She is both," Josef said. "It would be better to let her go. There can be danger otherwise."

"Danger from Deirdre?" Hayden sounded derisive.

"From her captor," Josef said. "There is hidden evil."

A stir of movement whispered around the room and Lili opened her eyes as if even she had been startled. The stunned silence that followed was filled with unspoken questions, disbelief—perhaps even fear. The latter came through like a throbbing pulse in Christy's temples, though she couldn't detect its source.

Again Lili closed her eyes and began to sway gently from side to side.

"You have other questions?" Josef asked.

Christy spoke quietly. "There is a crystal called a Herkimer diamond that my mother is holding. This stone appeared on a kitchen counter at Redlands this morning. Can you tell us how it got there?"

Lili moved, holding up the stone.

"A malicious spirit is among you," Josef said, and went on at some length in a discussion of such spirits.

"Does a name come to you?" Christy asked.

"A name . . . yes. The name is Rose."

"*Rose* put the stone on the counter!" Christy exclaimed.

"No. There are animals involved."

Floris broke in. "You mean my llamas? Rose and the llamas?"

"Yes. You will find the answers there, but you must know how to look. Where to look."

Floris fumbled in her bag and took out the needlepoint. "What about this? How did it come to my llama pen?"

"Guard against malicious spirits," Josef said portentously. "Do not open yourselves to evil."

"That doesn't tell us anything!" Floris cried.

Josef sounded fainter when he answered. "We are not om-
nipotent. We prefer to offer guidance. Not all can accept."

Hayden broke in roughly. "This is mumbo-jumbo—we're
not getting anywhere!"

Josef had begun to fade out. "I am sorry. It is necessary to
find your own way. The channel is growing weaker. We must
not ask too much on this occasion. She is very tired."

Josef was gone, and Christy felt the same impatience with
her mother's mentor that she'd experienced before. Josef
could confuse and even misdirect, though Lili claimed that he
only intended for them to do their own thinking and create
their own miracles.

Now Lili sat quietly with her eyes closed. She was indeed
tired, yet she would be aware of all that had transpired. Even
though she might not recall the exact words, the purport
would stay with her.

Slowly a feeling of desolation and helplessness crept through
Christy, shaking her physically. The pounding in her temples
was not her own fear but the echo of someone else's terror.
Someone in this room. Fog drifted before her eyes—that thick,
pale fog that often came before a vision. Gradually, as it
cleared, she saw again that high place of Nona's painting—the
cliff whose foot they had come to. But now Christy stood alone,
not on the path below but at the very edge of those high rocks
from which Rose had fallen. No one else seemed to be about.
The fear now was entirely her own.

A rainbow, rising out of mist, arched above the trees—a
band of radiant color across the sky. As the vision grew clearer,
the knowledge of her own imminent death was sharp in her
mind. When the rainbow faded, *she* would be gone. An instant
later the vision had vanished, and Christy sat trembling, her
hands tightly clasped together.

Lili moved, stretched her arms widely, and spoke to them
all.

"You didn't thank Josef," she said, gently reproachful.

"Thank him for what?" Oliver sounded as indignant as Hayden, yet he had asked no questions, thrown out no challenge. Nor had Eve. "Not one useful word came out of your friend, Miss Dukas. Is this what we were brought here for?"

"Perhaps no one asked the right questions," Lili said gently.

Hayden stood up, still angry. "I'm going home. This isn't the way to find Deirdre."

Victor, who had taken no part in what had happened, still sat cross-legged with his back to the hearth and the dying fire. "Maybe that's your fault, Hayden," he said. "When you let the shield come down, you'll hear what you need to hear."

Hayden swung around from the doorway. "What the hell do you mean by that?"

"I think you know." Victor sounded strangely sad, and Christy, watching with her heart as well as her eyes, was aware of a curious wavering in Hayden Mitchell. He seemed to get himself under control immediately, however, and spoke more courteously to Lili.

"I'm sorry if I've disrupted what you'd planned, Miss Dukas. I'm not up to any more right now."

"Hayden," Eve said, "Josef spoke the truth when he said to let Deirdre go. Isn't that what you must do?"

Hayden's anger flashed in the look he turned upon Eve. She raised her hands in a defensive gesture. "Hey—I didn't mean anything. Calm down!"

He gave them all a black look and went out the door. What a fiasco this had been, Christy thought, and wondered how her mother, who had roused all these emotions, could remain serenely calm.

Floris, who was paying no attention to anyone else, came to stand in front of Lili. "What did you mean about Rose and my llamas?" she demanded.

Lili shook her head. "You mustn't confuse me with Josef. I can't answer any of your questions myself. It's only when Josef speaks through me that answers may be given. But only as he chooses. He is very wise, you know. Sometimes the words he speaks lead us to think more deeply. He makes us look for answers that may exist close to us—even inside ourselves—but which we don't recognize. I believe he has stirred Hayden to some very deep and painful thinking."

"I've had enough!" Eve said impatiently, not really listening. "Oliver, please take me home."

Oliver seemed more shaken than angry. The mention of his wife's name seemed to have upset him "Yes," he agreed, "let's go right now." He walked out of the room without a good night to anyone, and Christy heard his footsteps sounding loudly on the wooden planks of the bridge.

Eve took her leave more apologetically. She spoke to Lili, waved her hand at the others, and went hastily after Oliver, lest he drive away without her.

When Floris hurried after them to ask for a lift, only Victor remained. He hadn't stirred from his place by the fire, and flames, leaping behind him in orange spears, threw his figure into sharp silhouette. Christy noted that from certain angles, and with certain lighting, Victor Birdcall could look like the portrait of some eagle-faced warrior from the past. Tonight the Indian connection was strong, and the words he had spoken to Hayden still puzzled and tantalized Christy.

When Lili stood up to stretch her arms toward the sky beyond the confines of Laurel House, it was as though she asked for help from the invisible heavens.

"The trouble is here on earth," Nona said wryly. "But Josef was right and you are tired now. So am I. This really wasn't a good idea. Everyone's more riled up than ever. Let's go downstairs and turn in. You staying for the night, Victor?"

He gave her his faint semblance of a smile. "I want to talk to Christy." He rose with a quick, lithe movement and stood rocking on the balls of his feet.

Nona said, "He's all yours, Christy. But watch out for redskins! Good night, both of you."

In contrast to her earlier guise of serenity, Lili's brightness and optimism seemed quenched, and she looked almost forlorn. Christy went to her mother quickly and put her arms about her, as she seldom dared to do.

"It's all right," she told her. "Something will come out of this, even if Josef wasn't very clear."

Lili rested her cheek against Christy's. "Of course. We must be patient. There was too much disharmony tonight. Too much anger and fear."

"Could you tell who was afraid?" Christy asked.

"No. There seemed a miasma—a sickness."

"Yes, I felt it too."

"Perhaps," Lili said, "that's what Josef intended—to bring the wounds to a festering that would expose the poison. Then the common good will result." She held up the Herkimer. "See! Its fires are dulled. You must return it to the Sun Wheel, Victor."

When he had taken it, Nona said, "That's enough for now. I'll go downstairs with you, Lili. Good night, Christy, Victor."

When they'd gone, Christy opened the balcony door, so that cool, Blue Ridge air could sweep out the smell of incense and whatever synthetic odors had mingled in the warm room. There was no trace of any ghostly heather scent now. When she closed the door and turned around, Victor was waiting for her. He had left his place by the hearth and stretched himself out in a chair.

"Go ahead—ask," he said.

Both his perception and his abruptness startled her. "You're such a secret man. You always know how to put a wall around yourself that not even Lili can penetrate."

His remote smile neither accepted nor denied. "Josef spoke the truth, but who will listen?"

"*What* was true? I don't think anything specific was said."

"What about the connection between Rose and the llamas?"

Christy thought of Donny and the manuscript Rose had left behind. She didn't want to give away the boy's secret, so she spoke cautiously.

"I believe that Rose was using the llamas in a book, though her manuscript has never been found."

"It won't be," Victor said. "Not until Donny makes up his mind."

"He's told you about this?"

"He left the manuscript with me. He thought I would make a good recipient for his secret."

Excitement quickened in her. "You've looked at it then?"

"Donny asked me not to."

Christy stared at him, and Victor met her look calmly. In the beginning she had disliked and distrusted him. But she had begun to reject her first careless impressions. She had never really looked deeply enough into Victor. He was secretive, yes, but a sense of respect and liking for him was growing in her. She could understand something of what Nona discerned in Victor Birdcall. He had lived through his own tragedy and found his own path toward healing.

"I'm glad you've kept your word to Donny," she told him. "He said he had those pages and that he'd put them in a safe place. He was going to get them for me, but I think he wasn't sure he wanted anyone to look at them. At least, not yet. Do you suppose they could possibly give any of the answers that Josef didn't manage tonight?"

"Josef told us a lot. He spoke of Deirdre needing to be released from her captor. That was pretty definite."

"If we take it literally. But he could have meant it in a more subtle sense—her spirit held captive on this earthly plane, perhaps?"

"That too. Sometimes I've almost sensed her about—at least some essence that stands for Deirdre. Not just her perfume or white dress. Those seem pretty obvious."

"You mean that one of us could have arranged the scent ahead of time?"

"Perhaps. There must have been opportunity."

Christy sighed. "I don't understand anything—yet I have an

almost mystical sense of Deirdre and what she was like, even though I never met her."

Victor was silent, as though he moved away into his own guarded thoughts.

"Anyway," she went on, "it's Hayden I'm sorry for. I don't know what he's fighting—aside from his own terrible loss that he can't accept."

"Perhaps he is the captive who most needs release."

"You told him he needed to let down his shield—what did you mean by that?"

"That's for Hayden to say. Good night, Christy."

She stopped him before he reached the door. "Shall I ask Donny to let us both see whatever it is Rose put into her manuscript?"

Victor's look seemed pitying—as though he had read her better than anyone else. "You need many answers, Christy Loren. Come and sit in Deirdre's Sun Wheel. You may find guidance there."

He went out the door, and the empty room closed about her —filled now with silent echoes of the words that had been spoken here tonight. They chattered through her consciousness, tugging, demanding—as though they cried out for an understanding she didn't know how to achieve.

Her brain, her very spirit, felt utterly weary, and she went downstairs to bed.

It was clever of me to steal that half bottle of Deirdre's scent. This afternoon, while Dukas was resting—for her big night!— and the others were out wandering around, leaving doors unlocked, I was able to drive up there and walk quite openly into the living room to sprinkle drops of perfume in the incense burners. A fine effect!

It's necessary to keep Hayden off balance until I can be sure of what I must do. Josef's cryptic remarks only muddied the waters. Just the same, he came too close for comfort—if someone had been able to translate. Dukas will be gone very soon, and Josef doesn't come in through anyone else, so that risk will be past.

Victor may have begun to suspect—something. But he won't act. His own experiences have made him wary. About Christy, I'm still uncertain. She's exploring too far afield, but she may be more sensitive than she's willing to accept. I should have acted more forcefully when I had the chance. If intuition really speaks to her, it might be all over for me.

Before I deal with Christy again, there is Oliver. He won't mean to speak out—he's too frightened. But if his fear overpowers him, then what? He isn't the man I thought he was, and his weaker side is disturbing.

Perhaps I have an amusing solution.

12

U P ON THE mountain the morning was glorious. The Shenandoah Valley lay distant, far below, the view shredded with mists that dissipated as the sun rose behind the house. This was a cliff house, with a sheer drop below Christy's window. Large black birds flew in and out of the crags below. They might be ravens, since someone had said there were ravens up here.

When she had showered and dressed, Christy went upstairs in search of coffee and found Nona in the kitchen. Lili was still asleep. She often stayed in bed late to recoup her energy after a session with Josef. Nona, in her dressing gown, with no scarf covering her head, looked tired and gloomy.

"What did Victor have to say after we left?" she asked.

Christy poured coffee for both of them and sat down at the counter. "Not very much. He seems to think Josef touched on some truths, even though we didn't understand what he was talking about."

"I don't like what happened," Nona said. "Someone got in here with Deirdre's perfume. I had a sniff at the incense burners this morning, and they'd certainly been scented. And not by Lili! Her part in all this is genuine as far as she knows. How much she fools herself we can never be sure."

"I don't know," Christy said. "Sometimes I wonder."

"Wonder what?" Her aunt was turning bacon with a fork, dropping eggs into the pan.

"Mostly about me, I suppose. When I was small I hated what my mother did because it always took her away from me. So I was jealous. Sometimes people made fun of her, and then I was ashamed. You didn't approve of her either, a lot of the time, and I was mixed up, confused. Perhaps I still am. Lili always seemed so happy in what she was doing—so serene. I wanted that for *me*. Instead, I had to share her with so many people who tugged at her and took her away from me—sometimes used her up, so she was tired and couldn't give me what I wanted from her."

"I know. I was jealous too—because I could never take her place with you."

"But you always had your own place!" Christy cried. "No one else ever gave me what you did. You were the one I could count on—when I couldn't count on *her.*"

Nona looked pleased as she transferred bacon and eggs to two plates and joined Christy at the counter. But talking about affection was not her thing, and she edged away from the personal.

"Victor must have said something more?" she prompted.

"Yes. He spoke about Hayden letting down his shield. What do you think he meant?"

"You'd better ask him—or Hayden."

That was what Victor had said, but she could hardly ask Hayden. He had seemed terribly disturbed last night, and torn in ways she couldn't fully understand. Losing Deirdre, perhaps not always loving her—but losing her, and never free of her—might leave him with a strong sense of guilt.

"I'm a total failure," she told her aunt. "I want to be useful, but nothing comes to me. Except for glimpses that only concern me, I don't see anything. Just when I might need—whatever this is—it vanishes."

"Need it for what?"

Christy recognized that challenging tone. "I know you've always set yourself against Lili's talents, and against whatever slight gift I have. Why? It's in you too—though you never acknowledge it. You paint mysteries on canvas."

"I'd rather see you happy than talented in that way," Nona said sadly. "I never wanted you to follow in Lili's steps. That road is fine for the dedicated woman she is. But I wanted a better life for you than she has had. *You* would know what you'd missed. I think you do know."

She was beginning to know, Christy thought.

Nona continued wryly. "I've always believed that this genetic trait is due to something askew in the brain. It can skip generations, and I hoped it would skip you."

"So I'm brain-damaged? Thanks! But what if this is perfectly normal for everyone, and just something that's squelched out of us by our pragmatic, left-brain world, so it doesn't develop?"

"God knows, I've tried to suppress it in you, Christy, and turn you in another way."

"Sometimes I wish you'd succeeded. I'm not happy being different, so if these visions stop, I ought to feel relieved. But I wonder if they can ever really be suppressed?"

"If a talent isn't used it grows weak, fades away. So why not let it go? That's why you came to Redlands, isn't it? To escape."

"Instead, I've become more involved than I want to be. Last night I saw a rainbow—a vision of a rainbow. And it seemed to mean my own death."

"Dismiss it," Nona said, but she looked concerned.

"I don't believe anything is inevitable. This may be a warning—something I'm to watch for. But I can still make choices. I must believe that!"

"A rainbow is for joy and promise," Nona reminded her. "It's a bridge to something wonderful, and I don't mean that pot of gold."

"I know all that, but I still felt afraid, even though I seemed to be alone in the scene that came to me. As though someone had been there and was gone, or as if someone were still coming. It isn't like a dream—I'm wide awake. A premonition has a different feeling from a dream. It's much stronger. And when this happened I was sitting right here among all of you."

"There was no resolution?"

"No. The fog that often comes with such pictures drifted in and wiped everything away. Nona"—Christy roused herself—

"I wish you would paint Deirdre again. Just paint her from memory and let your brush go where it pleases. You might be able to tell us something."

Nona stared at her, and then pushed her empty plate aside. "Believe me, *I* have never encouraged this—this parlor trick, or whatever you want to call it, in myself. It's a bit like automatic writing for me. Sometimes I can't help it. I don't even know what my brush is doing, or what will appear."

"Then try it for me. Try it now! I saw a pad on the desk in the living room. You could do a sketch of Deirdre, couldn't you? And just see if anything takes over."

Nona looked as though she might refuse. Then she shrugged and stood up abruptly. Christy followed her into the living room.

Apparently, Nona had been upstairs for a while, because the furniture was back in place, and all evidence of last night had been tidied up. She went to the desk and sat down, reaching for the white pad.

"I put this here yesterday, in case I wanted to make notes," she said. "But there was really nothing specific enough to set down. Lili often uses a tape, but I didn't bring a recorder with me."

Christy sat in a nearby chair and watched Nona as she picked up a pencil, examined the point, cracking her joints. That was something Christy had loved to request as a child, and she smiled to herself as she watched her aunt relax and close her eyes.

For once, Nona wasn't fighting whatever wanted to come, and in a few moments her pencil began to move on the paper. Christy could see that she was drawing a face, though from where she sat, she couldn't make it out clearly. The old feeling of excitement crept in, as it had always done on the occasions when Nona had been willing to try this.

Now her pencil moved swiftly and with confidence. A figure took shape, filling the paper, though Christy knew better than to get up and look. Any interruption or distraction would break that flow of pencil across paper.

It was not just an outline she was drawing, but a figure dressed in jeans. Christy could see that much, but she received no feeling of Deirdre's ethereal presence, and she was sure quickly enough that Nona wasn't drawing Deirdre at all.

The pencil faltered, scribbled a meaningless line, and then seemed to fall over on the paper—released by whatever power had moved it. Nona opened her eyes.

"My God!" she said. "Look what I've drawn!"

The sketch was not as skillful as Nona would have managed with her conscious ability and it had been hurriedly done. Yet it was quite recognizable as the portrait of a young boy. A boy with Hayden's face, as he might have looked when he was about ten or eleven.

"Now why did I draw that?" Nona asked of the air about her.

Picking up the pad, Christy carried it to window light and studied it carefully. The boy's face wore an expression of grief, and Christy saw that Nona had sketched a rabbit that he held in his arms. A very limp rabbit. She brought the paper back to her aunt.

"Now I remember!" Nona said. "Though I haven't thought of it in years. There was a summer I spent out in northwest New Jersey near the little Moravian town of Hope. I went there to be with an old friend who was ill and needed me. That was the summer when you spent a couple of months with your mother—remember? So you weren't with me. Hayden and his father lived on the next farm."

"You knew him before you came here? You never told me that!"

"It never came up. But that incident has stayed with me apparently. Hayden's mother died that summer, and he was brokenhearted. I never liked Bruce Mitchell, his father, and he didn't like me. But Hayden and I became good friends. The boy was lonely and unhappy, and perhaps I was a temporary mother figure for him to talk to. I could treat him as an equal—which nobody else did."

"And the rabbit?"

"That was pretty awful. It died cruelly in a trap. Hayden had named it Maxwell, and Max was the source of the worst quarrel I ever saw between Hayden and his father. I'd never known his mother, but I gathered from one thing and another that she possessed the same genetic flaw that runs in our family, Christy. Bruce hated it. He wanted to make sure no such nonsense cropped up in his son. So any hint of precognition, anything vaguely psychic, was stamped out of the boy. His father ridiculed and raged until all that went underground. His wife couldn't help when it surfaced, but Bruce would have none of that in Hayden."

"Just as you did with me—that is, discourage it. Though you never ridiculed or got angry."

Nona's chin came up and she grimaced. "I was never as bad as Bruce! I wanted to help you, not hurt you—though I may have been wrong too."

"Did Hayden see that his rabbit was going to die?"

"Yes. He told his father one evening just before it got dark. He'd had a vision of Max caught in a trap that Bruce had set out for beavers. He *knew* what had happened, and he led his father to the very place. The trap was hardly the humane sort, and the rabbit must have died painfully. When Bruce took it out of the trap and told Hayden to bury it, the boy just stood there with the rabbit in his arms and told his father what he thought of him."

Christy could remember with all of a child's hurt the death of her own little poodle, and how she had known that the accident had happened, and even where. How strange to have this in common with Hayden.

"Of course this was the beginning of a complete estrangement between Hayden and his father," Nona went on. "The boy hated him after that, and as soon as he was able he went off on his own. When Bruce died a couple of years ago, Hayden had never forgiven him. I think he blamed him in a way for his mother's death too. The one heritage he kept from his father, and that's been working in him ever since, is a rejection of anything psychic. Whenever this crops up in himself, he rejects and stifles it. And of course that made him impatient with Deirdre's whimsies—though perhaps it was the very quality that attracted him to her in the beginning. The same sort of magic he'd glimpsed in his mother—and had come to hate in himself."

"Was that what Victor was talking about last night? When he said Hayden needed to let down his guard?"

"It's possible. Victor can't know any of this, but he senses a great deal. I suspect that Deirdre, with all her other-worldliness, was the last woman Hayden would have wanted to fall in love with. Perhaps he was drawn to the same fragility he'd known in his mother. He'd been taught to abhor his mother's gifts, but he had loved her deeply. I think Deirdre, who was a gentle, rather helpless little thing in many ways, even tried in the beginning to be the sort of wife he wanted. But her own nature could never keep her on that course. The result for Hayden has been a great deal of confusion that he's tried to suppress. It's strange that I sat down here to draw Deirdre, and pulled Hayden out of my unconscious—or whatever—instead. The boy Hayden used to be."

This might have been a bridge by which she could reach Hayden, Christy thought. But instead, it was a further barrier, and explained some of his antagonism toward her. He hadn't wanted to ask for her help, yet had been forced to, and resented that very fact. All his deeper feelings and reactions were mostly submerged, hidden. Perhaps even from himself. So that much of the time only anger remained.

"Well!" That was Lili speaking suddenly from the doorway. "I see you didn't wait breakfast, my dears. And that's perfectly all right. I'll manage for myself."

Christy could never remember her mother looking like someone who had just risen from her bed. Her hair always seemed miraculously combed. And of course her dressing gown was a designer's item—green and floaty and trimmed with real lace. Even her bedroom slippers had satin heels, and her complexion was so beautiful that she needed no makeup to look perfect at any hour of the day. Though *she* didn't believe this, and always took a great deal of time to enhance it after breakfast.

When she held out her arms to her daughter, Christy went to her as she'd always done as a little girl, and allowed herself to be folded into Lili's sweetly scented embrace. This morning, however, her water lily perfume seemed a little cloying.

"I'll get your breakfast, Mother," Christy offered—as of course someone always did—and Lili thanked her affectionately.

"Just coffee and a roll, if there are any," she said.

But before Christy went to the kitchen, Lili noticed the pad in front of Nona, with its sketch of a young Hayden. "What's this? Is it one of your channeled drawings, Nona? Of course, it's of that young man who was here last night. The one whose wife is missing. Tell me about the boy and the rabbit."

"I don't agree that it was channeled," Nona said, but while Christy fixed her mother's breakfast, she repeated the story she'd told Christy earlier.

Lili said, "Mm," and "Ah," along the way, and thanked Christy when she brought her tray into the living room.

Bright daylight poured in from windows along the valley side, unshaded by trees, and the cool morning air was heavenly. It swept out what Christy still felt was a sort of miasma left over from the night before. There had been inimical forces in the room during the session with Josef, but she had no idea of their source.

Nona stood up. "I'd better get dressed. We'll need to start back before long. When is your limo coming to Redlands for you, Lili?"

"The time was to be this afternoon," Lili said. "But I'll call and tell Brewster to cancel. I've decided to stay for a while.

Can you put me up, Nona? I think Josef and I are not yet through with what is happening here, and I want to remain until this mystery concerning Deirdre is cleared up. I have a very strong sense that Christy needs my protection—so I really must stay."

Christy felt ridiculously pleased, as she always did when her mother interrupted her own life to take care of her daughter.

Nona was less happy. "I've got plenty of room. But don't expect to be waited on, Lili. And I don't want any of your entourage coming in."

"No waiting on. No entourage. I'll send Brewster home," Lili said meekly. "Besides, I want to know more about Hayden Mitchell. You're interested in him, aren't you, Chrystal?"

Nona said sharply, "Don't meddle!"

Christy felt no surprise at her mother's perception. She even wondered if she might talk to Lili openly about matters that troubled her—without having her consult Josef. She had never been altogether convinced about channeling. Was Josef simply another, useful part of her mother—even perhaps an unconscious part? Or was he really some outside entity who had lived in the past and whose present task was to be an adviser to Liliana Dukas? The old question. Yet there had been evidence at times of knowledge on Josef's part that Lili couldn't possibly have had. So was it ESP? Or what? These, of course, were questions that both believers and non-believers had wrangled about for years, and there were fanatics on both sides. Christy neither accepted wholly nor rejected. She couldn't explain what happened in her own clairvoyant experience. How *could* she know these things? Once Josef had said to her through her mother, "You don't need to understand." But she could never accept that. She *wanted* to understand—and that was impossible in this stage of existence. One had faith, or one didn't. An open mind helped.

Lili always knew a great deal about what was happening— too much! She looked at her daughter now with her special radiance and smiled warmly. "It will all come clear for you, Chrystal dear. Just be a little patient."

Nona went off to leave them alone, and Lili drew Christy into the living room. "Tell me," she said.

"I don't know how. I don't know where to begin, because most of the time I feel confused and discouraged and—helpless. I'm not patient, the way you are. How do *you* keep so calm, no matter what happens?"

Lili's smile was warm, loving. "I haven't always managed that. When all this started to come to life in me, *I* was frightened. I didn't know how to deal with it. But my mother had been there herself, and she helped me. She told me I needed to be quiet and go down inside myself, where I could ask for help. Not that it came to me right away. But one day I touched something. I reached a place where I could feel a special joy and serenity. It isn't always easy, and I still fail at times. I had to learn to accept myself. Accept my own gifts, so I could use them. You've fought yourself all the way. You weren't ready to change, and I had to wait. Now perhaps you are ready, and help will be there—when you accept. Accept and make peace with your own nature."

Lili put her hands upon Christy's, and strength seemed to flow from her touch. Christy relaxed a little, let some of the tension fade away. She had never felt closer to her mother.

"There is a Sun Wheel," Lili said. "I think you must go there. It has something to tell you. Go as soon as you can."

In some strange way all the old resentments, old jealousies seemed to lessen and belong to the past. Until now, Christy knew, she really hadn't been ready.

"I'll go to the Sun Wheel," she told her mother. "I'll go as soon as we return to Redlands."

Christy didn't wait for lunch with her mother and aunt. As soon as they reached Nona's house, she made some excuse to Nona and fled. She went across the valley on foot, climbing up the road that ran to Victor's.

She called his name when she reached his cabin but had no answer. On the mountainside above she'd heard a car following the higher road, but there had been no other sound on the sunny air except for a few lazy bird calls. Oliver Vaughn lived up there, but the woods were thick, and since he didn't like Victor, she wouldn't be disturbed. For a little while she would sit inside the Sun Wheel and let herself dream. She would think of her mother's words and try to find her own serenity.

White sand, circling the Wheel, shone in the golden brilliance of noonday. Victor's cabin stood just below the space where Deirdre had created the Wheel. On three sides of the clearing, woods formed a dark half circle. Sun rays slanted through erratically, touching tree trunks here and there with bands of cinnamon light. Only the Wheel itself was bright in full sun.

Christy chose her quadrant carefully and sat down on the ground within the boundaries of sand and rocks. This quarter held earth energies for the south. The color of the basic stones was white, and the segment stood for children, soft winds, enlightenment. She would be safe here. Perhaps a child who was waiting to be born would come and sit beside her within this Wheel—where they might begin to know each other and the child could make the right choice. A strange whimsy, when she had for so long given up the idea of marriage and children. Yet now it was comforting. She could almost feel the caress of the soft south wind against her cheek, and the loving touch of the child on her hand.

Victor had told her that when he came upon Deirdre that last time she'd sat in the area that stood for death and the unconscious. These symbols weren't necessarily sad. They could mean a merciful release into a happier existence. Perhaps that was what Deirdre had wanted. But why? Why would life on earth have become something from which she longed to escape?

Never mind—she hadn't come here to think about Deirdre, except incidentally. She needed help for herself. She rested her forehead against her knees and closed her eyes. Meditation was part of her daily ritual, encouraged by Lili when she was a little girl. It was something Nona believed in too: to go within and shut out the world in order to find one's own deeper peace. In many ways it was a form of prayer.

She relaxed slowly, allowing anxiety and troubling questions to flow away from her. Once she reached out to touch a white stone nearby, and its sun warmth seemed to fill her with life and hope. She wanted only to be quiet and empty herself. Only then would whatever might choose to speak to her come in. If she could reach that state of charmed serenity that always surrounded Lili, the Sun Wheel might bring her the enlightenment she longed for.

When the fog began to drift in, she tried to dispel its disquieting effect. *No!* she whispered in her mind. *Not now, not here.* But of course there was never any way to stop it when the mists started to billow around her. She could only sit helplessly and watch.

Then the mist lifted, cleared, and the vision came. Again she was on top of that cliff she meant never to visit. The arch of a rainbow curved above the trees—strangely ominous, since it always seemed to predict her own death. Then someone was there with her—someone who held her in a strong, murderous grasp, moving her toward the cliff's edge.

In terror Christy cried out in her real voice, and the fog rolled in, obliterating everything.

With her face still pressed against her knees, Christy tried to quiet her trembling. The longed-for peace the Sun Wheel had given her so briefly was gone. Shaken, she opened her eyes and stared at the figure sitting on the big stone in the center of the Wheel. Victor had stepped quietly into the circle and was watching her.

"You're all right, Christy," he said quietly. "Whatever it was that frightened you, it's gone now."

"It was the future." Her voice trembled as she answered

him. "This time I've seen something before it has happened. My own death. And very soon."

"Don't accept that," he told her. "Your gift hasn't been used enough, and you may have misinterpreted. A talent needs to be exercised, not resisted. Hayden fights it too—harder than you do. Then the pictures that come are confused and misleading—perhaps even prompted by your own fears. You both need to open yourselves to the light and accept what has been given you."

She tried to shake off the sense of horror and bring herself back to the present. "Talk to me, Victor. Have you thought any more about last night?"

He didn't answer. She saw his stillness—an alert, watchful stillness—and stiffened to a sense of present danger.

Victor lowered his voice when he spoke. "Don't move or do anything sudden, Christy. We have a visitor. Turn your head slowly and look behind you. But stay where you are."

She obeyed, turning until she could see the snake coming across the grass outside the Wheel. It flowed along in its own mysterious way, its head raised and moving from side to side, its small black tongue flickering, testing whatever lay ahead. Strangely, she didn't feel frightened now, even though she could see quite clearly the copper markings on the snake's head.

Making no sound, the creature followed along the white sand and rocks that marked the Sun Wheel's circumference. Now and then it paused to explore the air inside the rim of sand and stones, but it made no effort to come across the boundary. If Victor and Christy were anything more than rocks, the snake gave no sign. When it had examined a quarter of the Wheel's rim, it seemed to lose interest, and Christy watched it glide over the grass and disappear into the woods.

She turned to look at Victor. "It's strange, but I wasn't afraid."

"You knew you were safe," he told her. "There's nothing evil about a snake. It's only trying to live its own life, and it really has very little interest in us, unless we threaten it. Besides, it would never cross the Sun Wheel's boundaries unless we invited it in."

Christy looked at him quizzically. "I'm not that close to the mystical that I can trust what you're saying."

"That's true," Victor agreed calmly. "You've lived too long away from woods and hills and unobstructed distances. But the mystical lives in you deeply, and you need to allow it the freedom to grow."

She stirred uneasily, not wholly able to accept what he was saying. "Right here where there are woods and hills and distances—all this natural beauty—some terrible happenings have surfaced. Perhaps events we might call evil—though my mother doesn't believe there is any such thing. She guards against dangers, but she forgives too much."

"Perhaps it's unwise not to believe. Maybe we need to make more moral judgments—first of all about ourselves."

"That leaves the old, unanswered question," Christy said. "How does anyone judge wisely? When we pretend that evil doesn't exist, it can grow behind our backs without any opposition. Only I haven't any idea what's good and sound in *me*, let alone in others."

Victor gazed off into the woods where the snake had disappeared. "I expect we're all a mixture of good and evil. Maybe that's what our lives are about—growing and learning how to tell between the two. In the end, we have to make choices for ourselves. It's those who never accept the mixture who become dangerous."

His tone was almost sorrowful, as though the struggle he had made in his own life to find a choice hadn't always been sound. There was often a quiet wisdom in Victor Birdcall, but there was also a great deal of regret and self-blame.

"It's strange to be afraid of a rainbow," Christy mused. "In the visions I've had recently there's always a rainbow—and it seems to be a warning."

"Warnings may be good. They can be portents to help guide

us. In any case"—he smiled—"there's a concept others have offered that you might think about: *Dying isn't dangerous.* If there is nothing afterward, you won't know the difference. But, more likely, there are still more adventures ahead—and that could be interesting."

"But I want to do so much more with my life *now.* I haven't begun yet. Not really."

"Of course it's better to live—but without fear. And there's still time for you, Christy."

How blue his eyes were—how bright and deep. Eyes that had come to him from another heritage than his Indian side.

She smiled back at him. "You're so different now from when we first met. I didn't trust you at first, and now I seem to."

"Thank you. I don't care to be easily read. Perhaps that's one of my conceits."

They were silent for a little while, dreaming within the safety of the Sun Wheel. But that couldn't last, and Christy roused herself.

"Victor, what am I to do? How can I help Hayden and Donny? I care about them both—but I can't even help myself."

"There's a possible way," he said, pointing. "Go over there into the fire quarter of the west and ask for wisdom. When you've been told what you need to know, come into the house. I'll wait for you inside. Then you can tell me what you mean to do."

She felt comfortable with him now. "Thank you, Thunderbolt Man," she said, and stepped from the gentle south quadrant into the fires of the west. Victor went away and left her there, and she sat down again on the grass. This time she crossed her legs and rested a hand on each knee, palms up and open—in the way she'd so often seen Lili do.

At first she was aware only of the woods about her, with Victor's cabin below; aware of the point where the snake had entered and lost itself among the trees, quickly camouflaged. Far overhead man-made contrails streaked white paths across the blue of an otherwise cloudless sky. Then she closed her eyes and invited the western fire to fill her and bring the wisdom to act, and to overcome her own fears.

This time when the mists cleared she saw the past. A dark-haired woman sat sketching rather crudely with a pencil. She worked quickly, so that a llama figure emerged on the pad. The woman was trying to give it human characteristics, and she smiled wryly as she worked. Not a happy smile. Christy sensed that she was trying to draw herself—though she was a writer, not an artist. Those were Rose's big, dark eyes—in caricature. The llama lips smiled as Rose had done in those photographs on her book jackets. Then the sheet was removed from the pad, and everything faded away.

Overhead the sun grew hot, and Christy felt as warm as though the western fires of the Sun Wheel had lighted her from within. Her direction had been given. Now she knew what she must do, and there must be no more delay.

She went to the back door of Victor's cabin and tapped. The door swung wide at her touch and she stepped into a room that welcomed her. She had vacationed with Nona in Western states, and she recognized some of the objects Victor had chosen for his surroundings.

Before the hearth lay a Navajo rug of brown and beige earth colors, laced with a lightning slash of turquoise blue. Zuni dolls —kachinas—rested at each end of the mantel, with a pottery bowl in the center—perhaps from Taos. Over the wooden couch an Indian blanket had been spread, adding a touch of warm reds to the room.

Christy expressed her delight. "This is perfect, Victor. It suits you."

He looked quietly pleased. "When my wife and I lived in New Mexico our house was full of plastic and chromium because that was what she wanted. I didn't care. At that time I'd grown a long way from the reservation of my grandparents and I wanted her to be happy. Here by myself I have a few things about that I really like."

How deeply did he miss his wife? Christy wondered. How

had her terrible death affected him? Especially with the after-
math of false accusation and imprisonment. He must still be
trying to work his way out of that.

Behind the couch stood a long oak table, and Victor gestured
her toward it. "Is this what you want to see?"

Spread over the surface were a number of crude sketches,
and Christy knew at a glance that this was Rose's work. She
must have intended these as a base from which Nona could
develop her more professional drawings for the llama book.

"What about your promise to Donny?"

"You have his permission. He consulted with me this morning, and I agreed that it would be a good idea if you went
through Rose's plans for the book. He trusts you not to tell
anyone else about them yet."

Christy hesitated. "How can I promise that? What if I see
something that I'll need to tell Hayden about? Or Nona? Or
anyone?"

"Then I think you would need to talk to Donny first."

"Have you gone through the sketches yourself?"

"Donny said it was okay. I think you should look through
them now, Christy. Even if they don't trigger anything con-
sciously, they may prompt you to sense something I haven't
caught. They aren't happy drawings. They're not much like
Rose Vaughn as I knew her."

Victor drew a ladder-backed chair to the table and Christy
sat down to pick up the first picture. The stream that ran
through Floris's property was recognizable, and so was a
glimpse of the high steps that climbed to her house.

The Rose llama was the heroine of the story, obviously, and
Rose must have drawn her tongue in cheek—at least in the
beginning. The first sketch showed an affectionate creature,
eager to kiss anyone who came along. In the next drawing a
human figure—clearly Oliver, as Christy could recognize by
his handsome profile—stood at the fence, and Rose's long llama
neck reached over the top rail, and she was kissing him on the
cheek. It seemed a teasing gesture more than a loving one, and

Oliver's response seemed to be displeasure. Christy felt suddenly uneasy. Rose hadn't been joking in these drawings—there was a certain mockery here. Perhaps of herself, first of all.

The Deirdre llama was recognizable at once, and Rose had not been flattering. She was recognizable in her Deirdre role because she was dressed in lace and furbelows, and her llama hoofs wore open sandals, but she seemed a giddy, distraught creature. Fastened on her forehead like a diadem was a sparkling crystal. Rose had sketched in the rays that represented its shining center. The Herkimer?

Behind the Deirdre figure came a small boy llama, lovingly depicted as Donny—no satire here. Behind him pranced a small creature that was clearly a cat—Sinh pictured as herself.

There were no pages of text to accompany the drawings—perhaps Rose would have done those later. *If* she ever intended this as a book, which Christy was beginning to doubt.

As she turned the sheets, a male llama came trotting along outside the fence. He wore Hayden's glowering face, as he seemed to observe what was going on in the llama pen. Oliver appeared to be ordering him away, indignant with his presence, perhaps protecting the females.

The next sketch was of an adoring Eve llama, all her attention focused on Oliver. This seemed a cruel sketch, and Christy wondered about the friendship that was supposed to have existed between the two women, in spite of Oliver.

Christy held the sketch up to Victor. "This was never intended to be developed into a book for children, was it?"

"I'm sure it wasn't. I don't think it was intended for any publication. Maybe therapy for Rose. Keep going."

Christy picked up the next picture, startled. This was of Floris, and she was not portrayed as one of her own llamas but as an elderly witch. She wore a peaked hat, her chin elongated, as was her nose. She held the conventional broomstick in both hands and was waving it aloft. Rose had certainly not felt affectionate toward Floris when she drew this sketch. But who was the Floris witch threatening? There was no other figure in the picture.

Three more sketches remained. Again Eve appeared, and she was trying to kiss Oliver, though he didn't look interested. Rose had drawn the Eve llama with bangs and an untidy hairdo and, from under the frowsy hair, wide eyes looked pleadingly at Oliver. This was hardly unexpected, since Rose knew very well that she had taken Oliver away from her best friend, who had expected to marry him. Strangely, Oliver didn't seem to be interested in either of these two.

The next sketch was of a llama wearing an Indian kachina mask over his head and covering his long neck. He seemed to be an observer, taking no part in the action.

Christy looked at Victor, tapping the drawing. "Apparently Rose didn't think of you as a participant in whatever was happening?"

"She was right," Victor said. "Perhaps if I hadn't stood apart, tried not to get involved—" He shrugged and let the matter go.

The last finished sketch was of Deirdre, again as a llama. But, this was the strangest drawing of all, for this creature seemed frightened and wild-eyed. Her forepaws were trampling her own lacy garments, and the crystal diadem was askew over one ear. Nearby, the small boy llama watched her in terror, and he was crying. Sinh, still a cat, clung to Deirdre's shoulder with claws dug in, and her look was as wild as that of her mistress.

Only one more sheet with an unfinished sketch remained— just the face of Deirdre as herself, with tears rolling across her cheeks, and her mouth curved down in a mask of tragedy.

Christy stacked the sheets and set them down. "What was Rose up to? What did she mean?"

Victor gestured toward several objects hung in a row along one wall. They were Indian masks he must have collected over the years, and each one wore a different expression human, yet distorted.

"Yes," Christy said. "All those masks we wear! But Rose was

dipping behind the masks. She saw something ugly she was trying to set down. I wonder why?"

Victor returned the sketches to a large manila envelope. "She must have held in a lot of unhappiness she never showed anyone."

"If truth lies in these drawings," Christy said, "she was still in love with Oliver and he was pretty aloof and maybe upset about something himself."

"Don't try to read more than is there," Victor warned. "If you start to interpret, you may go down the wrong road."

"This might even mean that Rose was so unhappy and desperate that she committed suicide."

"Or that she had become such a threat to someone that she was killed deliberately? So now we're guessing again, and it's no good, Christy."

"There always seems to be a deep anger in Oliver," Christy went on, paying no attention because she had to speculate—she had to discover the key. "I wonder if Rose was afraid of him? And I don't understand the two views of Deirdre—the happy Deirdre and the one with the sorrowful, weeping face in the unfinished sketch."

"You'll never find your answers that way. You have the power to understand, Christy, if only you'll use it. Perhaps you have it even more than your mother. But you block yourself by trying to force your conscious mind to solve everything. Why are you afraid to trust yourself?"

She rested her elbows on the table and pressed her forehead against clasped hands. "Because I've never wanted this—gift. Even when I was a little girl, my friends thought I was weird. I always wanted to be like everyone else. Nona understood. She did her best to suppress this in me."

"Nona's a remarkable woman, but I think she didn't understand. Or maybe she wouldn't allow herself to understand or accept. In herself, or in you. The talent is there, waiting, and it's better to use it. Look, Christy—while I make some tea—you sit there and put your hands on that stack of drawings. Let *them* tell you."

For a moment she wanted only to push Rose's sketches away. But Victor had stepped into his adjoining kitchen and was paying no more attention. Hesitantly, she did as he'd suggested and rested her hands on the drawings. She closed her eyes and quieted her thoughts, allowing herself to open, to be inwardly ready for whatever might come. The only times she'd ever used this in the past were for the police—and on a few occasions here. But this seemed different. The sensation that trembled through her was something she'd never felt before.

This time there were no mists, no vision emerging. She was no longer Christy Loren. It was as though she occupied some other body, some other mind. Her thoughts were sad, frightened, confused. There was some terrible knowledge that she must resist and fight against. Danger was very near—a threat she didn't know *how* to resist. She must escape—flee from this prison that held her, though there seemed no way. Something, someone, stronger—someone ruthless—would never let her go. She had no key to the lock on the door.

A cry of agony sounded in Christy's mind: *Help me! Help me!*

Perhaps she cried out herself, as she'd done in the Sun Wheel, because Victor came quickly from the kitchen and put his hands on her shoulders. "It's all right, Christy. You're here. Nothing can touch you or hurt you."

She opened her eyes and looked at him. "Rose was afraid for her life. She knew someone would try to kill her. But that's all I know. For a moment I was inside Rose crying out for help."

"You didn't get any hint of who was threatening her?"

"Nothing," Christy told him.

"Then relax. Come and sit in my kitchen."

She sat at a square wooden table and drank raspberry tea Victor had poured into a blue mug. The bread he'd baked was sprouted grain and delicious. Since she'd skipped lunch the food tasted wonderful. She would think of nothing except how hungry she was. Victor had been wrong. There was no point at all to her encouraging her "talent." She only wanted to be through with all that.

Then, just at the moment when she rejected and denied, a new conviction possessed her, and shook her so that her hands trembled, spilling tea on the table.

"It wasn't Rose I went inside of just now!" she cried. "It was Deirdre!"

I know Rose was working on another book—a book about lla-mas. Before she put words down for the story, she used to draw little caricature sketches that an artist could later base real illustrations on. Once she showed me a single sketch. There weren't any llamas in that one—it was just Deirdre's face—like a mask—and she was crying. That was a face she never showed anyone, but Rose had guessed.

Rose let me see the sketch to let me know how much she'd suspected about what she called Deirdre's "pain and suffer-ing." Idiotic, of course. Deirdre never had any real depth for either joy or sorrow, even though she cried easily. But Rose told me there were more sketches that tried to tell the truth about Redlands. Now I wonder if any of those drawings might point to me.

Of course I never really intended what happened. It was one of those spontaneous explosions, for which I couldn't be re-sponsible. Rose brought it on herself. It happened suddenly, unexpectedly, that last time we walked together in the woods. I can still hear the way she screamed as she fell—a perfect pun-ishment for what she'd done. Of course there was no one about to hear her or see me there.

Later, after my exultation wore off, I was a bit shaken. I hadn't planned this and it happened too quickly for me to take precautions. I didn't remember the drawings until later, when I began to worry about them; about what they might reveal. But they didn't turn up among her things—I searched for *them thoroughly. They must be somewhere around—I don't think she destroyed them.*

Rose was very close to Donny. I never liked that, because you can't trust small children. What if she let him keep them for her? I wonder if I can find out without giving everything away?

If he has them, *he must never put those sketches in Christy's hands. Especially not that one of Deirdre crying. I know who can help me—who* must *help me. Guilt makes a wonderful weapon. I'm glad it has never been a problem for me. I'm certainly not to blame for what has happened. People bring disaster upon themselves.*

I still have that amusing notion to try, and I think now is the time.

13

"HELLO? HELLO?" The call came to them from outside the cabin, and Victor went to let Eve in.

Rose had caught Eve's characteristics very well in her drawings. At the moment she looked much like the frowsy-haired llama in the sketch. She seemed surprised to find Christy in Victor's cabin, though she hardly greeted her, being anxious to pour out her concern to Victor.

"Have you seen anything of Oliver? I've just been up to his house, and I can't rouse him. He told me last night that he was going to stay home and work on something he's writing. And his car is outside. But he didn't answer when I called and knocked. I know he was upset over what happened on Wintergreen."

"I haven't seen him today," Victor said, sounding curt. He didn't like Eve—with good reason—and resented her intrusion.

Eve hardly noticed because of her own distraction. "Will you come up to Oliver's house with me, Victor? I really think we should go inside and have a look. But I don't want to do it alone."

"No," Victor told her flatly. "Oliver wouldn't welcome my snooping around. And I don't think you should go up there either. Let him alone."

Christy had been watching Eve, but now something drew her attention to Victor. His guard was up again, as though he protected himself in some way.

Eve said, "Look, Victor, this isn't my imagination. Oliver and

I have been friends for a long time. I've known him since Rose and I were young. I'm very worried about him."

"Maybe you should leave it alone," Victor said. "Let him work it out in his own way."

Eve moved impatiently about the room, though she hardly seemed to be registering what she saw. Rose's sketches lay on the table, but fortunately Victor had returned them to their envelope. Christy could imagine how eagerly Eve would have leafed through those drawings.

Now she took down one of the Zuni dolls and examined it—an action that merely occupied her hands, not her mind. "He's in terrible trouble—I'm sure of it. He needs our help."

"Maybe it's trouble he wants to keep to himself," Victor said flatly. "He won't thank anyone who barges in to interfere."

Eve set the doll back in place and swung around. "You know something, don't you? You've seen something? You're close enough to his house."

"I don't look where concealment is intended," Victor said. "I mind my own business."

Christy asked a question. "Eve, is it something connected with Rose's death that's worrying you?"

"I thought *you* were supposed to be psychic!" Eve snapped. "So why don't you tell me?"

"It doesn't work that easily—not on demand."

Eve began to search through her jacket pockets almost frantically. What she drew out was a small silver lighter. "Oliver forgot this the last time he visited me—just a few days ago. He smoked that pipe of his a lot and used his lighter. Here, Christy —hold it in your hands and see if it tells you anything."

Victor saw Christy's hesitation. "Maybe you'd better try. Perhaps we'll know then if we should interfere."

Her fingers closed upon the lighter as Eve pressed it into her hand, and at once the throbbing started in her temples, the feeling of nausea. She sensed water—a lifeless body in water. Death. Murder? The lighter burned her fingers as though she touched flame. She flung it from her, and dropped onto the couch with its red blanket that now seemed on fire. Yet at the same time she shivered with cold.

"What is it?" Eve cried. "What did you see?"

For a few moments she couldn't speak, and Victor came to sit beside her. "Think of the Sun Wheel and let yourself be quiet. Tell us what you saw, Christy."

Somehow she managed to steady herself. "I saw something dead floating in a pond. I couldn't see clearly and I don't know if it was Oliver. There was an awful feeling of fright, of violent death."

"Where?" Eve cried. "Where is this pond?"

"I think I can find it," Christy said, helpless to resist the tide that swept her along. She had no choice. This was like all the other times when she had led the police to a body. The headache, the nausea, the urgency that she was forced to follow—all were the same.

Victor changed his mind. "I'll come with you," he said. "Shall we go in my car?"

"No. We must follow the path above your house. Yes, Victor, please come with me."

When Christy and Victor hurried out the back door, Eve followed, frightened and anxious.

A narrow, winding, uphill path overgrown with vines, as though little used, drew her along. She had known it would be there. The climb was steep and Christy was breathing quickly when she stepped into a clearing around what must be Oliver Vaughn's house.

"There's no pond up here!" Eve cried.

Christy stood looking at the gray-shingled house while a dreadful anticipation grew in her. It was always like this. The tension increased as she neared her goal—increased until it could be released in discovery.

A flight of stone steps led to the front door, and she went up them quickly. The house was silent—lifeless. That was the way it should be—a *dead* silence.

"You said a pond!" Eve's voice shook, and Victor touched her arm.

"Steady," he said. "Let Christy do her thing."

The front door was unlocked—which wasn't unusual—and Christy went inside. She crossed the living room with the others following, and started up the stairs. She was hardly aware of the bedroom she walked through—a bedroom Oliver must have shared with Rose. The bathroom door stood open, and she knew now why she had seen water. Not a pond.

"In here," she said.

Victor went ahead of the two women and stood blocking the door. "Maybe you'd better not come any further."

Neither Eve nor Christy paid any attention. They both pushed past him into the room.

In death, Oliver was no longer a beautiful man. He lay naked in the tub, and a bar of soap had been dissolving in the water near him. He was not floating—the water was too shallow—but lying back, and his features were contorted in terror. Worst of all, he was not the only dead thing in the water. A copperhead snake lay under the surface—as lifeless as Oliver.

When Eve would have rushed toward the tub, Victor held her back. "There's nothing you can do. We'll go down to my place and call the sheriff."

He pushed Eve out of the house and caught her arm as she stumbled on the steps. When he looked back at Christy, she nodded.

"I'm all right. Go ahead."

The throbbing in her temples and the sickness had stopped, as always happened once the horror she'd been directed toward was fully exposed. Only then could she be released. She felt weak and hardly able to think, but the pain and distress were gone. Yet this experience was worse than the others, because this was the first time she had found someone she had known in life.

Passing the Sun Wheel, Christy longed to step into its safe boundaries and let its healing power flow through her. But she knew she must never take such turmoil into the Wheel. First, she must cleanse herself of what was seared into her vision. There was a ritual she had worked out, and a prayer she could say, but those would come later.

When Victor had phoned the sheriff's office, Christy called her aunt and told her what had happened. "No, we don't know how he died. There—there was a copperhead in the water with him. I suppose he could have been bitten."

Victor shook his head as she set down the phone. "I don't think so. I didn't see any of the signs of swelling, and if he'd been bitten he'd have gone for help as fast as he could. Christy, are you able to carry this any further and tell us how it happened?"

Eve was in a state of shock and she hadn't stopped pacing the room, but now she came toward Christy anxiously.

But Christy shook her head. "I don't know how, Victor. The pictures always stop after someone is found. There's nothing more."

Victor poured brandy for all of them, and Eve drank hers at a swallow.

"He had a bad heart," she said miserably. "Rose told me that once, though Oliver always kept quiet about it. What if the snake got into the water and frightened him to death?"

In the end, that was the verdict at which the police arrived. Oliver had died of a heart attack, and the doctor in Waynesboro, to whom he had been going for several years, verified the heart problem. As Eve had said, it was quite likely that the copperhead had slipped into the tub and frightened him. Though copperheads disliked water. Where the snake had come from was anybody's guess, but not unusual in the area. Sometimes snakes crawled into houses when no one had any idea how they got in. The official verdict was death by accident. No one suggested that the snake might have been put deliberately into the water with him.

For Christy, however, the suggestion of murder had been

powerful, and she at least had no doubt. But there was no point in saying anything, when only her vision was involved. She had the strong feeling that Eve knew more about Oliver than she was telling. Even though Eve managed to evade all questions and seemed stunned by her own grief, Christy sensed conceal-ment. It was enough for the police that Eve, who had long been Oliver's friend and his wife's friend, should have been concerned about him and had asked Victor and Christy to go up to his house with her.

Though of course Christy told Lili and Nona of her premoni-tion, and Nona decided to tell Hayden. No one else knew. Floris claimed that her animals had been strangely restless around the time of Oliver's death. They had hummed in alarm, with no visible outward cause to upset them. But llama emo-tions weren't likely to be used as evidence.

A few days after Oliver's death, Hayden phoned Christy and asked if he could talk with her. She agreed to have dinner with him, not altogether sure whether she looked forward to being with him or simply dreaded whatever he might have to say.

A strange thing happened shortly before Hayden called for her that evening. Donny turned up on the back deck outside her room, tapping on the glass doors. Sinh had come with him, and she let them both in. He didn't explain his presence at once, and she let him watch while she fastened on the dangling amethyst earrings her mother had given her long ago. She could remember her mother's words.

Amethysts help you to get in touch with your own inner being. They open up one's psychic centers, and they guard against outward manifestation of harm. Wear them for protec-tion.

Tonight she had need of amethysts.

Donny said, "My mother used to let me watch when she combed her hair and put on her earrings."

Christy knew he had come for some special reason, and she waited, giving him time. Sinh seemed as uneasy as Donny, and carefully avoided Christy. She sat by the door, her blue eyes regarding the room suspiciously.

"I saw my mother again," Donny said. "I saw her this morning, and she told me she knows who put the snake in the water with Oliver."

Christy made no foolish effort at denial. She sat very still, watching the boy's reflection in the dressing-table mirror. "Did she tell you who it was?" she asked.

Donny shook his head. "She said it was better if I didn't know, and she said I shouldn't tell my father I'd seen her. But I need to tell somebody, and nobody else believes that I really do see her."

"*Are* you sure it was your mother, Donny?"

"I never see her close up, because she always stays back in the trees. I just see her moving in the shadows. But I know it's my mother. I know how she sounds."

"*You* would know her voice, if anyone did," Christy said.

"She won't let me come close or touch her. But this time it seemed as though she'd run away from something and was scared she'd be caught. I had the feeling that she was awfully frightened. I want to help her, but I don't know how. I tried to ask Victor about this, but he's acting strange and he doesn't want to talk about her at all."

"Thank you for telling me, Donny. I wish I could really help you."

"I heard Nona tell my father about the way you knew ahead of time that Oliver was dead, and you knew where to look. So why can't you find Deirdre? I mean really find her, so I can be with my mother again."

He came so close that Christy caught his outdoor odor—a small-boy-in-from-playing odor. But Donny was not like any small boy she'd ever known, and she didn't dare hug him casually. He always seemed to stand apart on his own—independent, yet touchingly in need. When she saw Hayden tonight she must talk to him about his son.

She tried to explain. "Those times when I've held something

of your mother's, I never received any pictures that would lead me to her."

What she had received was the strong feeling of death, but that was something she couldn't tell Donny. Not until she was sure.

The boy went toward the sliding doors, picking up the cat, who perched willingly on his shoulder. Donny nuzzled her, and Sinh began to purr like any ordinary cat.

"Once my mother said that if she died she'd like to come back inside Sinh. Do you think she could do that, Christy?"

That conceit had already occurred to her. However, Donny didn't really expect an answer.

He went on softly. "Sometimes I think she really is dead, and it's only her spirit that comes and talks to me." He slipped through the doors and disappeared, the cat clinging to his shoulder.

Christy closed the doors upon the twilight of early summer and the uproar of crickets and tree frogs, wishing more than anything else that the mystery surrounding Deirdre could be resolved. But visions seldom came to her in words—only in pictures, and whenever she tried to concentrate on Deirdre, the glimpses that appeared were quickly erased by mists, leaving her with a sense of confusion.

Before she went upstairs to meet Hayden, she took out the drawing Nona had done of him—boy and rabbit—and folded it into her purse. She had saved it from that morning on Wintergreen, not quite sure why. Perhaps merely because it paralleled in Hayden her own childhood experience, and she wondered if she dared show it to him.

Nona was busy in the kitchen when Christy went upstairs, and Lili lent her presence, if not her help, at the kitchen table —something she always did gracefully. On this visit Christy had grown closer to her mother, and she was grateful for the new understanding between them. Lili would always remain elusive, but for the first time Christy recognized that her mother was there for her in a time of need. But now she was growing restless and ready to return to her own busy life. It was time for her daughter to let her go. Oliver's death had sent Lili into several sessions with Josef, but he had been philosophical and non-specific about the whole event. In fact, he seemed to regard the matter with a certain distaste. To Josef, death had little significance, though he regretted the rather messy ways in which earth mortals died.

When Hayden arrived, his mood seemed quiet and subdued. Christy had seen little of him since Oliver's death, and he'd never talked to her about it. She'd have liked the chance to open up with him, and perhaps tonight . . .

However, when they were in his Jeep following the winding mountain road to Nellysford he had little to say, and Christy grew uncomfortable, wondering why they were doing this and what he intended.

The Stoney Creek Café was popular locally, not only being the nearest restaurant around, but because it was attractive with its decorations of pottery and baskets, and with friendly service and good food. They sat in a booth where they could talk privately, and since they were early, the rooms were quiet.

When they'd ordered, Hayden seemed to make an effort—as though the subject he wanted to talk about was distasteful but necessary.

"Nona told me, Christy, about how you and Eve and Victor found Oliver. She said you'd had one of those experiences when you knew exactly where to look. Can you tell me about it?"

She had wanted to talk to him, yet now that he was probing so earnestly, she felt unsure.

"Nona's already told you. So what do you want to know?"

He sought for words. "I don't mean just about what happened—though it must have been pretty bad. I mean—how did you *feel*? How did the picture come to you?"

"Eve gave me a lighter of Oliver's and the moment I took it in my hand I knew he was dead—*in water*. It was there in my mind—though not clear in detail, since I thought it must be a pond of some sort, not a bathtub. As for how I felt—if you mean literally—my head hurt and I was nauseated. That often happens. The pressure isn't released until I follow through and go wherever I am led. I have no choice if I want the pain to stop. I never know ahead of time exactly where I'm going. I'm somehow pulled in a certain direction, as though I followed a compass inside me until I come to whatever is to be found."

Hayden listened gravely, and she wished she had more to offer—both to him and to Donny.

He puzzled aloud. "Yet, though both your mother and you feel that Deirdre is dead, your compass doesn't work to find her. I wonder why not?"

She shook her head unhappily. He was there across the table, and they were separated by a gulf. "I don't know. Whenever I try to focus on Deirdre, there's such confusion, something so frightening, that I never find a clear direction I can take."

He seemed less impatient now, more thoughtful. "I've been wondering if I could do this myself, Christy. Victor thinks I have it in myself to find the way. But I have no idea how to coax it out of hiding—if it's there at all."

"Sometimes meditation can help," Christy said. "Going down into the quiet inside of us—letting everything else go. Then, sometimes, pictures come—for me, at least."

"Those are only words. They don't tell me how. Though I'm ready to try anything."

"That sounds desperate—and desperation never works."

He shrugged and let the matter go.

A waitress brought fresh green salads and a lazy Susan of assorted dressings. When she'd gone, Christy told him of Donny's visit and the boy's continued conviction that his mother was alive and that he'd met and talked to her.

"I think he wants to tell you," she finished, "but he's afraid you won't believe him. This time he said something strange— that Deirdre had told him she knew who put the snake in Oliver's bath, but she wouldn't tell him who it was."

"My God! I wonder if that's possible, and she really is alive? I'll talk to him tonight."

"Only if you can do it gently, I don't think he really knows anything, but it might be a relief for *him* to talk to you."

"I've lost touch with my son," Hayden said sadly. "Maybe I should never have doubted him. Once, late at night, when I was downstairs, I had the feeling that Deirdre was on the deck watching me through the windows. But when I went outside no one was there. Afterward, I wondered if I'd fallen asleep on the couch and it was only a dream. I've had some strange dreams lately. Christy, you told me about your recurrent dream. Have you had it again?"

"Yes. And I've seen places similar to the one I've dreamed about. I'm always going down that red path with high walls on either side. I can hear footsteps and I know someone is following me. Yet lately, I don't know whether it's the follower I'm afraid of, or some hazy figure that waits for me ahead. I only know that I wake up terrified."

Absently, she touched the earrings Lili had given her, and Hayden noted the gesture.

"Amethyst," he said. "I can remember that my mother wore amethyst a lot. She told me that it was for protection against evil."

It was reassuring that he could speak to her like this, not dismissing his mother's belief. After a moment he went on.

"I had a dream recently that seems to have some of the same elements as yours. I was walking through woods toward that rocky cliff from which Rose fell. I seemed to know that something terrible was happening there—something that would destroy whatever happiness might still be left for me in the future. You were there. Somehow you were a part of it. You were with someone that I thought was Deirdre. Either your death or hers was about to happen. It was as if you were trying to save each other, and I had the overpowering sensation of being too late. Then I woke up and couldn't even be sure what it was I'd feared so terribly. Can you make anything of this?"

She was silent, sensing the man even more than his words. When she didn't see him for days, she thought about him, and watched for any glimpse she might have of him. Yet now that she was with him, she must be constantly on guard against her own feelings. Chemistry! But only for her and not for him. Because there was still Deirdre—whom he loved and did not love, but from whom he would never be released until he knew what had happened to her. And perhaps not then.

"I can't make anything of anything," she told him wearily.

"I know. That's the way I feel most of the time. There have been two deaths, probably three, in this small community in a short period of time. Two supposedly accidental, and one unresolved. Don't you sense anything at all about this, Christy?"

She answered almost without volition, automatically, surprising herself. "I believe someone pushed Rose Vaughn so that she fell to her death. I don't know what happened to Deirdre. I only know that I felt a terrible sense of evil, of wicked intent, when I held her scarf in my hands. And I know that murder was the cause of Oliver's death. That came to me clearly before we found him. Someone put that copperhead into his tub and he died of fright." She had said nothing new, yet the words had poured out of her as though they must.

When her hands began to shake, she set down her fork, able to eat nothing more. Hayden reached across the table and took both her hands in his own warm ones.

"I'm sorry, Christy. I shouldn't have done this to you. You never asked for any of this. But I don't know where to turn or what to do. The sheriff's satisfied and won't look any further. But there is *something* loose among us. That's true, isn't it?"

She drew her hands away gently because if he went on holding them she might start to cry. Senselessly—because she was sorry for herself, and there was no point in that indulgence. She wanted so much more from him than what he considered a comforting gesture.

"Why *don't* you try to solve this yourself, Hayden?" she asked directly.

Quick irritation sounded in his voice. "What am I supposed to do?"

"Let your father's side of you go—all that anger that comes too quickly and only defeats what you truly want. Go back into the feelings your mother left you. Nona told me about that summer she spent in New Jersey. The summer your mother died—when Nona first got to know you as a boy, and met your father." *And your rabbit died,* she thought, but didn't speak the words.

By this time their meal had been more or less eaten, the table cleared and coffee brought. Hayden stirred his coffee inattentively.

"Nona shouldn't have told you any of that," he said, still irritated.

Because it was so personal, hurtful, private? Probably all of that, yet he needed to talk and let out some of that old turmoil and pain. He needed to share feelings so long held back, whether he could accept that or not. Christy took the folded drawing from her purse and spread it open between them on the table.

"Nona sketched this up at Wintergreen after everyone else was gone. Sometimes she does these automatic drawings— letting whatever wants to appear come out on paper. I asked her to see if she could find Deirdre that way. Instead she did this of you. She told me about the rabbit, and how you knew ahead of time that it had died. The same thing happened to me when I was little. I had a pet poodle I loved a lot—and it was killed by a car. When it happened, I *knew*— and that was when my mother realized that I had her gift. If that's what I'm supposed to call it. Perhaps you do have this too, even though Nona said your father was set against it. Victor says that such a gift needs to be exercised. Nona's discouragement may have kept mine from being as useful as it might be. As your father's did with you. But it's there inside us, Hayden, and I don't think we can help by suppressing it. If we both let down our guard and let it come, perhaps we'll find out about Deirdre."

He listened without interrupting and without his usual impatience, staring at the drawing of the boy and the dead rabbit. Christy watched his face as she talked, and for once all his defenses were down. His expression had changed from quick anger, until by the time she'd finished he looked almost like the young boy in the drawing—lost and lonely and sorrowful.

"I don't know where to begin," he repeated. "I don't know how."

"Maybe you start by praying a little. Ask for help. It's there. Ask what you can do. And I'll do the same. We both need to stop fighting this."

"It's not your problem," he told her. "You'd be better off going away. You're there in that dream I had, and you're in danger—as you are in your dream."

So absorbed were they that they didn't see Nona until she stood beside their table. "Thank God I found you!" she cried. "Lili's outside and she's frantic. Josef wants to talk to you right away!"

I'm not sure what to do—though I'm in no immediate danger of discovery. I didn't intend for him to die. I knew Oliver was afraid of snakes, and when I dropped that dead one into his bathwater, I thought I'd give him a good scare. Then he wouldn't do what he threatened, because he'd be afraid of me —of what I might do next. I had to keep him under control. But he went into a heart attack and died before I could rescue him.

Luckily, the police never got the whole picture. Though copperheads hate water, it all seemed too obvious for any serious investigation. Snakes sometimes get into houses, and no one knows how. If others are suspicious, they're not talking. Though that worries me. What if they're plotting something? Oliver always did his best to keep me posted—now I must work in the dark. There are matters to take care of before I can leave safely.

Of course the Wintergreen affair was a fizzle. Theatrical but pointless. Josef isn't a very good alter ego for Lili to use. He's pompous and hates to be clear. Oliver thought it all nonsense, yet because of me he was getting frightened.

Now I must find those drawings before anyone else sees them. I wonder if I dare repeat my performance with Donny and ask him for them? The mimicry is almost perfect—he hasn't caught on to me yet. I've managed to convince him that if he comes too close I'll disappear.

One thing went very wrong. Deirdre got away from me for a short time, and she talked to Donny. Not that it really matters, because no one will believe a little boy. Still, I must be on guard, so that it doesn't happen again.

I must also hunt for the book that Oliver showed me that time, and then hid from me. He had it marked up with notes in the margin, and it was supposed to worry me. He even said he might mail it anonymously to Hayden. He really thought he could hold that over my head. A stupid man, Oliver, though I thought him so beautiful at first—so fascinating. It's just as well that he's gone. I was mistaken about him from the first.

Once the drawings and the book are out of the way, I can take the next step. I've given Christy enough rope. None of these psychics are effective. Deirdre believed in all that, but I don't. Josef is as phony as the rest. And Deirdre is where she can't get away from me again.

Sooner or later I must be rid of her entirely. She's more dangerous to me than Christy. The problem is—how? She must be disposed of without leaving a trace, so the mystery of her disappearance will never be solved. But that's not easy—though I can't leave this place until it is done.

14

T HE STRIP of stores that edged the shopping center in
Nellysford was divided at one point by an alley that had
been made into a small park. Low wooden benches invited,
and new plantings made it an attractive spot. The entire shopping area was well lighted, and tonight a big moon sailed
overhead, silvering the dark hills beyond the highway.

Liliana Dukas sat on a bench, waiting for them. For once she
hadn't dressed for the occasion, but had come in slacks and an
embroidered Filipino blouse under an open cardigan. The eve
ning was cool and clear and this space seemed set apart from
shops and shoppers. No one else was using it at the moment,
and Nona led the way to where Lili waited.

She looked up and smiled at her sister. "Good! You found
them, Nona. Josef knew you would. Do sit down, all of you, and
I'll try to reach him."

Christy sat opposite her mother, and Hayden slid along the
bench beside Christy. Nona seemed uncomfortable and unable to sit still. She walked up and down beside the benches,
her tension evident.

Once more Lili went through her ritual of prayer and request for help. Then she sat very still with her hands folded in
front of her. The silence grew endlessly long. Christy watched
cars turning in and out of the parking spaces nearby, yet they
seemed to occupy a different, faraway world. Only this small
circle waiting for Josef seemed real. Though when his voice
came through Lili, Christy jumped in spite of herself. Hayden
put a quieting hand on her arm and they listened intently.

"You have embarked on an earthly search," Josef proclaimed. "It is necessary to find that for which you search as quickly as possible. Much harm has already been done, and one of you is in grave danger."

Josef's voice faded out, and Nona spoke for all of them, since Lili, in a sense, was elsewhere.

"Can you tell us which one is in danger?" she asked.

"You will know when it is time. Your paths lead toward the same goal in different ways. Once they converge, there is danger and possible death. But there are always free choices within the pattern."

Once more Christy felt impatient with Josef, and she wished Lili were not so devoted to this particular entity.

"You're talking in riddles, Josef," she told him. "I think you enjoy riddles. Tell us what to *do*—where to look. Help us to find the way!"

He didn't seem annoyed by her words, but then that was one of the virtues of existing on another energy plane. One was never upset by foolish mortals.

"Part of the answer lies with the llamas," he said. "There is a woman who will try to prevent you from finding what you seek."

"Do you mean Floris Fox?" Nona asked.

"You will find the answer with the llamas."

"But we don't even know what we should look for!" Christy cried. "Help us, Josef!"

Josef was silent and they couldn't be sure if he was still listening.

Hayden asked a question, sounding matter-of-fact. "You said *part* of the answer lies in the llamas, Josef. Where will we find the other part?"

"There is a man. He is bound by his own fears and his own beliefs. He is of American Indian heritage. This man knows more than he understands, and he keeps his secrets well."

"You're talking about Victor Birdcall now?" Nona said. "Do you mean that he's not to be trusted—that he is part of the evil things that have happened?"

"This you must find out. He has yet to speak out about what he has seen."

Josef went away with his usual aggravating suddenness, and Lili stirred and stretched, looking a little dazed, as she always did after such a session.

"I heard it all," she told them. "But I don't understand any more than you do. Please take me back to your house, Nona. I think it is nearly time for me to return to my own life. Josef will have nothing more to say. He has given you something to work on, and he knows you must finish this on your own."

Christy and Hayden walked with her as Nona led the way to the station wagon, bright with its brave rainbow decals. When they'd watched Nona and Lili drive away, Christy spoke helplessly.

"What do you make of all that?"

Hayden's smile was wry. "As Josef says, there is always a choice. Victor or Floris—which one do we talk to first, and when?"

"He didn't really say we should talk to Floris," Christy pointed out. "He only spoke of the llamas."

"Who aren't going to tell us very much. So we'd better try Victor. Shall we see him tonight? It's not awfully late."

"Yes, let's. He may really have seen something he isn't talking about, since his cabin's pretty close to Oliver's house."

They drove back through the mountains, the lights of little houses along the road shining in the darkness, and the Jeep's headlights carving the way ahead. Dark hills and valleys rose and fell mysteriously around them in the moonlight, sometimes without any habitation at all.

When they reached Redlands and followed the way across the valley up toward Victor's, they could see the lights from his cabin through the trees. He must have heard them pull up in the clearing in front, but he didn't come to look out. They went up the steps together, and Hayden knocked.

Victor opened the door, and Hayden and Christy stepped into the main room of the cabin. He had lighted a fire as the night air cooled, and its flames cast shimmering shadows over the papers he had spread out upon the floor. Christy recognized Rose Vaughn's rough sketches for her book.

"Perhaps that's what Josef meant," she said to Hayden. "Not the real llamas, but these."

Victor stood beside them. "Another interview with Josef?"

Hayden nodded. "Yes, and he told us to come to you. What is all this?" He gestured toward the drawings.

As Christy explained, Hayden knelt to look at them, picking each up in turn. He smiled sadly at the first Deirdre sketch.

"Rose caught her very well. Deirdre would love this. She could laugh at herself. Sometimes."

"I wonder how well you knew Deirdre?" Victor asked softly.

Addressed to Deirdre's husband, that seemed a startling question, but Hayden didn't look surprised. "Sometimes I didn't know her at all. And often, just when I believed I could reach her, she slipped away and eluded me."

Christy dropped down beside Hayden so that she could study Rose's sketches again. There was the Deirdre llama, coquettish in lace and ribbons. Then the later one with her crystal diadem askew, her fragile garments trampled, and Donny nearby crying, Sinh on his shoulder, looking wild as she watched her mistress. This drawing troubled Hayden, though he didn't comment.

"What did Josef come up with this time?" Victor asked.

"He only mentioned your Indian background," Hayden said. "He told us that you know more than you understand—whatever that means."

"Or perhaps I understand more than I really know." Victor went to lean against the mantel, his arm resting between a Zuni doll and the Indian pottery. He seemed to have gone off into one of his own deep silences.

Christy's impatience crept into her voice. "Don't go inscrutable on us! If you know anything about Oliver that would help, please tell us."

For a moment longer he stood looking into the fire. Then he

went to his desk across the room and picked up another draw-ing. "I didn't show you this one, Christy. But now you'd better see it. Though I'd rather not have shown it to Hayden."

Christy took the sketch and studied it in dismay. Rose had drawn the Deirdre llama again, this time with long, fluttering lashes and a look that was somehow adoring as she followed a male llama along the fence of Floris's pen. The male llama, however, was not Hayden but Oliver, Rose's husband. And he didn't seem indifferent.

She showed it to Hayden, who responded angrily. "That's crazy! Deirdre never looked at Oliver twice. She detested ev-erything he stood for."

"Read what's written on the back," Victor said.

Christy turned the drawing over. Across the reverse side of the rough sketch, Rose had written a few words: *Oh, Oliver, how could you?*

"This is idiotic!" Hayden took the drawing and tossed it aside. For a moment, Christy thought he might stalk out of the room.

Victor said wearily, "Come and sit down. I never wanted to talk about any of this. I didn't want to know what was going on. But since it's possible that Oliver killed her, you'd better know."

"Killed who?" Christy demanded. "Deirdre?"

"Rose, of course," Victor said. "Because he was obsessed with Deirdre, as she was with him. She told me as much one time when she came up here to her Sun Wheel. I tried to stop her from telling me, but I can understand what happened. Oliver *looked* like a hero out of some legend. Rose knew what he was like and she loved him anyway. But when she found out about Deirdre it must have been too much, and he had to be rid of his wife. I don't *know* this—I only understand that it would have been possible. That's what obsession can do."

Hayden listened grimly. "I don't believe this, Victor. I knew Deirdre well enough to be sure she was incapable of obsession, except with her own spirit world. You've gone down the wrong road."

"I wanted to stay out of this," Victor said. "It wasn't up to me to tell you after she disappeared, but I glimpsed Deirdre up there at Oliver's a few times. I was out chopping firewood, and I saw her through the trees."

"But you told me that the figure Donny saw that time wasn't Deirdre," Christy reminded him.

"That's the strange part." Victor shook his head as though he wanted to clear it of cobwebs. "When I saw her move, I didn't think it was Deirdre, though the woman dressed like her. I did know that Oliver had someone up there with him after Rose died. And as long as he was alive, I couldn't interfere. The problem wasn't mine to work out, Hayden."

"Thanks a lot," Hayden said.

"I'm not trying to defend my position," Victor told him. "But maybe I know more about circumstantial evidence than you do. I know about the wrong conclusions people can leap to. Rose suspected—as you can tell by those sketches. Sure, it looked obvious—but it wasn't up to me to expose whatever was going on."

"Uninvolvement isn't a virtue," Hayden said harshly. "Not when all of us were out searching for Deirdre, including Oliver!"

Christy still knelt on the floor before Rose's sketches, but now the voices of the men seemed to fade away. The room had begun to fill with mist, closing in around her, hiding Hayden and Victor from view, forming a frame, as if she looked through a window. The scene itself was misty, as though it might be raining. Someone was there in the center of the picture, covered by a long raincoat with a hood that shrouded the face. Who this figure was she couldn't tell, but he or she was digging with a spade. Christy had the strong sense of something being either buried or dug up, and she watched for some revelation. Then a second figure came out of the mists, moving lightly on delicate legs—a graceful young llama that gave her a clue to the setting.

Fog erased the pictures as though someone had closed the window, and Christy returned to the present. Both men were watching her.

Victor said, "You went away, Christy. What did you see?"

"Someone was in the llama pen," she told him. "Someone who was digging—either to bury something or to dig something up. I don't know what it means."

"Well, we can't go digging up the whole llama pen to find out," Hayden said impatiently. "Though if the figure was Floris, I suppose we could ask and see if she'd tell us something."

"I don't know that it was Floris. It could have been a man. I don't even know if it's something that has already happened, or an event that's still ahead."

"That's a big help!" Hayden was still upset by Victor's revelations.

"I'm sorry," Christy told him. "Lili says this happens often with psychic messages. Unless there's some evidence in what's communicated to give a time, there's no telling if it's past or future. Or even something that's happening right now."

Victor looked out the window. "It's started raining since you came in. So if you saw someone in a raincoat, perhaps whoever it is is burying something now."

"I don't think so," Christy said doubtfully. "I remember now that there was a sense of daylight—perhaps around dawn."

Hayden dismissed this speculation. "I don't think you're right, Victor, but I think we should go up to Oliver's and see if we can find any evidence of Deirdre being there—of having been there. If there's nothing, then you're wrong and we can forget it. Can we get into his house?"

"I have a key," Victor said. "Since it's been standing empty, it's been locked up. There's a distant cousin who now owns the place, and I've agreed to look after it for now."

"Then let's go," Hayden said.

When Victor had picked up the drawings and put them away, they went out into the drizzle to the Jeep and drove the long way around to the upper road. Oliver's house was dark, with a deserted look about it. Victor unlocked the door and turned on lights. Remembering the last time she'd come into this house, Christy glanced around uneasily.

"Suppose we take separate routes to save time," Hayden suggested. "We'll each look for traces of someone who might have stayed here besides Oliver. We can watch for anything that might be unusual or out of order."

Christy had no wish to go upstairs, so she chose the kitchen area. With one exception everything there appeared to have been put away since the last time Oliver had used it. However, a paring knife lay on a counter, with a potato beside it. The potato had been cut in two, and if it had been there for long it would have blackened, but the cut part was only a little brown. Someone had used this kitchen recently.

Hayden called from another part of the lower floor. "Christy? Come here a minute, will you?"

She walked through the living room, which seemed in order, except for an old newspaper or two, and table surfaces that had gathered dust. When she stepped to the door of what must have been Oliver's study, she could see a good deal of disorder —probably natural for a man who was busy with his work. She remembered that someone had said he was writing a book.

"Look at this, Christy!" Hayden gestured toward a row of volumes along one wall. "Oliver had a whole collection of stuff on occult and psychical phenomena—parapsychology. Pretty strange for someone so set against the whole subject?"

"Perhaps they gave him ammunition for his arguments. Hayden, did you know what sort of book he was working on?"

"He never talked about it to me."

In the brief silence that followed, Christy experienced an instant of suspended time. This sort of thing was coming more often now—probably because she was so entirely involved. A sense of foreknowledge filled her. No mists, no visions, but only an intense fear—an anticipation of some horror she couldn't place. Then it was gone as though it had never happened. She knew only that it had to do with what Hayden had been telling her—something about Oliver's research for a book.

Hayden noticed nothing as she went on. "Nobody has mentioned a manuscript being found, so I don't know what happened to it, if there really was one."

"That's because he burned it," a voice said from the doorway.

They looked around, startled, to see Eve Corey watching them.

"What are you up to?" she asked. "And who's walking around upstairs? I went over to your house to talk with you, Hayden, and Leonie said you'd gone out for dinner. I could see lights in this place from across the valley, so I drove over. Would the sheriff be interested in what you're doing here?" A clear challenge sounded in her voice.

"What does it matter?" Hayden said. "Go ahead and call him, if you want to. But first, maybe you can help us. What do you mean about Oliver burning his manuscript?"

Eve looked more than ever like the llama sketch Rose had done of her, Christy thought—with eyes that bulged a little, and a skittish air, as though she might take off at a trot at any moment.

Instead, as if to quiet herself, she sat down at Oliver's desk and clasped her hands together. "I don't know why he burned it. I was a good friend—for longer than he knew Rose—and sometimes he talked to me more than to anyone else. I was here the day he took up the pages he'd written—he hadn't done all that much, really—and stuffed them in the fireplace. I had the feeling that it hurt him to burn them, but I think he was afraid in some way of what he was writing."

Victor had come quietly into the room behind Eve, and he stood with a finger to his lips, not wanting her to know he was there.

"Did you ever think," Hayden asked Eve, "that Deirdre

might be hiding here in Oliver's house after she was supposed to have disappeared?"

Eve hesitated a moment. "Why on earth would you think that?"

"Victor believes that he saw her up here," Christy said quietly.

"That Indian!" Eve said. "I wouldn't be surprised if *he* put that copperhead in the bath with Oliver! He's the one we should all be afraid of!"

Her vehemence was too great, Christy thought, and wondered how she might get Eve to open up.

Though Victor still didn't move, Christy saw his eyes darken, and she thought of Donny's Thunderbolt Man. Then he went away as quietly as he had appeared, with Eve still unaware that he'd been there.

Eve began to think out loud. "There was a book that Oliver used a lot as reference. That's the space on the shelf where it always stood. It was a big tome on abnormal psychology, and I remember a chapter on siblings that seemed to interest him especially. Once he went down to talk to Floris Fox about some of the examples in that chapter."

"Why Floris?" Hayden asked.

"Because she comes of a whole family of siblings—she had seven sisters and brothers. So she knew all about the quarreling and the jealousy—and sometimes affection. She even had a couple of sisters who fell in love with the same man, and they haven't spoken to each other in years—though neither one married him. I went along with Oliver that time when he talked to Floris about her family."

"I don't know if that has any bearing now, Eve," Hayden said. "We came into the house to see if we could find any trace of Deirdre staying here since Oliver died. Victor thinks he's seen her, but *I* don't believe this. Whatever happened—if she was alive—she wouldn't come here."

"There's a cut potato in the kitchen," Christy said, "and it hasn't blackened. So someone has been here."

"Then let's go on looking," Hayden decided. "You might as well help us, Eve. Since you knew Oliver pretty well, perhaps you're better acquainted with the house than we are."

"I knew Rose when she lived here." Eve sounded defensive. "I know where she hid a few things from Oliver. He was pretty scornful of her children's books. They were beneath his notice, so she'd work when he was off at his teaching. Then she'd get everything out of sight before he came home. It's funny her llama book never turned up. Even though she never showed it to me I know she was working on it, and after she died I really looked for it."

Neither Christy nor Hayden said anything. Eve went into the living room and stopped in surprise. Victor Birdcall sat on the sofa, looking through a newspaper that was weeks old.

"What are *you* doing here?" she demanded.

"Victor has the key," Hayden said curtly. "He let us in."

Abruptly, Eve changed her mind about whatever help she might have offered. "I'll go along home now. I only came over because I saw the lights up here and thought I'd take a look."

"Don't go yet," Christy said quickly. "You spoke about a place where Rose used to put her work, so Oliver wouldn't find it. Can you tell us where that was?"

Eve hesitated. "I suppose it doesn't matter if you know now. There's an attic, with old trunks and boxes and stuff. Oliver had a dust allergy, so he never went up there. But that's where Rose kept her work when she knew he'd be around. Then there wouldn't be any put-downs."

"Show us, Eve," Hayden said. "Come up there with us."

"No, thanks. I've had enough of this. I'm going home."

She walked out of the room abruptly, and they heard her slam the front door.

"Let's have a look at the attic," Hayden said. "There's nowhere else to search. How do we get up there, Victor?"

Victor showed them where stairs led up from the second-floor hallway. He had brought a flashlight, and he went up first, while Hayden and Christy climbed the steep flight behind him. The door at the top was locked and there was no key. Experimentally, Victor reached along the ledge overhead and found it. The key turned silently in the lock, and Victor went ahead to switch on an overhead bulb that dangled from the raftered ceiling.

Shadows came to life in the big, unfurnished space, and a wave of stale air greeted them. Up here, rain sounded noisily on the roof.

Trunks, boxes, pieces of old furniture, and discarded household items were piled everywhere. A clearing had been made for a table that held a covered typewriter, some notebooks and pads, and a jar of pencils. No work in progress was in sight. Christy felt a new disliking for Oliver because of the way he'd treated his wife's very real gift.

"She used to carry her portable typewriter downstairs so she could work in the kitchen when Oliver was out of the house," Victor said. "It wasn't that he minded what she was doing, though maybe he was a little jealous of her success—he just poked fun at whatever she wrote, and that could damage her confidence, in spite of her talent."

At the far end of the attic several trunks had been piled up, forming a wall that hid from view what lay behind it. On top of one trunk stood a table lamp, an electric heater, and a fan. Christy went quickly around the trunks and stood looking at what lay beyond. A futon had been placed on the floor, with a pillow and blankets, offering a sleeping place. Against the wall stood a cracked mirror, and a wire had been strung to hold hangers with a few articles of clothing.

"These aren't Deirdre's things," Hayden said.

"They wouldn't be, Hay," Victor reminded him. "When Deirdre left, she didn't take much with her, did she? Except maybe this?"

He had found a rolled-up bundle on a dusty table and he shook out a long white caftan. Whoever had masqueraded in the woods must have worn this gown. It was the same garment that had lured Christy down from the rear deck at Nona's house. She couldn't remember now where she'd left it after they went to the place where Rose had died. She hadn't wanted to ever touch it again, and she didn't touch it now.

Their light-fingered, malicious spirit had clearly brought the gown here, and now the question rose once more as to whether it had been Deirdre in the woods, or Deirdre hiding in this house. Someone had certainly been camping out here, and if not Deirdre, then who? But of course it must have been Deirdre!

They were inside Oliver's house tonight. I could see them through the kitchen windows, though I didn't dare watch for long. There was no way to keep them from going to the attic, where I've hidden since Oliver died. After Rose was gone, of course, I lived downstairs with him for a time.

It was a good thing I persuaded Oliver to burn those pages of the book he'd started. He told me what he was writing about—obsession. He thought he knew enough to write about it. I know a great deal more. I was obsessed by him for much too long a time. Deirdre never liked him. In her way, I suppose, she really cared about Hayden—who would have been my enemy if he'd known about me. I've always pretended in order to keep what the spy stories call my "cover." Deirdre will never dare to betray me. She knows what I can do, and how much stronger I am than she is.

Oliver was such a gorgeous man. I could never stand men who were ugly. He was sensual, strongly sexual, and I wanted him as I'd never wanted any other man. That was obsession. But in the end he proved to be weak and ineffectual. Would he have done to Rose what I did? No—he'd never have had that sort of passion. In his mind, where he thought he was so securely intellectual—he was nothing—an empty shell. He would have betrayed me in the end, out of basic weakness. Just the same, I only meant to frighten him.

He had his uses for a time and was some protection for me, but that came to an end as I began to know him. I suppose he was obsessed with me in his way, since he couldn't get me out of his life. And since he couldn't escape, it would have been much better for all of us if he'd killed himself.

It seemed such fun at first—playing Deirdre's spirit self in the woods; leaving Rose's slippers around for Victor to find, and planting the needlepoint in the llama pen. But I'm bored with those childish tricks, and I must get away—find a place where I can live safely. I can't take Deirdre with me. My little sister has become too great a burden. I've kept our secret well over the years—since she never wanted to acknowledge me. But now time has run out, and it must be done, once and for all, though I'm still not sure exactly how.

Perhaps Deirdre and Christy at the same time? If I can coax them out together. Christy won't be suspicious, but Deirdre will know what I intend. I wonder if Donny can be used to help me? From a distance he still thinks I'm Deirdre. That beastly cat knows better!

15

WHEN THEY left Oliver's house, Hayden seemed lost in some inner maze of his own. The shock of learning that Deirdre must really be alive, and that she'd been hiding from him—living with Oliver—perhaps had even been the cause of Oliver's death—was more than he could understand or endure. There was nothing anyone could say, no comfort to be offered. He was alone with a terrible enigma he still had no means of solving. There would be no use combing the woods for Deirdre in the rain—she could have gone anywhere, concealed herself in a hundred places in or out of Redlands. There were even caves in the mountains, and she was an outdoor creature.

Victor took charge quietly. "Come down to my place for a drink, Hay. You can stay the night, if you want, and tomorrow you can decide what's possible. She may come back to Oliver's during the night, and we can find her in the morning."

"Thanks, Victor. First, I'll drive Christy back to Nona's, and then take you up on staying here. Donny will be okay with Leonie. I ought to stick close to where she's likely to appear. If I could just talk with her . . ."

When they left, Victor stood in his lighted doorway, watching them drive away. He must carry his own guilt, Christy thought, for not bringing his suspicions into the open. If he'd acted, Oliver might still be alive. But perhaps it hadn't been possible for him to behave in any other way. There were those who believed that everyone was bonded into a pattern accepted at birth. But where did that leave free choice?

"We *can* make choices." Hayden's words seemed to read her thoughts—but she didn't think he was talking about Victor.

"I know," she said. "Lili believes there's a master plan, but that every move within it isn't ordained. It's up to us to decide what to do. Lili knows how to manage that with the greatest assurance. I seem to wind up in a state of confusion."

Unexpectedly, he reached out to touch her arm. "You do all right. Better than I've done."

He drove the rest of the way to Nona's in bleak silence, and she didn't speak again until she got out of the Jeep. "I'm sorry —about everything," she told him, knowing how inadequate words could be. He only nodded and drove away.

No one could help him now. No sympathy could reach him, much as she longed to offer it. She went into the house feeling almost as dazed as Hayden looked.

Lights were on in Nona's kitchen when she went along the deck, and through the bay windows she could see Nona and Lili at the table with cups before them. Lili's drink would be herbal tea, but Nona seemed to be drinking black coffee. When Christy went through the door, prepared to resist the questioning that was sure to greet her, Nona put a finger to her lips.

"Ssh—it's Josef."

Christy sat down quietly and watched her mother. Lili's eyes were closed and she breathed deeply, swaying a little. This was the time to ask Josef a few questions herself, Christy thought, waiting for his voice.

After a moment or two he spoke. "Good evening to my friends."

Only Nona said, "Good evening," on cue. Then she spoke directly to Josef. "*You* wanted to talk with us."

"To Christy," Josef said. "She is here now. She must listen carefully. There is something to be done at once."

"I will listen," Christy said.

Josef went on. "You must go to the house of the spirit woman Go by car. Go quickly."

"You mean Deirdre's house? What must I do there, Josef?"

"You will know. Take your aunt and your mother with you. Lili will help you. Good night to you for now."

Not at all satisfactory, Christy thought, but she'd better do as Josef said.

Lili shook herself and returned to the real world. "Let's go," she told them briskly.

They took the station wagon, driving the short distance, as Josef had directed. Lights burned in several rooms of Hayden's house.

Leonie met them at the door, looking frightened and uncertain. "Please go upstairs right away. Donny is asleep in his room—don't wake him up."

Christy ran up the stairs ahead of the others. She had no doubt at all where she must go. Deirdre's door was closed. Christy opened it without a warning knock, and stood with Nona and Lili behind her, looking into the room.

Several lamps had been lighted and the woman sat in her favorite chair. She had taken one of her own filmy gowns from the closet and put it on over jeans that showed at her ankles. The crystal Christy had returned to Donny rested in her cupped hands. She sat watching them quietly, almost as though she had expected them to come.

"I didn't know where else to go," Deirdre said. Tearstains had dried on her cheeks, and she looked forlorn and helpless.

This was Hayden's wife, and for a moment an intense unhappiness filled Christy—until pity for Deirdre surfaced. Pity for the sadness and fear that possessed this wraith of a woman who sat before them.

Lili knew what to do. She went quickly to drop to her knees before Deirdre, taking her hands in hers, crystal and all.

"You are safe now. Nothing can hurt you. If there is anything you'd like to tell us—any way we can help you—we will listen."

Lili carried the power of healing in her hands, and Deirdre seemed to relax a little at her touch. When Lili put an arm around her, she leaned into it.

How lovely she was, Christy thought—in an ethereal sort of

way—as delicate in her appearance as she'd been described, and as Nona had painted her. Her violet eyes, still brimming with tears, were fixed on Lili's face as though she might draw sustenance from someone so strong and confident.

Yet in the end, while Lili was still murmuring words of reassurance, Deirdre gently withdrew her hands, set the crystal aside, and stood up. Sinh, who had crouched unnoticed on a bookcase, startled them all by leaping onto Deirdre's shoulder and practically circling herself around Deirdre's slender neck. Deirdre reached up to caress her, and the cat purred and rubbed her head against Deirdre's chin.

"I'm sorry," Deirdre whispered softly to the cat, and then released clinging claws and set her on the floor. "I must go now."

Nona said, "Sit down, Deirdre, please. No one is going to force you to do anything, but it will be better if you talk to us, let us help you. This is Liliana Dukas, of whom you may have heard. She's Christy's mother, and Christy is my niece."

"I know all that," Deirdre said. "But I must go now. It isn't safe for me to stay in this house. *She* mustn't find me here."

"She?" Nona repeated.

A terror close to hysteria shone in Deirdre's eyes. "This time I got away, but she'll find me. She always does."

"Tell us who you mean, dear?" Lili asked, her tone calming.

Deirdre was far from calm. "No! She'd punish me. I can't tell anyone."

"If we know who you're talking about, she can be stopped," Nona told her.

But Deirdre was beyond reason. She ran toward the door, and Christy moved to block her way.

"Wait, please. Hayden's at Victor's now. We can phone and ask him to come home. He'd be here in minutes. And he only wants to help you, Deirdre. You must know that."

"Not any more. Not after Oliver. So many horrible things have happened and *she* says it's my fault. I have to save myself and stop her. If I can find the courage. I've never been brave."

"First you must see Hayden," Nona said firmly. "I'm going to call him now. He has a right to help you."

"No—I don't belong to Hayden! We lost each other a long time ago." She moved away from Christy and raised her arms in a wide arc. "I belong to the woods and the mountains—to moonlight and rainbows. They don't frighten me, and that's where I must go. She can't follow me there."

"It's raining hard," Nona said. "You can't go out in this."

"I don't mind the rain. I can hide better in a storm. It was foolish to come here—I always do foolish things."

"Deirdre," Christy pleaded, "what about your son? Donny misses you terribly. Don't you want to see him before you go?"

She shook her head wildly. "There's no time. It's better for him if he doesn't see me now."

Lili went quickly to the closet, took out a long green raincoat and helped Deirdre into it. At least she wore heavy shoes. When Christy stepped aside, unable to stop her now, Deirdre ran toward the stairs.

"We have to let her go," Lili said. "She must meet her own destiny. Her own karma."

Christy had little use for destiny at the moment, and she hurried downstairs after Deirdre. She was in time to see Hayden come through the front door. He stood still when he saw Deirdre, and spoke quietly.

"I saw the lights from Victor's, and I thought I'd better come."

Deirdre faced him down the long room for only a moment. Then she fled toward a door to the rear deck and disappeared into dark, slanting rain.

Hayden went after her and down the back steps. They could hear him crashing around in wet brush down the hill, the sounds gradually diminishing. The three women waited under the overhang of the back deck, listening to the rain. But Deirdre had circled around to the front, where Hayden's Jeep stood in the driveway. They heard it start, heard Hayden shout, but by the time they reached the front windows the car's headlights were moving away at a greater speed than was safe for these roads.

"You can take my car," Nona called to Hayden.

He came up to the house to join them. "It's no use. Even if I could catch her, I might do more harm than good. I don't think she'll go outside of Redlands. There's something holding her here. I feel that strongly. What did she say to you upstairs?"

Christy told him. "She talked about a 'she' who seems to have been holding her captive in some way. But she wouldn't tell us who it was. It can't be anyone who lives here, can it—not anyone we know?"

"The evil don't wear labels," Nona said. "Masks can fool anyone, and I think we've been fooled by someone here for a long time."

Lili said with her usual assurance, "There is no evil. There are only misguided souls whom we must pity and help."

"While they go around murdering people?" Hayden was impatient again. "Anyway, there's one thing I haven't followed through on. Christy, you had a vision about someone digging in the llama pen—has anything more come to you?"

Christy shook her head. "I'm sorry—nothing."

"Then I'm going down there now and see if I can find an answer."

"In the dark, in the rain?" Nona protested.

He paid no attention, and Christy said quickly, "Let me come with you. Perhaps something will filter through if I go down there. We don't have any time to lose. I have the feeling that Deirdre is desperate enough to do anything."

Hayden found Christy an old raincoat, and Nona gave him the keys to her car. "Don't worry about us. We'll stay right here, or walk home if it stops raining."

Christy glanced at her mother as she went out. For once, Lili did not look serene. No one had taken her good advice, and she had no more ready answers. Apparently, Josef too was silent.

Tension showed in Hayden's grip on the wheel as he drove, and Christy felt increasingly fearful, though she had no focus for her fear. Like Hayden, she knew that Deirdre must be helped somehow, and that they must follow any means of rescue they could find.

The stream at the foot of the hill rushed along noisily at high speed as they crossed the bridge. In Floris's house above, lights shone through the rainy darkness, and Floris came quickly to let them in.

No, she hadn't seen Deirdre, she said in answer to Hayden's question, though she didn't seem especially surprised to learn that his wife had been roaming about in the woods.

"I was sure I sensed her around a few times," Floris said. "Maybe she even brought the cat here. She should have been born a deer—or perhaps a llama. Though my llamas have better care than Deirdre seems to have had."

There was criticism of Hayden implied in her words, but he paid no attention. At his urging, Christy described the flash of pictures that had come to her—of someone digging down in the llama pen. Perhaps within the last twenty-four hours.

Again, Floris didn't seem surprised. "The llamas have been restless on and off, so I knew something was up. They're in the barn now, and I thought some animal had stirred them up. It's only when they stop humming and begin to quack like ducks that I know there's real trouble."

Hayden borrowed two flashlights, and they went down to where the animals had been closed into the barn for the night. Beyond the main pen was a wide stretch of meadow, but the picture Christy had received was of the pen itself.

When Hayden played his flashlight over the area, it didn't take long to find the muddy corner where earth had been disturbed. Rain was no longer a downpour, but a steady dripping from trees sounded all around. The air felt cool on Christy's face, and the smell of the woods was fresh and pungent. But there was something else out there among the nearby trees—a *presence*. It came to her strongly—someone watching. Perhaps Deirdre herself? But any move on Hayden's part would only precipitate flight, so she said nothing.

With a spade borrowed from Floris, Hayden thrust deeply into the soft red earth, striking something almost at once—something buried hurriedly near the surface. He lifted out a plastic bag and held it up to Christy's flashlight. The bag contained a large book.

"Let's go see what we've found," he said. In the barn the llamas hummed among themselves, and eyes looked out curiously, caught in the passing beam of light.

Once more in the kitchen, where Floris spread newspapers over a table, Hayden examined his parcel. The book was thick, and obviously scholarly, and Oliver Vaughn's bookplate showed on the inside cover. Looking at the title, Christy saw that it was the volume on abnormal psychology that Eve had mentioned. The section on siblings opened to a marker, and Oliver had made notations in the margin—his script cramped and hard to read.

Floris looked over Hayden's shoulder uneasily. "Oliver came down here one time to talk about the problems I'd had growing up in a large family. He was mostly interested in how I felt about sisters. I told him that sisters come in all varieties, so most anything goes. I think he was planning an article or something on the subject."

"Thanks, Floris," Hayden said. "I'll take this along and have a closer look."

Floris came with them to the door, looking past them, as though she sensed something out among the dripping trees. "Lately I keep seeing things," she said.

If it was Deirdre, let her be, Christy thought.

When they reached Hayden's house, he found that his Jeep had been returned to the garage. It was wet, and muddy, but how long it had been there, there was no telling.

They hurried inside and Leonie came to let them know that Miss Harmony and Miss Dukas had gone home when it stopped raining. Hayden told her to go to bed—he would look in on Donny later.

When he'd turned on more lights in the living room, they

saw Deirdre. She lay in shadow on the sofa at the far end, where Leonie hadn't noticed her. One hand was tucked under her cheek, like a child, and her hair and clothes were soaking wet. If she had gone on foot, Christy thought, she might have been down there in the woods watching, and still have come back here before they could make the trip by car.

When Hayden touched her shoulder, she started up in fright. "It's all right," he told her gently. "You mustn't run away any more. Tonight you will sleep in your own bed."

For a moment she stared up at him, her eyes wide and doubting. Then she seemed to let go of all resistance and he gathered her slight body into his arms and carried her to the stairs. "Wait, please," he said to Christy over his shoulder.

The book that had belonged to Oliver lay on a table, where Hayden had placed it. Christy reached to pick it up, and the moment she touched it a sense of warning flashed through her. The book was dangerous—to someone. Without a doubt, she knew that this volume held answers that would illuminate everything. Someone had been frightened enough of its contents to attempt to hide it.

But why in the llama pen? Why not in a dozen other hiding places?

She sat down beside a reading lamp and turned to the marked pages about siblings. Oliver had checked several paragraphs concerning the possessive older sister. In themselves, the passages seemed innocent enough. Perhaps he'd really been interested in the article he meant to write, and nothing else. But she knew there was more. The warning that there was a threat to someone in these pages had been clear. Perhaps to herself, as well as Deirdre?

When Hayden came downstairs he looked depressed, gloomy. "I've put her to bed," he said, and came to sit across from Christy.

She tapped the open book on her lap. "Did Deirdre have a sister? An older sister?"

"It's strange, but I'm not really sure. She loved to tell all sorts of stories about her childhood, and I could never be certain which ones she was making up. I do know that Deirdre's mother was her father's second wife. His first wife had died, and there may have been a half sister. Sometimes she claimed there was, though she said the older girl had quarreled with her father and gone to live with an aunt. The aunt has since died, so that story could never be checked. Other times she'd deny having any sister. Once when I asked questions, she begged me to let it go. I suspect that the sister got in touch with her at one time and said something that alarmed Deirdre—perhaps even threatened her. But whenever I tried to pin her down—just so I could help her—she would say she had no sister, and slip off in her own elusive way."

When he came to a pause Hayden got up to light the fire against the evening's chill. As warmth spread through the room, he drew Christy to the couch before the hearth and sat beside her.

"Deirdre's is a very gentle madness," he told her, watching the flames. "I've known for a long time that there was an imbalance there, but it always seemed harmless enough. I know there were times when she grew too keyed up and excited. She'd be full of talk about moonlight and rainbows and all those eerie tales her Irish nanny had filled her head with as a little girl. Most children outgrow fairy tales, but I don't think Deirdre ever did. Besides, there was always something enchanting in that childlike quality. She refused to see a psychiatrist, and I never pushed. But now, what if she's no longer harmless? What if her mind has taken some manic turn, so that she's out of control?"

He looked somber, hopeless, and Christy could only listen as he went on.

"I've always felt that I could never put her away in an institution, where she would be restrained and given drugs; confined between hard bare walls. How could I do that to her bright spirit? She was such a delight when I first knew her. Mischievous and entrancing, but never malicious. It wasn't until after Donny was born that I began to realize that I'd married an enthralling child-woman who would never grow up. There was nothing dangerous about her. In fact, she was loving toward everyone, though perhaps too easily influenced by others at times. Eve Corey would use her—boss her around, until I put a stop to that. Rose understood her better and was always kind. And Deirdre was comfortable with Nona, and sometimes listened to her. But now—I don't know what's happening, or how she could run off to Oliver. I suppose an—illness—like hers doesn't stay the same. It can take turns for the worse without reason. Yet I can't see her harming Rose—or Oliver."

"Did she talk to you just now, while you were putting her to bed?"

"A little. She pleaded with me to let her stay and sleep in her room—where she would be safe. *Pleaded*, as though I were a stranger and this wasn't her home. She's pitifully afraid of something, but the moment I ask questions, she slips away from me. I had the feeling that she's afraid for her life. All I can do is stay home and watch over her for a few days, try to get the truth out of her. That's the only way I can help her."

"I'm sorry," Christy said. "I'm so terribly sorry."

He took her hand and held it for a moment against his cheek. "Thank you for staying," he said. "Thank you for being here."

Events would have to take their own course, and she could only watch for some way to change what needn't be inevitable —now that she was forewarned.

"I can get back to Nona's by myself," she told him. "It's not raining, and you mustn't leave the house now."

But he wouldn't let her go alone. It would only take a few moments to drive her over. When they reached the house, he left her and went straight back to Deirdre. Once more, Christy found herself watching until his headlights turned up his own driveway.

Then she went inside to warmth and light. Nona and Lili were waiting for her, and she knew the time had come to tell them everything.

She shut me in and got away!

I never thought she could be that strong. She wants me gone —dead. I know that very well. It will come down in the end to a life-or-death struggle between me and the sister I've always hated. And I will win.

But first I must find the means to get out of the prison in which she's tried to lock me. The same place where I held her.

ᕗᕗᕗᕗ **16** *ᕗᕗᕗᕗ*

CHRISTY faced the two women, knowing that questions were ready to pour out of them.

"I'll tell you," she said, sitting down at the kitchen table. "But please don't ask me anything or give me advice. I'm too tired and confused to deal with anything more tonight. I just want to talk a little, and then go to bed. In the morning you can say anything you please."

So they listened, and except for exchanging a look now and then, neither one interrupted. And if Lili consulted Josef, she did so after Christy had gone down to her room.

She got ready for bed quickly, telling herself that she wanted to think of nothing further about this whole crowded day. She had no answer to anything, and she saw how bitterly and finally Hayden had been trapped. Just as she was trapped, since there was no way out of his caring for Deirdre for the rest of her life. She must not think of her own premonitions of some danger. Not unless they could, in some way, be used to help Deirdre and Hayden.

Tonight her one comfort was the memory of that moment when he had held her hand against his cheek. With the tenderness of that gesture, he'd told her what he couldn't put into words. If Deirdre had been less helpless, less totally dependent on him to keep her from further "escapades," then there might have been some hope. But if Deirdre had committed murder when it came to Rose, and if she had put the snake in Oliver's bath—there would be some terrible times ahead for Hayden.

After a long while, weariness brought restless sleep, though for once no dreams. By the time the sun touched the tops of the trees near the lower deck, she was wide awake. Awake, but far from ready to deal with whatever this day would bring.

When she'd showered and dressed, she went upstairs to find Nona getting breakfast. Lili never rose early unless she had to. Nona said her mother was leaving later on, anxious to get back to all that waited for her in her own life. She was unable to do anything more for Christy.

"Josef thinks you'll be all right on your own now," Nona finished.

For once, Josef was right. Christy had no need to lean on Lili or ask her advice. They had drawn closer on this visit than ever before. In her own way, Lili loved her daughter, but she could never play the role of mother for long.

Nona continued, "As soon as you've eaten a batch of my blueberry pancakes and have come to life a little, you and I are going over to Hayden's. Lili can fend for herself."

Christy wasn't sure she was ready to see Hayden yet, but when Nona took over in that tone of voice, it was useless to oppose whatever she planned.

At least, morning was a time for hope. The mountains around Redlands stood against a washed blue sky, poplars and oaks a furry fringe along high ridges. Cows were out in the lower meadow, and a bright red cardinal sang its morning song in an oak tree. A mockingbird was awake too, mimicking cheerfully.

When they started off on foot for Hayden's, Christy matched Nona's stride mindlessly. She didn't want to ask what Nona intended, she didn't want her own thoughts to start tormenting her again. All that was ominous still lay ahead, but she would deal with it later.

Hayden came down the steps to meet them, and obviously none of the problems that weighed on him had lifted. He looked as though he'd had little rest last night.

"Donny doesn't know yet that his mother's home," he told them. "He's out playing, and Deirdre is still asleep. Once she knew I'd stay on guard, she seemed able to let go. When I left her room for a shower and breakfast, I locked her in." He looked at Nona apologetically. "I have to do this. She can't be trusted not to run away again, and perhaps do herself harm."

"Of course," Nona said. "Christy has told us about Deirdre, and that's why I've come. I want to take over for a while, Hayden. You and Christy both need a break. Forget about everything here at Redlands and take Christy off somewhere pleasant. When you come back you'll feel better able to decide about the future."

Hayden managed a smile. "Thanks, Nona. I accept—if Christy will too. And I know where we can go. Not far away, and not for long. But first come upstairs with me so I can let Deirdre know I'm not abandoning her."

They all went up together, and Hayden unlocked Deirdre's door. She sat up in bed as he came in, and looked past him to Nona and Christy.

"Good morning, everyone. I've had a wonderful rest." She reached out her arms happily to embrace Hayden. "Darling— you must be horribly tired. I know you stayed with me all night, and that was kind. But now you need a rest from *me*. I'll be perfectly all right."

"Of course you will be," Nona said briskly. "I'm going to stay here for a while, to give Hayden that rest he needs. That is, if you're willing to have me."

Sinh had come into the room with them, and she was stalking about as though on unfamiliar territory.

Deirdre sighed. "Poor old Sinh! You don't trust me, do you? But I'll try to stay home now. I was very sick for a while, but I'm much better now, and I think I'll sleep a while longer, if nobody minds."

The cat, however, looked as though she didn't believe a word of this, and went haughtily out of the room.

Hayden kissed the cheek Deirdre raised to him and accepted another hug. Armed with reading material she'd picked up downstairs, Nona sat down in Deirdre's armchair.

"When you want to get up," she told her, "let me know. I'll ask Leonie to bring your breakfast here. Donny doesn't know you're home yet, but when you're ready we'll bring him in."

As Christy followed Hayden out of the room, she glanced at the book Nona had picked up and saw that it was the one they'd dug out of the llama pen last night. Good! Now Nona could read about siblings, and perhaps she could come up with some new ideas.

Once more in the Jeep, Hayden followed the road that dipped into the valley, ran past a little lake, then up toward the farther high ridge—a mountain much higher than on Hayden's side. When they were near the top, Hayden parked under pine trees and they got out to climb the rest of the way on foot.

Beyond a stand of birches stood a high outcropping of rock, where they could sit and look out over the countryside. This was nowhere near that other pile of rock that Christy had grown to fear.

From up here the high ranges of the Blue Ridge stood clear, with mists floating below, so that peaks seemed to rise from a white sea. Below the driftings of cloud, the foothills crowded in, offering blue-green views in all directions. Just beyond where they sat hawks soared—twenty or more, playing on currents of air. A lovely sight. Inwardly, however, Christy was aware only of the man stretched out beside her, aware of her own pulse beat because of his nearness.

Nona's house and Hayden's were both visible on a much lower level across the valley from where they sat. They looked like miniatures from this height, with nothing stirring around them, so that the scene seemed dreamy—almost like a make-believe stage set. Christy knew only that she was waiting.

Hayden appeared less tired now, as though he had shed the burden of Deirdre's problems for a little while. He held his hand toward Christy, questioning, and she put her own in his. His warm fingers closed about hers, and when he began to speak, his voice was so low that she bent her head to catch his words.

"I recognized you the moment you walked into my life," he said. "That time when you were with Donny reading to the cows. I didn't want to recognize you. At first it was easy to deny and set myself against you. I can't do that any more. What lies ahead may be rough going, Christy. But I know this now—I want you with me—somehow. I want you to be there."

She answered easily, warmly. "I want to be there, Hayden."

His hand tightened around hers, and he raised it to his cheek. "Deirdre changes with every hour. Sometimes she needs me, and sometimes she doesn't want me near her. This long period while she was gone has made me think about her in new ways. During that time I asked myself how I would feel if she were dead; how I must act if she were found alive. It began to seem that her death would mean a release—but I couldn't wish that for her. Now that she's returned, I know I want to care for her, and I always will. She's like a child—like a helpless, injured daughter. What I feel about you, Christy, is totally different. These days I'm filled with too many if-onlys, and that does me no good. I'm not sure what lies ahead, and it's not fair to ask anything of you. But I don't want to be fair—I need you. So if you're willing . . ."

She knew how willing she was. Up here in this clear mountain air his words brought joy, and a lifting of her spirit.

Hayden moved suddenly, standing up. "There's a car down on my driveway. I can't tell from here whose it is."

A small figure—man or woman?—got out and went up on the deck, to disappear into the house. The lovely moment between them was lost for now, and Christy stood beside him, all her senses alert to new alarm.

"We have to go back," she said. "I can feel that something's about to happen. Something you need to prevent."

He didn't question her certainty, but before they started down, he held her to him and kissed her hair, her eyes, her mouth. That was all they dared for now, and they went down to the Jeep together, their hands touching as they hurried.

Hayden drove, but the rain had settled the roads, and no

clouds of dust rose behind them. There was no time, Christy thought—no time! Already they might be too late. Events were quickening, and Deirdre must be their only concern.

The roundabout way took no more than fifteen minutes, and they rushed together into the house, to be met by silence. Upstairs, Deirdre's door was locked from the outside, so Nona must have gone out. But when Hayden opened the door and looked in, Eve Corey sat on the edge of Deirdre's bed, and Deirdre was gone.

Eve grinned at them sardonically. "Good! I need to be rescued. I couldn't make Leonie hear me—she's doing laundry in the basement, or something."

Hayden brushed her words aside. "Where is Deirdre? Why isn't Nona here?"

"When I came in a little while ago," Eve said, "Nona had just had an urgent call from Lili. Josef was warning her about something. So I offered to stay with Deirdre until she got back. Deirdre wanted to talk, and I sat down and listened. She seemed to be getting too excited, and I wasn't sure I could handle her. She was talking about the Sun Wheel at Victor's, and how it might help her. I told her she should wait till you came back, Hayden, and she seemed to accept that. She got up and dressed in jeans and a sweater, and then lay down again. But when I turned my back, she dashed out of the room and locked me in!"

"The Sun Wheel—that's where she's gone?" Hayden demanded.

For just a minute Eve hesitated, and Christy heard the pause uneasily. "That's what she told me," Eve said.

"Will you stay here, Christy?" Hayden asked. "In case Deirdre comes back. I'm going over to Victor's right away." He rushed off, and minutes later they heard him start the Jeep.

"I'm sorry," Eve said, though she didn't sound especially upset. "There were a lot of things I wanted to ask Deirdre, but there wasn't time."

Moving about Deirdre's room, Christy was aware once more

of Nona's rainbow painting. She remembered the tiny face Nona had caught among the trees, and which Donny had seen. Looking for it now, she found it easily. A face that bore a resemblance to Deirdre, though the expression was sly and far from innocent. Had Nona, painting automatically, glimpsed the sister Deirdre had rejected?

She turned back to Eve. "I'm glad she told you where she was going."

"She didn't." Eve went to a window to watch Hayden drive away.

"What do you mean?" Christy cried. She thought of the way Deirdre might have frightened Oliver with that snake, and that Eve had loved Oliver. So it might not be wise to trust anything Eve said about Deirdre.

Eve turned, her smile unpleasant. "She hasn't gone to the Sun Wheel, but I had to convince Hayden, so I could get him out of the way. I don't know where Deirdre has gone, but I know what she wants to do. There's a payment she needs to make—and I don't think we should interfere."

Christy took her by the arm. "Tell me what you're talking about! Tell me exactly!"

"Hey!" Eve shook off her hand. "I'm willing to tell you, now that Hayden's gone. There's nothing you can do except sit down and listen."

Eve dropped onto the bed again, and Christy seated herself reluctantly in Deirdre's chair, stirred by an impatience that urged her to action—if only she knew what action to take. Sinh crawled out of a corner and sat at her feet, mewing.

"It was the book that made her decide," Eve said. "Nona was reading it, and she left it like that—open and face down." Eve pointed to where the big volume lay on the floor. "Deirdre knew that Nona had found the place Oliver had marked, and that she would tell Hayden. Deirdre asked me straight out if I knew that Oliver had made notes in this book, and I said that Oliver had told me a little that night when he drove me down from Wintergreen. At least, he told me his suspicions. Deirdre almost cried when I mentioned Oliver. I couldn't feel sorry for her, somehow. She said someone ought to read what was in the book and maybe try to help her. She'd meant to take it to Floris, but someone was up there in her house, so she buried it in the llama pen, meaning to get it later. Though I suspect she didn't really know why she buried it—she's been off in outer space for some time. She said it was as though someone told her to bury it—forced her to."

Eve paused, and Christy prodded impatiently. "Never mind all that. Tell me what else Deirdre said."

"She said, 'I know where I can meet her. I know where she's sure to come. And I know what I need to do.' Then, before I could guess what she intended, she ran out of the room and locked me in. So when you and Hayden came, I decided to throw him off. He'd try to stop her—and that shouldn't be allowed. Anyway, it's too late now."

"I must find her!"

"How are you going to do that? She could be anywhere."

Christy didn't trouble to answer. She picked up Deirdre's nightgown that lay across the bed, and returned to Deirdre's chair. Sinh watched intently, and she spoke to the cat with a strange sense that the animal could understand.

"Can you help me, Sinh? Can you help me to help *her?*"

Sinh mewed again and rubbed her head against Christy's ankle.

The gown still carried a trace of Deirdre's heathery scent, and Christy held it in her hands and closed her eyes, letting everything around her slip away. The cat leaped onto her knees and rested its head on the folds of the gown. Perhaps, between them, they could find Deirdre.

As the picture came into Christy's mind, the mists flowed in gently, leaving their center clear, so she could see Deirdre standing alone, waiting. Then, as foggy edges moved back, Christy knew where she was, knew the terrible threat to Deirdre. For a moment longer she sat very still, with an inner listening. It was as if she heard her mother's voice speaking words that gave her strength and direction.

Go deep inside yourself and accept, Chrystal. Make peace with yourself. Then you can act.

A quiet recognition of her own powers flowed through Christy, filling her with a sense of confidence. She knew what she must do, knew she must act swiftly before it was too late. As she moved, Sinh flew off her lap and Christy ran to the door. Eve called after her, but she paid no attention, rushing downstairs and out the front door.

This place was one she could reach only on foot, and she ran with a new, tireless energy. Past Nona's without a glance. Past the cabin where she'd sheltered with Victor. Turning away from open sky and mountains, and down through the darkness of the woods.

Clouds had covered the sun again, and the path ahead grew misty. But these were real mists, with a hint of red earth showing through at ground level. Columns of trees on either side formed a high wall, and she knew she had been here before, not only in her dream but in her waking hours.

She slowed her progress, lest she run into a rock or trip over a fallen log. The only part of the dream that was different was that she heard no pounding footsteps following her.

When she came into an opening in the trees and found herself above the high pinnacle of rocky cliff from which Rose had fallen, she knew this was her destination. Deirdre stood near the edge—stood still, as though she waited. Almost as though she knew someone would come.

Christy ran to throw her arms about Deirdre's slight body and draw her back from the edge. Deirdre went limp, weeping helplessly as Christy held her.

"You have to let me go," she whispered. "This is the only choice I can make."

"No! There are always other choices, other ways! Hayden wants to help you."

Deirdre looked sadly into Christy's face. "Hayden deserves

happiness—and it can't be with me. Christy, let me go. Let me go before *she* comes back!"

"Your sister?" Christy said gently. "Tell me about your sister."

"There's no time," Deirdre said. "I know she's coming."

She began to struggle in Christy's grasp, moving nearer to the place where the rock pitched downward. Then, even as Christy tried desperately to hold her, she saw the change that began to happen in Deirdre—as though a terrible metamorphosis was taking place. The soft contours of Deirdre's face hardened, her eyes turned dark with hatred, and the woman in Christy's arms struggled with a strength greater than Deirdre's. She could never hold this woman who was *not* Deirdre. There was no time to understand—but only to know that there were two women in Deirdre's frail body, and the other was the stronger of the two.

Christy was being pulled toward the edge, and in a moment she would be thrown over—to her death far below. But now, strangely, as though she were in her dream again, she could hear feet beating heavily on the earth. Someone was following, after all.

When Hayden hurled himself into the clearing, she felt no surprise. He snatched her from Deirdre's grasp, drawing her back from where the cliff plunged down. She stood trembling in his arms, and they both stared at Deirdre—who was changing again. Changing into the gentle sister, who only loved and would harm no one. She smiled at them both—a smile of happy triumph.

"Look!" Deirdre cried, and opened her arms wide.

Christy and Hayden looked toward the sky to see the rainbow curving above trees and rocks, rising from the mist to paint a tremendous arc across the heavens. An arc that held all the colors, as though they had been set there and would never fade.

Deirdre's arms seemed to embrace the glowing arc. "Do you

see what it means? The green is for healing, the pink is for joy, and blue is for—peace."

She looked at Hayden with love and stepped out into space as if beneath the rainbow, disappearing into the mists below. The two who were left stood in shocked silence. As mist blew aside in a light wind, Deirdre's slight body could be seen lying far below, unmoving. She had known, and she had chosen, taking her "sister" with her.

But now, with her own special sense, Christy saw that something strange was happening to the earthly body Deirdre had left behind. Two wisps of vapor rose from her inert form and separated, to float away in different directions. One seemed to lift upward toward the rainbow that still arched across the sky. The other drifted off into the woods and disappeared.

With a wonder she did not question, Christy knew that Deirdre was safe. About the "other" she couldn't tell. Only *she* had seen those two wisps separate. Gently, Hayden released her, and as she moved farther from the cliff's edge, she saw the woman who stood near the woods watching.

Lili was smiling with her own radiance. "I came as soon as I sensed something wrong. But you're fine, and you didn't need me, Chrystal."

"I couldn't help her." Christy moved toward her mother, and Hayden came with her. "I couldn't help Deirdre," she repeated sadly. "She chose the rainbow."

Lili looked up at the sky where the colors held clear, and she seemed to understand.

"There were two Deirdres," Christy said. "While she lay on the rocks down there, the two separated." She turned to Hayden. "I saw it happen—their spirits, like wisps of smoke, rising in different directions."

Lili nodded sadly. "Sometimes two souls are born into one body. They can be so opposite in nature that they struggle against each other all their lives. Deirdre chose to free herself in her own way. I thank God, Hayden, that you got here in time to save my daughter."

Hayden said, "Sometimes I sensed that there were two—but I didn't understand. There was—deception. And I was fooled."

"You mustn't blame yourself," Lili said. "How were you led to come here?"

Hayden put an arm around Christy as though he couldn't let her go. "I went to Victor's because Eve told us Deirdre had gone there to the Sun Wheel. She wasn't there, but Victor told me to stand inside the Wheel and ask for help. So I went into the quadrant of the western fire and asked for wisdom. Right away, Christy, I knew your danger. And I knew the place. I have Victor to thank for making me listen."

"The time was right, and you were ready to listen," Lili said.

She stepped to the edge of the cliff and looked down sadly. When she had spoken a few words of prayer, she turned toward the path up the hill. "I'll go back now, and find a telephone. You'll stay, Hayden?"

Hayden nodded, and Christy waited for him while he climbed down the cliff to Deirdre.

Good and evil, she thought. All human beings were a mixture of the light and the dark. In Deirdre the separation had been extreme, dividing into two parts, each trying to defeat the other. In this strange way the split had become absolute, and perhaps Deirdre's real goodness had won.

I don't know where I am, or what has happened to me. Something is terribly wrong. Everything around me is familiar, but I seem to be floating, drifting. I can go anywhere—but no one sees me or speaks to me. There's no sense of time where I am, and nothing is solid around me.

I have seen Donny, but he never sees me. He is not my son—he is Deirdre's, and she is no longer with me.

Will I go wandering down the years like this? Through the meaningless centuries? Always searching, though I'm not sure for what?

Those two will be happy together in each other's arms, but I feel nothing about them any more. Only the sight of a rainbow fills me with sadness. Then the loneliness comes in and I stray through the woods, hoping that someone will see me, speak to me. But no one ever does.

17

DAYS HAD passed since Deirdre's death. Lili had stayed on without explanation. For the time being she appeared to have cut all ties with her own life, and she made an effort to be as little trouble to Nona as possible. It was as if she knew she must wait because there were still unfinished matters at Redlands, and perhaps she would be needed. For Liliana Dukas, she was unusually quiet.

During those days Christy came to feel closer to her mother than ever before. Closer than she was able to feel with Hayden. The way Deirdre had died seemed to place a block between them and, like Lili, Christy could only wait.

One evening when those who had been closely concerned had gathered at Nona's, Eve clarified for them some of what had happened as far as Oliver was concerned. He had been caught, trapped, by the *other* Deirdre, though he didn't realize the truth for a long while. When Deirdre told him she had pushed Rose to her death in order to free him, he was horrified. But he was still held in the thrall of his own terrible obsession, even though he'd grown afraid of the changeling Deirdre. He began to read about divided personalities, about jealous siblings, and even about obsession. All too late.

"He told me a little that last night before he died," Eve said. "I think he believed that he might help the two personalities to merge and recover. Then he'd have sent the real Deirdre back to you, Hayden. I cared about Oliver, but I thought his feeling about Deirdre was a lot simpler than it turned out to be. I suppose I was too angry to be of much help. Rose was my friend, and when she died, I know Oliver was devastated. But I didn't understand all the reasons why.

"When he talked to me that last night, he swore me to secrecy until he could find a way out. Think of the horror if the real Deirdre had been arrested! I'm sure the other one would have gone into hiding and let her sister go mad."

Hayden made a despairing sound, and Christy watched him unhappily as Eve went on.

"Then Oliver had a heart attack because of the snake, and I guessed what might have happened. But I had no proof. Nothing I dared go to the police with. I thought of talking to Hayden, but that would open a whole new nest of vipers. Again, the real Deirdre would be blamed. So I acted a lie too. I needed to see the change for myself, but Deirdre kept out of my way and, like Oliver, I waited too long."

A few questions were answered during that sad evening when they listened to Eve, but Lili was the only one who commented.

"It's still not finished," she said. "There's something more to come."

Donny was the most stricken, the most frightened. Since his mother's death, he had slept in Hayden's bed, and one night he sat up suddenly in the early hours, no longer terrified, but smiling.

"I was walking in the woods," he told his father. "I got up in the night and went outside and I found my mother. I think she was calling me, and she didn't run away this time. She sat close by on a rock and talked to me. She said everything was fine for her now, and I mustn't cry for her, because she was happy and had other things she needed to do. So I should be glad for that, and learn how to let her go."

The next day, relating this to Christy, Hayden said, "At first I thought he'd had a comforting dream, though I didn't tell him that. Then, in the morning when we got up, I saw grass stains and red earth on his bare feet."

Christy felt no surprise, no doubt. From her own storytelling experience with children, she knew how close the young were to the mysteries of being born. It was only when the "real," left-brain world of grown-ups took over that they lost the power to see. Now it would be a little easier for Donny.

Nothing was easy for Hayden. He continued to be torn and unable to find his own peace. Christy knew he was still tied to the unresolved past, still reproaching himself. Though she longed to help him, the way was never clear, and he held everyone off. There was too much guilt in him, and she had no way to get past his self-blame for not recognizing what was happening to Deirdre.

Now and then Christy walked alone in the woods, more apart from the others than when Deirdre had been alive. Often she sensed that something drifted near her, just out of sight among the trees—something utterly lost and sad. Perhaps Hayden could never be entirely free until this unhappy presence was released.

The time came when she knew she needed her mother's help. One morning she found Lili sitting alone on the steps to Nona's deck, and she sat down beside her. They were both quiet for a little while, because there could be communion in silence. During these days of waiting, Christy had found a new respect and admiration for her mother. They could be friends now, as they hadn't been when she was young. Lili's way was not Christy's, but by letting old judgments go, she could come lovingly close to her mother. This took nothing away from her affection and gratitude for Nona—and her aunt seemed to understand.

When the quiet between them had lengthened as they sat together on the steps, Christy began to pour out what was troubling her.

"I've almost seen her down there in the woods. Not Deirdre—the other one. I don't think she knows that the body she shared with Deirdre is dead. Is there any way we can help her to find release?"

"Perhaps if we act together," Lili said, "we can find a way. Hayden must be part of whatever we do. He's still at home this morning—I saw him outside a little while ago. Perhaps you can ask him to come with us. And there's something else—do you know where Deirdre's crystal is—the one with the inner phantom?"

"I know where Donny keeps it. He's back in school now, but I don't think he'll mind if I borrow it."

"I'll wait for you," Lili said.

Christy found the crystal easily, and Hayden came with her without asking questions. It was almost as though he too had been waiting, and expected whatever was about to happen.

Once more they started along the fateful path through the woods, this time to the foot of the rocky cliff. The small clearing had been cleansed by rains since Deirdre had lain there, and purified many times over by the sun. Yet it seemed to Christy, with all her senses alert, that a lingering sadness haunted this spot.

"Do whatever you are prompted to do," Lili directed her. "Go inside yourself and ask."

Perhaps if she could do this, Christy thought, it might be possible for Hayden too to leave the past.

She stepped into full sunlight and held up the crystal in the fingers of both hands, so that it pointed toward the sky. Negativity seemed to flow away from the space about her, as though it could not face this radiant light. In her hands the crystal felt warm, but no throbbing energy filled it now. Sunlight washed over its planes, striking rainbow colors, and deep within the stone the "phantom" seemed to move as she watched it.

Words came into her mind as clearly as though she spoke them aloud. *I know you are there and I want to help you. You aren't tied any longer to the body you shared with Deirdre. You are free now. Let your earthly life go.*

A questioning word seemed to whisper through Christy's mind: *Atonement!*

She spoke her answer silently. *There's no atonement for you here. That lies ahead when you can accept fully what you must accept.*

A drifting of mist near the edge of the woods seemed to thicken and come closer to where Christy stood. Hayden and Lili stood back in silence, watching. Christy closed her eyes and a vision came into her mind. She could see broad stairs climbing up and up, until they vanished—perhaps into some other plane than this earthly one. Christy herself seemed to stand at the very foot of the flight, and her own spirit beckoned to the other Deirdre. The prayer that filled her was for release from evil, and a return to all that was good. Sensing, more than seeing, she was aware that the drifting of mist was floating up the stairs.

The way up is open now, she said in her mind, and held the crystal still higher, her eyes fixed upon it. The phantom within the stone shimmered in the light and began to change. In wonder, Christy saw what was happening. Even as she watched, the form that hid inside the stone grew less distinct. Slowly the shadow blurred—and was gone. The vision of a broad staircase was gone as well, and only the crystal shone clear in her fingers—with no lingering shadow within.

"Look!" she cried to Hayden and Lili, and held the crystal toward them. No lost spirit lingered in the woods, and a wonderful sense of peace flowed through her.

Lili's smile was loving and proud as she embraced her daughter. "It's time for me to return to my own work," she said, and she moved up through the woods without looking back.

The haunting was over.

Hayden came to stand before Christy, once more marveling. He touched her cheek with the back of his hand, finding its contour and the line of her jaw. Her lips trembled, and he kissed her, stilling the tremor. For a moment he held her quietly, his cheek against her hair.

They started up the hill together, climbing silently until they came out under that great open sky, with its scalloping of mountains at the horizon. The only shadows around them were cast by clouds.

Christy still held the stone that had been symbolic of Deirdre's life. Both Deirdres were free now, and so was Hayden. He put an arm about her.

The way was open to all the discovery of each other that lay ahead.

PHYLLIS A. WHITNEY was born in Yokohama, Japan, of American parents; and also lived in the Philippines and China. After the death of her father in China, she and her mother returned to the United States, which she saw for the first time when she was fifteen. This early travel has exerted a strong influence on her work; many of her novels are set in areas she has visited in Europe, Africa, and the Orient, as well as in the places she has lived.

Phyllis A. Whitney is the author's maiden name. (The "A" stands for "Ayame," which is the Japanese word for "iris.") She is a widow, and lives near her daughter in Virginia. In 1975 she was elected President of the Mystery Writers of America, and in 1988 received the organization's Grand Master Award for lifetime achievement

Since 1941, when she attained her first hardcover publication, she has become an international success. Over thirty-five million copies of her novels are in print in paperback editions. Her novels for adults now number thirty-three, and her devoted following has made bestsellers of most of these titles, including *Feather on the Moon, Silversword, Dream of Orchids,* and *Flaming Tree.*